Praise for *HIDDEN*

"Engrossing [and] provc   ts. Clare animates her tale with ɛ   sets the groundwork for a sublime   ...ᴜ passion."

—*Kirkus Reviews*

"Sensual and riveting. Kelli Clare brings a fresh new voice with this romantic thriller filled with intrigue and surprises."

—J. Kenner, *New York Times* and
#1 international best-selling author

"Darkly intriguing and scorchingly sexy. A perfect combination of mystery, intrigue, romance, and action make this a must-read. The premise is electrifying, the romance is sizzling, and the storytelling is top notch. Kelli Clare is a dynamic new voice in the genre."

—Julie Ann Walker, *New York Times* and
USA Today best-selling author

"Captivating and provocative. Clare deftly weaves a sensual tale loaded with passion, intrigue, and high-stakes action. *Hidden* is a fast-paced romantic thriller that'll wrap you up and won't let go until the last satisfying paragraph."

—Kerry Lonsdale, *Wall Street Journal* best-selling author

"A propulsive, thrilling read filled with action, romance, and intrigue. Passion and lies make this thriller irresistible. Loved it!"

—Kaira Rouda, *USA Today* best-selling
author of *Best Day Ever*

"This is beautiful writing . . . a distinctive voice. Clare has a strong narrative gift. I was totally drawn in."

—William Bernhardt, best-selling author of
the Ben Kincaid legal thrillers

HIDDEN

HIDDEN

A Novel

KELLI CLARE

Published by SparkPress, a BookSparks imprint,
A division of SparkPoint Studio, LLC
Tempe, Arizona, USA, 85281
www.gosparkpress.com

Published 2018
Printed in the United States of America
ISBN: 978-1-943006-52-6 (pbk)
ISBN: 978-1-943006-53-3 (e-bk)
Library of Congress Control Number: 2017963117

Formatting by Kiran Spees
Author photo by Carli Felix

This is a work of fiction. Any references to historical events, current events, real people, or real places are used fictitiously. Other names, characters, places, and events are products of the author's imagination, and any resemblance to actual events, places, or persons, living or dead, is entirely coincidental. Eastridge is a fictional estate, and resemblance to any existing properties is entirely coincidental.

In loving memory of my grandmother

"Don't bend; don't water it down; don't try to make it logical; don't edit your own soul according to the fashion. Rather, follow your most intense obsessions mercilessly."

–Franz Kafka

In my dream, I watch my fate play out like some gothic horror movie. I see my own green eyes, filling with terror and tears as I fall to my knees, submitting to the command of invincible blue eyes. Those eyes rage with fiery madness, and his face twists into something else, something evil. He thrusts his arm high above his head, a deadly blade in his cruel grip. He is going to take my life. I wake, screaming, to find those same blue eyes—now attentive and worried—staring into mine.

One

THE FIRST TIME I saw Will Hastings's handsome face was in late July after the annual Blessing of the Fleet. His bold gaze burned into mine from the opposite side of Water Street. The highland band, piping loud and marching through the center, drew the post-ceremony procession to a close, granting me an unobstructed view. A slow smile touched his lips, and despite the stifling summer heat, it drove a sensual shiver through me.

He was magnificent, the kind of man you would never find living in small-town New England. He could have just stepped right off the cover of *GQ Magazine*. I'd never seen a man so tall, with shoulders so broad it made me wonder if he had to have his shirts custom tailored. His taut, cut biceps emerged from the sleeves of a beautifully faded indigo T-shirt tucked into close-fitting jeans. Most women would pay a fortune for the highlights that seemed to flow naturally through the waves of his dark blond hair. His jawline was strong and commanding, reminding me of paintings I'd studied in college of ancient Roman gladiators.

The parade had ended, but Jess and I hadn't moved from the curb. My best friend released her wavy red hair from its loose bun and lifted her face to the late-morning sun, and I stared at him. She opened her eyes to drink from her raspberry mimosa and elbowed me.

"Who's he and why are you staring at each other? Wait—is he . . . ?"

My eyes skipped to Jess to deliver a dirty look. "The guy who

1

followed me home the other night. Yes, I think so. Maybe I'm wrong. Maybe he's staying nearby." When I refocused across the street, he was gone.

"And maybe you should say something to someone, report it to the police."

"You know, paranoia is my sister's thing, not mine. I'm not sure I feel threatened. Besides, aren't you always saying I should be more open to meeting new people?"

"I haven't seen you outwardly curious in a while, and yeah, you do need to get out of your artsy little head. Just be careful. If it happens again, promise you'll do something about it."

"I will. Promise."

I struggled with reconciling his presence in town and the sense that he watched me. After all, it was summertime. Stonington was a historically rich town, a cultural treasure, and the only one in Connecticut to face the open Atlantic waters. It attracted countless visitors. It was common to see tourists milling around town taking photos or wandering the streets at night, unaware most businesses closed long before ten. Stonington was also a colonial fishing town, and outsiders came from far and wide to work for the commercial fleet. This wasn't the first time a man from one of the crews or a tourist had looked my way.

The next day, after the last of my noisy day campers had gone, I locked the art studio door and headed for the fishing pier to sketch. It was either that or listen to another of Jess's lectures. She'd go on about how I wallowed in self-imposed loneliness and how it left her alone to test the waters in the pool of datable men. The pool was small—it was blue-plastic-toddler-swimming-pool small—and I didn't need to dip a toe to know there was nothing left in it for me.

The pier was a respite from my grandmother's and sister's intrusiveness as well. Gran and Isobel were all I had, and they meant well. Trysts with my art kept me sane, human.

I looked out over the harbor and spotted *Neptune* trudging her way in. The sailboats beyond paled in her presence. I don't know what it was about the old girl, but I loved that fishing boat. Her emerald-green hull had become chalky over time, and the once black and white hoists and booms were covered in rust, but she was still glorious against the backdrop of the sea. I sat and lost myself in the sketch.

No more than ten minutes had passed when the pier thrummed with the pounding steps of the lumping crew as they made their way to the dock. With a soft curse, I pulled the cover over my drawing and watched the deckhands secure *Neptune*'s lines.

"Hello."

My shoulders jerked. I arched my neck back and blinked at the man looming above.

"Didn't mean to startle you," he said. I don't know which was more surprising—his deep, thunderous tone or the English accent. A rich, masculine scent rolled down his corded arm and circled my head when he offered his hand.

I stood without taking it and dusted off my backside. Even when standing, I had to lift my chin to meet his eyes. I was five and a half feet tall, and he towered a foot above me. I stared at him and explored those eyes. They were gunmetal blue, his gaze invincible.

"Hi. It's . . . you—from the street. You were staring."

He offered no apology. Instead, he extended his arm to offer his hand again, palm facing up this time. "Will Hastings." A seductive smile played with the corners of his mouth, one side curving higher than the other. His commanding presence saturated the space around me. Power. He was power.

I bit my lip and presented my hand, distantly aware I'd edged closer. "Ellie James."

With a firm grasp, he held my fingers as he studied me. "Christ, you're lovely."

The gravel texture layered in the sound of his deep voice captivated me, as did his choice of words. My pulse sped. No words came to me. I dropped my eyes, but they were drawn back to his in an instant.

Will Hastings pressed his lips to my knuckles before releasing me. "I'll see you again." After taking a few steps back, he turned and strode away, joining the rest of the crew to unload *Neptune*'s catch.

"But . . . wait," I called through the heat of my blush.

He tossed back one confident word. "Soon."

It was impossible not to glance once more in his direction before heading up the pier. He watched me over his shoulder with powerful arms raised high, prepared to lift the next teeming crate from its moving hook.

I reminded myself to breathe and exhaled, withdrawing from my daze.

That night, when I couldn't sleep, I pulled out my pad and finished the drawing from memory, coercing life into the old fishing boat on paper. I flipped the page and continued, allowing my mind to create whatever it wanted to see in the moment. It wasn't long before Will's eyes stared back at me. I held up the sketch and angled it left and right, considering the penciled likeness. It jumped out at me then—his gaze revealed something more than I'd realized at the pier. Something dark.

That darkness drew me to him, even on paper. But there was something more, an alluring energy, and it drove images into my head of tangled sheets and sweating, entwined bodies.

I shook my head to clear it, deciding to go to the family cottage soon. No one else used the place anymore. It was quaint and private, no fishermen, no tourists, no onlookers. I missed the beach there and needed to step into the sea. An empty feeling, a profound void caused by the lack of a genuine soul-deep connection lingered in my spirit. The Atlantic soothed me, filling that void with comforting messages from a faraway land I imagined reaching out for me.

I walked the pier several times over the next few days and visited *Neptune*'s dock, hoping to run into Will. He wasn't there, but that was hardly surprising. He was too polished, too smooth. It was clear he was more than a longshoreman in for the season. Our paths never crossed. Still, the ache low in my abdomen assured me of his presence.

My curiosity became a preoccupation, and it haunted me. I wanted nothing more than to know why I was drawn to him. I searched the streets for him. Needed to see his eyes again to resolve what my mind had shown me only on paper.

By the time Thursday finally rolled around, I'd grown irritable, frustration grabbing hold and biting hard. God, I needed to get a grip. I was getting ready for my shift at Nick's, still preoccupied, finding it difficult to focus on anything other than getting to work, when Jess texted to let me know she was running late. Jess and I tended bar there in addition to our day jobs—mine, teaching and selling art, and hers, perioperative nursing. It was the night of the annual event celebrating the restaurant's long run in the community, and it would draw people for miles throughout New London County. Locals, fishermen, and tourists alike.

If my gut was right, and Will Hastings was still around town, I would see him there. Maybe then the possessed mood that kept me from sleeping would subside.

I pulled the red T-shirt with the restaurant's logo over my head, tucking it into cutoff jean shorts, and brushed through my long brunette layers once more. Another touch of shimmering nude lipstick, and then I slipped out the front door and headed down the sidewalk toward Nick's.

—

Josh Mendes insisted on getting in the way of my mission. One of Ed Sheeran's songs followed him in from the restaurant's rear patio where the twenty- and thirtysomethings hung out. He stood in silence, staring as I mixed and poured cocktails.

"I'm a bit busy, Josh. Do you want another beer?"

"Yeah." He grabbed my hand when I reached for his empty. "Come back to me, Ellie. We could be good together if you'd give it another shot. Let's try again."

We had dated on and off in the three years since I'd come home from UConn, and never got it right. He was a good man, a lieutenant with the local police department. I wanted to love him, but it never came to me—that collision of fiery emotional and physical bliss I refused to live without. Josh needed consistent encouragement, and I'd grown tired of managing the intimacy between us.

I pulled my hand back and grabbed a clean glass, filling it with Guinness. "Please don't. I can't do this conversation again. Nothing has changed. I'm sorry."

"If there's something I can do to change your mind, you know I'll do it."

"I know." I offered his beer with a friendly smile before turning away. When I glanced at the wall of mirrors to see if he'd moved on, I found Will staring back at me. Every part of me tensed, my pulse quickening from the intensity of his focused eyes. I spun and scanned the crowd. I couldn't let him get away.

We locked stares again. I searched for the dark, menacing trait that had nagged at my subconscious. It was there, but it didn't frighten me. It filled my senses and fueled my curiosity. This man would never need encouraging. He canted his head, signaling for me to follow him out the rear exit.

"Cover me for a bit, Jess. I need to do something."

"What are you up to, Ells?"

"I'll be out on the patio for a few minutes."

She bumped her hip against mine as she passed. "Got it."

The terrace was crowded, though Will was easy to find. He leaned against the building's brick wall with his arms crossed over his chest and feet spread wide. I pushed my way through the sweating mob of drinking and dancing revelers, staying close to the wall, but lost sight of him when someone grabbed me and pulled me into the mix. The guy who'd snatched my arms released me abruptly and stepped back.

Will was behind me. "Turn round, Ellie James," he said close to my ear. The warmth of his breath on my neck caused goose bumps. His words held no hint of intonation. It was a command.

I turned to meet his eyes.

He flashed his brows and rubbed his chin, a glimmer from one of the sun's last rays bouncing off his platinum Patek Philippe watch.

I ignored the odd fluttering in my stomach and waited.

He stepped closer, compelling me back against the wall. One of his hands rested against the bricks near my head. His eyes never left mine.

"Who are you?"

"I told you my name."

"Yes, but why are you here in Stonington?"

"Business. I have a job to do."

"At the pier?"

A smirk dominated his lips, his face. "No, not at the pier."

That assuming smile made him impossibly more handsome, and almost unmade me. I wiped my sweaty palms on my hips. "Why did you introduce yourself to me?"

He shrugged but never broke eye contact.

"Have you followed me?"

"Yes."

"Why?"

"You should talk to your sister about that. I'd rather she filled you in."

"What does that mean? Do you know my sister?"

"Not personally."

"You're making no sense."

Another shrug. As he glanced at my mouth, his eyes grew possessive, and I was mesmerized. I wanted to reach up and touch his five-o'clock shadow. His virile scent intoxicated me. It was sensual and earthy at once, like sandalwood and peat. Peat—he was a scotch drinker.

He cocked his head and flashed a satisfied smile.

"Where can I find you?"

His smile dissolved, and his eyes burned deeper into mine. "Stop looking for me."

I matched his determined stare. "Stop following me."

"You don't have to look for me. . . . I'll find you again, Ellie. Just talk to your sister."

Neither of us moved. Was I breathing? Finally, he dropped his arm and stepped back.

"It's getting dark. You should go inside."

My body submitted to his suggestion before my brain could catch it. I stopped and looked back after several steps. He was still there, watching me with his arms folded against his massive chest. Our eyes connected again. He'd be back.

When I reached the door, I glanced over my shoulder one last time, but he was gone. I spent the rest of my shift trapped inside my head, confused by what had happened on the patio. Only one thing was clear—I wanted to see Will again.

I shot a quick text message to Isobel, asking if she knew him and if she planned to meet me at closing as she typically did, but my sister never replied.

Jess gripped my shoulders and shook me, causing the beer in my hand to spill. "Ellie, did you hear me? I have to go. The emergency department needs all surgical staff at the hospital STAT. There's been some kind of street fight on the north side of town. Josh was dispatched to the scene. It's about time to close anyway. You'll wait for Isobel?"

The street and the house were quiet as usual. I waved goodbye as I turned the key, unlocking the front door. Josh had sent one of the rookies to drive me home from the bar. He gave a nod and accelerated. The patrol car sped down the street, heading north with its flashing red and blue emergency lights engaged, back into the odd chaos of the night.

There were no lights on.

There was no aromatic bouquet from Gran's evening chamomile to greet me.

There was no one around to witness my terror when I stepped inside and found my sister and grandmother lying on the floor, holding hands in an ever-widening pool of deep red. The cross of Saint George drawn in blood sullied their beautiful faces. They'd been shot.

Gran was already gone.

Isobel blinked her hazel eyes and tried to tell me something. She tugged on the scrap of paper sticking out of her front pocket until her strength was exhausted, her arm dropping to the floor. A fading whisper floated away on one of her final breaths. "Find Lissie. Get out. . . ."

I screamed at her, screamed for her to stay with me, and then fell to my knees between my dead grandmother and dying sister, clutching their combined hands in mine.

Then they were both gone.

Blood soaked my bare legs as I rocked back and forth. I gagged on the coppery scent filling the foyer. Stinging tears flooded my eyes. Pain-filled moments that felt like an eternity dragged on until

Gran's old clock chimed eleven times, forcing me to dismiss the pain. Fear for my life and Lissie's took its place. I had to find her.

I grabbed the crumpled paper hanging from my sister's jeans. It wasn't a scrap at all but a thick sheet, and when I unfolded it, Will Hastings's eyes stared back at me. Something senseless, something I couldn't rationalize that was neither right nor wrong skipped through my mind and banged around inside my skull.

Isobel had taken my drawing. Beneath his picture, she'd written a name—Ethan—and some numbers. Ethan? I shoved it into my pocket and jumped up, causing myself to slip in blood, righting myself briefly only to stumble and crash into the center table. I anchored there for a moment to catch my breath. My hands trembled, my mind reeling, unable to compose complete thoughts. *Run.*

I ran up the old Victorian staircase and called out for Lissie. Her bedroom was at the back of the house, and when I got there, the door was open. I burst through and pounded the side of my fist against the light switch.

The room spun. I reached for the doorframe and pulled in a deep breath to combat the sickening rush of adrenaline. I called out again. "Lissie, are you here?"

There was no reply—no sound at all. No sign of her even after searching beneath the bed and in her closet. I hit the hallway and headed to Isobel's room, but Lissie wasn't there either. My own room was just as empty.

A sob pushed upward into the back of my throat as I raced to the last bedroom. It was there, in Gran's room, where I heard a thump against the wall. Everything in me froze. Then it came again— another soft thump against the far wall.

I sprinted across the room to the walk-in. Lissie screamed. She was crouched in the corner of the secret room at the back of the closet. Her hands covered her head. She hid in the same little room where Isobel and I had hosted clandestine tea parties with our dolls

when we were children. I didn't know my sister had shown Lissie
our hiding place but thanked God she had.

"Lissie, sweetheart—" I lowered myself in front of her, peeled her
hands from her head, and lifted her chin so she could see me. She
lunged like a wild animal and wrapped both arms so tightly around
my neck I had to loosen them to breathe.

We were in danger—the rolling in my gut was proof. The best
course of action would've been to get out of the house, but for several moments, I couldn't move. I could do nothing more than hold
my trembling niece.

Isobel's last words were instructions. Find her daughter and run.
I needed to move.

I listened carefully for sounds anomalous to the old house. There
was nothing more than the soft whistling from the air ducts. "I need
to call for help, then we're going to leave," I whispered. "But you
must stay here while I get my phone. Understand? Do not move. I
won't leave without you." I didn't want her to see, didn't want the
image of her mother's lifeless body burned into her memory.

I pressed Lissie into the corner and exited the secret room.
My fingers dragged along the top of the door casing until finding
the key I used to open the large trunk tucked in one corner of the
closet. I opened a black box and removed Pearl, and then rummaged
through the trunk until finding a loaded magazine with six rounds
and jammed it into the gun.

Pearl was a pretty little twenty-five-caliber automatic pistol. A
gift to my mother from my father, so I had been told. It had engraved
nickel plating and a mother-of-pearl stock. Natural patina added
beauty to the piece. I wasn't unfamiliar with the gun despite the fact
I'd never before carried it. Gran tried to give it to me several times,
though I'd refused her each time. Isobel would have taken it—had
she not already had two of her own.

My sister was prepared for all unknowns as if Earth's destruction were coming. Not only had she owned guns, but she'd also practiced weekly at the local shooting range. "Why can't you listen for once? Take it, and after you learn how to use it, we'll get you something more useful. Do it, Ellie. Take the gun," she'd insisted after our grandmother tattled on me.

We celebrated her thirtieth birthday two weeks earlier. The three years that separated Isobel and me seemed like three decades. We couldn't have been more different.

I stuffed the gun into the waistband of my shorts at the small of my back and tiptoed out of the closet, pulling the door shut and listening before I entered the hallway. In Lissie's room, I made quick work of stuffing a backpack with some of her things before creeping to mine where I added my phone charger and car keys.

My cell phone was downstairs in the foyer. I sidled down the wooden stair treads with my eyes focused upward on the wrought iron and crystal chandelier. It was on the floor near their bodies, so I crawled past the ornate twin entry doors but kept my head turned away. Vomit burned my throat as I beat it back down. I reached out and fumbled until making contact with the phone. Once it was in my grip, I hung my head and fought my body's overwhelming urge to faint.

I needed to get up, get us out.

It was too late. A floorboard creaked behind me. The pounding of my heart flooded my ears. Someone was in the house. I'd screwed up—we shouldn't have still been there.

"You shouldn't be here," the intruder's voice echoed.

Two

My captor pulled the gun from my waistband and lifted me from the floor, covering my mouth with his hand so I couldn't scream, and carried me from the bloody foyer into the living room. He was unwilling to remove his hand from my mouth or allow me to turn and face him, but I knew who it was the moment he touched me.

"Don't make a sound. You can't overpower me, nor outrun me."

That rumbling voice. Will. *Ethan.*

"I'll remove my hand if you assure me you won't scream." My back was pulled tight against his chest, and both of my arms were restrained by one of his. "Be calm and quiet."

I wanted to scream but nodded in agreement to his terms instead. The power surging through his huge body was irrefutable. He didn't need a weapon. He could snap my spine with ease. I didn't know if he was Will or Ethan, murderer or not. Oh, God, I'd left Lissie. My mind and body were breaking down, and disjointed thoughts created more confusion than I could sort through.

My knees buckled, and I fainted.

When I came to, he held me in his arms, and my head rested against his chest. His steady heart thundered in my ear. His lips were parted, and his gaze burned into mine.

I wasn't able to push out words or sound.

"They'll come back for you. You must let me help—I can get you out of here. I'm not the enemy. . . . I'm here to protect you. Can you stand?"

"Yes," I whispered, hoping I was right. Hoping my legs would hold me.

He set me on my feet and steadied me and then cradled my face in his hands and stared into my eyes again. "I know you're confused, but I won't hurt you. Not ever. I swear it."

I swayed, still groggy. My head spun. "You didn't do this?"

"No." There was something convincing in his eyes. It was fierce but honest and certain—strong and compassionate, like the feel of his hands on my face. I'd misread the darkness that lurked within those eyes, in his soul. It was driven by an intense protective instinct, not menace.

I chose to trust him despite the alarm surging through me.

"Lissie—she's still upstairs."

"There's someone else in the house?"

"She can't see this. She's just a little girl." I pushed back tears.

"Go to her now. I'll follow." He released me without allowing much space between us.

I grabbed the backpack from the bottom step and threw it over my shoulder as we headed up to get Lissie from Gran's closet. The tired staircase groaned under Will's weight.

He spoke into a communication device as we climbed. "Car to the front . . . be ready to roll. Need cover upstairs. There's another survivor."

When we reached Lissie, she was curled into a ball. Her hands covered her head again, and she wept. I squatted and tried to pull her to me, but she resisted. "It's time to go. Come on, sweetie. Come to me." She wouldn't come out of her fetal ball.

"There's no time. Move aside."

I searched his eyes for reassurance and stepped aside.

He lifted my niece with speed and a firm gentleness, and after she'd curled back around herself, he shifted her into one arm. Smaller than average for her seven years, she looked like an infant against his broad chest. She whimpered when we covered her head with a blanket and pushed out a little hand seeking mine. I held it tight while she dug her nails into my flesh.

"Walk slow and stay close to me." His warm hand covered the small of my back.

A brawny man with black, buzzed-cut hair appeared at the bottom of the stairs with a large pistol drawn. I stiffened as my heart forfeited another second of my life.

Will nudged me forward. "It's okay. . . . Ben's with me."

As we descended, I focused on Ben to keep from looking at the horrific sight of my murdered family. He had a thick, oblique scar that slashed across his forehead, and he was dressed like a soldier, wearing a dark T-shirt, military trousers, and black combat boots.

The two men flanked me, shielding me with their bodies as they moved us from the house to the black Hummer waiting in the otherwise empty street. Will opened the door and pushed me into the back, slid Lissie onto the seat next to me, and climbed in. "Move it. Drive north then head west to Lords Point," he said as he cuffed the driver once on the shoulder.

I pulled Lissie to my lap and held her quivering body to my chest as she cried for Isobel. Once the car was on the road, I closed my eyes, battling hard for control of my own emotions.

"You'll be safe for now at your beach cottage."

I nodded. I didn't know where else to go—there was no one left, nowhere for me to turn.

Though I could feel his eyes on me, scrutinizing every breath as I struggled to keep it together, we rode in deafening silence until reaching the main route.

"I'll keep you safe, Ellie."

I turned to the window and focused on the blurred, passing terrain, fighting tears. One word. That's all it would take for me to break apart.

He slid closer and closed the gap between us. "Look at me," he ordered in a soft tone, placing his hand on the back of my head. I turned to meet his eyes. Neither of us spoke. My eyes dropped, and I swallowed against the thickness at the back of my throat. The pressure of his hand remained steady as he lowered it to my nape. I pushed my eyes up, and his were still there—waiting for mine to come back. We were stuck there for a moment.

"I swear I'll protect you."

"Who's Ethan?" It was a quivering whisper.

"My brother."

"He knew my sister?"

"Quite well. They met in London."

Isobel spent an entire summer studying in London eight years ago.

I dug beneath Lissie to pluck the sketch from my pocket and held the paper at an angle so he could see only the name and numbers. "Is this his phone number?"

"Yes." He let his hand fall. The strength it provided fell with it.

"None of this makes sense." The first tears tumbled free, and more quickly followed in an unbroken stream. I knew I trusted him, but I wasn't sure why. Isobel had ties. I trusted her. What would I do without her? I choked on the silent panic strangling me.

The back of his fingers lingered near my cheek. He was about to wipe the tears, but changed his mind and let his hand drop again. "When you're safe, we'll talk. I'll explain."

I wiped at the burning tears, tilting my head toward the young driver. "Who's this?"

"John. He's my youngest brother."

"How many?"

"There're four of us. John is seventeen. Thomas twenty-eight. Ethan's thirty-four."

"And you?"

"Thirty-two."

John peered into the rearview mirror and revealed eyes almost identical to Will's. The one difference was John's youthful innocence. A sharp breath stabbed my lungs. I looked down at the little girl curled on my lap and then stared back at the mirror, comparing his eyes to hers. I'd been staring at the same eyes on my niece since her birth.

Will still watched me. He shifted his weight. "How old?"

I studied his eyes and made the same comparison. "She was seven in April."

He turned his head and cursed under his breath. When he came back to me, he found the single tear that loosed itself before I could stop it and wiped it away with his thumb.

That one tear unleashed another round, and as the watery pain streaked down my face, it hit me—I was responsible for Lissie's life, but I didn't know how to be that for her.

"What's going to happen? To their . . . to them?"

"They'll be held at the medical examiner's office while police look for you. Ben will go back to ensure authorities find them. I don't want our location traced by phone." He tucked a finger under my chin and lifted my wet eyes to his. "I won't leave you alone in this."

I believed him.

Even though it was fleeting, relief washed over me as we pulled up in front of the seaside cottage. It was my safe place. The haven where I always ran when something in my world failed, when I was broken. But this time, I wasn't alone.

The edge of the sea reached up to soothe me, knowing I was adrift with grief as it cleansed the blood from my legs. I stood in the water with my arms outstretched and eyes shut tight, inhaling the salt-laden breeze as it whipped my hair about. Breaking waves rolled in and pushed me back as if to save me. I was lost.

"How do I get through this?" I whispered into the familiar briny depths.

Will stood nearby. He refused to let me out of his sight, refused to allow me beyond arm's reach, and he'd tried hard to convince me to stay inside, but I needed to feel the sea.

Two hundred feet behind us were several cottages nestled high among boulders and stones. At the foot of the hill, sea oats grew tall along weatherworn fencing. The cottages had white-painted cedar-shake siding as was traditional for Lords Point, but each had varying shades of gray and brown caused by winter beatings. Mine stood out only because of the flickering lantern in its kitchen window.

"We should go inside and talk while the young one sleeps. There's something you should have been told long ago," he said.

The moment I stepped out of the water, his hand was low on my back, guiding me up the rocky hill path. His touch was warm and strong, filled with energy, similar to the summer storm about to hit the beach. His presence was powerful. It tugged at me, drawing me to him.

Inside, Will leaned forward at the edge of the sofa and raked long fingers through his hair as he stared at me. "You noticed the cross?"

I sat at the opposite end with my legs pulled up and the side of my face resting against the soft back cushion. "Yes." Their faces. The blood.

"It's a signature—a calling card."

I lifted my head and swallowed a ragged breath. "You know who did this?"

"What do you know of your lineage?"

"What? My sister was just murdered, and you want to discuss my lineage?"

He raised a brow and waited.

"I know my grandparents were English. My grandfather's parents settled here just before the turn of the twentieth century."

"And your parents?"

I shrugged. I never knew my parents. "There was an accident. I was just two. They'd taken a trip abroad without Isobel and me. The plane went down. My grandmother raised us."

"I'm sorry for that, for the losses you've suffered. You're English. Raised here, but your blood is pure. What do you know of your surname?"

"It's a name," I snapped. "What's there to know? Look, it's pretty clear I'm uninformed where my family tree is concerned, so if you know something, please just tell me."

His eyes shifted back to the floor, and he shook his head, cursing under his breath as he had in the car. It was his thing—raking his hair and cursing beneath his breath. It was . . . sexy.

When I realized he was watching me stare at him, it jolted me from my head, and I snapped again. "What does this have to do with what happened to my family?"

Will took my hand, his attempt at patience. He took a deep breath through his nose and let it go. "Christ. Did they tell you nothing?"

I watched his every move, studied him, waiting for him to say something more. His moods shifted fast and without warning.

Another call on my cell from Josh went unanswered.

"This will sound mad, but I give you my word it's the truth. The ancient blood running through you has been hunted and eliminated for generations."

"What do you mean *hunted?*"

"A covert order of British assassins believes your blood is a threat to the Crown. They refer to themselves as the Order." He went on after assessing my silent emotional deliberations. "Your ancestors and mine made a pact that's been in play for centuries. The terms were designed to protect your bloodline. My family was contracted to defend yours."

I pulled my hand away. Was he joking? What he said sounded

insane, even as he said it with absolute conviction. "You're right, it sounds ridiculous . . . like a story by the Brothers Grimm, but go on."

"My job is to keep you alive."

"Well, I guess you've done that. So you'll be leaving."

"I won't be going anywhere without you." His words were sharp. He meant it.

"You're telling me that my life has been a lie—some tragic, untold fairy tale, and Prince Charming has at last been dispatched to rescue me. What do you expect me to do with that?"

"Never confuse me with the good guy. I'm not some fucking prince, and this has nothing to do with fantasy." He paused. The same hand he'd held mine with was now fisted. "Do not doubt my word when I give it." His anger was palpable. He'd absorbed mine and made it his.

I had an impulsive urge to soothe him. Touching the inside of his wrist, I encouraged him to open his hand, and when he did, I slipped mine back into his. "Suppose I believe. Why is this important? Does the Crown even have power?"

"The Crown makes countless moves by way of royal prerogative, without consulting commons or public." His thumb caressed the bright blue veins on the inside of my wrist. "Jesus, you're delicate."

I narrowed my eyes.

"The queen is aging and unwell. Most countrymen find her heir to be a self-indulgent arse. The prince's outspoken positions on great issues are unpopular. Public mood could become unstable when he inherits. That's the driving force behind the Order's renewed focus of its objective."

"Preservation of the reigning bloodline."

"Yes. The elimination of all threats."

"Political complicity, that I get. But secret societies that execute families? It feels too Shakespearean, if not medieval."

"American culture is in its infancy compared to most civilizations, and most Americans know nothing about their heritage or its histories."

Others may have been offended by the remark, but he was right. I'd studied art history for six years before earning my master's, and ancient European cultures were esoteric. "How far back does this conflict go?"

He hesitated in thought, something dark filling his eyes.

"Tell me everything, Will." I touched his forearm and dragged my fingers to his palm.

He stiffened, his gaze locked on my hand. "I believe the first group of assassins emerged soon after the death of Queen Anne—that was three centuries ago."

"So you're saying this . . . this ancient Order survived three centuries and now wants the prince to inherit, feels just in safeguarding the Crown's sitting bloodline, but public opinion is low. There's worry of a referendum or perhaps another heir coming forward. Got it. But I don't understand how my family was drawn into this. Please. I need to know."

"Yeah, you do." His long fingers curled onto mine. "Your father was the last successor of King Edward the Fourth's patrilineal descent."

"What?" I stretched my brain to recall the significance of Edward IV's reign. It had been eclipsed by the Cousins' War. York versus Lancaster and then the Tudors. "Patrilineal? But none of his sons survived."

"One survived. Your English history lessons here in America are wrong."

"This is crazy. My last name is James. And historians at the nation's most prestigious universities still debate over who murdered Edward's sons, the princes in the Tower."

"Richard lived."

"I'm sure many descendants of the Plantagenet dynasty still live."

"None like you. You're a direct descendant of the one successive line of a beloved king. And in the eyes of the Order, that makes you a threat to the Crown."

"And since I'm female, since my father had no sons, I'm the end of the line."

"Yes."

"This is insane. How can it be? And that's an archaic, sexist notion, by the way."

The corners of his mouth twitched as if he were amused. "You asked for the truth, and I gave it to you."

"And my sister, she died for this." The last four words faded to a whisper. I winced in pain as the image of Isobel and our grandmother lying dead filled my mind.

"I'm sorry."

"It's too much. I can't. . . ." I shook my pounding head, holding it between my hands, pushing back at the agony and that gruesome image.

His hand went to my arm, his touch hesitant as he tested my reaction. "I'm here."

"Will, I don't—" *I don't know what to do.* I couldn't get the words out before the sob trapped in my chest finally broke free and released my heartache. I closed my eyes, but tears raced down my cheeks anyway. My body trembled, and my teeth clattered.

My family was gone. Oh, God. They were dead.

Will wrapped a throw around my shaking body as he gathered me in his lap and pressed my face to his chest. "Shhh. I'm here now. Never leave you again. I'm here," he said, purring the words against my hair.

I padded across the wood floor and pulled the semiopaque white sheers back from the doors. Golden beams of sunlight radiated through the east-facing panes of glass. My throbbing head tortured me, allowing thoughts and images from the day before to collide into one another as they whirled around inside my mind.

Ben was on the other side, standing guard. He raised one hand in greeting and gave a quick nod. I stared stupidly before opening one of the doors wide and stepping out onto the veranda.

"Where is he? Where's Will? I need to see him."

Both hands went back to the impressive-looking rifle strapped to his shoulder. His muscled body tensed. "He'll be back soon. Stay inside until he returns. Please." When I nodded, his face and shoulders relaxed.

"Why don't you sit down? There's no need to stand."

Ben shook his head and pulled his phone from a pocket. He removed his dark Oakleys to read a text message. His eyes crinkled, and a smile lifted his face, causing the scar on his forehead to pucker. I turned to go back inside, but he stopped me. "Wait. Here. . . ." He was beaming as he extended his phone and revealed a picture.

"She's beautiful. What's her name?"

"Chelsea."

"Well, Chelsea certainly has striking eyes. She's gorgeous. You must miss her."

"Yeah. We celebrated her third birthday end of May." He looked down at his boots and forced his feelings to retreat.

I noticed his empty mug on the side table. "More coffee?" Maybe he'd talk if I pumped him with caffeine. I wanted to know more about everything, more about Will.

He nodded. "Yes, thank you."

"Be right back."

I went inside and pulled the curtains back across both doors for privacy. Lissie was still sleeping. It was close to seven, but she was used to sleeping until nine or later during the summer months. I brushed my teeth and changed out of dirty clothes.

John was in the kitchen. He was dressed like Ben but wasn't armed with a rifle. A handgun was on the counter in front of him. His broad shoulders and chest—even the same sun-kissed, dark blond mane—reminded me of his brother, though he stood only five feet ten or eleven. "Ellie," he said by way of greeting before he stuffed his mouth with sausage.

Finding him in my kitchen surprised me, and for some reason, it warmed my heart. I wanted to smile, but couldn't yet find that strength. "Where is Will?"

"Back at his place. Thought he'd be back before you woke. But don't worry, you're safe. We won't leave you alone."

"So he said."

I busied myself making a fresh pot of coffee and rifled through tall cabinets on tiptoes searching for a thermal carafe. Coffee was essential for survival, and it had to be steaming hot. Once I'd filled the carafe, I composed a meager smile for John, and then stepped out onto the veranda again to continue my conversation with Ben.

"When did the three of you arrive in Stonington? Sugar? Cream?"

"Black. Will came over in May. John and I joined him near the end of June when Ethan sent us to bring him back." He sipped from his steaming mug.

"Yet a month has passed, and you're all still here."

He raised and dropped his free shoulder. "An army couldn't have moved him."

"How does this work for you guys?" I sat and invited him to do the same.

He remained on his feet and removed his sunglasses to knife me with his dark stare. "Listen, it's not my place to have this conversation with you. I know you need a distraction, but—"

"And will he? Have this conversation with me?"

"I think he will."

We both stared out to sea and worked at our coffee. A laughing gull filled the air with its raucous call, then swooped down to pluck a dead fish from the seaweed washed ashore during the night's storm. The sulfuric odor of the decaying algae drifted along the breeze. I wrinkled my nose.

John burst through the door. "There's a policeman in the drive."

Ben barked orders. "Get back inside and cover the young one. Do not leave her. Ellie, you must answer the door, but don't allow him in. I'll stay close to you, just don't give me away. We can't allow anyone to know we're here with you."

"But—"

"Damn it, don't make me ring Will. There's no time for it. If you don't open the door, the police will come in."

"Okay," I snapped.

He was on my heels as I headed for the front door. He rotated his rifle so it rested on his back and drew a pistol from his belt, hiding just out of view with his gun sighted on the policeman.

I swallowed hard and opened the door.

After flashing his badge and identification, Detective Parker apologized for the early hour and told me he'd been transferred in from Mystic's police department a month prior. One hand gripped the frame so I couldn't close the door and the other was pushed down into his trouser pocket, jangling keys or coins or something metal.

"Of course, you're new to town. I'm sorry. I know the uniform, but I don't remember seeing you at Nick's."

He squinted.

"Nick's—the local favorite, town's watering hole? Everyone on the force comes in for a burger and chowder. I've worked there for years."

"Yes, that's right. I mean to stop in soon." His eyes shifted and strained to see beyond the open door.

Confused, I stared at Parker and waited for him to speak again.

He hadn't yet articulated the reason for his visit, and considering the circumstances, I found it unsettling. I reminded myself Ben was nearby. It was odd, but the presence of an unfamiliar English soldier was more comforting.

"Is it okay if I come in, Ms. James?"

"I'd rather you didn't. What is it? Do you need me at the station?"

"Are you alone?"

"Yes."

He worked harder at jangling whatever he carried in his pocket. "No need to come to the station yet. In fact, if you plan to come back into town, call me first. We'll see that it's safe." The detective handed me a card with his handwritten cell number on it. "Maybe you need to see to funeral arrangements or something. I can escort you."

"Shouldn't you be more concerned with the investigation?"

"We're doing what we can, but there isn't much for investigators and forensics to work with." He stared behind me into the cottage again—he knew I wasn't alone.

"If there's nothing more you can tell me, please go. I'd like to rest."

"Of course. You have my number." Parker extended a firm handshake, one meant to intimidate. "A word of advice: don't leave this county."

I closed the door and tossed a nervous glance at Ben. A stinging sensation gnawed at the pit of my stomach as I headed for my bedroom. Did the police consider me a suspect?

Three

Lissie poked her head into the shower. "Aunt Ellie, I'm hungry." Then she sat on the toilet seat lid and waited for me to finish. I'd seen her sit in the bathroom with Isobel that way hundreds of times.

"Okay, sweetie, I'm almost done, then we'll have breakfast. Wait for me—don't leave the bedroom until I'm ready. How are you feeling?"

"I'm . . . I don't know. I wanna cry."

"It's okay to cry." I quickly rinsed the conditioner from my hair. "And it's okay to be sad. I'm sad, too. You know that, right?"

"Are those guys still here?"

"Yes. Do you remember their names?"

"Will."

"Will, yes. Ben is the one with dark hair. John is the youngest who looks like Will."

"Are they good guys? Like superheroes?"

I pulled back the shower curtain and slipped into my bathrobe. "Well, no, but they are here to help us." I took hold of her chin, thumbing the little dimple there, and placed a kiss on her forehead. "I know you're sad and scared. Me, too. I don't have any answers yet, but I promise I'll figure this out. For now, I think we're safer if they stay. I'll never leave you, Lissie. I love you."

It was the first time those last three words left my lips in that order. Ever.

I knew nothing about being a mother, and I couldn't have been more unprepared even as her aunt. Isobel once told me you need only know love to be a parent. "That counts me out," I'd said, confessing to never having loved anyone other than her and our gran. And even that had never been a close, affectionate love. Maybe it was my fault—maybe my heart didn't know how to love because I never gave it a chance, painting my view of life within the boundaries of my mind rather than living it. I'd been raised without parents by a preoccupied English grandmother. Maybe it was their fault for abandoning me. Or maybe I was just a cold bitch and didn't have it in me.

I closed my eyes and shook my head to clear my mind. "Let's get something to eat, pretty girl." I managed an authentic smile when she looked up at me with those beautiful blue eyes.

Lissie finished her scrambled eggs and glass of milk in a hurry before she broke down and fell into one of her emotional fits. This time, I understood the meltdown. She was a child abandoned, left with nothing more than pain and the idea of solitude.

"Momma's never coming back . . . she's never coming back . . . my momma . . ." She stuttered through the same words several times, bawling as heartbreak pulled her under. It was the worst thing I'd ever seen.

I dropped to my knees and held her as tightly as I could.

God, tell me what to do. Please help me help her.

Her sobs eventually slowed to soft weeping.

Will walked in as I dried the last of her tears with a kitchen towel. His jaw dropped and his eyes grew wide when she spun and pegged him with her puffy gaze. They stared at each other—with the same eyes.

When she turned back to me, her eyes revealed the same striking intensity as his. I wanted to ask what she'd found there in his. Wanted to know what it felt like for her. Did she recognize herself in him? Instead, I hid my surprise behind a reticent smile. "I have art supplies in my closet. Go to my room, choose your colors from the shelf, and wait for me. I'll be there soon."

She stared at Will as she pranced from the kitchen, resilient and cheerful once again.

"Are you all right, Ellie?"

I nodded but avoided his eyes. I'd fallen apart on him the night before.

He came around the center island. "You're sure?" The tenderness in his voice was soothing. I shut my eyes and tried to absorb it. "Hey." He closed in and lifted my chin, forcing eye contact, and without doubt, expecting more tears. There were none.

"Ben told you—about Detective Parker's visit?"

"Yes. And you're all right?"

"I'm fine. He thinks I had something to do with it."

"Did he accuse you?"

"It's the way he looked at me."

"I'll look into it. He hasn't yet reported your location. When he does, they'll be all over this place. Stay close to me. The local media outlets reported you missing—taken. I want them to run with that idea until we're gone. I have someone conducting surveillance in town. Still, we can't stay here long. You understand that, right? I need you to trust me."

I studied his eyes as they studied mine. I didn't know what to say. Didn't know what to do. Where else could I go? Pain, confusion, and loneliness haunted me, but when he was close, when he touched me, my mind rested. I would stay close to him. And trust him. I nodded.

"Lissie's beautiful."

"Her eyes. She looks a lot like—"

"Ethan," Will finished. "I don't believe my brother would bail on his own child." He shook his head. "Not if he knew. Let's keep this between you and me for now. I need to talk to him before jumping off with it."

—

Goose bumps ran up my arm as I sat outside on the beach with Will, even as the golden sun heated my skin. Will's spice mingled with the seaside scents and drifted on the ocean breeze, whirling around me. We watched Lissie sort through her collection of shells and stones.

"How long have you been here?" I wanted to hear it from him.

"Arrived the first of May."

"How long have you been watching me?"

"Every day since." He straightened his back and met my eyes. "But I've seen you before. You've seen me."

"What do you mean?"

"You deserve the truth, Elle."

"When?"

"My father told me about you when I was five and reminded me often how I would someday protect you. There was no imminent danger at the time I came over, and he'd forbidden it, but I needed to see for myself you were real—that the training had purpose. It all seemed mad to me then, as it does for you now. You were seventeen."

There was sincerity in his eyes. His words held me captivated. I wanted more. There had to be more, so I encouraged him. "Go on. Tell me, Will."

"You were with a group of girls walking along Water Street, laughing and eating ice cream. There was a town celebration, and the crowd was heavy. You were shoved, and I caught you." He pushed his stare to the horizon with unfocused eyes and a self-indulgent smile. "You looked up at me and apologized three times. I could never forget those green eyes."

A sharp breath pierced my chest. I remembered.

When his eyes came back to mine, the smile was gone. "Four years later, I came back. It was impulsive, ego-driven. I beat a man for following you from a pub across your university campus."

"You did that." My voice was a whisper.

His eyes were charged with emotion. "If you hadn't turned back, I would have killed him. He was planning to hurt you."

The man had threatened to find me after I snubbed his advances in the bar. Jess and I found him on the ground—half dead—and called campus police.

"How long did you stay?"

"About ten days. Would have stayed longer if Ethan hadn't ordered me home. We'd just completed the business plan for our private equity firm, and I'd ditched him." Will stood and offered his hand. "Back inside. It's getting late."

Back in my room, after I checked on Lissie once more for the night, I could only stare at the bed. Going near it would be to fall into a dark, isolated hole with no way out—a feeling that began to haunt me during my last year at UConn. Panic slinked around my neck and worked to suffocate me. I put out a hand, reaching for the wall.

I needed air, needed the sea, needed . . . something. Couldn't breathe.

Will appeared on the other side of the glass-paned doors as though he were responding to my silent plea. He opened one side and extended his hand, waiting without a word to see if his offer would be accepted. I placed my hand in his. He led me to the double-wide chaise, where he gestured with his head for me to sit and handed me an open bottle of red wine.

I wiggled into an awkward position on the edge. "Thanks. Being confined indoors is hard. I'm used to being outside, day and night."

"Unless you're with me, you must not come out of the cottage."

"I know." I tipped the wine bottle, sipping politely at first, then gulped until I had to come up for air. The edge had to be alleviated somehow—before I melted down like Lissie.

When I offered him a drink, the corners of his mouth twitched. He took a swig and returned it to my hand, and then watched me pull deep from the bottle again three more times. I sank into the downy cushions with a light head. His lips curved into a full, crooked smile as he grabbed a throw from one of the chairs and covered me.

I was tipsy, liquid courage warming me, so with a flirty smile, I held out the wine bottle but without fully extending my arm—it was an invitation. I needed the peace his closeness provided. With a raised brow, he accepted the invite, placing the bottle on the table before he dropped into the cushions next to me. He lifted his arm, and without hesitation, I rolled into his side and placed my head on his chest.

"Sleep," he commanded.

Settled against the warmth of Will's body, I slept soundly for a few hours in the cool night air. No doubt the rolling and crashing of waves had been a lullaby, but he'd been my anchor. I woke before he did and stared at his rugged, beautiful face. Golden stubble highlighted his jawline and long, dark lashes touched his cheekbones. I closed my eyes and remembered the younger version I'd bumped into ten years earlier. His hair was lighter and his face clean-shaven, but the same charged eyes stared back at me. He was well-built even then, a little leaner, and stood at the same imposing height. My strawberry ice cream dotted his black T-shirt.

He stirred, twisting from his back to his side, and pulled me closer. He was . . . aroused. As he shifted his weight and settled, the chaise's wood frame creaked in complaint.

"Will?"

"Yeah?" He opened his eyes and stared back at me.

"Tell me what's going to happen. I don't know what to do."

"Let me take you to England. I have the resources there I need to keep you safe." The suggestion rolled off his tongue with ease.

"But my life is here. I don't know how to live anywhere else. The beach, the art gallery, my friends . . ." I winced. None of it mattered without my family. Will tightened his embrace and waited while I bitch-slapped grief again. "You must have a life of your own you'd like to get back to?"

He glared at me. "Your protection is my priority. Nothing else is as important. I'll be with you or near you—"

"For how long? How long will this go on?"

He shrugged. "It may never end."

"That's . . . that's—"

"Who we are. We're bound, Elle. Neither of us can change that. I understand you haven't had time to come to terms with it, but know that I'm telling you—warning you—if you run, I'll follow. If you insist on staying here, I'll stay. Assassins will continue to search for you. I'll protect you no matter the location, but I believe England is the best option, and I'll work hard to convince you of it. The two of you will be safe at Eastridge."

"Eastridge?"

"Name of the house."

"How long will you give me to consider it?"

"Not long. There isn't much time. They're going to come for you."

I shut my eyes, overwhelmed by the thought of anything beyond the moment we were in. The future—the next day—was too much to consider. I wanted only to lie there wrapped up in Will, soothed and protected.

"What's this?" He touched the white butterfly-shaped birthmark on my neck.

My eyes popped open. His touch was rousing. "The butterfly? It's a birthmark."

He traced it several times with his fingertip, sending shivers along my spine. "Not a butterfly," he said with a slight shake of his head. His long finger wandered away from the birthmark and made its way to my bottom lip. His eyes came back to mine. Then he moved that finger and placed a warm, soft kiss in its spot.

It was easy to give myself permission to melt into his body since he already held me in his strong arms. I touched his cheek. "Do it again."

Will threw his legs over the side of the chaise with a hoarse curse and gave me his back. "Go inside and stay there."

"*What?* No." I was confused and defiant.

He lowered his head into his hands. "Please."

I leaped from the chaise and blasted through the door, not bothering to close it after it banged into the wall.

Will came back from an exhaustive shoreline run and kept his back to me as he crouched with his elbows against his thighs to catch his breath. I watched the muscles in his back expand and contract and his shoulders rise and fall, and my frustration peaked. I needed either a knockdown, drag-out fight or to be taken hard in bed. He'd made it clear he wasn't going to touch me again, so a fight he would get.

"Where's my gun?"

His head snapped in my direction. "It's my job to carry weapons, not yours."

I narrowed my eyes. "It's mine, and I want it back."

Rising to his full height, he turned and stood with his feet spread wide and arms folded over his chest. "Do you know how to use it?"

"How hard can it be?"

He darted up the veranda stairs and stopped short only to hover over me like a storm. "As long as I breathe, you'll not carry a gun. You'll not touch one or even look at one unless you've learned to use it properly. When you're finished behaving like a fucking brat, we'll talk about what needs to happen next."

"Me? You big bastard!"

"Brat," he repeated.

He was sweating, and his spiced, scorching heat turned me on. Recognizing the distraction, I stifled a moan and vowed to fight harder.

"Your move." He cocked his head.

I considered slapping the smug expression off his face.

He shook his head in warning before jerking me to his chest and resting a cheek on top of my head. "Your burden is heavy. Let me bear some of it. You don't need to worry about weapons and protecting yourself. I won't let anyone hurt you. I won't leave you."

I clutched his sweat-soaked shirt with both hands. I thought I should cry, but no tears would come. There was no swelling in the back of my throat. No sob tore at my chest. I didn't feel the sadness or grief I should have, not when I was in his arms.

"We need to focus on you. I know you worry for Lissie, but she'll be fine."

"Fine?" I glanced inside where she lounged on my bed with her tablet.

"She hasn't been discovered. Even if so, they may not care. Her lineage is matrilineal."

My fingers hadn't released his shirt, nor had he removed his arms from around me. I lay my head back on his chest to think. "Do you truly believe she's not on their radar?"

"Yes."

I lifted my chin and searched his eyes—he did believe it. Still, I would insist on actions that wouldn't risk her precious life.

Later, when Lissie slept, I approached him from behind and whispered next to his ear. "Will, take me out to the beach." Even closer, I breathed, "Please."

He dropped the newspaper and came around the chair. "Stay close to me, Elle."

Elle he'd said again, not Ellie. It was the intimate version of my name for him—the version he shared with no one. He took my hand and led me through the kitchen and down the rocky hill path to the beach.

It was an unusually warm evening, even after the sun went down hours before, but the cooling sea breeze balanced the heat. As we walked along the shoreline, he threw rocks and cursed. Finally, his thoughts spilled out and ended with a sharp command. "It would be easier for us both if you'd choose to go to England free of my coercion, but we're running out of time. I've been placating you. It's wrong for me to gamble with your life. You have forty-eight hours to get used to the idea. Then we go."

I pushed aside his edict without responding. Didn't want to think about it. He didn't need a reply anyway. His words were a decree, not an attempt at conversation—not that he'd get away with that.

We sat at the water's edge; some moments we filled with small talk, some with silence. I leaned back on my elbows and lifted my face to the moon where it hung in the deep-blue sky, surrounded by twinkling stars. The tide swept over my legs.

"You should roll up your pant legs." I'd already convinced him to take off his shirt.

Will's sculpted body seduced my creativity on more than one level. His chest was a smooth canvas, beautifully flawed by two scars. The largest was five inches in length and slashed across the middle of his right pectoral muscle. The other was about three inches long, located at the top of his ribcage beneath the left pec. High on his right deltoid, he was inked with an artful master-piece though void of color. It was a shield and within its detail were vining roses, a heraldic lion, and the Latin word *defensor*. *Defender*.

I slid my gaze to his face and found him watching me. He stared with hunger, his pupils blown. "Even warriors have to play now and then, right?" I leaned forward and slipped my hand into the water to splash him.

"Keep it up, woman, and this one will show you how we play. I'm not sure you'll like it." He winked and flashed a grin. It was the first time he'd stowed his commanding tough guy and allowed me to see how lighthearted and charming he could be.

I splashed him again.

He rolled up his jeans as I splashed him once more, but instead of extending his legs to the water or retaliating with a splash, he stood and pulled me up with him. That wide grin returned to his face, and he maintained a firm grip on my arms as his eyes moved over the water.

"You wouldn't!" I pulled back, laughing, but he held on tight. I shrieked as he swept me off my feet and stepped into the sea.

He kept walking, grinning. "I would." His cuffed jeans were wet to his knees.

"Will," I shouted through my laughter, hammering on his chest with my fist.

He put me down in water that reached the hem of my shorts. I stepped back, and with a bit of luck, found a shallow spot where I kicked water up at him. Lunging, he tossed me over his shoulder and stepped out deeper into rolling waves.

"Okay, okay, you win! Go back!"

He carried me in closer to the beach and allowed me to slide down the front of his hard body. "I always win, Elle. Always." His hands never left my waist.

"We'll see." Tumbling waves struck my knees. He watched as I dragged my fingers over the scars on his chest and upward to his shoulders and the shield. I couldn't stop touching him, caressing the length of his neck. "Kiss me, Will."

My defender leaned in and erased the distance between us. The hunger was there, burning in his eyes. He wanted that kiss as much as I did. But then he only shook his head. "You're too exposed out here. I need to be more focused." His breath brushed my lips.

"Then kiss me inside."

He shook his head again and pulled me out of the water. Will had found ways to touch me, to put his arms around me, to feel my skin. And he'd also found ways to validate each touch—keeping me together when I crumbled was part of the job. But when he'd stretched that as far as he could, he pulled back and punished us both. He denied his desire for me, though we both felt its constant pull.

I was ready to push him. "Why won't you touch me?"

He stilled, his mouth open but no words forming.

"Kiss me. Save all of me."

Glints of moonlight played in his eyes as he stared into me. "You mistake me for one of those good guys you belong with. I'm not that. Not principled, nor heroic. I destroy things, destroy people. I take what I want and don't care who objects or who is ruined in the process."

He takes what he wants. He doesn't want me. The unspoken words messed with my head. I knew they were wrong, but couldn't make them stop. My eyes dropped to the sand, and my arms tightened around my middle. I was wounded and angry.

"Look at me, Elle." He grabbed my chin and forced my face to his. "Look at me."

I did.

"Ask me if I've taken lives. Ask me if I'll kill again. How many lives do you think I've ruined in my business dealings? Ask me."

"I won't ask. I don't care," I said in defiance.

He still held my chin. "Don't you? You should." His fiery eyes burned deeper into mine.

"I don't."

"You're so stubborn."

"So."

His lips were parted as he stared at mine. "I hurt people, Elle. But I will never hurt you. Not you—not ever." He ran his thumb over my bottom lip.

"Keeping me alive and well is your sworn duty."

"It is."

I pushed his hand away. He'd taken something from me, and I planned to take it back. "As you've said, we're bound in a way that can't be undone, not until one of us is dead. So what difference does the rest of it make? But if you see me as an obligation, not someone you want—if I'm undesirable to you, then it makes sense for you to keep your distance. Because after all, you take what you want."

"What? You don't know what you're saying." Will raked his hair. "You're the only one I've ever desired." He cursed and paced through the sand in a wide circle around me until calming himself. "I don't want to hurt you."

It would have been easier to walk away and let him win. Easier to guard my heart against the danger of more wreckage. The problem was, my heart was already in too deep—it wanted to know him. I needed to know him. I stepped closer.

Will retreated, and I stepped close again. When he recognized my resolve, he stopped moving and allowed me to place my hands flat against his chiseled abs. He glared at me, his eyes mirroring my own determination.

"Tell me, Will. How will you hurt me?" I lowered my chin and met his stare from beneath my lashes.

His eyes narrowed further. "What are you doing?"

I shrugged. "You'll hit me?"

"Never." He clenched his teeth and flexed the muscles along his jaw.

"How then, how will you hurt me?"

"Stop this."

"I'm not finished. What about—"

"You deserve better than what I am," he snapped.

There it was. The choice he'd taken from me. My decisions were mine. All of them. I'd never allow anyone to take that away from me.

"But do you want me?"

"Yes."

I pressed myself against his rigid body. I stroked the back of his neck and played with the ends of his hair. His body responded, his eyes burning and his arousal straining between us. Although his arms remained at his sides, his hands were no longer balled into fists. He'd lowered his head during my attempted interrogation. His mouth was close to mine.

"*Elle.* You're playing with fire. Pushing me this way is reckless."

His rumbling voice, the gravel, it made me ache. I wanted to kiss him—wanted his hands on me—and I wanted to slap his face, but did nothing.

I reproached in a soft manner near his lips. "Reckless or not, here's the thing. I decide the level of emotional risk I'm willing to assume. You manage the physical risk . . . for now. I've accepted that. Everything else is still mine." I pushed off against his chest with both hands and walked away. "I decide what I deserve," I shouted over my shoulder, heading down the beach.

"That's far enough, goddamn it," he shouted back.

I turned around, and as I continued walking backwards, I flipped him off. I had the urge to run as I spun back in the other direction. I wanted to run away from him, from the responsibility of caring for Lissie, from my whole lonely, screwed-up life. So I did run. I sprinted along the beach, not caring if someone was waiting at the other end to kill me. I ran and freed myself from it all, if only for a few moments.

I never looked back. I just ran.

Will grabbed me from behind and lifted me midstride. "What the hell are you doing?"

"Let go of me, you gigantic ass!" I twisted and kicked at air.

"Give me your word you'll not run away from me again."

"Go to hell."

Without warning, he tossed me over his shoulder and headed back to the cottage. One arm restrained both of my legs beneath my thighs, and he used his other hand to gather and hold my wrists behind his neck. "Christ, Elle. You have an awful temper."

I called him names and demanded he let me go, but he ignored my insults and walked until we reached the cottage. I pounded on his back with my fists when he let go of my wrists to open the kitchen door.

"Stop this or I'll smack your arse," he threatened.

"You said you wouldn't hit me."

"I won't, not that way, but I will smack your arse if you don't quit this tantrum."

I pushed harder. "Fuck you, Will."

He set me on my feet with a furious jolt and pushed my back against the wall. His body was tight against mine—he was aroused again—and he held my wrists to his chest. His charged eyes rested on my mouth. "I'm beginning to think that's exactly what you need—a good, hard fucking. One you'll never forget."

"Let's go," I challenged. I chewed on my bottom lip and matched him stare for stare.

Ben came into the kitchen, reversing his direction as soon as he realized what was going on. He didn't say anything, but the raised brow and snicker said enough. He'd heard everything.

That was all Will needed to remind himself a good, hard fucking was exactly what he wouldn't give me. "Go to your room." He released my wrists and stepped back. "Do not leave this cottage." Then he strutted down the hallway and went back to his stack of newspapers, confident I would do as he'd commanded.

Four

I POUNDED THE SIDE of my fist on the doorframe. The police believed we were missing—we'd have to skip the funeral. Not only had the Order taken our family from Lissie and me, but they also stole our opportunity to say goodbye. Inside my mind, I imagined Reverend Archer's prayer as he committed the bodies of my grandmother and sister to the earth for rest and their souls to our Father in heaven.

No one was positioned on guard outside my bedroom doors. I needed a human connection, so I headed to the kitchen, but no one was there either. There were no men eating, drinking, cleaning weapons, or reading newspapers. The full moon tugged at me through the window, and the energy of the riotous sea called out.

I left through the kitchen door and made my way down the uneven path to the beach, seeking freedom from the endless mind clutter. My tired legs carried me knee-deep into the sea, where my lungs finally filled with ease again. Brisk water struck my thighs. "Just a few minutes to clear my head," I said to the sea. "He'll come quickly and haul me back inside anyway—no doubt he's already headed this way."

For a moment, something blocked the soft glow cast by the veranda lights. When the light was obstructed again, I turned and stared but found nothing.

I closed my eyes and inhaled, taking a deep breath through my nose, refocusing on the sea. I extended the length of my arms backward and pulled in another vigorous breath. Before I could exhale, a thick arm squeezed my neck and prevented it.

A crude whisper in my ear told me not to move, and then cold steel replaced the arm.

My body and mind failed me. I couldn't move. Couldn't think.

An assassin was behind me, pressing a large knife into my throat. He slogged through climbing waves, dragging me into deeper water. His blade's smooth edge chilled the skin where it demanded the attention of my throbbing carotid. Blood pulsed violently through my veins. Pain twisted inside my chest.

"You'll die tonight, and this will be done at long last." He filled his other hand with my hair. "I don't even have to spill your blood out here in this mad sea." His accent was thick and inarticulate. I couldn't place it.

I still held my breath. Both lungs burned, pleading with me to use them. I released the breath I'd held hostage and my choking gasps were followed by a loud, exhaled cry.

"Shut your fucking mouth. No noise." He yanked hard on my hair, pulling me off my feet.

My blurred vision improved as oxygen reached my blood once again. I heard the respiration of my own lungs and the thumping of my heart inside my head. It grew louder. I could no longer hear the crash of waves. It was my turn. I would follow my sister in death.

The executioner moved another step deeper into the sea. "You made this too easy, standing out here alone while your men are distracted by mine. What a daft girl you are."

When he pulled me deeper, I stumbled on a slimy rock and lost my balance. Another wall of waves rolled in as I fell forward and sank into the water. The force pulled me under, pulled me from his grasp, and dragged me several feet away from him, several feet closer to shore.

He lumbered through waves and jerked me upright by the hair.

I gulped air and vomited seawater. The brine burned my sinuses as I choked on both.

"Ready for more? Take one last look at land. You'll never see it again." He turned us toward the beach and wrenched my head up. He stopped with a sudden lurch and pressed the blade to my throat again.

I gasped with such brutal force salt blistered my lungs.

My defender stood before us.

Clouds pushed back over the horizon and allowed me to see Will clearly in the light cast by the moon. His posture was tall and erect while his stance was wide. His fists were balled into lethal weapons. The muscles in his jaw were clenched and his chin jutted. Veins bulged and throbbed in his corded neck and arms. His eyes flashed with fury and the promise of death. He was a dangerous storm in his own right.

"Focus on me, Elle," he thundered above all other sound. "Look at me. Only me."

Locked into his fiery stare, terror fled from my soul, and I was soothed by those raging flashes of emotion in his eyes. Maybe I was sick for feeling that way—maybe my mind was broken. Either way, that fire in his eyes was my salvation.

Cloud cover rolled in, and Will became a dark silhouette against a blanket of stratus haze. I felt the intensity of the assassin's stare as he locked on Will's hulking, shadowed form. I searched the darkness until I found Will's eyes again. He nodded. Strength climbed from my quivering stomach. I elbowed the assassin twice in the abdomen.

He grunted and grabbed his gut in reflex, losing his grip on the knife. It fell from my throat into the water. I dislodged my lower body from his. He still held the ends of my hair firm in his other hand.

"I can snap your neck just as easily, bitch," he spat through his teeth, jerking my head back. The stink of cheap bourbon and garlic buzzed around my face, and I gagged. Before he could secure my body against his again, a sharp pop and its echo rang through the night. Then another. The second bullet hit the assassin in one of his legs and caused him to jerk and contort.

"Hold, goddamn it," Will shouted over his shoulder.

The assassin steadied himself using my shoulders. He shielded his body with mine.

I couldn't breathe, couldn't draw breath or release it.

He was strangling me.

Will charged, his eyes burning with rage and teeth bared. A bellow tore from his throat. His powerful arms ripped me from my captor's hold and thrust me toward the shore.

Punishing waves dragged me close to dry land. I forced my exhausted body up on all fours and clawed my way through sand, stones, and rotting seaweed onto the beach, and collapsed. My lungs purged seawater and filled with air at the same time. I lay there gasping and choking, closer to death than I'd ever been, the side of my face pressed into wet sand.

Then everything went black.

I regained consciousness in Ben's arms as he carried me into the cottage. He placed me on the sofa and wrapped my soaked body in blankets, keeping close. Too close. He scrutinized my actions as though he expected something from me. I trembled with cold and shock but had nothing else to give. My soul was numb.

Clashing male voices rumbled from the kitchen, snatching my brain from its fog.

"Stay here, Ellie. Do not move," Ben ordered as he jumped up and headed that way.

"Where is she?" Will snarled.

"Calm down and think. You'll scare her. You're covered in—"

"Get out of my way, boy."

I kicked the blankets to the floor and staggered in the direction of his voice. Ben and John barricaded the doorway with their bodies. Were they protecting me from Will? I knew he would never hurt me. I pushed at their backs. "Move. Please!" I pushed again, but they were solid. "Please, let me through." It hurt to speak. My throat was torn up.

In the small gap between their bodies, I saw Will look down at himself. His soaked shirt was stained with blood. He pulled it over his head and wrapped it around his mangled fist. "I won't say it more than once. You will not touch her, and you'll move out of her way as she's asked you to do." His tone was calm, but he was primed for attack if he didn't get what he wanted.

Ben and John stepped aside, and I exploded forward, racing to Will. He caught me and lifted me into his arms. Warm lips rested along my temple as he held me tight against his bare chest. My heart raced. It was then I realized how far gone I was—I'd fallen hard for the dangerous man who'd just killed another to save my life.

His rasping whisper swept over my ear. "Are you hurt, baby? Did he hurt you?"

"I'm okay." I swallowed against the burn.

"Never do that to me again, Elle."

He pressed those lips into my skin, allowing his soft kiss to linger there at my temple. In the heat of the moment, he'd been unable to keep his feelings in check.

His hand was a mess. Will's weapon of choice was his fists. He preferred to beat his enemies to death—time permitting—rather than shooting them. After a brief argument, he allowed me to clean the wounds on his knuckles and wrap his hand with gauze. He'd taken life with those bare hands and didn't want me to touch them, didn't want me close to the death he'd caused. But what he'd done couldn't change how I wanted him. And, God, I wanted him.

"Why is it you're good at this? You've had practice with someone else?" Will snapped. He raised both brows and waited for the answer he wouldn't get.

"You're well acquainted with ice, I suppose." I pressed a frozen compress to his hand harder than necessary.

"Ow." He feigned a grimace he couldn't sustain. "Merciless woman." His lips twitched until he let them curve, and then he winked.

I smiled, too. "I agree to go with you to England. Our passports need to be picked up from the house in town. I won't go back there, but I'll give you the code for the safe."

I couldn't see any other path forward. We had no one left in Connecticut. If Lissie was Ethan's, she had a family there—a father, a grandmother, and three uncles. And I wanted revenge. The yearning took me by surprise. It burned slow somewhere deep within me and continued to rise. In England, I could sort through the mess and find the answers I needed. I could learn to fight. I could plan retribution against those who took my family from me.

Will gave a clipped nod and checked his watch. "Plane leaves in sixteen hours."

Will rushed into my bedroom just as I'd finished packing and pulled me to his side. "Police are headed this way."

I ran to the living room and peered out the window. "It's Josh. He won't bother coming to the front. I should meet him out on the veranda before he gets to the door."

"No. You're not going out there. We don't know why he's here."

"He won't hurt me. Let me talk to him. I'll convince him to let me leave."

Will grabbed my wrists and yanked me close to his chest. Jealous rage filled his eyes. "What makes you think he'll let you go? I sure as hell wouldn't."

"I'm not with him anymore—and *no one* owns me," I snapped.

He opened his fingers, releasing my wrists, and stepped back.

Ben looked outside. "The two of you need to go out there and explain what's going on. Unless you plan to kill him, there's no other way. Good news is, he's alone."

I edged closer, stepping back into the space of Will's dark energy. His breath warmed my face. "Ben's right, we must tell him. Promise me, Will. Promise you won't hurt him."

"For you . . ." He tucked a lock of hair behind my ear and nodded. "But let me be clear. If he is aggressive with you in any way, all bets are off."

We stepped out onto the veranda.

"Why haven't you answered your goddamned phone? You've been here all this time? State police are due tomorrow to begin searching the water for your body. What the fuck is wrong with you?" Josh shouted. "Your family was murdered, Ellie—but you know that, don't you? And still, you're here, shacked up with—"

Will moved so fast there was no time to stop him. They were toe-to-toe. "Watch your fucking mouth when you speak to her, cop."

"Vá se foder." It was the Portuguese equivalent of *go fuck yourself.* "I saw the two of you outside Nick's that night."

Will's chest vibrated.

"Josh." My voice was hoarse but confident. "Give me a chance to tell you what's happened. Please."

"Listen to what she has to say. Her life's in danger. She was nearly killed last night, and they'll come for her again."

Josh's eyes fell to the bruises on my neck before meeting mine. His face softened.

I held Josh's stare. "Go inside, Will, please. Let me tell him what he needs to know."

Will did as I asked but didn't go far. The rumble of his deep voice passed through the wall that separated us and soothed me. I was safe, protected.

Josh sat on the top step of the veranda next to me. He watched the cottonlike clouds drift lazily over the Atlantic and listened as I shared my story. A story I hadn't even fully grasped. It was surreal—I'd fallen down a rabbit hole.

"Jesus, you've had me so worried. Thought you were dead. Lissie's unharmed?"

"Physically, yes. I'm sorry. Sorry to put you in this position. Especially when—"

"Don't say it, Ellie. I know I've lost you. You don't need to say it."

"I won't survive without him. If I stay here, authorities won't believe me, and they'll win. They'll take my life, just as they took Isobel's."

He closed his eyes. "Go then. No one will stop you. I give you my word."

"Don't sacrifice your career, Josh. Do whatever you have to when I'm gone."

"Go tonight. I'll make my report in the morning. I can't offer more time than that. My superiors will try to force you back once you've been located. There's nothing I can do to stop them."

"But the government needs an indictment to extradite, right?"

"Yeah, but Connecticut could ask the State Department to revoke your passport during the investigation, potentially provoking deportation."

There was nothing more to be said, nothing that would provide comfort for either of us. We sat still and quiet for some time, his arm around me, my head resting against his. He hushed me each time I tried to speak and eventually walked away without another word.

Will's fist smashed through plaster at the same time I opened the door and stepped inside.

"Stop it, Will. It's done. He's gone. We're free to leave."

He closed in fast and pushed his way into my eyes as if he were inspecting my soul. Satisfied with what he found, he said, "I'm sorry. Let's go now, before you change your mind."

"I'm guessing you wouldn't handle that well. I'll get Lissie."

Lissie was on the airplane—the private jet Will hired—exploring with John. Will and I stood on the tarmac while Ben sorted through customs documentation with the pilots.

"Ready?" Will asked. His hand covered the small of my back.

"I'm ready." Terrified but ready. I bit my lip and avoided his eyes. Flying was a nightmare for me, and I'd failed to tell him how sick I might become if the meds didn't knock me out. I'd seen several doctors for it, and they'd concurred. It was all in my head, a phobia. Knowing my parents died in a plane crash was the root cause.

"What is it? Are you okay?"

I glanced at the plane again. "Fine." Anxiety slashed at my empty stomach.

After following my nervous glance, he stepped in front of me and hovered above. "Why didn't you tell me? How bad is it?"

"I've taken something. With luck, I'll sleep until we land. We should go. I need to check on Lissie, and they're waiting." I flashed an uneasy smile and eyed the pilots where they stood near the foot of the steps.

"And they'll continue to wait. What can I do to make it easier for you?"

"I don't know that anything else can be done."

"Anything—just say it. We don't leave until you have what you need." The back of his fingers brushed my cheek.

"There's nothing, but thank you."

His fingers brushed my battered, discolored throat, and then his fingertips and his eyes rested there.

"Will?"

"Yeah?"

You're what I need.

"Elle?"

"I'm sorry for the way I behaved."

"Don't be. You'll never have to apologize. Not to me. You *should* be angry. I've been a fool." His hand moved to the back of my head. He pulled me close and lowered his mouth to mine. And then he kissed me.

When he released my lips, my soul mourned the loss. We stood motionless, like we had turned to stone, each of us locked in the other's gaze. Will's eyes pleaded for forgiveness before he took my lips between his again. I touched his face and nodded, forgiving him.

He threaded his fingers deep into my hair and slanted his mouth over mine, pushing past my lips with his tongue. The intense, unyielding way he kissed me made his intent clear—he was driven by his desire for me and nothing else. And he was taking what he wanted. Something in him had shifted after I was attacked on the beach, and again after Josh showed up.

As the sun's last ray dove below the horizon, Will and I tasted each other for the first time in a stormy but deliberate tangle. We didn't stop until we shared the same sustaining breath.

His fist tightened in my hair as he pulled back and stared beyond my shoulder. Those fiery eyes pushed back into mine before he placed one more lingering kiss on my mouth. "Someone's here to see you off." He let go and stepped back. Although Will's eyes were still locked on me, the next words he spoke were meant for Ben. "Handle this for me." Then he walked away.

The pain on Josh's face was unmistakable. It twisted my gut and tore at my conscience, though it had no impact on my heart. Hurting him was never my intention, but there it was—deepened by the intense, passionate moment with Will he'd just witnessed.

"I couldn't leave it the way we did. I shouldn't have walked away earlier."

"I'll never forget all that you've done for me, Josh."

"Don't go. Please don't go. Get in the car. I believe you. I'll convince the chief and protect you—I promise."

Ben's thick arm held the car door shut as Josh tried to open it. "Don't do it, cop. Say your fucking goodbye so we can get her to safety."

Josh's hand moved to his hip. He was out of uniform, but he still carried. His arm dropped when he realized he had reached for his gun.

"I'm going. Lissie deserves a better life than what I can give her here. My staying would only turn Stonington into a war zone."

His aggrieved brown eyes pleaded. "I don't know how to live without you."

"You do. Take care of Jess for me. I can't communicate with her right now. I won't put her at risk." I put my arms around him and rested my head on his shoulder.

"I'm begging you." He pulled me tight against his body and pressed his cheek to mine. "Don't go."

"Ellie," Ben said in warning.

I didn't need an explanation to understand why his warning was serious. The next time Will hit something, it wouldn't be a wall. But I had to say goodbye—Josh deserved as much.

My lips pressed their last kiss to Josh's cheek.

In the next moment, as I was about to step back from Josh, we were ripped apart, and he sailed several feet through the air before skidding over asphalt on his back.

Will pinned me against a metal building and held me there with his body while his hands possessed the long layers of my hair. He'd flown across the tarmac with unbelievable speed and force. "Do you want him?" he asked in a low, menacing tone close to my ear as he pushed his growing arousal into my stomach. "Do you?" His nostrils flared with each breath. Muscles along his jawline contracted.

I explored the darkness that consumed his eyes. His scent messed with my head, causing my brain to interpret his fierce nature as therapy for my restless spirit. I was distantly aware of the other two men arguing behind us.

"He's not hurting her," Ben said as he shoved Josh against the hood of his car. "That will never happen."

Will purred as he nipped at my earlobe. "I'll kill him."

Panting and aroused, I gripped his neck with my nails. "You won't. I want you."

Five

WILL BACKED AWAY from me and offered his hand. When I took it without hesitation, he guided me across the tarmac, and as soon as we reached the jet, he let go and busied himself with luggage and the pilots. I couldn't take my eyes off of him. Sensing my stare, he stilled for a moment and then reconnected, his expression revealing penance. "Go on in, baby," he said softly, tilting his head toward the plane's entrance.

I watched Will conduct pat-downs on each of the pilots through a smudged window.

"You're getting used to his way." John winked like a miniature version of his brother. A tight smirk similar to Will's tugged at his mouth. The girls must have loved this kid.

"Is there another way?" I tasted my lips. The rich flavor of Will's declarative kisses still lingered there and on my tongue. The jealous fury and the subsequent remorse I'd seen in his eyes filled my mind.

Lissie raced up and down the aisle wearing a backpack filled with her favorite stuffed animals, her activity dragging me out of my head. The Dramamine would soon slow her down.

"Come here, girlie, let's make up your bed so it's ready when you're sleepy."

The plane had a full galley and two separate areas with luxurious white leather seating and glossy walnut paneling. The first seating area had four individual reclining seats and two collapsible tables. John helped me berth one seat flat for Lissie. I hoped she'd sleep the duration of the flight and then some, though it would be noon in England when we arrived. The second area had a plush pullout sofa and entertainment center. At the back was the lavatory, and even though it was small, it was as luxurious as those you'd find in an upscale hotel.

Ben came in and conducted a sweep of the rear cabin, and when he positioned himself in the cockpit, he looked as if he belonged there.

"He flies, doesn't he?"

"Royal Air Force pilot. He's conducting a preflight check and looking for anything suspicious," John said.

The precautions Will had undertaken were serious and alarming—it exposed the enormity of what we faced. I corralled Lissie and sat her on my lap, and John positioned himself in front of us as the two pilots boarded, his protective stance obvious. The pilots inspected the cabin before settling into the cockpit for departure preparations.

Will entered the cabin last with the large, black duffel that held their weapons thrown over his shoulder, ducking beneath the six-inches-too-short ceiling. As he headed for the rear seating area, he grabbed my hand and pulled me with him.

Lissie followed and leaped between us as soon as we sat on the sofa. She was already at ease with him—she'd found her very own superhero. He pushed a wild lock of hair out of her face. "When you wake, we'll be across the sea. Your castle awaits, princess."

One beat of my heart was forever lost.

"Are we going to see a real castle?" Her eyes and mouth were wide with excitement.

"Something like that, but first you must sleep."

"Get ready for bed, Lissie." I pointed to the lavatory she'd already surveyed twice. "Your toothbrush is there."

Will pressed back against the sofa and took me with him, tucking me snug beneath his arm. The jealousy and anger were long gone, tenderness overriding. "We'll take off once you're both settled. You sleep here, baby."

Snuggling into his body felt as natural as being home. I sensed it was that way for him, too. Awkward moments didn't exist for Will and me. We were equally attracted to each other. Equally comfortable touching the other. I burrowed deeper into his warmth and teased. "Good—keep me close to the lav."

The muscles in his shoulders and arms tensed. "How bad, Elle?"

"I don't know. I've never flown on anything like this. Are there any stops?"

"No stops. We'll be in the air for seven hours." He released a heavy breath and then captured my hand and kissed it. But that wasn't enough. It would never be enough. I couldn't wait for him to kiss me again, to feel his lips on mine. It was challenging to think of anything else.

Lissie was out sooner than expected. She'd curled up between us and lost her battle with sleep. Will carried her to the front, and I tucked her into a mountain of blankets and stuffed animals. We then settled on the pulled-out sofa with our legs stretched over the length of it. Will with his scotch, and me under his big arm with my ginger ale. I was preparing for the worst.

The pilots received authorization from the control tower and fired the engines. They waited only for Will's word.

"Ready to do this?"

"As ready as I can be." I'd hoped to be sleeping, but the sandman refused to come for me.

He shouted to the front, "Let's go."

Ben tapped on the clear panel that divided the cockpit from the cabin to signal the pilots and then closed the privacy curtain between the front and back seating areas.

We taxied down the runway within seconds.

"Maybe you just need a distraction," Will said with a raised brow and crooked smile. He stared at my mouth.

I stared back at his. "Maybe."

"Let's give it a whirl, shall we?" He set our glasses aside and laced our fingers. "You're okay with the way I kissed you earlier?"

"Yes." I couldn't curb the disobedient smile. "Do you plan to do it again?"

He rolled onto his side and slid an arm beneath me, using it to pull me close. His lips hovered above mine. "You have no idea."

My stomach flipped. Butterflies, not nausea.

Will dragged his fingers down my leg until he reached my toes. He hesitated for a moment before he closed his hand around my foot and dragged it up, bending my knee and spreading my legs. His hand slid to my thigh. He rotated his wrist until long fingers extended beneath the hem of my white denim shorts. "You really should wear more clothing when you're near me." His voice grew deeper with each word, the texture more distinct.

I grabbed his face and drew his mouth to mine, breathing my words onto his lips. "I'm fully clothed."

"I have your bare arse in my hand, so it's not enough." Then he sucked and pulled on my lips with his until he felt like slipping his tongue into my mouth to explore mine. His kiss was like velvet—smooth and self-indulgent. It was luxurious and addictive. He was attentive and generous.

The diversion tactic was working. We were in the air, and I could think of only one thing: Will. Touching him, and being touched by him.

"No more holding back," he said in my ear. A trail of heat blistered my skin where he kissed his way from there to the edge of my blouse. His hand left my behind and worked the buttons.

"No more," I admonished.

"Won't make that mistake again, Elle. I'll give you whatever you want." I reached for his hard length after he pushed it against my body. He caught my fingers and kissed them before imprisoning my hand above my head.

I wanted him. "I—"

He shut my mouth with his. Urgency burned in his eyes when he pulled back. "I need you to think this through. Maybe you have, but you must be certain. We're already bound, but if we do this—once I've had you—it can never be undone. There'll be no one else for either of us. Never again will another man touch you, not as long as I breathe. You need to know how it'll be with me. Make sure that's what you want. Remember who I am, what I've done. What I'll do." Warning was written in his eyes.

I'm the bad guy. You must be okay with that. And I was.

"Will—"

He pressed his lips to mine. His mouth dragged over my cheek to my ear. "Hear me out," he whispered. "You're right, I want you. Bloody fucking hell I can think of nothing else. I need you to be the one to make a clearheaded decision. If you want me, if you choose me, or if you fail to make a decision at all, I'll take what I want. And that's every piece of you. If you decide otherwise, I'll protect you but from a distance. Can't be part of your life that way. Can't be near you and not have you. So choose, Elle, choose what you want, and be absolutely sure. Whatever you decide, baby, I'll give it to you. You have my word."

What he had failed to realize was I'd also fallen beyond reason. We were in the same crazy place. Still, I wanted to give him something to ease his worried soul. My fingers played along his jawline, my nails scratching through his slight beard. "I have thought about it, and I know what I want. I always know what I want. I choose you, Will."

He pushed the unbuttoned blouse from my shoulders. His illuminated eyes swept over me from head to toe. "You're so beautiful. Feminine and delicate. Perfect."

I'd been blessed with exceptional metabolism and long legs.

Will pressed my back to the cushions and positioned himself above me. His fevered lips were on mine as he finessed open the button on my shorts. "I'm going to take this off. I want to see more." He stared into my eyes as he tugged down the zipper.

I nodded. I was his for the taking.

"I need to touch you. Waited so long." He used his kiss to burn a path from my mouth to my stomach and slid the shorts over my hips and down my legs.

I moaned and arched against his mouth. I needed him. Nothing else mattered. The taste of scotch on his tongue, his virile scent, the feel of his hot mouth on my skin—God, I was high.

When he came back to my mouth, I yanked at his shirt until he pulled it over his head. He pushed his hand down into my lace panties and slid two fingers inside me, drawing a sharp cry from my lips that he smothered—no, swallowed—with his kiss. "Christ, you're so wet, baby. Smaller than I expected. So tight," he murmured, circling higher with his thumb as he moved his fingers in and out of me. He tested me. Watched me. Pushed me.

No words formed in my head as he increased the intensity of his touch. Pleading for release from the ache he caused, I pulled his face down to mine and cried the one word my brain had retained. His name.

He smirked against my mouth.

I writhed beneath him and cried out again, this time climaxing—shattering into billions of tiny fragments of myself. He owned me with his kiss, thrusting deep with his tongue, swallowing every sound I made.

"You are mine. You'll never let another man touch you again." Not just words. It was a command, and he wanted confirmation I wouldn't break it.

"You. Only you," I whispered, lost in his charged eyes.

He acknowledged our agreement with a bow of his head and kissed me once more before he stood. "Leave it," he ordered when he saw me reach for my blouse.

I snuggled into the blanket, sipping ginger ale, and watched the muscles in his shoulders and back ripple as he stretched the way a lion might when rising from his den.

Before Will closed the dividing curtain on his way back from the front of the plane, he turned and snapped, "What?"

John extended his phone. "Ethan says he's been trying to reach you for an hour."

Will didn't take the phone. Instead, he shut the curtain and picked up his own, thumbing Ethan's number as he sat down next to me. "What is it? When? What the fuck does that mean?" He took my hand and kissed it as he listened to his brother.

Panic rushed up my spine. They were talking about me.

"Wait a minute," Will said into the phone. "You okay, Elle? Your skin is on fire."

I shook my head, increasing the dizziness that buzzed about my brain. I kicked and thrashed against the blanket to free myself.

"I'll ring you later. Handle it, Ethan. I have to go."

"Why does she want me dead? It's absurd to think I'd move for the throne." The thought was random, incoherent—or maybe it was appropriate, I didn't know.

"The queen's been known to get her hands dirty, yes, but not this. Not murder."

A cold sweat consumed me. I prattled on like a child. "Why won't she make them stop?"

"You're not well, baby. We can talk about this later."

Beads of sweat formed above my top lip. I covered my ringing ears. "Medicine."

Will raced for my bag. The cabin spun faster. I collapsed backward onto the pillows. His words—whatever he'd said—and the fumbling of his hands through my things sounded as though it had come from the end of a long, echoing corridor. He placed an arm behind me and held a small pill on his palm.

I put it in my mouth and swallowed three times before it went down. "Too hot," I said hoarsely and collapsed against his arm. I had no other layers to remove.

"Be still. I'll get something cold." He placed me gently on the pillows and moments later appeared from the lavatory with small towels soaked with cold water. One he pressed to my forehead and the other to my neck.

"Get me some ice," he shouted, jumping up to meet Ben at the curtain.

"How bad is it?"

"I don't know. Be sure the pilots avoid turbulence if possible. Keep your eye on the young one." Then he was back at my side, placing ice inside the towels.

I grabbed a cube from the bucket and popped it into my mouth.

"What else can I do to help you?" Will backed away when I reached for him. "I can't hold you—my body heat will increase your temperature."

Nausea hit fast and hard, taking control of my body. I covered my mouth and clawed at him and the cushions in a desperate attempt to get to the lavatory. He got it and carried me the few feet to the door, gently setting me down inside.

I fell to my knees and retched without control into the toilet, bringing up what little there was and then nothing more than stomach acid. Will was on his knees behind me. He held up my hair and convulsing body.

"Jesus, Elle. When did you last eat? You're ripping your gut to pieces."

I was sicker than I'd ever been. It was stupid of me to not have eaten, to not have taken a larger dose of meds. I gagged up stomach acid until there was none, and then dry heaved for another ten or fifteen minutes before finally collapsing into Will's arms. The tempo of my heart was erratic, and my weak body listless.

Will settled on the floor and held me, his big body half in and half out of the lavatory. He ran his fingers through my hair and soothed me with his protective whispers.

The next phase moved in and racked my body with violent tremors. Disjointed thoughts overwhelmed me. I was frightened. My blood turned cold. A heavy blanket tightened around me, suffocating me. My mind rebelled against the attack but my body had no fight left. "Not yet. Don't kill me," I whispered.

"Baby, it's me. Look at my eyes." The blanket was Will, his warm arms and body wrapped tight around my frigid frame. "Your mind isn't clear. We need to get fluids back into you." I dug my fingers into his arm. "I won't let go, Elle. I promise." He pressed my face to his bare chest and kissed the top of my head. Then he shouted for Ben.

Ben appeared like he'd been standing there all along. He held out a blanket and turned his head while Will wrapped it around me. "We're still four or five hours out. If she could sleep through the rest of—"

"Too late for that. Find me something with electrolytes—anything. Grab my phone."

Ben tossed Will's phone. "Should be an electrolyte replacement with the first-aid gear. Be right back."

Will barked through the phone at his younger brother back in England. "Thomas, get a paramedic to the tarmac on standby. And not some fucking ambulance driver. The signal is weak—you're breaking up. Bad enough. Not sure she'll keep it down. Get on— damn it!" The signal dropped. He lifted himself and me at once from the floor and lay me on the sofa bed.

Acid burned my throat. The irregular rhythm of my heart fluttered inside my ears. My pounding head was more than I could tolerate. I couldn't slow my breath or the trembling of my cold body. An involuntary whimper slipped past my lips.

Ben was back with a bottle of cloudy water. "Get in there and hold her against your skin. It's the only way she can warm up."

Will nodded. "Lissie?"

"Sleeping soundly, but John's a bit unnerved."

"Give me a few minutes then send him back."

Ben cleared his throat. "Ethan called me."

"What for?"

"He wanted to know how far gone you are."

I couldn't see their faces, but it was obvious by the tension-filled silence they'd communicated something without words.

"Don't worry about it. Sounds like he's over it," Ben said as he headed back to the front.

"Fuck him if he's not." Will took off his jeans and climbed in with me. His skin seared mine when he pulled me to his body and wrapped his scorching arms around me. The kiss he placed on my forehead was like fire. He pulled the blanket over us and shifted his weight. "Try some water?"

I shook my head.

"I'll give you a little more time, then you must."

"Will?" John said hesitantly.

"Get my phone." He angled his chin toward the lavatory. "You have control up front?"

"Yeah. How is she?"

"Not sure. Pull it together—I need your help. See if you can get a signal and get Thomas on the phone. When we arrive at Gatwick, stay with Lissie. Take her to Ethan's car. She doesn't know anyone else other than Ben, and he needs to get to his daughter. Mum will be there to help."

"Ethan's car? You don't want her with you, close to Ellie?"

"It may frighten her. Get straight, boy. I've got this. Now go on."

John pushed his shoulders back and walked away with confidence.

My icy body melted further into Will's heat. Trembling slowed to shivering, and at some point, soothed by the thundering of his heartbeat against my face, I fell asleep. He woke me frequently to make me drink the electrolyte-enriched water. I drank with success three or four times, but the last time, a wave of nausea rolled through my wasted body.

"Going to be sick," I croaked.

Will wrapped me in the blanket and lifted me, sitting us on the floor again near the toilet. He gathered my hair and waited patiently while I heaved up the water I'd taken in. I fell back against him and fainted.

"No—open your eyes goddamn it, Elle," he ordered, lowering my head.

I tried but failed to focus on his eyes.

"Do not do that to me again. Understand?"

I had nothing left to give. I closed my eyes, my fate resting in his hands. Senseless, daunting thoughts ran wild inside my head, tormenting me, knowing I couldn't fight back. The lyrics dark and eager, convincing me I couldn't feel my heart, that someone was killing me.

My mind was broken.

Thomas called. "You're still about an hour and twenty out. The pilot is making good time so maybe less. Paramedic is there waiting. Did you get fluids into her?"

"A few ounces she just tossed."

"There's nothing else you can do other than keep her conscious until the paramedic can administer to her intravenously. Don't let her pass out. Sleep should be okay, but not fainting."

"I want you all at the tarmac. Bring mother to help John with

Lissie. I need you with me, Thomas. Search the paramedic before you bring him on board."

"We'll be there, but need to leave now. You may be in before we can get there."

"Let Mum ride with Ethan and don't wait for them. Drive my car. I'm quite serious when I say I need you here when we land."

"Ah. Got it."

That was the last thing I heard before I fell asleep—or passed out, I don't know which.

Six

AFTER THE PARAMEDIC administered fluids intravenously and the tachycardia ceased, Will carried me from the plane to his shining black Jaguar. The car suited him well—strong, smart, sexy. "I've got you, Elle. You can trust me," he whispered as he sheltered me in his arms.

I was comforted by the car ride, the smooth roar of the engine, the luxurious floating of the wheels over asphalt, the security of Will's embrace. I'd curled around him on the back seat while Thomas drove through the lush green countryside to Hastings, an ancient seaside town at the east end of England's southern coast, two hours south of London. The house was located on the eastern ridge above the sandstone cliffs overlooking the English Channel.

The reason Will favored Thomas's help was obvious. Thomas was the closest in size and strength and had a similar disposition. He had a powerful build like Will and looked a lot like him, though the way he carried himself was different and he was an inch or two shorter. Thomas was the only one able to hold Will in check on a physical level, and he'd done so when Will went after the paramedic.

I'd fallen sick on the plane, but that wasn't the worst of it. I'd also fallen apart.

In the coming days, repressed grief and fear came forward as a destructive cyclone of emotion. My mind fought back the one way it knew how, forcing a mental lockdown.

But after four long, rainy days, the sunshine radiating through the windows finally drew me out of bed. I counted them. Nineteen deer frolicked across the boundless lawn of the estate, their spirits wild and free. One small doe stopped and fixed her eyes on my window. Through her, my soul looked back at me. It scorned and provoked, and pushed me to let in the pain.

As if she were satisfied with the message she'd delivered, the little female ran back to the herd and left me staring at my reflection in the pane of glass. It was clear there was only one way to free myself from the darkness I'd fallen into. Feel the pain. Acknowledge it, so it would leave me. Before that moment, my broken mind had refused to embrace the idea.

Will wound his arms around me from behind and watched the deer play.

"Will, go on. Do something for yourself today." It was time for me to get it together, and I had to be sure I mended with my own pieces, not his.

"I can stay. Try the medication. Please, baby."

I sent him away after soaking his shirt with a rainstorm of tears. The first since the night my family was murdered.

He'd stayed in that room with me for days, working hard to protect me from grief and depression. He allowed me to absorb his strength and fuse with his soul. It was the only way to be free of my pain. From the moment we arrived in England, he'd accepted the burden and carried it as his own. There was nothing more selfish than what I'd done to him.

I shoved the numbness away and pulled the pain inward. Every splintered piece of my heart cut me deep, and those cuts bled heavily. My soul bled for Isobel. She was too young—my sister's life ended far too soon. It bled for Gran. Her death was unintended. She'd been in the wrong place at the wrong time. My soul bled for the parents I'd never known. And for all the years of my life when I wasn't alone—the years I had with my sister and my grandmother—but still felt as though I had been.

I cried with the force of someone who was drowning. Snot and tears mixed together in my mouth, choking me. I screamed soundlessly and writhed as pain and loss ripped through my hemorrhaging spirit. Fear and anxiety were all that remained when I found the strength to pick myself up from the floor. Fear and anxiety could be managed.

Steam would provide relief for my raw throat and gritty, swollen eyes, so I turned on the hot tap and stepped into the shower. Fresh linens covered the bed and a silver tray filled with sandwiches, cheeses, and fruit was on the table when the rose-scented steam and I emerged from the bathroom an hour later. Will had warned me about the efficiency of the household staff.

I slipped into my white silk robe. When I pulled the pins from my hair and let it fall, my mind drifted to Will. He'd return soon. A tiny flutter tickled the walls of my stomach. As if summoned by some intuitive force, he pushed through the door with a bottle of scotch in one hand and a bottle of red wine in the other. He poured without words as he watched me, evaluating my mood, watching it brighten before his eyes.

What we shared in the days prior was intimate and beautiful, chaste. His kisses had been tender and sweet and his arms a sanctuary. But that was about to change. Neither of us could wait another moment to lose ourselves to that one incomparable connection we hadn't yet made.

A smile tugged at his lips as he stalked across the room and towered above me with a glass in each hand. He waited for me to meet his eyes. "When I said you're mine, I meant it. No one and nothing takes from me what is mine. You *will* come back from this, Elle. Back to *me*." His voice was strong as it delivered his first command since we'd arrived. There would be no more pleading on his part.

"Drink." He put the wine in my hand.

As I measured the determination in his eyes, I sipped and waited for his next words.

"You'll eat with me tonight. Now—or in an hour, but you'll eat before this night is over." He nodded at my glass. "Another."

I took another drink and stared at the man who threatened to smack my ass for poor behavior back in the States, the man who shattered me blissfully on the plane using nothing more than his fingers. The man I wanted more than anything.

His brows flashed. Had he read my mind?

One of those long fingers guided the glass to my mouth before he went to refill his own. While at the table, he lifted the bottle of medication his physician had prescribed for me and examined the label. Then he stared at me, pushing deep into my soul. Without moving his eyes from mine, he dropped the bottle of antidepressants into the wastebasket.

He shot his whisky and came back to me. "You haven't said a word, but your eyes tell me everything. Those bewitching green eyes." Will swept tresses of hair out of his way and threaded his fingers through the back of my layers. He pulled my mouth to his and sucked hard on my lips, murmuring against my mouth. "Mine."

The wine glass slipped from my hand, splashing red at our feet. Neither of us cared. He opened my robe, and it slid from my shoulders. It fell to the floor on top of the mess and revealed my bare body. I reached for him, my heart fluttering, but he stepped back.

"I want to look at you." The blue of his eyes was lost. "Christ, you're lovely." The same words he'd said when we met in Stonington on the pier—said with the same charged eyes.

My lips curved into that same nervous smile.

"You know what will happen if I don't leave this room."

I nodded.

"And that's what you want?" His tone suggested it was something I shouldn't want, something that should offend me.

"Yes, that's what I want. You, Will."

He erupted—became an explosion of fiery emotion. He tore the shirt over his head and dropped his jeans as he consumed the space between us. I gasped at the sight. He was enormous. His erection was enormous. My body quivered like that of a virgin who'd never seen a man before, but my desire for him countered the nervousness.

Will smirked.

Then he lifted me into his arms and carried me to bed. He pushed his tongue past my lips as he fell on top of me. Our kiss was a firestorm of pent-up emotional and physical desire. It boiled in our blood. It was bone-deep. His skin burned into mine until I couldn't tell the difference.

We ignored the persistent banging at the door until we couldn't.

He leaped from the bed like a starved animal and shoved into his jeans. "What the fuck do you want?" he snapped at his brother after nearly jerking the door off its hinges.

"*Jesus.*" Ethan hesitated. "We're going to lose Stanbury if you don't speak to him now. There's nothing more I can do. He agreed to stay if you get back to work and handle his offshores. Otherwise, he'll pull everything."

Will pushed his fingers through his hair and looked back at me as he spoke to Ethan. "I'll be down in a minute. I'll take care of him." He closed the door and tugged on his shirt. "We're so close, baby." Those rasping words swept over my ear before his lips rested at my temple.

"Take care of your business. I'll wait for you."

"Promise me you'll eat." He plucked a juicy raspberry from the tray and stuffed it into my mouth and then pressed his lips to mine. "I'll speak to Mrs. Bates about your green salads."

I fell back against the pillows, beaming as I recalled the incredulous look on his face when he'd realized the kale and avocado salad

I'd eaten at the cottage was something I delighted in as a main course.

Before he stepped through the doorway, he glanced over his shoulder and found my smile. "There you are," he whispered.

Will was gone all night and left the estate before dawn for his office in London. It was easy to forget about his professional responsibilities. Easy to forget his career was something other than fighting my personal death squad.

I woke late that morning and lay there, thinking about the days that had passed.

While he stayed in bed with me through those dark days, working hard to keep me from falling deeper into the wicked depths that reached for me, he'd spoken about his family and his business. He and his brothers had gone to Oxford, where he'd earned his MBA. He and Ethan then cofounded a private equity firm and maintained positions as active partners.

The lockdown in my head had kept me from responding, but I was right there with him as his captivating voice led me through the stories that made him who he was.

He'd described the firm and how it functioned. He and Ethan focused on different aspects of the business, each with a management team that worked beneath him. Ethan conducted research and sourced both investors and investments, while Will negotiated contracts, closed deals, and monitored portfolios. Ethan did most of the initial networking, but Will had the golden touch when it was time to close. It made sense. Will was commanding and charming at once when he wanted something. I couldn't imagine him being denied.

The London financial community hailed them as the youngest founders of one of its most successful private equity firms.

Although Richard Hastings—a decommissioned foot soldier for

MI5—had raised his sons as warriors first, he'd also valued higher education. Ethan completed his MBA two years ahead of Will. Thomas held a master's in mathematical finance and would soon join his brothers in business.

Lissie slipped her angelic face into the room and grinned like the devil. "Aunt Ellie! Will said you feel better. You wanna come on my tour?" She needed me. I'd let her down.

"Definitely. Come in. I'll get dressed quickly."

She giggled as someone chased her away.

Mrs. Bates pushed into my room with a housemaid tight on her heels. "Up with you, dear. It's nearly twelve. You must be starving. William said you'd eat for us today. Lily, say hello to our young lady of the house." The house manager's lilting Irish accent was hypnotic.

"What? No, I'm not that. I'll come down to the kitchen after I dress—if you'll tell me where to find it." I clutched the sheet beneath my chin. It smelled like Will.

"No need, Ms. James. I have a tray ready for you now," Lily said in a small voice. Her accent was different than Will's aristocratic posh. She was from North England, maybe Yorkshire.

"Ellie," I corrected. What the hell? *William* was in big trouble.

"Don't blame him, dear. I do things my way round here." Mrs. Bates could read my face as well as anyone. She muttered to herself then. "It's time one o' them lads attached himself. Lord knows Mary could use a daughter."

"Honestly, Mrs. Bates." I pushed my hand against my forehead. "This is all a bit much."

She tossed my robe on the bed and eyed the mess she found beneath it. My cheeks heated. She canted her head and her eyes hit the bathroom door. "Don't mind us. Go on then." The two of them stepped into the corridor, so I launched into my robe and ran to the bathroom.

When I came out, I found the bed made and dozens of fragrant white and blush pink flowers—*roses?*—arranged around the room. Some were in clear crystal vases and some in beautiful vintage urns. I tugged at a snowy-white flower in the blue porcelain urn, plucking it loose from a cluster that shared one sturdy stem. I held it under my nose and inhaled its rich fragrance, sighing as I waltzed across the room to soak up the sunshine.

He hadn't bothered with a card.

"*English* roses, dear. That lad will give you nothing but the best," Mrs. Bates said with a clever smile as she pulled the door shut.

A satisfied smile claimed my own face when the image of Will's magnificent body filled my head. It wasn't just the way he looked. There was something about the way he moved. The way he said my name. It changed me, took me to a carnal place within myself I never knew existed. When he came back from London, I'd have all of him.

The text alert on my phone startled me. There were seven voicemail messages and three times as many texts. I'd contacted the carrier to extend my coverage while Will loaded the car before we left Lords Point, though he had cautioned me not to take my friends' calls—to keep them safe. To keep us all safe. I didn't read the text messages because it would reveal that I'd opened them, but no one would know if I listened to the voicemail.

"It's Jess. You're scaring me, Ells. Josh says you're safe, but I need to hear it from you. Call me back, damn it."

"I did some digging. I know who he is, which means I know where you are. I never thought—at least his resources are immense so he should be able to keep you safe. He better." It was Josh.

"Keep your eyes and ears open. You're a suspect now. I'll do what I can to lead them in another direction, but you left me with nothing useful. Ask him if he can do something about that. Stay safe." Josh again.

"I miss you. I know you're with him. Do you love him? Come home to me, Ellie." His words were low and slurred this time.

"I know you would tell me to trust Josh. He says this is for the best, that I should let go. Well, what if I can't? Am I supposed to just pick someone else to be my best friend, to be my family, and pretend you were never here? Damn you, Ells. Damn *him*." Jess's voice broke on the last word.

The last two messages remained unheard. I couldn't bear to hear any more of the pain I'd caused. In order to live, I had to hurt others—had to be a suspect in the murder of my own family.

I reminded myself to feel the pain. Tears spilled down my face while my stomach rolled with nausea. I threw my phone at the wall, and it damaged the cream-and-gold floral damask wallpaper.

Seven

I STARED AT THE nineteenth-century oil painting, *William the Conqueror at the Battle of Hastings,* hanging above the bar in the billiard room. I couldn't tell who'd painted it but planned to research that when I could. Was it a cosmic coincidence or fated historical repetition? Will Hastings had indeed conquered. He swooped in to save my life and took it from me at the same time.

"You're late," I whispered behind my glass of Dom Pérignon circa 1998.

Earlier that day, after Will called and said he was driving back for the night, Thomas convinced me to dress for dinner and have drinks with a few of his friends afterward while I waited for my conqueror to return.

I'd occupied myself with the exploration of Eastridge while Will was in London. Lissie provided me with not one but three "super-secret castle tours." God, I'd missed her. Will's mother had looked after her. The day I sent him away, Will had shown Lissie the house and encouraged her to claim it as her own castle. He lavished free rein upon the girl.

Eastridge was a stately eighteenth-century Georgian country house built of native stone. It was an elegant mansion renovated for modern comfort in recent years, though the old charm of the soaring, ornate plastered ceilings, original oak floors, and baroque-styled wall panels had been preserved with care. Stunning original fireplaces graced most rooms, as did ancestral portraits and other timeworn paintings.

The grand cantilevered staircase had been restored to its original splendor. It seemed to float high above the central great hall, and at the top it split the first-floor corridor into north and south bedroom wings. Balusters, newels, treads, and even the substantial but graceful winding handrail were all made from Scottish oak and detailed with simple but elegant carvings.

There was a huge modern kitchen with pantries, an informal dining space, and a comfortable family lounging area on the ground level extending across the back of the house, occupying what was once a drawing room, music room, and large library. A large drawing room and library combination and a formal dining room were located to the right of the central hall while a billiard room with a full custom bar occupied space to the left. The basement had been converted to a training center with a gym the size of a professional regulation basketball court.

Because of Ethan and Will's financial success, the house remained a private home. Many comparable estates were forced to open for the public to generate income for maintenance or were turned over to the National Trust for preservation.

Will was there—I could sense his presence without seeing him. I dropped my pencil and picked up my champagne, and then turned in his direction, pitching a slow, coquettish smile.

He stood with his hands in his trouser pockets and leaned on one shoulder against the casing of the billiard room doorway. He wore a three-piece dark blue Italian suit with plaid detail so fine you could see it only when you were close to him, a crisp white shirt unbuttoned at the neck, no tie. His usual five-o-clock shadow was a five-day beard and his thick mane was slicked back instead of swept to the left. Charged eyes scorched a path into my soul.

The whole room became *him*.

One of the girls visiting with Thomas's friends whimpered. She was right. He was sexy as hell. I only just suppressed the sounds of my own pleasure. Will was the kind of man who enjoyed the chase as much as he did his prize's submission, and I had no desire to deprive him of either. I leaned back against the bar where I'd been sketching on a napkin and took a sip from my glass. I watched the smile dangle from the corner of his lips as he crossed the room.

I'd dressed for him. It was the first time he saw Miss Fancy Pants.

Gran used to call me that, though she was the old pot calling the kettle black. My grandmother was the most elegant and fashionable woman I'd known, and she'd taught Isobel and me well. "Our style must be quite lovely and conservative at once," she had explained as she peered over the rim of her red-framed readers and flashed a tight smile.

My scarlet sleeveless dress was a fitted sheath that hit below the knee except where the right front slit sneaked up my thigh. My nude, strappy Louboutins were the perfect complement.

Will closed in, leaving little space between us. He took the drink from my hand and finished it himself. The most handsome man I'd ever seen leaned in close to my ear and sent a chill along my spine. "*Elle.* I'll make it up to you." His lips brushed along my cheek to the corner of my mouth before he straightened his back and stood at his full height.

"You better." I placed a kiss on the underside of his bearded jaw. "Have you eaten?"

He shook his head and pushed his hot gaze down into mine. His masculine scent filled my senses. My knees threatened to buckle. He lifted my hand and pressed his warm lips there. "You're beautiful."

"Thank y—"

"If you two are quite finished, where's Ethan?" Thomas interrupted, startling me.

Will turned to him with a raised brow.

"Right." Thomas refilled my glass and poured double shots of whisky for himself and Will.

"Need to fight before I head back to the city. On the mats at six, brother."

They threw back the scotch and pounded their glasses on the wooden bar. That was enough. I wouldn't share him any further until morning. I tugged on Will's hand and led him toward the kitchen. Mrs. Bates had left a plate warming for him, and she'd shown me where to find it and how to turn off the oven. But once we were out of sight, he backed me up against the doors beneath the staircase and kissed me.

"I'm taking you to my room tonight." His lips were devoted to the base of my throat.

I ran my fingers through the back of his hair. "The boys' wing. How very *not* English."

Will's hot gaze dipped and continued to move down the front of my dress. "You can worry about my virtue later, baby," he teased. "I need to be inside you. Rather not wake the house. I *will* have all of you tonight." He dragged his eyes back to mine and pushed his arousal into me.

I pushed back. "Dinner for you first. Seems you'll need your strength. With your impending fight and all."

He grinned. "Did you wear this for me?" His hand found the slit of my dress and glided up my thigh. A soft moan escaped me. The back of his fingers brushed the edge of my panties. "Is that a yes?"

Remembering where we were, I pushed his hand away and then stumbled on my words. I don't know why. It had made him happy, and that was the point, wasn't it? "I haven't been myself since—I do prefer dresses and—yes, of course. I wore it for you."

He tucked a finger under my chin and caressed my lips with his thumb. "Good. I'm going to buy you many more." As he lowered his head to kiss me again, Thomas rushed into the hall calling Will's name. "Better be important, goddamn it," Will snapped at his brother but kept his head lowered, his eyes on my mouth.

"Someone's on property—on foot."

Will's head jerked in Thomas's direction. "How many? Where?"

"I can see only one man. If there are others, they're obscured beyond reach of the cameras. Top of the ridge, northeast corner."

"Put John on monitors and comms. Suit up. We're heading out." He pulled his phone from his breast pocket and punched two words into a text message: SIX HALL.

A knot twisted in my gut. "What is it, Will? Tell me what's happening." I gripped his arm with a shaky hand to steady myself.

"What's about to go down is precautionary, nothing more. I don't want you to panic, Elle." As the words left his mouth, he moved us aside, and three men burst through the basement door. Another came from the front entrance and two more from the billiard room.

Soldiers, not men.

It was the Six—Will's private army. Six former soldiers of the British Armed Forces, skilled marksmen and combat fighters who trained at Eastridge every morning. To the public, it was a security team for the estate and its properties, but these men understood their real purpose. Will employed them for my protection, to help keep me alive.

Six soldiers surrounded me in a tight circle, their broad backs forming an impenetrable barrier. Each held a pistol in a low-ready tactical position until Will commanded them to stand down and conceal.

I could do nothing more than stare at them with my dry mouth hanging wide.

"Baby, the Six are here for your protection. They won't leave you until I return. Remember, precautionary this time—that's all." He placed a quick, hard kiss on my still gaping mouth and then traded his jacket and vest for a leather holster that held two daggers.

Will and Thomas disappeared through the foyer.

—

"He's just a kid. Because of his German descent, he believed he was expressing what he thought was a clever political position—but he now knows better. He's straightened out now."

"Why would someone of German descent misconstrue the Order's mission?"

Will kissed my neck and purred. "Come with me to bed, baby."

"As soon as you tell me what I want to know." I hugged his neck tight and fluttered my lashes. "Please."

He swept me into his arms and walked toward the staircase. "On the way. Short version."

"Deal. Start talking." I grazed his earlobe with my teeth.

"Order is short for the Order of the Electress. It's an unsanctioned, rogue faction of the Order of the Garter."

The Order of the Garter was a noble Arthurian-like knighthood led by the sitting sovereign. The irony was that my ancestors founded it, and the enemy chose it to hide behind as it eliminated my bloodline.

I kissed Will's neck as he climbed the stairs. "Go on."

"Mission is to preserve the present monarchy—that you know. Succession of the throne is limited to Protestant descendants of Sophia of Hanover. In the absence of legitimate issue from William the Third and Queen Anne, as granddaughter of James the First, Sophia was next in the line of succession. Sophia became the Electress of Hanover through marriage and Queen Mother to George the First. Anyway, that kid has no idea what the Order's about. He made the connection only to Hanover."

Will didn't need to explain Hanover. I'd run across the information in one of the old books in the library. It was the birthplace of King George I, the first Hanoverian monarch to rule Britain. Hanover was a German kingdom that no longer existed, though the great city itself remained the capital of one of Germany's northern states.

"So Germans rule England?" I asked.

"In a manner of speaking. Understand now why your blood is both revered and loathed?"

"It makes more sense now, yes. One more thing . . ."

"No more talking, baby."

"Why the daggers and not a gun?"

He ignored my question.

My lips lingered at the corner of his mouth before I breathed the words onto his skin. "I want to know."

"A bullet through the head is merciful. Those who hunt you will suffer."

Then he pinned me against the bedroom door he'd just locked, and took my mouth with his. I'd never been kissed by a man so fierce, never knew passion so raw and powerful could be expressed in a kiss. I wanted his power. Wanted to breathe it and feel it inside me.

I tugged the shirt from his shoulders and dragged my lips over his magnificent chest. He fisted my hair, twisting it through his long fingers, and pulled me back to his mouth.

"*Elle*. I need to be inside you. I'm mad for you." His deep voice was feral. The sensual way he said my name unmade me. It was an imperious purr.

Oh, God.

I spun and lifted my hair so he could unzip me. Goose bumps trailed behind those velvet kisses as his mouth followed the descent of my zipper. He grasped my shoulders and turned me back to him, causing my dress to hit the floor and pool at my feet.

There I stood before him, weak with anticipation, wearing nothing more than the red Chantilly lace bra and panties I'd chosen for the dress, for him. He stared. His illuminated eyes lingered, sliding up and down without care. A blush warmed my cheeks. He purred my name again, and the blood rushed to my core.

I was out of my mind for his touch. I wanted to feel his skin on mine. More than that, it was a need, something I began to ache for while he was away in London. I stepped out of my shoes and fallen dress, anchored my arms around his long neck, and melted into his body as I inhaled the warm scent at the base of his throat. His full bottom lip caught my eye. I lifted onto tiptoes and nipped it.

"Ten years—that's how long I've wanted you. I swear you're a witch."

"So be it," I teased with a wicked smile.

He moved our bodies with speed and grace as though we were one, like a predator stealing its prey. My back was pressed against the wall, and he was against me. A guttural vibration moved upward, rumbling in his chest until a growl caught at the back of his throat. Capturing both of my roaming hands and holding them in one of his above my head, he dragged his other hand from my lips down to my thigh and kissed me hard.

I moaned against his mouth.

A framed picture loosened from the wall. Will instinctively batted it away before it hit me and sent it crashing to the wood floor.

I locked my legs around him when he lifted me into his arms and carried me to his bed. He sat down at the edge and pulled me tight against his erection, and as I straddled his lap, he filled his hands with my hair again and kissed me until we shared a single, ragged breath.

I bit his neck, and he tossed me onto the bed and prowled up my body. He was so far gone he didn't realize he was crushing me with his weight. I pushed hard against his chest and dug my nails into his flesh. He lifted and effortlessly supported his weight.

Smooth lips slid down my neck to my breasts and sucked and pulled on my nipples through the lace. He came back to my mouth and claimed it as he dragged his fingers down the front of my body. He stopped only when he reached my panties. With one powerful tug, he snapped the lace and tore them off.

I cried out when he pushed his fingers inside me. "So tight, baby." He pleasured me with his thumb as he had on the plane. His fingers moved in and out, and he pushed me higher as he increased the intensity. Another cry parted my lips and swept against his as I came.

"I need you." His words were desperate but controlled. That massive body stilled, and he waited with burning eyes for my response. The growl lying in wait at the back of his throat vibrated.

"I'm yours . . . take me." It was nothing more than a whisper, but inside my head the words screamed. Because he made me feel. Because my soul was no longer uninhabited.

I reached down between our bodies to help get his trousers out of the way. As soon as he was free, I wound my fingers around him, sliding my hand up and down his length.

He groaned, a throaty sound of torment and pleasure. The band of my bra abruptly contracted before he captured my hands and confined them above my head once more. He released them when he took control of the rest of my body, anchoring me tight in one arm and yanking the lace from my chest with the other. His knees pushed my legs open wide. Cool air hit my wet core, driving my need for him higher.

My back arched of its own accord as his voracious mouth moved over my body. I moaned, pleaded with him, begged. But instead of pushing himself inside me, he slid his hand between my thighs and pushed his fingers into me again. "Will, please. I need you now. . . ."

He shut my mouth with his. "You're small. . . . I don't want to hurt you, baby." His voice was all gravel.

Will was huge—he was power, and by comparison, I was small and delicate. But I didn't care. If he hurt me at first, it would be good pain. "Please, Will . . ."

He smirked against my mouth, pleased with my desperation for him, and then kissed his way down the front of my body. Heat blasted through my blood. My hips bucked when he gripped them with his strong hands and drew me to his mouth. He buried his face between my thighs.

"Oh, God," I cried out, panting and pulling his hair. Each time he intensified the pleasure, I pulled harder. But it was Will's name I cried as my body shattered, fragmenting into billions of pieces against his mouth.

When he finally shoved inside me with one fierce thrust, his mouth owned mine and he swallowed my scream. He buried his face in my hair as his enormous body shuddered with need. He forced himself to remain still and cursed against my neck as he kissed me there, buried deep inside me. He filled me completely. I could feel him throbbing—he was a second heartbeat within my body. Those white-hot eyes burned into my soul when he lifted his head and found mine.

Will's embrace tightened as he balanced his weight and mine and then dropped his face down into my neck again. "*Christ* . . . you're so tight," he mumbled while battling hard to find the strength to calm himself, wrestling with self-control.

I clung to him with all that I had when at last he moved inside me. I cried out as he stretched me. Though he'd commanded my surrender, he held back. I could feel the restrained power surging within him. Before my brain could stop it, my body arched up against his heavy thrusts and writhed beneath his dominance, pushing him to let go of more. "I want more, all of you," I demanded.

And just like that, he gave me what I desired. He covered my mouth with his, the kiss intense as always, but different. It was a claiming kiss. Our teeth banged. My bottom lip split and bled from the force. His chest vibrated. "You're mine," he said as he sank deeper inside me. He drove hard and fast, filling me over and over until everything we were had burned away. We became something else, something we'd never before been separately.

We were remade.

Another orgasm—an unexpected culmination—ripped through me. I screamed his name against his lips, my body and soul shattering a third time.

Every muscle in his body tensed. He lifted his head and threw it backward. The growl once lodged at the back of his throat broke loose, morphing into a roar as he came. His breath was heavy as he dropped down and burrowed into my hair again. When the shuddering of his body settled, he turned his face and kissed my neck, kissed my butterfly.

"I'll never let you go, Elle. Never."

I was breathless. Thunderstruck by his storm.

Will rolled onto his back and pulled me to his chest. "Sleep well, baby. You're safe." And in his arms, he owned my body and possessed my rousing soul with strength and tenderness.

Will was already downstairs in the gym by the time I woke. I had slept dreamless in his arms through the night. There were no nightmares—no knives, no distorted faces, no death. There was only Will.

He planned to leave for London after he trained with Thomas, and I couldn't bear the thought of not kissing him once more before he left. I leaped out of bed and found my dress where he'd laid it neatly over the back of a chair and hurried down the corridor to my room.

"G'morning, dearest. Lily will get on with breakfast soon," Mrs. Bates lilted as she misted the roses with cool water, doting on them with the affection of a proud parent.

"Mrs. Bates, really, I don't mind having breakfast in the kitchen."

"Neither you nor dear Mary will be subjected to breaking your fast with those lads or the children," she harrumphed. "Ladies of this house will be afforded the respect of privacy in the morning hours. I'll see to it."

I picked the same fight with her every morning, battling an antiquated custom, and every morning she refused to yield. I could demand what I wanted from Will, but I decided instead to make an effort to accept the traditions of his family home while I was there.

"All right, you win." I flashed an honest smile and headed for the shower, though I rolled my eyes at the thought when I stepped under the spray of warm water.

John was headed up the staircase as I headed down. His sweat mixed with the trickle of blood from a small cut above his eye.

I stopped short. "You're hurt?"

He dabbed the laceration with a fingertip and grinned. "That's nothing. It happens."

I lifted a brow. "Which one?" Will and Thomas were massive by comparison.

"Thom. Did you see how the rain cleared out? The weather is perfect."

"Don't tease me, John. Where is Will now?"

"Going at it again with Thomas, repaying him on my behalf, I think."

As John resumed his climb three stairs at a time, sunlight burst in from the foyer. Eastridge was a fantastic house, but I needed more. I needed that sunshine touching me, warming me. Needed to walk along the edge of the sea and feel its energy. South East England was known for its verdant landscapes, quaint villages, and charming coastline, and I wanted to see it for myself. I stuffed my phone in my back pocket and hit the foyer, hoping for one or two breaths of fresh air.

"I can't let you out, Ms. James," one of Will's soldiers said as he stepped in front of me. A rifle hung from his shoulder and rested against his back. His expression was sober, but his eyes were kind. He smelled of evergreen and new leather.

"Are you serious?"

"Sorry. You'll need to speak to Will. His orders. Shall I take you to him?"

It wasn't his fault, but I snapped anyway. "Count on it. Yes, take me to him."

We headed for the double doors beneath the staircase in the central hall. At the bottom of the stairs was a fluorescent-lit corridor full of closed doors. The first three were solid wood with no visible handles. Electronic pads were mounted to the right of each. We walked farther down the corridor where two sets of steel doors led into the gymnasium. He pushed one open wide and waited for me to pass through, following as I made a beeline for Will.

Will stood with Ben and Thomas at the far end of the gym, toweling sweat from his face and neck. He saw us and sprinted across the pale wood floor. "What happened? What's wrong?"

"This happened." I pointed at his sentry.

He dismissed his soldier with a slice of his chin. "Why are you upset? You know what we're up against. There'll be a guard at the door from now on. Joe was doing his job."

I hooked my hands on my hips. "I only wanted some fresh air. I wasn't going to leave."

Will closed the gap between us and forced me to meet his eyes. "Did he touch you?"

"What? No."

"I'll do whatever is necessary to keep you safe, and you will cooperate."

I narrowed my eyes. "I'm not your prisoner."

"Goddamn it, Elle." His jaw tightened and eyes flashed, warning me he was prepared to fight and win. "We've been through this."

"You—" I halted my argument. I wouldn't fight with him.

Couldn't bear the idea we'd be distant in both the physical and emotional sense while he was away. My hands left my hips and moved to his corded forearms. As I traced the bulging veins there, I changed course and made a gentle demand. "Take me to the beach, Will."

His face relaxed as he exhaled. A bead of sweat fell from his forehead and landed on my cheek. He was thoughtful for a minute before nodding. "After I finish here and make some calls. I'll drive back to London later." He wiped the drop of sweat from my face with his thumb.

"Really?"

He lowered his head and pressed his salty lips to mine. "I'll deny you nothing." Then he grabbed the phone from my pocket and shouted for Thomas.

"Oh. I listened to the messages." My eyes dropped to the floor. "I'm officially a suspect now. Josh wants to know if you—" I didn't know how to finish the sentence.

"I know. He called me, found me in London at my office. It's all right." He pulled my chin up. "U.S. police demand you be interviewed. My lawyers will make certain it's conducted by the London Metropolitan Police Commissioner. He's an appointee of the queen, and we know she doesn't want an investigation from abroad any more than we do. If we grant this request, I think they'll drop the matter."

"What do I say?"

"The lawyers will prepare you and do most of the talking."

"But—" I tried not to panic, my body vibrating with the need.

"Baby, you didn't do anything wrong. You're the victim here, not the criminal. I'll get the cop anything else he needs privately. He and I agreed to clean it up, and we will. I promise." He handed my phone to Thomas. "Destroy this and make the account go away. Remove her online presence."

Thomas was a genius with devices, the internet, and computer systems. He and one of his closest friends from Oxford could hack anything. He would break into the phone company's data and the social media sites to remove all traces of me.

Vanished, just like that. Gone like the rest of my family.

Thomas swiped through my apps quickly before popping the SIM card. "I'll get you another phone this afternoon. You can still follow Jessica's tweets, but wait for me to set it up so it's secure."

Eight

I was shocked at first but ultimately thankful for the way Lissie spoke to Mary with such ease—Grannie, as she and Chelsea, Ben's three-year-old daughter, called her.

Mary Hastings was a gentle, loving woman, and I couldn't imagine any child rejecting her kindness. It must have been difficult for her to hold back with four warrior-born sons. Even so, there was no doubt she had still imparted her love and strength. The tenderness Will drew from his fierce depths for me was proof of his mother's influence.

It was written on my heart how unprepared I was to raise a seven-year-old. I'd ruin Lissie on my own. Her growing relationship with Mary relieved me of the pressure and allowed me time to search for the best path forward for Lissie and me. If there was one. My role in her upbringing would change if Ethan was her father. I would no longer be her guardian.

I inspected Lissie's hands after she scrubbed the purple finger paint from them. "Good job, girlie. Paint's all gone."

She smiled at me with Ethan's eyes and Isobel's mouth.

"Your turn, Chelsea." I lifted the toddler to the sink and washed her hands. "Good?"

"Good!" she squealed, clapping her hands under the running water.

"You're getting Auntie all wet, silly girl."

"Me, too!" Lissie shrieked.

The three of us giggled as I shifted Chelsea to one hip and reached for the faucet.

Will caught my hand and pulled it back. He kissed my fingers and shut off the water himself. "Ready, baby?" His grip was firm as he eliminated the space between us.

Chelsea twisted, uncomfortable with the closeness of the giant looming above.

"Come. Let's go," the giant said before he bent and placed a kiss on my lips.

I stared up into his magnetic smile, stunned by his display of possessive affection.

Mary stood at the center island slicing bread and cheese for the girls. She narrowed her eyes and scolded her son. "You're old enough to know better, William. Go and wait for Ellie in the hall."

Will scowled at his mother, and as he left the kitchen, he mumbled an apology to her.

A giggle escaped my lips. I covered my mouth before another slipped out.

"It's all right, dear. That one," she said, gesturing with knife in hand in the direction he'd gone, "has always been a handful. Stubborn like his father and equally lionhearted." She smiled then and stared at nothing with distant eyes. Her unfocused face was beautiful. It was clear she was caught in the memory of her late husband.

I gave her another moment. "Does he look like Richard?"

"Quite like Richard. In fact, he's the spitting image. His walk, even his voice. All four of my boys have their father's eyes."

My gaze shifted to Lissie. I wasn't sure if Ethan had discussed it with anyone other than Will, so I self-corrected and hoped she hadn't noticed. It wasn't my place to tell her.

"Hastings eyes are hard to miss. There's a fiery element. Only it's—"

"White," I finished.

"Yes, white. Like lightning. You know, dear, when he came back from America the first time, the clarity in his eyes was unmistakable. We knew then if the conflict with the Order resumed, it would be Will's war, not Ethan's. We didn't know how it would unravel, just that it was so. I suppose Richard knew in his heart long before that—he'd always been much harder on Will."

"Will's a good man with a good heart despite the cards he's been dealt, the game he's forced to play. His tenderness with me is unmatched. You know that, right?"

She smiled wide, and a twinkle bounced around inside her honey-brown eyes. "I do. Go on, Ellie. He's done his time."

The back staircase was perfect for my escape from the kitchen. I stepped into faded denim boyfriend shorts with split side seams and black strappy heels. It wasn't necessary but still I pressed at the lower hem of my sleeveless white blouse. I tossed lipstick and sunglasses into my black leather shoulder bag before dashing out the door.

Will waited in the grand hall as his mother had instructed. He met me at the bottom of the stairs wearing one of his confident smiles. His brows flashed, and he rubbed his chin. "Christ. *Elle.* Your legs are a mile long. Maybe we should just go upstairs. We can go out another day."

"Oh, I think we'll do both." I flipped several glossy strands of hair over my shoulder and treated him to a slow, mischievous smile. "Beach first."

"Not until you kiss me." He lifted me from the last step.

"If I do that, you'll not want to leave. Swear we'll go."

He nodded.

I hooked my legs around his hips and cradled his face in my hands, and then slanted my mouth over his, tickling his lips with my tongue. He opened wide and thrust his tongue impatiently against mine. When he was satisfied with his victory, he put me down but didn't loosen his grip on my waist.

"Beach, baby?"

I thought about it, shaking my head as though the image of us tangled up in bedsheets could ever be erased from my mind. A cocky grin slid across his face.

"Yes, to the beach." I pulled back and dragged my eyes to the bulge that would soon push above the waistband of his jeans if he didn't cool it. "And if you're a good boy, maybe we'll use that later."

"Witch."

He patted my ass as we walked out the front door.

I was outside Eastridge for the first time since arriving in England. It was seventy-eight degrees and not a cloud floated in the sky. The glorious sun caressed my skin the minute we stepped through the doorway. I took in the flourishing landscape and decided to paint it someday. An airy bouquet of earthiness after a long rain, fresh clipped grass, and lavender wove itself through my senses. I inhaled deeply, pulling in a faint, salty nip of the sea, and smiled.

Thomas pulled up in a black Range Rover with dark tinted windows. Ben rode shotgun. John sprinted out of the house behind us and pulled open the car door before we reached it. I cuffed him on the shoulder and winked, receiving a sweeping grin and countered wink in return. Will and I climbed into the back. He locked his arm around my waist and slid me closer to him after John piled in on the other side.

"Weapons?"

"Secured. You don't want any of the Six?" Thomas looked at Will in the rearview mirror.

"Not this time. Let's roll."

Anxiety made its move. I squeezed Will's thigh and chewed on my lip. "Is it safe?"

He tightened his arm around me. "The locals aren't aware you're here. There might be some initial confusion, maybe apprehension, but these people aren't the enemy. They'll support you, even protect you—once they get used to the idea. We've done some recon. There's nothing to indicate assassins are here, but it won't be long before they show up. I want you to experience Old Town before that happens."

I took a deep breath and forgot to release it.

"Breathe, baby. I won't let anyone hurt you. Someday you'll walk the streets of London with me." He winked and confidently kissed my forehead.

The four of them were armed only with their fists, which in itself was a weapon unequaled, though I had no doubt Will would carry a gun wherever and whenever he felt compelled, without concern for the law.

I exhaled and nodded. I trusted him. If he said it was okay, then it was okay.

"I'm going to teach you how to use a gun. I bought one for you. You'll handle it only when I give it to you."

"What?"

"I'd be a fool not to teach you."

A gun wouldn't be much use for me, not in the UK, where firearms possession was broadly prohibited. Will's family was well connected, and he knew how to find policy loopholes, but his methods wouldn't work for a foreigner like me. Still, I understood where he was coming from—I'd be exposed to guns, and I needed to know what to do should one fall into my hands.

"I should learn to fight."

"No way," he snapped.

"But—"

"No." His back stiffened, and he shook his head. "I won't see you beaten and bruised."

I leaned over his lap and gawked at the passing scenery. Wild forget-me-nots bloomed along the edge of the forest, bumblebees buzzing about the blossoms. Several deer loped throughout the trees. "We'll see."

Thomas drove north down the ridge until the estate ended near Old London Road, then headed south into the heart of Hastings. They referred to the area as Old Town. It could have been the model for Stonington, though it had an edgier feel. It was like the ancient town dangled from a precipice, but worked hard to hoist itself up as it evolved alongside a younger, more hip generation.

The streets were filled with people and celebrations. There were vendors selling drinks, food, fresh-caught fish, and crafts. Local artists painted portraits for those who posed. Solo musicians and traditional marching bands dueled for attention. A carnival queen and her court paraded through the cobblestoned streets.

Parking was limited, and many streets were closed for the town's annual festival. We pulled into a small, gated lot behind a charming pub with a bedazzled crown sculpture mounted above its front entrance.

Will caught my unasked question. "It's one of Ethan's investments. His partner runs it."

A cute girl with short, blonde hair stepped out of another car and sidled up to Thomas. She was fashion-model thin and six feet tall with heels. He took her hand.

"Ellie, this is my friend, Kirsty."

She presented me with a timid smile and nod. "Quite nice to meet you."

I returned the smile but saved my perceptible American-accented words for later when she was more comfortable.

We walked down a quaint, narrow alleyway with stacked Tudor-style buildings on both sides. Ben and John walked in front while Thomas and Kirsty brought up the rear. The alleyway ended after a few short blocks at the fisherman's beach—the Stade. We crossed a road filled with more people, vendors, and musicians. Not far to the west was the historic pier, reaching proudly into the English Channel even as it endured the workmen and machinery of a substantial renovation. The remains of William the Conqueror's castle sat high upon the west ridge beyond the pier.

The Stade was a shingle beach alive with fisheries, net houses, merchants selling fresh catches, and of course, fishing boats. *Neptune* would have fit in well.

"No sand?" I stopped and slipped out of my sinking heels.

"There's a bit out close to the water." Will canted his head toward the channel.

I took a barefoot step. "Ow! Is this pebble beach part of the ecosystem or was it placed intentionally?"

"Shingle. It's natural." One corner of his mouth curved with amusement just before he swooped me into his arms and headed toward the water. When he put me down, my feet hit soft, golden sand.

It frustrated me when he wore his dark aviators. I counted on reading his expressive eyes. We often communicated without words. "Take them off, Will," I demanded.

"Better?" He hooked the sunglasses on his T-shirt and his strong hands on my bottom to pull me closer.

I locked into his gaze and nodded.

"Have you been eating, Elle?"

"You know I have." I pulled his face down until his lips burned against mine.

"You've lost weight since leaving the States. I won't have you lose this sweet, plump arse. It fills my hands perfectly." He squeezed to demonstrate.

"Plump? What—"

"I didn't say fat. I said perfect. *Christ.* You're beautiful." He took my mouth with his and pushed our kiss deep and hard. We broke the kiss and panted against each other's lips. "I can't get enough of you, baby."

"So you won't be leaving tonight?"

A huge, eye-crinkling smile ate up his face. "Is that an order?"

"Not at all. You give the orders around here, so I hear." I kissed his cheek then tugged on his arm. "Let's walk. I want to see more."

It wasn't an order, wasn't a demand. It was a suggestion. Suggestions left him an out when he needed one. I recognized how serious he'd become. From the moment he made his decision to take what he wanted on the tarmac in Connecticut, he was all in. He had already worked to move mountains to give me whatever I demanded. Yes, I suffered when he wasn't there at night. Missed his raspy whispers in my ear telling me everything was okay, the fire in his eyes when he looked at me, his equal measures of tough guy and tenderness, and the security of his arms. And I battled horrific nightmares without him. But I wouldn't use it to hold on to him. I needed to be certain he was making choices, not fulfilling obligations.

Will grabbed my hand and pointed east. "I have something to show you down there."

We headed down the beach away from the activity, soon coming upon a quiet expanse of shoreline beneath the ridge. Striking eroded walls of the sandstone cliffs were carved by the English Channel's tempestuous disposition. It was gorgeous.

We dropped our things and he led me into the water. He pointed above the cliffs. "Look high above the cliffs on the ridge, to the right of the three Wellingtonias. Giant sequoias I think they're called in America."

I stepped back until the tide swept over my knees. Beyond the trees, the house's second story and chimneys came into view. I stepped back again until water reached the hem of my shorts. There.

Eastridge was perched high above where we stood. She was an elegant stone fortress standing tall and proud, announcing her presence to all who dared look her way.

"How beautiful," I breathed, mesmerized.

He tugged me closer to the beach as an aggressive tide swept in, and kissed me.

A burst of cool sea air washed over my flesh and left behind a blanket of goose bumps. It tickled my nose and ears, and carried a whispered message as it had back on the coast of Connecticut. I arched my back and let go, trusting Will to hold me while I closed my eyes to send my reply, acknowledging that it had found me. My spirit skipped beyond the channel and reached out to the Atlantic Ocean. My hair floated behind me with the next hard-driving breeze. Something peaceful, something honest staked a claim in my unguarded mind and heart.

Will smiled and reeled me back in after I opened my eyes. He pressed his forehead to mine. "You were never lost, Elle. It's all been here, waiting for you. *I've* been waiting for you."

The restrooms at Ethan's pub were set back in a wood-paneled alcove for privacy. I opened the ladies' room door after freshening up and smacked into the chest of a strange man. He was intentionally blocking my path. His funky breath stunk of onions and dark stout.

"Haven't seen anything like you round here before. How 'bout a drink, hen? Just you and—"

A huge arm appeared like a snake coiling around his neck. It cut off his sentence and his oxygen. Will jerked the guy away from me and slammed his face into the wall. He held that face to the wall while he spoke. "Do we need to discuss this or are we done here?"

"We're g-good, man. D-done," the guy stuttered. When he peeled himself from the wall and turned to go, blood dripped from above his eye and nose. He scurried away after Will signaled with his chin for him to move on.

"You okay, baby?" Will hovered without touching me.

"Yes, I'm okay."

Thomas came from behind. "You busted his nose quite good."

"Makes him pretty fucking lucky then. If he pulls that again, he won't walk away alive."

"She's beautiful. Better get used to it when you take her out, brother."

"Yeah. Stay with her for a minute." Will ducked into the men's room. The guy's blood was splattered on one of his hands.

I stared at Thomas. My chest tightened.

"That was no one, Ellie. Nothing for you to worry about. He's just a pissed local, who thought he might have a shot with the most beautiful woman he's ever seen." He winked.

I smiled hesitantly at Thomas. Then I stepped backward into the safety of Will's arms as he came up behind me. My chest split with relief.

From the table, I explored the homey atmosphere, the artful, hipster charm of the decor. In addition to the tables with board games painted on them, there were a couple of snugs with leather seating. The generous bar was crafted by hand from reclaimed wood. Old fireplaces anchored each end of the pub. Works for sale by local artists filled the walls, and daily newspapers and books were scattered about.

I thought of Nick's and the similarities. I thought of the old Victorian house in Stonington where I grew up, and the cottage at Lords Point. The gallery where I worked, the kids I taught. The stars over the open waters of the Atlantic at night. I thought of everything I once loved in Connecticut. But truth be told, I didn't miss any of it. I was too busy falling in love with England. Here, the reminders of abandonment and heartbreak were distant, and I could see tomorrow. I snuggled deeper into Will's side for reassurance.

He leaned in and kissed the tip of my nose. "You're reflecting a lot today."

"I'm—I think I'm happy here. It feels right."

A gratified smile possessed his face before a seriousness chased it away. "So I can stop worrying that I might have to chase you round the globe?"

"Yes."

"And you'll let me know if that changes?" He brushed his lips over mine.

"Yes."

With tenderness and discretion, he kissed his way down my neck. "Ready to go home?"

I twisted to see his eyes. "You need to start for London soon?"

"I'm not going. Can't sleep apart from you tonight." His gaze jumped to a yellow envelope placed on the table in front of him by the server. "What the hell is this?" he snarled.

"I don't know, sir. A man paid me fifty pounds to put it in front of you."

"Show me," Will commanded.

"I can't. He ran out the back door when I came over to your table."

Ben flew to the back and burst through the door. He stepped back inside seconds later and shook his head. It was too late. The man was gone, camouflaged within the festival crowd.

Will opened the envelope and pulled out two large photos. Both were taken from an elevated position and showed him carrying me from the plane. He was flanked by Thomas, Ethan, John, and Ben—an obvious protection detail. The Cross of Saint George was stamped on the front of each. He tossed the photos into the middle of the table, pushed back against his chair, and stretched. "War it is, motherfuckers."

Thomas picked up the photos. "I guess it's on then."

They knew where I was. Assassins had watched Will carry me onto English soil. I swallowed hard and battled anxiety and fear as they worked to overwhelm me. They lurked in tandem and courted my mind, waiting for an opportunity to steal the kiss that would seal the deal. I shook them from my head, refusing to hide, choosing to fight. I corrected my posture, and took a deep breath and released it. Despite my best effort, one traitorous tear found freedom and rolled down my cheek.

"You're safe—I promise." Will caught the tear before it dropped from my chin. "No one will get past me. Not ever." He rested his lips along my temple. "I swear it, Elle. Please trust me."

I sniffled and then smiled. His commitment to me was unreal. It was beyond comprehension. "I trust you." Our lips were a perfect fit. It was hard to keep them apart, so neither of us tried. "Take me home, Will."

After Ben inspected the car, he pulled up to the entrance, and the rest of us climbed in. He hit the lock button and met Will's eyes in the rearview mirror. "Left side of the street, dark sedan, two men. Drive or fight?"

Will's attention shifted to the sedan. "Drive, then fight." The muscles in his arms tensed. He'd tucked me into both tight. "Open the cache, John. Pull out two Glocks."

Ben pulled away from the curb and headed out of town, the dark car following close. John lifted the mat and a panel beneath his feet and retrieved two pistols. The youngest Hastings inserted a loaded magazine into each gun and handed them off to his brothers.

Will cuffed Thomas's shoulder. They didn't need words. The two of them acted and thought like one well-oiled machine. Thomas gave an almost-imperceptible nod.

I stared straight ahead, choking back the fear that swam in my blood. Illuminated clouds hung low in the magenta-and-blue twilight sky, the sun having dipped below the horizon moments before.

Will strengthened his embrace. "Thomas and I are going to jump out. Stay in the car. John will restrain you if you try to get out." His tone was hawkish. He lifted my chin and stared hard into my eyes, seeking obedience.

"Okay," I breathed, my heart banging against my sternum.

Will's arms tightened even more, creating an impenetrable cocoon. "Prepare yourself, John. You keep her in this car—by force if necessary." Then he lowered his head and planted a soft, haunting kiss on my mouth.

Ben accelerated. So did the car on our tail. He hit the brakes. Both cars skidded, tires screeching as rubber smoked and burned. Metal crunched and glass shattered as the sedan plowed into the back of us.

Will absorbed the impact I should have felt.

Ben threw the Rover into reverse and accelerated again, pushing the sedan until it dislodged from our bumper and lurched sideways, sliding into the gravel at the edge of the road. Will and Thomas were out of the car at once. In the time I'd twisted and tracked them through the broken rear window, they had torn the two men out of that dark car and held them at gunpoint.

Ben remained behind the wheel with the Rover still running. "Shit!" He slammed the gearshift into Park. As he leaped out, he shouted at John and me to stay in the car.

John held my hand, the sweat of our palms mingling. "Oh, shit. Look up ahead. . . ."

I turned and saw a police car approaching from the opposite direction. It sped up and abruptly engaged its vibrant emergency lights. Wine rebelled in my clenched stomach. I tucked my head between my knees and fought a wave of nausea with measured breaths.

Ben jumped back into the car and handed the guns to John. "Pull the mags and get those back in the floor. *Now.*" A blast of crisp air slapped my face. He'd put the windows down. "Ellie, sit up straight and don't give us away with panic. Will can fix this. This is an unfortunate car accident—nothing more."

Nine

B<small>EFORE</small> W<small>ILL</small> <small>LET</small> go of my hand at the top of the stairs, he placed a tender kiss on my palm. "I need to touch base with Ethan and reach out to some clients. No more worrying, Elle. It's been handled. See you in a bit."

A hot bath with soothing essential oils helped ease the tension in my mind and body. My strength had crumbled once we made it back to Eastridge. I'd sobbed, and Will had soothed me, promising me things I wasn't sure anyone could ever deliver.

He was sitting in the armchair talking on his phone when I came out of the bathroom. His voice was low as he spoke to Ethan. "Their information is on the police report. Shouldn't be an issue. They were unarmed messengers. I was clear. They understand further involvement will cost them their lives. Need to get Thomas a new car."

I'd taken nothing into the bathroom with me other than the clean bra and panties I wore. I shrugged to myself and paraded toward the closet. I didn't make it that far. Will cleared his throat and summoned me with those long fingers. "Turn round," he commanded when I stood in front of him.

I obliged, giving him the "plump" view he desired.

He continued his conversation with Ethan as he stared at my ass. After he'd filled his eyes, he filled his lap with me, making sure my backside was snug against his erection. "I'll ring you back later. Something just came up." He disconnected and tossed his phone onto the table.

"Really? Something just came up?"

"You've been tormenting me with this pretty arse all day, baby." He gripped my hips and ground himself against my lace-covered cheeks, his words warm against my hair. "Give me what's mine."

"Take it, savage."

A primitive grunt came from his chest as he moved us across the room. The back of my legs hit the mattress, and I fell onto the bed. He pulled himself into check as he stripped. "You're okay, baby?" His eyes were fierce and filled with heat but softer than the night before. "Last night, I mean. Did I hurt you?" He supported his body above mine and inhaled against the skin between my breasts, exhaling the word, "Jasmine."

He had hurt me with his first thrusts the night before. Even so, I wouldn't concede to it. Yes, he was significantly bigger than I was, but once he'd stretched me, it was a-ma-zing. And more than that, it connected us on an emotional level never before equaled. I needed that from him. "Do it again. Fill me. Make me feel."

There was no time for pomp and circumstance. We shared the same urgent sense of desperation—I needed him inside me, and he needed to be there. My fierce defender gathered my wrists above my head in one of his hands. "When I'm inside you, you'll surrender to me completely. Every time, Elle." Then he eased into me one rock-hard inch at a time. I panted and moaned, insane from the intense desire he stirred in me. His tender, possessive whispers brought me to tears. "My angel . . . you're mine. . . . My beautiful angel . . . never letting go . . ."

When he finally pushed in deep, he swallowed his name as I sobbed it, and then he kissed the tears that had slipped away from me. "Let go, baby. Give yourself to me." And as I gave up everything he claimed, we burned to ashes and became one breathless, sated existence. He maintained mind-blowing control, covering my mouth with his to absorb my loud cries and quelling his roar when he came.

I'd fallen asleep on his chest, but found him in the chair with his laptop when I woke, stuffing half a sandwich into his mouth. Documents and newspapers were spread about the floor and hanging from the chair.

"I kept you from your work."

"Stay beneath that blanket until I'm finished." He looked up over the screen and winked.

I wrapped the sheet around myself and headed for the bathroom. My stomach rumbled before I could get the door closed.

"You'll eat, woman," he called through the door.

I was starved. While eating, I watched Will harness his intense physical energy and apply it to his intellect. He was as intelligent as he was strong. After a call, during which he spoke only French— God, that was sexy—and another to Ethan, he stood and stretched. The movements were graceful and majestic; he was a magnificent lion.

"I have something for you." He gathered two old books from behind the chair and set them next to me on the bed.

"What's this?"

"Look through these and see if anything stands out. Don't push me for an explanation until you've done that." He countered his firm words with a soft kiss. "I need to go down to the gym and run. Be back soon."

The books were heavy and quite old. One was a colossal tome covered in worn, brown leather with black leather straps that buckled to hold its contents securely within. There was a golden three-budded cross made of tarnished metal fastened to the cover by rivets. The same metal was used for decorative corner pieces.

The other book was smaller and less ornate. It was covered in black leather dappled with shades of gray caused by time and wear.

There were two aged, red satin ribbons dangling from within its pages. I opened to the first ribbon-marked page and began to read. The print was small, imperfect, and faded. I skimmed most of the page, reading the last paragraph out loud:

Our rightful King Edward V and his brother, Prince Richard of York, were held captive in the Tower of London by their uncle, Richard, Duke of Gloucester, after the death of their father, the king. It is known the boy king met his death in the Tower by natural cause whilst the prince was removed in secret a fortnight thereafter.

I flipped to the next bookmarked page and read more:

Prince Richard remained in hiding in the South of France, under the care and keep of Charles VIII and Louis XII, where Richard's royal lineage began. He took a wife of noble French blood, and she bore him three sons and one daughter.

Will had already explained it to me. He didn't need to provide proof. He'd given his word, and I believed him. But there it was in black and white, journalized centuries ago.

I picked up the giant tome and unfastened its buckles. "Okay, big guy. What story do you have to tell?" It was full of genealogical charts and maps, not at all what I'd expected. Some with pages of explanation, some without. I leafed through, unsure where to stop and read. I thumbed through the pages until landing on Edward IV and slid my finger delicately over the decomposing page to Richard's name. "There you are—Prince Richard, Duke of York." Somehow I'd still expected Richard's chart to end there.

Richard had his own page.

My eyes roamed that page, following the faded, blotted columns of names downward until I reached the bottom where the last several generations were scrawled more legibly in crisp ink. I sucked in a sharp breath, but shouldn't have been surprised by what I'd found.

My great grandfather changed our family name to James when he and great grandmother settled in Connecticut in 1898. He was born John Plantagenet. Just as overwhelming was the sight of the final names listed on my family tree—my parents: EDWARD AND ELISABETH JAMES. There was a footnote at the bottom of the page:

EDWARD JAMES WAS THE LAST BORN MALE HEIR OF THE SUCCESSIVE PATRILINEAL DESCENT OF KING EDWARD IV AND HIS SECOND SON, PRINCE RICHARD. HIS GRANDCHILDREN, MALE OR FEMALE, WILL NOT BE KNOWN AS HEIRS TO THE THRONE UNLESS HIS DAUGHTER ACQUIRES IT AS RIGHTFUL QUEEN.

Tears threatened, but I pushed them back and summoned anger in their place. I dragged my finger, indelicately this time, from the top of the page to the bottom. They were all gone. Only a footnote remained. The pain caused by my sister's death returned and ripped through me.

I compelled myself to allow the pain its due, binding myself to the anger.

My throat tightened, and I clenched my jaw. My mind swam. I cursed. If it weren't for that damned footnote, Isobel would be alive, and assassins wouldn't be hunting me. There had to be another living bloodline stronger than mine. There must be someone else. It was the only answer.

I flipped through the tome, back to King Edward's page. Richard had been the only surviving son. But what about brothers? "Where are your brothers, Edward Plantagenet, mighty king?"

Of course, there were two, which I should have recalled from my studies. King Richard III had several children, though none who were legitimate had survived. And then there was George Plantagenet, Duke of Clarence, drowned in a barrel of wine for treason. He'd had one son and one daughter—both deprived of their inheritances by Edward's act of attainder before his ill-timed death. Both executed by a Tudor king.

The Tudor kings had suffered acute paranoia, which was the only reason for those executions. That paranoia was Richard's fault. He hadn't had the courage of his father to fight. Instead, he and his supporters bribed imposters to keep the Tudors busy while he tucked tail and hid among the French like the coward he was. Bastard. Richard had allowed the burden to fall on his own sons, who ultimately bound themselves to a line of warriors named Hastings.

But, what of George's living heirs?

George's daughter, Countess Margaret Pole, lived until executed at the age of sixty-eight. She'd had children, surviving sons and daughters. Margaret's was a matrilineal line of the Plantagenet dynasty, which must be why her bloodline was never hunted by the Order. Still, I was curious. Where were her descendants today?

My finger drifted along the descending names on the countess's page. Two generations beneath her own name was something I hadn't foreseen. I swallowed hard and whispered that name. "Hastings." My eyes dove to the bottom, leaping ahead of my brain, and there he was: WILLIAM RICHARD HASTINGS. I tossed the old tome to the foot of the bed as though it had burned my fingers.

Will's body filled the doorway. "You all right, baby?"

I shook my head, my stare still locked on that tome. "Is this . . . real? It's all true?"

He responded with a low "Yes," but remained where he was.

I pulled my knees up to my chest and rested my chin there. My head was swimming with information—full of confusing mind clutter. No words came to me.

"You chose me, Elle. Are you still sure? Now that you know who we are."

"Yes," I snapped. My eyes whipped around to find his. "You doubt me?"

He stalked from the door and pinned me beneath him on the bed. He kissed me like tomorrow might never come. "Your life will be harder with me in it, not easier. And now you know why." He was driving at something, but I wasn't able to piece it together. There was too much banging around inside my skull already. And then that kiss. . . .

"It's too late now. I warned you." He sat up with his legs crisscrossed and jerked me on top of him. "It's too fucking late." I locked my legs around his lower back as he pushed wild locks of hair away from my face. The position was comforting and intimate. Sensual.

"I don't understand. What are you saying?" My hips rocked without permission.

Strong hands stilled my body. "Don't do that." His expression softened. "We need to clear this up first."

He wore no shirt, only running shorts, which made me incapable of coherent thought. I pressed my lips to his and stayed there until he pulled back.

"What is it—what are you trying to say?"

"Now you see, it could all be yours. Do you want it, baby? I need to know. I'll share you with Britain if necessary, if you choose it, but I won't give you up."

"*What?*"

"Whatever you want, I'll find a way to give it to you."

"That's crazy, Will. I just want them to leave me alone. And you. I want you."

"You become a greater threat to the Crown if you're involved with me. My blood and yours together—that strengthens your position."

"I don't care."

"I'll fight for you either way, because I can't live without you. Just need you to tell me which endgame you desire." He wasn't going to let up until I'd shown intelligible consideration.

"Have you left anything else out?"

"There's nothing else. I'll never lie to you."

I believed him. He was no liar. Will was loyal to the point of obsession. I pulled his face into my hands. "Then why not tell me sooner you carried the blood?"

"Ethan leads this family. We're old school here, Elle. I must respect his position, even when I don't agree with his decisions. He believes you'll grow paranoid like your sister." He stared into me with those beautiful blue eyes.

I winced at both the softness of his eyes and the thought of Isobel. It was an accurate description of her behavior. I thought it was the pregnancy that had changed her, but it was London. Whatever she experienced when she was there with Ethan had altered her.

"What do you believe?"

"I believe you're strong and growing stronger. It's a quiet strength, but it's absolute, baby, and it powers mine. It's the loveliest thing I've ever seen. In time, you and I will end this war."

I was stunned by his words and the confidence behind them. I couldn't move my gaze from his. I'd never seen myself through someone else's eyes. Will showed me a woman with fire and determination who was forgiving and capable. No damsel in distress stared back at me. But the truth was, I'd stolen glimpses into the most vulnerable part of his soul, and that powered my strength, emboldened me. I lay my head on his broad shoulder.

"The endgame I desire is you and me, nothing more. Fight for us, Will."

Will's response was delivered in an unyielding, breathless kiss. His tongue filled my mouth, and his arms pulled me deeper into our tantric position. Together we deepened our kiss. My hands were in his hair, his were in mine. His erection jerked between us.

"*Elle*. Never leave me. Say it," he commanded.

I whispered close to his ear, "I'll never leave you."

He pressed me back against the mattress, and a growl moved up his vibrating chest and ripped from his throat as he removed the silk chemise from my body. "I'm going to taste all of you—every beautiful piece of you."

My back arched and pushed me closer to him. It was never close enough. I was desperate for him. I would never leave him.

As though something troubling jogged his memory, he lifted and rolled to his side. His eyes pushed white heat into mine before he burned a path down to my breasts. That gaze slid over the curve of my hips. Steady hands caressed the length of my legs, and then he dropped his head and placed a gentle kiss low on my stomach.

"You're so exquisite. I know it hurts you. I don't know how to make it not."

"You can't, Will. That's not something you can fix. Time can. Maybe. It's only for a moment, then it feels incredible." I grinned and drew one from him.

His mouth covered mine and two long fingers pushed inside me, and then another, working to stretch me, luring a soft cry from my throat. "Always wet when I touch you, baby." It was true. I wanted him always. I took his heavy arousal into my hand, but before I could stroke, he captured my hand and kissed it.

"Don't push me. I can't maintain self-control when you do."

"Then don't. I need you."

"My control is determined by yours, baby. It hangs by a thread. Let me love you my way, Elle. Submit to me."

Will was huge and his body was more than strong. The power

that coursed through him had to be managed, and his need for dominance controlled. My pushing was a show of impatience, not an objection to that need. Because once he kissed me, touched me, there was nothing that could keep me from surrendering to him. There was no help for it.

I nodded. "Do it now, love me now. Please." I would plead. I would beg. Whatever it took. The craving for him was deep-rooted in my gut, and it never diminished. He'd planted the seed when he kissed my hand on that pier.

The sheets rustled, tangling as his body blanketed mine. He kissed me with a smirk on his lips, and then dragged his mouth along my skin until he reached his destination. His hands gripped my thighs and pushed them open wide, and he carried on with his original plan—to taste every beautiful piece of me.

As I shattered in ecstasy, he shot up my body. He covered my mouth with his and shoved deep inside me with a savage groan before the contractions of my orgasm had finished. He cursed against my neck, his trembling body forced still.

"*Christ.* I'll never get over that."

My nails ravaged his back, drawing tiny beads of blood, and I bit his shoulder as he moved in and out of me. I arched against him, pushing and grinding. He slowed and commanded my surrender. "Stop fighting me, baby. Let go." His authoritative but gentle words resonated, forcing me to see what it was he needed. It wasn't control of me; it was control of *us* once he was inside me. When I submitted, he was able to rein himself in and take us to a beautiful place neither of us had ever been without the other.

He filled me over and over while creating that erogenous friction in all the right places. I squeezed him with my knees and cried out against his lips. He was a god—the only man I'd ever had who could shatter me that way. He failed to hold his roar in check as he followed me over the edge.

The roof could have fallen in, the outside world ended. But not our world. I knew when Will wrapped me in his arms, and together we drifted toward sleep, our world would survive, no matter the odds. No matter the cost.

Dreams plagued me through the night, even as Will held me with sheltering arms. But it wasn't the same murderous faces I'd grown used to in my sleep that pursued me this time. The tome was a living, breathing demon that night, and its contents haunted me. Its words and the voices of its inhabitants had burrowed into my brain. In this dream, I watched my fate play out like some gothic horror movie.

"Your Grace." I directed my eyes to a dirt floor strewn with sweet-smelling rushes dotted with delicate purple blossoms and curtsied low in front of the Duke of Clarence.

"Your death shall come as have all the others. You will not survive. My grandsons cannot save you." A wooden dais creaked under his weight as he climbed down. "Kneel and raise your eyes to mine."

As my chin lifted, I saw my own green eyes, filled with terror and tears. I'd fallen to my knees, submitting to the command of George Plantagenet. His blue eyes were familiar, invincible, raging with fiery madness. His face twisted into something else, something evil. He was going to take my life, his arm thrust high above his head, a blood-stained sword in his cruel grip. . . .

A scream burst from my quivering lungs. I clawed at him. I kicked and writhed. I threw myself to the edge of the bed and sent a lamp crashing to the floor. It was Will who reached for me, not his fifteenth-century ancestor.

"I'm here. It's me. Come to me, baby," he pleaded, his expression worried.

"I'm sorry." I wiped at the tears and crawled back into the safety of his arms.

He cooed and stroked my hair. "You don't need to be sorry. Not ever." Then his tone shifted, resembling the barbarity of his ancestral grandfather. "I'm going to kill them all."

Ten

BAD COMPANY SHOUTED from the speakers and fifteen balls broke with a sharp crack as Will and I entered the billiard room. Ethan was home from London. It was the first time I'd seen him since Will carried me from the plane.

Ethan tossed his cue on top of the table and pointed behind the bar where Thomas lowered the sound system's volume. "Hello, darlin'," Ethan drawled before taking my hand and moving his gape from head to toe, finally landing on my eyes. "Christ."

Will tensed, his fists tightening as he measured his brother's bad form. I slid my hand up his arm and gave his biceps a light squeeze. Ethan was testing him.

Ethan crossed his arms over his muscular chest and grinned. He was broad like his brothers, though he stood no more than six feet tall. His hair was brown, and he had a rather large knot on the bridge of his nose—maybe it had been broken a few times, but his eyes and grin were indistinguishable from Will's.

My God, Lissie looked so much like him.

"Glad you're home, Ethan. I'll leave you two to your business, but at some point I'd like to talk about Lissie." Ethan nodded, and I released Will's arm and curled up on the sofa, content to be alone with my thoughts and sketchpad. I could feel them both watching me as they discussed China's stumbling stocks and its impact on the European market. A nervous client worried it would affect his in-progress leveraged buyout.

It was Lissie's face reaching out from the paper when Will dropped onto the chesterfield next to me, and I lifted my pencil. "Your talent is remarkable, Elle." He studied my drawing, wearing a smile that was handsome as hell. "Tell me what you need to start painting again."

"Late mornings flooded with light from the northern sky."

Ethan sat on the sofa across from ours. "This room then." He winked. "Next week will be quite busy for us, darlin'—in London. I need my brother to get focused and close some business. Hoping you can help me with that."

I turned to Will. "Take me with you."

"I'll be tied up with new investors, baby."

"Take me. I don't want to be so far from you all week."

"You'll stay here."

I narrowed my eyes, but since he wasn't leaving for a few more days, I let it drop. I'd hit him with it again later when we didn't have an audience. My brain shifted gears. My mouth opened, closed, opened. Unbidden words finally escaped. "Lissie looks like you, Ethan."

Ethan jerked his eyes to the floor.

"Is she yours?"

He shrugged.

"It's likely?"

He made eye contact. "Yeah."

"Do you plan to tell her—if she's yours—and raise her? Do you have a plan?"

"Yes. When I confirm she's mine, I'd like your help telling her."

I swiftly deflated and withered beneath Will's arm. Ethan's response should have pleased me, but instead, it sliced into my heart, carving out another piece of wreckage.

"I won't take her from you, Ellie. She needs you. I know that."

"You really didn't know?"

"I never would have abandoned them. Blood is blood, always to be protected, no matter the circumstances."

He said all the right things. Still, anger whispered in my mind, reminding me how horribly the loss of my sister's life hurt. I snapped. "Why weren't you there for Isobel—at the end?"

Compassion filled his eyes, and he dismissed my aggression for what it was: heartache. "I'm sorry. Should have been. I'm so sorry."

My throat began to close up. Tears would fall if I didn't move on. I blinked them away and changed the subject. "Have you issued other commands that require Will to keep something from me? If so, release him now."

Ethan looked at Will, a wide grin spreading from his mouth to his eyes. "He doesn't follow orders anyway. Maybe yours, but not mine."

Will wore the same amused grin.

"This isn't funny. Stop it—both of you."

"There's nothing more, Ellie," Ethan said.

"Will?"

"I'll never lie to you, baby," he said low in my ear as he wound his arms around me.

They still grinned, compelling me to narrow my eyes in warning. Ethan winked and strode back to the pool table. He and Thomas became dark silhouettes against the gray afternoon light pouring through the bank of windows.

Will leaned in and sealed his mouth over mine. The tenderness of his kiss was intoxicating. He lingered at my lips and didn't care that his brothers watched. Maybe that was the point. A dreamy sigh slipped out as I gave his face a gentle push away from mine.

"I promised to spend time with the girls. Lissie will be waiting."

"Take them out for a walk, just stay in the east and south gardens."

"It's okay—I can go outside?"

"I'll send out the Six."

"You'll be watching the security monitors when you should be working," I teased.

My defender, my brilliant lover, conceded with a nod.

The boys' club talk began no sooner than I'd left a kiss on his cheek and headed upstairs to find the girls.

"Christ. What a lovely bit of trouble. I see why you've gone mad."

"Touch her and die," Will snapped back at Ethan.

"Don't stir the fucking beast. I want to play cards tonight," Thomas quipped.

The exterior of the weapons room was deceiving. It never occurred to me it was anything more than a storage room. Will placed his hand to the electronic pad on the wall, and the door slid open with a whoosh. We stepped into a narrow but deep, cavernous room. The door slid shut on its own with another gusting whoosh of air. It was time for my first shooting lesson.

"Ready to do this?"

"I'm ready."

The first area where we stood was the weapons vault. There were shotguns, rifles, handguns, and daggers hanging on walls and resting on shelves. He pointed out the licensed weapons. The pistols he planned for us to shoot were illegal, as were most of the weapons.

Nothing he showed me in that room mattered. Nothing he did or said registered in my mind as a deal breaker, nor did it scare me. My feelings for Will were irrevocable. His cutthroat tactics, his crimes— his sins—couldn't change that. Maybe I was sick. I'd considered the idea once before. Maybe it was love. I'd never been in love before, but I'd heard it was blinding that way.

There were heavy wooden worktables and metal stools running along the north and south walls before we reached four steps that led down into the shooting pit. There was one large, central worktable in the pit and targets positioned at different distances and angles.

Forty slight clicks echoed through the pit as he filled the magazines with ten rounds each and then inserted one into the Glock 26 he'd bought for me. He released the slide, and it sprung forward into its locked position. It was the first time I saw a gun in his hand.

"There's no manual safety on this pistol. It's automatically disengaged when the trigger is pulled, reengaged when the trigger is released."

"How safe is that?" I bit my lip and fidgeted—my nervous tic.

"Quite safe. It won't fire unless you pull the trigger. Keep your finger off the trigger unless you mean to pull it, baby." He pointed to the parts of the gun as he explained everything.

"Got it."

"Christ. This is mad."

"You don't trust me?"

"I do. It's just this isn't what I wanted for you." He stared at me. "Watch me first."

He picked up his much larger gun and positioned himself in front of the target. His feet were spread the width of his squared shoulders, and his arms were extended with soft elbows and locked wrists. His T-shirt clung as he moved and flexed, revealing sheets of hard muscle beneath. Those low-rise jeans hugged the curve of his perfect posterior and muscular thighs.

I reveled in every detail.

He looked back over his shoulder and shook his head at my flirty smile.

I winked.

The corners of his mouth twitched, and then he turned and fired fifteen times. He created one jagged hole in the center of the target.

It was my turn. Will positioned me and stood against my backside to guide me. He adjusted the earmuffs he'd put on my head and placed my finger outside the guard, keeping his on top. "Pull once." His finger moved mine to the trigger.

I pulled. And flinched. I may have closed my eyes.

He slid his hands back and rested them on my shoulders. "Don't close your eyes. Use the sight. Do it again."

I fired again. The second time wasn't as intimidating. I fired three times more without hesitation.

His hands moved down to my hips, and he pressed a fevered kiss on my neck. "Empty it."

I grinned and pulled the trigger five times.

Will reached around my body to remove the empty magazine and insert another. He kissed my neck again and pointed to a different target. When his hands were back on my hips, I aimed and fired ten rounds. After the fourth repetition, he pulled the pistol from my hands.

My head was light—I was high.

He caught me as I jumped into his arms and smashed my mouth to his, demanding his enslaving kiss. His talented mouth claimed mine the way only he could. It was fierce but smooth, unyielding, and without breath. He set me on the table and pushed my legs open wide. His strong hands grabbed my ass and pulled me tight against the growing bulge in his jeans.

I kissed his throat, growing more intoxicated as his pulse leaped beneath my lips.

"I need you, baby. Taking you here. Now."

Ethan cleared his throat.

"Goddamn it." Will closed the three buttons on my blouse he'd undone, leaned in with his head hanging next to my cheek, and splayed his hands against the table on either side of me. "What?" he snapped.

"The door has a lock. Next time you might use it. Jones insists on a face-to-face today. I'm leaving in ten. Decide what next week looks like so plans can be made. I'll be back in the morning."

Will glared over my shoulder at his brother. "You already know what it looks like."

"Sure about that?"

"I'm right here—stop talking about me as if I'm not," I snapped.

Will straightened his back and pulled me from the table. He stared at me through narrowed eyes. "My answer hasn't changed."

"Nor has mine. I want to go. Thomas and Ben could take me shopping while you're working." I volunteered them only because I knew if Will were to come around, that's how it would go down anyway.

The door whooshed, but neither of us looked in that direction.

"Shopping?"

"Yes, shopping. And I'll be overwhelmed with nightmares without you."

"You still have them when I'm here."

"Fewer."

"How do you expect me to accomplish anything if I'm distracted with worry? Billions move through the firm, and I need to—*Jesus Christ.* You're asking me to leave you in a public house, and worse, on the streets of London. I won't do it."

"You can focus on work. I promise. Thomas and Ben protect me when you can't. And what about the Six? Here or there . . . what difference does it make?"

He planted his feet wide and crossed his arms over his massive chest. His tone became acerbic and measured. "I can control this fucking environment, that's the difference, woman. I said no."

I walked away, and he let me. When I glanced back, he'd started cleaning the guns.

We didn't speak until late that evening. We were at an impasse and one of us needed to give in, but it hadn't yet become clear who that would be.

Will slipped into bed behind me after spending the rest of the day in the training center. He pulled me into his shelter and wrapped himself around me. "Don't be angry with me," he rasped in my ear after pushing my hair aside. "I watched a man nearly take your life. I can't stomach the idea another might get that close. I won't lose you, Elle." His words were as tender as the warm kiss he placed on my neck.

A tear fell onto my pillow. I squeezed my eyes tight and swallowed hard to push back the rest. I understood where he was coming from. My rigid body relaxed into his heat, and my hand slipped into his, lacing our fingers. He was going to win.

I recalled his mother's lesson a few days earlier. At the time, I'd assumed she was disciplining Will. But the lesson was meant for me, her message suddenly clear: *he'll get what he wants because that's who he is, but you must be strong enough to make him work for it, so he never takes you for granted.* Only a mother could steer a daughter that way, through coarse waters she'd already navigated. Mary had no daughters, and I had no mother. It was a first for us both. Lissie's face flashed through my mind. She'd need that from me.

I quashed the intense desire to turn to Will. He'd get his victory in the morning.

He kissed my shoulder before we drifted to sleep in a tangle of arms and legs.

I had planned to catch Will before he went to the gym, but he didn't wake me, so I'd missed him.

Mrs. Bates and Lily barged into my room and conducted their usual routine.

"I'd rather have breakfast with the girls this morning."

Mrs. Bates stared at me with her hands on her hips. "With the children, you say?" She was a large, disciplined Irish woman, and she took sass from no one. She was traditional and stubborn. Perfect for Will and his brothers. Not so much for me. But then her eyes softened. "Go on then, dearest."

In the kitchen, we polished off every pancake and slice of bacon put in front of us, but only after we made smiley faces with fruit and pats of butter. With breakfast finished, I kissed both girls and hurried from the table, leaving Nanny Sue with the mess. I needed to let Will off the hook. He'd done his time.

I darted out the door and bounced off his chest. I'd have fallen on my ass had he not caught me. "Will, I—"

His hands gripped my bottom and jerked me up against him. Unbridled desire surged through his body, and the white fire in his eyes burned into me. I locked my legs around his hips and held on for the ride as he swept us from the hall to the privacy of the drawing room. In a flash, my back was pressed to the wall as his mouth covered mine, taking what was his. His kiss was bruising. I surrendered, falling deep into his fierce affection.

"You're avoiding me," he said close to my ear before sucking hard on my butterfly.

I panted, laboring to catch my breath. "I was just going to look for you."

"Guess we should talk about this."

"Can't think. Put me down."

As soon as he allowed me to slide to my feet, I ducked beneath his arm and moved to the bank of southern windows. I basked in the late-morning sunshine, touching my swollen lips, wanting more. He stared into me before heading to the chesterfield, where he'd been waiting with his stack of newspapers. The room smelled of fresh ink, scotch, and old books. And Will.

"You'll do as you're told when necessary?" His tone was sharp but layered with resolve. He was giving in, even though it displeased him to do so.

I was still high and pleasantly surprised, but also annoyed. He would read everything on my face, so I turned and searched the lush landscape for my doe. What would she tell me to do?

A newspaper thumped as it hit the table, and his scent reached out for me. "Elle." He was moving closer. "You must agree."

Irritated by his shift from desirous to stern, I faced him and pushed back, punishing him. "Define 'when necessary' if you think you can."

He cursed under his breath and raked his hair. "It's quite simple. Obey when I ask something of you."

There were two words in the English language I hated to hear—no, and obey. My chin jutted. "I think what you mean is I should trust your direction if exposed to danger."

"When. Not if. The threat is substantial, though you still deny it."

I wasn't in denial, not after what happened on the beach at Lords Point. I shook my head, and whispered, "I don't."

We stood unmoving for several moments. Our stares were an even match. We did that a lot, stared into each other. In those moments, words meant nothing. They didn't exist. Through my eyes, he dove beneath the surface of his fear and mine, and found something deeper that neither of us could live with. My death at the hands of our enemy terrified us, but beneath that trepidation lurked something else: irreparable change—the consequence of my necessary imprisonment. Confinement would alter me. I would suffer a slow and painful emotional death. It would leave behind nothing more than an empty shell. We'd never make it as a couple that way. I'd never make it that way.

We remained still without words, and together understood what we hadn't been able to reconcile as individuals—living was more than assuring breath. We knew what we were up against. The risk of future encounters with assassins was unavoidable.

"All right. I get it, baby. I'll do whatever it takes."

It was a rare gift, his ability to decode the messages hidden on my pages. The vulnerability of it was unsettling, but it's one of the things I loved most about him. He could reach me where no one ever had.

With a leap, I closed the gap between us and wound my arms around his neck. "Thank you, Will." The words and the flood of tears choked me. I buried my face in his shirt and waited for the thundering of his heart to reset me.

He protected my exposed soul in his arms and waited with me. "I'm sorry. The thought of . . . it rouses the brutality. I can't lose you."

In a day, my life had become mired in grief, confusion, and fear. I was thrust into a world of murder and violence. Sometimes the struggle to rise above it was so heavy it overwhelmed me to the point of near destruction. I'd lost myself to its darkness once. There was only one thing solid enough to pull me out and keep me out—Will's belief in my strength.

"Who won?"

"Fuck off, Ethan," Will said.

When my well dried up, I lifted my puffy face and kissed his neck. He and Ethan would discuss security detail for London and then move into business. I didn't want any part of it, so I headed to my room.

"How does she do that?" Ethan teased. He sank into the chesterfield to take his crack at the stack of newspapers.

"She's stubborn." Will never shared what went on between us. Our relationship was ours alone, and he didn't care what anyone thought.

"And so the king of stubborn learns to compromise. I like it."

Glasses clinked. They were breaking out the scotch before noon.

"Don't press me, brother. You won't be afforded the same."

"You're fooling no one—there's more to it than what you say. The depth between the two of you is, well, impressive. Don't let her go, brother." Ethan hesitated. Paper rustled. "She's quite worth the trouble. I see that now. And Christ, those eyes."

Glass pounded wood. "You better never touch her, Ethan."

Another glass hit the table. "I think we're all quite clear on that point."

I ran up the stairs, away from the sounds of their pissing match. The Hastings brothers were alpha males—all four of them. It was like living with a pack of wolves where the males continued to battle for alpha position. Ethan yielded to his brothers more than I imagined Will might. But when it came down to it, sibling rivalry and egos were set aside, and the eldest male was given his due.

Will soon texted me. It was just two words, but I knew exactly what they meant. I dove on the bed with my tablet to search Bond Street.

"Thank you, God," I said when Jimmy Choo appeared as one of the listed retailers. Shoes and me, we had a thing.

When we'd left the States, I brought with me only what I had at the cottage. It was enough, but wasn't much in comparison to my well-stocked closet back home. Will offered to take me to Stonington for more things before we headed to the airport, but I'd refused to go back.

"I'll buy you whatever you want in London," he'd promised. It was a sincere gesture of pure intent. I had no doubt even then he would give me the moon—rip it to pieces with his bare hands and lay it at my feet, if that's what I wanted.

"Your protection is more than enough. I can take care of myself otherwise, but thank you," I'd said.

He had let it drop there, but the spark in his eyes warned me that wasn't the end of it.

I had a feeling that conversation would soon resume.

Eleven

Our party left for London that evening in four separate cars.

"We'll go in my car—just you and me," Will said. "We'll have drinks and something to eat at the hotel. Ethan can handle the security logistics."

I squealed. "Will! Is this . . . are you . . . have you planned a date?"

"Yes." His cocky wink made my stomach flutter. "I'll need to run some numbers later with Ethan, but you first, baby." He grabbed our bags and headed out to bring the car around.

Will tucked me into his sleek black Jag like the well-bred gentleman he was and then jumped in, wasting no time as he sped down the ridge for Old London Road and the A21. Ben and two of the Six rode with Ethan in his Mercedes. The rest of the Six tailed us in the estate's Land Rover. Thomas headed out in his own Rover and planned to stop for Kirsty.

The scent of heaven's woodlands drifted across the car. My tongue swept over my lips as I thought about how well he kissed them. His eyes burned into me. Mine fled from the fast-moving English countryside to him. God, he looked amazing behind the wheel. He drove just as he did everything else—with aggression and arrogant confidence, fully in command.

Through my stare, I willed him to me.

He leaned over and kissed me. "Red."

"What?" I breathed against his lips before he moved to refocus on the road.

"When you go shopping, get another red dress."

"Favorite color?"

"Only when it's on your body. And, as you know, that now belongs to me."

I couldn't hold it back, a laugh slipped out. "You're quite full of yourself tonight."

A big, easy smile covered his face, though he kept his eyes on the road. He reached for my hand as he settled deeper into his seat and accelerated.

We pulled up in front of an elegant boutique hotel located just a few blocks southeast of London's Manchester Square. Will opened the door and took my hand but hesitated after I stepped out, allowing me a few moments to take in my first sight of the streets of London.

A west-pointing street sign caught my attention. "Wallace," I whispered, dazzled. The Wallace Collection was a significant assemblage of art that included original paintings by the old masters and a large exhibit of eighteenth-century French works. An artist's dream. My dream.

The satisfied grin on his face gave him away—he'd anticipated the moment. "If everything goes well, I'll take you through."

I touched his cheek and rewarded him with an affectionate smile. His hand found mine and pulled my fingers to his lips. Several unexpected camera flashes went off from the opposite side of the street. Will wasn't bothered by the intrusion in the least, and though it was something I wasn't accustomed to, I also dismissed it.

The hotel doorman approached. "Mr. Hastings, sir?"

Will nodded. "The three cars behind me as well."

"Shall we park the cars for you?"

"No. We'll park and manage the bags. Thank you."

The young doorman bowed his head and opened the hotel entrance wide.

Joe Wright, leader of the Six, jumped out of the Land Rover and sprinted over, reaching for the key to Will's car. "I'll park the Jag so you can get her off the street. We'll set up and see you later."

Will placed his hand on my lower back and ushered me between stately white columns into the grand Victorian building made of red brick. As we passed through the door, he put cash in the doorman's hand. Not for service, for silence. He guided me across the polished marble floors of the quaint lobby to a library-esque lounge styled in rich woods and earth tones. He then gestured for me to sit on a sumptuous tufted sofa in a semiprivate space reminiscent of an old snug.

"You've been here?"

"Yeah, belongs to one of the clients. It does quite well, so I want one of us with you at all times. Even on our floors. Red or white, baby?" He pulled out his phone and read a text message as he sat.

"Red. What do you mean *our floors?*"

"Ethan cleared the fourth and fifth floors. Sleeping rooms on four. Five is one large suite that we'll use for a private lounge."

"Is that necessary?"

He leaned close and inhaled, and my breath quickened in response. His voice dripped with the same deep gravel he used in bed. "Yes, it's necessary. Don't be con—"

He stopped midsentence and turned to the bar server, who had coughed to draw his attention. "Chateauneuf-du-Pape *et* Laphroaig . . . ," French and Gaelic in the same sentence, both pronunciations flawless, "and don't clear your fucking throat for my attention again."

When he spoke French, it rolled off his tongue beautifully. I'd heard him use the language during business calls. It was typically followed then by "those fucking French."

His focus jerked back to me. "Wouldn't bring you otherwise.

Don't be concerned about the indulgence when it's of no concern to me. Ethan and I make a lot of money, and we spend a lot of money. Get used to it." Then he retrieved my glass of wine from the fearless-turned-apprehensive server's tray and handed it to me.

"Occasionally your arrogance is off-putting, you know."

"Yeah." He never denied it—his ego was too big for even him to dismiss. "Taste," he commanded, and as he studied my face with a raised brow, I did taste it.

The wine was delicious. Its alcohol content was higher than I was used to, but he knew that when he chose it. "Very nice, thank you." I smiled.

His face lit with satisfaction, and then he took his scotch from the tray and sent the server away with a food order.

"Where are the others?"

"Inspecting the rooms and setting up shop in the security office. One of ours will monitor the surveillance cameras inside and out at all times, and another will patrol the property on foot. Just you and me for now, baby."

"And you'd rather see to my intoxication than check things out for yourself?"

"I'll do that after I carry you to bed." He smirked.

That small, haughty smile unmade me, sending shivers along my spine. My unruly body prepared itself for his, heat building between my legs. I slid my hand to his inner thigh.

His hand captured mine and squeezed. "You need to be careful out there tomorrow, Elle. Told you—I can't live without you. Better make damned sure you come back to me unharmed."

"You've covered the bases. And that's part of the plan, right? Expose me to the public. Pull in allies."

"Introduce, not expose. There's a difference. It won't be me out there with you, and I don't like that. You pushed me, baby, hard. I wanted more time to implement."

"If you really don't want me to go without you, I won't. I trust you, Will."

He kissed my forehead and then pulled me against the sofa beneath his arm. "We'll give it a shot. I must learn to trust Thomas."

"You trust Ben."

"I do, but it's not the same. He's not blood. As close as we are, there's no guarantee he'd risk himself the way my brothers would. Enough of this talk—it's spoiling date night."

We laughed out loud. Although I feared what we both knew was out there lying in wait, my spirit was light and my heart filling with something I'd never known, never expected.

"I'm so happy it's you. I can't imagine getting through this with anyone else."

He pressed his lips to mine. "I won't let you down."

"I know."

"I'll be tied up tomorrow and most of the following day. We'll see how the rest of the week goes. Thomas and Ben will take you shopping. Two others will follow. You must do as you're told, Elle. Promise me. I have business matters to handle, and if I'm distracted . . ."

"What will you promise me?"

"Anything you want." He swallowed what was left of his whisky and held up the glass in his surly way to call for another. "Give me your word."

I sipped on my Chateauneuf and stared at him.

"Give me your fucking word, Elle."

The server was back with two more drinks, again holding the tray near Will.

He jerked his chin toward the cocktail table. "No more wine. Keep the scotch coming." When he didn't get anything from me, he took my glass and set it on the table. "You must promise. You understand what we're up against. I've left Ethan to run the company for months, and I need to take care of some clients this week. I can't accommodate tantrums or avoidable distractions."

What crossed my mind next took me by surprise. I looked up at him from beneath my lashes. "Stay with me every night—even if you come back late or you're working on something. Even if you don't wake me, be there. With *me*."

He nodded. "That's it?"

"No other women, Will." The bitter taste of regret abruptly filled my mouth. Jealousy had never been something that possessed me. But there it was. Women looked at him like they wanted to devour him, and I hated it. He was mine, damn it.

"What?"

"That's what Ethan does. Sleeps around when he's here."

He fought to suppress it but couldn't stop the grin that tore up his face. "*That's* what you're worried about?"

"Well, yes."

That wicked grin remained on his face. As handsome as it was, it irritated me, and I snapped at him. "I won't have it, Will. It's the one deal breaker." There. I'd discovered one.

Will pulled me tight against his body, filled a hand with my hair, and kissed me hard. He angled his head and thrust his tongue deep, tasting me, possessing me. I whimpered, falling into his impassioned kiss. When we broke, he pressed his lips softly to mine several times before he loosened his grip on my hair and rested his forehead on mine. We stayed in that position for God knows how long, wrapped up in each other. There was nothing else.

A thought entered my mind but was lost before I could make sense of it. Anything outside the space we shared became pointless. His hand still owned the back of my head, preserving the contact between us. It was an incredible, intimate moment, and a rare display of intense affection for a prominent Englishman in public.

"Only you. I swear," he breathed. He caressed my lips with his thumb and then placed one more soft kiss there.

A woman with long, silver hair arranged two elegant place settings and platters of food on the cocktail table before us. "Carry on, loves," she said as she gestured with her hands in a way I didn't understand, then she disappeared.

Ethan approached as though he'd come from nowhere. His words destroyed the peace we'd found. "All clear. Go to the security office and see to your men. They need to see how serious you are about this. We'll stay with her until you return." He dropped two key cards on the table. "Yours opens everything. The blue one is for your room, Ellie."

Will nodded at Ethan. "Eat, baby. I'll be back soon."

Ethan and Thomas moved the surrounding leather club chairs closer. Ethan pulled out his phone and scrolled through his email.

"So. Shopping," my stand-in defender said with a wink.

They all had the same eyes, and the same wink, which they shared often. The flirtiness of it was atypical for well-bred Englishmen. I loved that these brothers chose to show, rather than suppress, their affection. It made me wonder if their father had done the same.

"Sorry, Thomas. I know you'd prefer to spend the time doing something else, but I insist on shopping, and he insists it be you in charge of my safety. You'll bring Kirsty?"

"He's right. Until things settle, it must be one of us. Don't give me the slip, Ellie," he warned. "She can come if that's what you want."

"Don't force her. She doesn't seem all that comfortable around me. Can you keep up?"

"I can shop with the best—just wait and see."

"What is this, and how do I eat it?"

Ethan looked up from his phone for a moment and chuckled.

"Yorkshire puddings. Those are sweet," Thomas said, pointing to one platter. "What are you drinking?" He scooped a pudding from the other platter, soaked it with gravy, cut it into small pieces, and then handed me the plate.

Mary Hastings may not have had much to do with the training and education of her sons, but she had taught them good old-fashioned chivalry. Her boys opened doors, held jackets, presented flowers—and prepared Yorkshire puddings.

"Chateauneuf." I took a bite and moaned, stuffing another into my mouth without delay. "This is delicious." It was made with beef and watercress.

"Great pairing. Makes you sleepy."

"He plans to work through the night," I muttered through a mouthful.

"We'll see. Maybe not after that snogging."

"Thomas!" I felt my cheeks burn and diverted my attention back to the plate. I'd never heard the term before, but the meaning was clear.

Will looked down at me with his handsome smile before resuming his seat on the sofa. He canted his head toward the bar and sent his brothers away, determined to finish what we'd started. My date picked up one of the sweet Yorkshire puddings and held it close to my mouth. Once I bit, he shoved the rest into his mouth and watched for my reaction.

It was a little bite of heaven—sweet, moist bread filled with toasted coconut and warm, melted chocolate. "That is so good. You'll make me fat with your English food, Will." The dribble of chocolate on his mouth was utterly kissable. I dabbed at it with my napkin.

Will leaned in and sucked a bead from my bottom lip. "Next time, do it this way." He demonstrated again. Sensing my undeniable arousal, and after adjusting his own, he smirked. "Drizzling some on your lovely naked body in my bed . . . also acceptable."

He definitely knew how to read me.

The rest of the party drifted in, pulling club chairs with them as they arrived. Drinks flowed, and the guys carried on in a raucous manner. The camaraderie was remarkable. It was a blend of brothers by blood and brothers-in-arms, but a band of brothers nonetheless. I thought of the tattoo on Will's shoulder. His father inked the same shield on each of his sons when they turned eighteen. It was a traditional rite of passage for a warrior-trained Hastings male, and it committed them to the ancient dynastic pact meant to keep me alive.

Content and heavy-eyed, I snuggled into Will's side and placed my head on his chest. My fingers gripped his shirt. His heartbeat and voice—both rich, intense—soothed me.

"See what's up over there. Tell him I'll break his fucking neck if he doesn't turn his head," Will said, stirring me from my bliss.

"That son of a bitch. I warned him earlier to stop staring." Thomas stood and headed for the bar.

"You know he's not coming back without throwing a punch," Ethan snapped.

Will shrugged.

"Arsehole. You had to turn him out like yourself."

"Someone had to teach him. He's quite good backup."

Seconds later, the gawker's head jerked, and he flew back against the bar. As Thomas grabbed him by the throat, two other eager men arrived to help their friend.

"Will, go help him," I groused.

"Nah. He can handle those three," Ethan said.

Four more made their way to Thomas's fight.

Will sprang into action. "Six," he commanded. "Get the fuck up, Ethan."

"Six" was the one-word command Will used to send his soldiers to me. Four of the Six who were with us at the time closed in around me without delay.

Ben was already on his feet. The three of them jumped into the fight, as did several more from the bar. Someone within the fray shouted, "You bloody bastards think you own everything!"

Fists and bodies flew, and blood splattered. Tables crashed. Chairs sailed through the air, the wood pieces splintering upon impact where they landed. Women shrieked, but not me. Though my heart raced from a stab of adrenaline, I watched the brawl quiet as a mouse, flanked by former soldiers of the British Armed Forces. I flinched once or twice when one of ours took a hit, but I'd seen worse.

A chair crunched against Will's back. It was the only hit he took. When he turned to face the man who wielded the seat as his weapon, the guy tossed it away and sprinted toward the exit.

Kirsty arrived, weaving through the chaos. Her eyes were the size of golf balls.

"Come sit with me, Kirsty. It'll be over soon." I pushed at one of my immoveable guards in a failed attempt to let her in next to me on the sofa. "You've never seen them fight?"

Will wrapped a bar towel around his red-stained knuckles. He pulled me close and kissed the top of my head. "Let's go upstairs to the room, baby."

"This is fast becoming an expensive week even by my standard," Ethan said. He chuckled as he gazed around the bar and then slapped Thomas on the back. "Felt good. I needed that, brother."

"You pussy. You didn't even want to get up," Will countered.

I pulled back and lifted my chin to see his face. "All right. Boys' club is done for the night. Don't you two have work to do?"

The hotel owner and two policemen walked in.

"Handle that, will you," Will said as he cuffed Ethan on the shoulder and led me out of the lounge with his arm secured around my waist.

"Are they going to arrest you?"

He looked down at me with an incredulous smile and shook his head as we stepped into the elevator. The moment the doors closed, he swept me off my feet.

"What are you doing?"

"I told you I'd carry you to bed. I'm a man of my word, if nothing else."

I laughed.

"Haven't seen you laugh this much since—"

"Don't say it, Will." It was nothing more than a whisper.

"Did the fighting scare you?"

"No." My need for him displaced fear and logic.

Will pushed through the door of our suite and kicked the solid wood base of the bed before he placed me on top. The same fingers used minutes before to beat others slid sensually along the arches of my bare feet after he removed my blue suede strappy heels. "Christ. Even your feet turn me on." He purred my name and blasted me with the white heat of his eyes as his body covered mine.

"How much time do we have before Ethan shows up?"

"Not enough." He pushed his tongue past my lips and owned me. His hard length throbbed as he rubbed it against my body and grumbled. "Goddamn it, not enough." Then he hesitantly lifted himself from the bed and adjusted his arousal. "You'll be the cause of my ruin, woman."

I whined in protest, but received nothing more than a wink and a crooked smile.

"Sleep well, baby. I'll be on the other side of this door."

Will and Ethan spent the next few hours drinking and working on their business strategy for the week in the sitting room of our suite. I could hear their voices—the thunder of Will's and the smooth roll of Ethan's—but it didn't stop me from drifting into sleep.

A shrill scream burst from my lungs as my body jerked upright.

Will rushed through the door. He shot across the bed and tried to pull me close while I pushed and kicked like some wild, cornered animal to get away from him. "Look at me, Elle. It's me. Just look at me, baby."

His voice blasted through the walls of my mind's trap. I found his eyes and collapsed into his arms, gulping air through my dry mouth. "S-sorry."

"Jesus fucking Christ. She doesn't deserve this."

"I'm going to find every last one of those fucks and end this."

"I'll be there at your side when you do, brother. You have my word." Ethan patted Will's shoulder and then slipped out of the room without another sound.

Will climbed into bed and pulled my quivering body to his, his generous arms sealing me tight in his strength. I slept there dreamless through the rest of the night.

Twelve

I STARED INTO THE mirror and ran my fingers through my long, brunette layers. It was the perfect time to make a change. I was coming to terms with the real me, or the new me—I didn't know which it was, but it didn't matter. The important thing was I understood the evolution that continued to strengthen and define me.

The hotel concierge rang back and confirmed an immediate appointment at one of London's finest salons. Fact was, the Hastings name turned heads and moved mountains throughout South East England. London was no exception.

Thomas's text alert chimed: DO NOT OPEN THAT DOOR UNTIL I'M WAITING ON THE OTHER SIDE. TEXT ME BACK WHEN YOU'RE READY TO GO. T

I replied immediately: READY NOW. He was at my door within seconds.

"Can we get coffee to go? I should be at the salon within the next thirty minutes." I forgot myself for a moment, pushing through the center of my four-man protection detail, heading for the elevator.

"Hold it, Ellie. Don't walk off like that. You must behave with me as you do with Will."

I turned to him with hands on my hips and a raised brow.

"You know what I mean," he said. "And wait—salon?"

"Yes. Salon."

"Christ. You're not going to make this easy, are you?"

Ben snickered as he recognized the same complaint he'd heard from Will but pulled himself together fast after meeting my narrowed eyes.

I handed Thomas a slip of paper with the salon info and a list of the shops I wanted to hit. He looked up twice before he finished reading. "Let's get on with it then. This'll take two full days." He pressed the elevator button and held out his big arm, corralling me behind him as the doors opened.

"Done by tea tomorrow. I promise."

He and Ben glared over their shoulders, but both men softened when they found my sympathetic smile. As we stepped outside the hotel entrance, Thomas grabbed a newspaper and cursed. The bar fight had made the front page of the city's most infamous tabloid. So did an intimate photo of Will and me taken in front of the hotel the night before. The caption and write-up speculated about the Hastings Group CEO's long-awaited return to London and how his prior absence may have been related to the "mystery woman" in the photo.

"Will set up that photo. I'm sure of it. Let the fun and games begin," Ben said.

Thomas tossed out the paper. "Some warning would have been nice."

We walked a few blocks and turned many heads, my entourage of guards and me. As soon as we arrived at the salon, Thomas and I were greeted by the owner and delivered to a plush lounge where we were plied with mimosas and quiche. Ben and the others waited in the coffee shop next door.

When I finally dragged my dazed stare from the mirror and climbed out of the luxurious swiveling chair, Thomas was looming possessively, his gaping mouth saying nothing. He'd never gone far, never allowed me out of his line of vision.

My boring brown tresses had been transformed by one of London's renowned artistic colorists into bouncing waves painted with shades of swirling caramel and flaxen. From a distance, I looked like a blonde.

Thomas extended his hand. "Lovely. My brother's a lucky man."

I offered my hand and a blushing smile and allowed him to lead me through the salon, but dug my heels in when we reached the door. "Hang on. I need to check out first."

"Already done. Let's get to the shopping."

"Wait—what? Done?"

He pulled me outside into the beckoning sunshine.

"But—"

"No."

I refused to move my feet.

"You can't leave a paper trail with your name, so your credit cards aren't to be used. Do you think Will's ego would allow for it even if there were no security issues? You're his. Get over the money thing."

"But Thomas—"

"No. Move your feet, or I'll lift you." He sounded like Will.

As we walked, I pouted. And then I scowled.

"Listen. I know things are different in America. Independence being the theme of fucking everything. Try to remember where you are now. I suppose it comes off paradoxical, but it's the way of England's old blood. We're progressive and traditionalists. Some things never change and some things change rapidly. When it comes to caring for our women, you'll find most lean traditionally. That's why my brother will never allow you to pay for your own things. And you shouldn't bust his balls over it. Don't mess with his ego that way, Ellie. It would be the same with me."

"So you buy Kirsty's things?"

"Not quite. Our relationship isn't the same as yours. If I were to decide she was the woman for me, then yes, I would."

"Is she going to be—the woman for you?"

"I'm happy with her in the present, but I don't see her as my future."

"Ugh."

"What?"

"She's in love with you, Thomas."

Again reminding me of Will, he cursed under his breath.

After a late lunch, we left Jimmy Choo and the shops of New Bond Street for the dress boutiques of Old Bond Street. Thomas and Ben might never walk into a designer dress shop again. I'd potentially ruined them for their future wives, dragging them into many boutiques and trying dozens of dresses at each before deciding what I wanted.

I reached for his arm. "Take me back to the hotel, Thomas. I'm tired."

"It's about time." He winked and then placed his hand low on my back. "Let's go. They'll deliver your packages to the hotel."

"Hang on," Ben said. "We've got company outside. Let me grab the other two and have a look before we head out."

Thomas peered out the shop's display window. "Too late. They clearly know who she is. It's too thick—I'll take her back in a taxi. The three of you should meet us at the hotel entrance for cover."

The moment we stepped out the door, we were hit by the flashing of cameras and shouts of the notorious London tabloid paparazzi. My stomach lurched and anxiety hummed in my ears.

"Ellie, pose for us, love," someone shouted.

"It's her . . . it's the last white rose!"

"Are you here to claim the throne?"

Paparazzi surrounded the four men who surrounded me in a tight circle. When they couldn't get a direct shot, they lifted their cameras on poles above our heads to snap photos.

My chest tightened. I couldn't breathe.

My protectors batted cameras and shoved photographers.

"Back the fuck up," Thomas said as he stiff-armed an aggressive photographer. "You all know you're going to get your snaps so back up and give her some space."

A man pushed a mic into my face. "There's a photo circulating of you and Will Hastings. Are you a couple? Why are you with his brother? Have you come for your inheritance?"

Thomas batted the mic down. "She and my brother are together. I'm protecting her from people like you—that's why she's with me now. No other comments will be made."

"Let her speak, Hastings," someone shouted.

Others from the street joined the melee. People shoved. Shouted.

Their voices rang in my ears like echoes moving through an empty tunnel. Panic consumed me, and I clutched Thomas's shirt, my knuckles turning white.

As he locked me inside his arms, Thomas shouted at Ben, "Where's the taxi?"

Paparazzi reinforcements arrived. Photographers were fighting other photographers. Punches were thrown, as were cameras and phones.

Thomas pushed me into an alcove. He pressed my back to the wall and used his own body to shield mine. "I'll get you out of here. I promise. Hold on to me." I pressed myself to his chest, drawing ragged breaths through my open mouth.

Ben appeared behind Thomas's back with the two other men. "Let's move. Follow me. I'll clear the path. Taxi's one block south. We need to move now. This isn't going to ease anytime soon."

"Ellie, I'm going to be right beside you. You're going to feel me on you, touching you. If you need to hold on to me, then do it. You must not get separated from me. You will stay on Ben's heels. Do not veer—stay on his fucking heels."

I wiped at the tears running down my face and nodded.

"No more crying. Getting out of this is nothing compared to last night," he teased.

—

It was past three when Will slipped into bed and pulled me close. We were face to face, and our bodies were pressed snug with our arms and legs woven together like the threads of a tapestry. I buried my face at the base of his neck.

He lifted locks of my hair and inspected the color, twisting some around his finger. "There's a beautiful blonde in my bed." Exhaustion was apparent in his voice.

I pressed a secret smile against his warm skin. "How did you know it was me?"

He cupped my chin and pushed my head back to inhale against my throat. "As beautiful as you are, I can identify you by your scent alone."

"That's creepy, Will."

He inhaled again and moaned.

I dragged my fingers along his jawline and smoothed his beard. He hadn't trimmed it for several days, so it was longer than his usual stubble. "You're tired."

"Yeah."

We joined our lips, resting them in mutual tenderness, and closed our eyes.

"Baby, I was lost before you. So destructive. You saved me." His whisper relaxed into sleep.

He was already gone when the rain pounded against the windows and lightning streaked through the London sky, illuminating the dark morning. Thunder cracked again, the thrill I used to feel with it insignificant after falling for Will's thunderous heartbeat and voice.

I sat up with a start and choked on nothing.

My dreams had been pleasant instead of horror-filled. And lucid—I'd been in and out of consciousness, aware that I was dreaming. At one point, it seemed as though my father stood next to our bed. He hadn't said anything, though he never did when I dreamed of him.

It was difficult to sort through the reality of those hours. Did Will really say the words or had I been dreaming? *Baby, I was lost. . . .* That's what my brain heard, but my heart insisted there had been more. *I love you.*

Then I found the crimson rose he left on his pillow. Will had showered me with roses at Eastridge. He'd filled my room with combinations of beautiful white and pink English roses. The brute was a romantic at heart. But this rose on his pillow was unlike the others. I lifted the long-stemmed beauty to my nose and breathed in its fragrance.

"My God. I can't sort through it. Did he say he loves me?" I tried to reason with my abstract-driven mind. There'd been times in my life when I'd feared something, and when it came to pass, my brain locked down and blocked it. Is that what I had done? "Stop obsessing and get moving, Ellie. And stop talking to yourself."

Thomas waited in the hall with coffee in each of his hands. "We'll take my car today and leave from the owner's private entrance."

We collected my dresses from the boutiques where they'd been fitted overnight but not yet delivered, hit a few more shops, and finished up with afternoon tea as promised. The lounge was fully restored to its original grandeur and filled with tea-loving patrons.

Ethan was back and joined us for the hotel's popular Gentleman's Tea—translation: whisky and meat available. He summoned the hotel manager and insisted she sit at our table.

I sipped on my Earl Grey and sampled fancies and classic scones while listening to Ethan's demands for a sumptuous spread and

well-stocked bar for our private fifth-floor lounge. He and Will were
hosting a cocktail party for new clients that evening.

"Champagne fountain?" the manager asked.

"Oh, why not? We made a lot of money this week. Let's celebrate."
He dismissed the woman with nothing more than a nod of his head,
and then turned his attention to me. "Dress to the nines tonight,
Ellie."

"It's okay for me to be there?"

"Quite. Our guests are looking forward to meeting Will's
American sweetheart."

"What?"

"Sharing some personal details is important in this business—
especially when we're working to hook investors. They want to know
we have lives outside the firm."

"Which one of you did the sharing?"

"Couldn't have stopped him from going on about you had I tried."

I smiled at the thought, missing Will.

Ethan stood and offered his hand. "Come, darlin'. You and I have
a meeting with the commissioner."

"Commissioner? Wait—where is Will?"

"Do you think you'd benefit from his inability to control himself? His innate drive to protect you won't be restrained, not even in
the presence of the authorities."

Tears stung the back of my lids. How would I get through the
interview without Will?

"He had no choice, Ellie. I demanded this, and that he not discuss it with you in advance. He doesn't have the ability to say no to
you. I won't have my brother investigated. Or worse."

I slipped my hand into Ethan's and nodded, barely breathing.
He was right. I had to push back at the fear, at the anxiety rushing
through my cooling blood, and trust him. We couldn't risk Will's
freedom, and allowing him to participate in an onerous situation

with the head of the Metropolitan Police would be an absolute gamble. Ethan led me to a private room near the rear of the hotel where patrons weren't permitted. He never let go of my hand.

The interrogation was gentle. Typical procedural questions, Will's lawyer pointed out. Commissioner Brown had been kind, offering sympathetic smiles and gestures as he laid out his questions. I liked him from the moment he'd entered the room. He had a stocky build and comforting blue eyes. It went unsaid, but it was clear there was some level of friendship and respect between him and Ethan.

"Reiterating once more for the record, you arrived home at approximately ten minutes before eleven p.m., and at that time, when you found your sister and grandmother lying in the foyer, there was no one else in the house."

"Other than Lissie, that's right."

"These questions have been asked and answered. We're done. Send my regards to Stonington's captain," Ethan said.

"Thank you, Ms. James. And again, I'm deeply sorry for your losses. I'm quite offended by the insistence of the American police that we put you through this." Brown bowed his head, and with that, he and his two quiet but observant detectives left the hotel.

"Have a soak and get dressed," Ethan said, waiting for me to pass through the door of the suite I shared with Will. "He'll be here soon, eager to get his hands on you I expect. You did well." He kissed my hand, and I closed the door, anxious to be alone with my thoughts and settle my mind before Will arrived.

The hot bath had been both relaxing and reinvigorating. I finished dressing and gazed into the full-length mirror while waiting for Will.

My curve-hugging cocktail dress was a silk sheath covered in fine metallic embroidery with embroidered trim along the hem, shoulders, and V-shaped neckline and had a silk-banded waist. Sparkling metallic Choos complemented the dress well. My gaze wandered from the shoes. My green irises popped against the characteristic smoky eyes I'd created with multiple shades of deep plum shadows and liners. I'd given the upward-curving outer corners more drama than usual.

I'd never done anything as expressive with my hair. Recalling Will's amorous behavior early that morning after he'd crept into bed forced my lips into a mischievous smile, and my reflection nodded with approval. "Here's your red dress, warrior."

Ben's knuckles rapped against the door. "Ellie, open."

I jerked it open wide. "Where's Will?"

"He said he couldn't reach you. Everything okay?"

"Yes. Oh—I misplaced my phone. Thomas said he'd check the car. Where is he?"

"Ethan wanted to talk to him before Will gets here."

"Will was supposed to be here by now."

"He's tied up with a contract negotiation, but he'll be here soon. He said he'll meet you upstairs."

"Is he angry with Thomas?"

"I don't think he's angry with any one person. It's the whole situation. What happened yesterday was out of his control, and we all know that doesn't work for Will. Control is his thing, right? You can bet it won't go down that way again. He's better equipped to deal with the press than the rest of us anyway. Jesus, I need a drink. Let's go up."

I tossed lipstick into my clutch and grabbed my sketch portfolio.

The view from the rooftop terrace was amazing. The warm sun was setting over Manchester Square. I sketched the London skyline to the north where I could see the graceful steeple of the historic Hinde Street Methodist Church. It had an octagonal tower and spire set above four solid peaks with finials at each corner. The midsection had narrow semicircular arched openings, and the lower section had semicircular arched windows and Corinthian columns that supported the two levels above.

I knew the moment Will had arrived. He filled the doorway, watching me.

It was impossible not to smile when I stole a sideways glance. He wore an elegant, gray Italian suit tailored for his body and a fiery stare. I wanted to run to him but managed to wait it out, allowing him to come to me. When he stepped out onto the terrace, my protection detail moved inside with haste.

Will's body heat and his irresistible scent closed in from behind, and then his strong arms were around me. My skin prickled with goose bumps. Reveling in his presence, I let my head fall back against his shoulder.

"I've missed you, Will."

He inhaled through my hair and fingered some of the flaxen tips before he pushed them out of his way. He traced the butterfly on my neck with his finger and kissed it with eager lips. "Kiss me, baby." As he said the words, my heart flipped.

I turned and found white fire in his eyes.

There was no time to waste. He bent and owned my mouth, his tongue running along my bottom lip before pushing inside to find mine. When he was satisfied with the depth of our kiss, he broke and moved his charged gaze up and down my body. "You're so much more than just beautiful. . . . My angel." Then he hauled me back against him, pushed his rigid length into my stomach, and slipped his tongue past my lips again. One hand applied pressure to my nape so I couldn't escape his kiss, and the other moved up my thigh beneath the hem of my dress. "Need you," he purred. "Need to be inside you."

"Me too," I breathed against his lips. The terrace spun. I was high.

"Will," Ethan snapped from inside the open door.

Will ignored his brother and pushed another kiss deeper, pushed it beyond a kiss. Neither of us would be satisfied until we shared the same breath. And we did.

"Ethan said the interview went well."

I nodded, still panting from that last kiss.

"I'm going to take you home tonight. I'll bring you again, but for now I want you back at Eastridge. One day soon I'll shut down Hertford for an evening and give it to you."

Hertford was the historic mansion in Manchester Square that housed the Wallace Collection. I peeked around his shoulder at the square, its lush gardens and the mansion silhouetted against the glowing amber backdrop, and smiled. "I know." He would. He'd stop time for me, if he could.

He pressed his smiling lips against mine.

"What's going on? Tell me, Will."

"The questions the paparazzi asked, knowing who you are—the press didn't have that information yet. It was fed to them with intent."

"You mean the Order was behind it?"

"Had to be. We'll leave after the cocktail party."

"They're getting closer."

"Make no mistake, they're coming."

A cold rush of anxiety slid through my body. He felt it and strengthened his embrace.

"You'll be safe at Eastridge. I know that mess with the photographers scared you yesterday, and I'm sorry, baby. The press will be an issue for us, but I'll manage it better in the future. I won't allow that to happen again."

"Are you coming back?"

"We'll have to work this out. I know you don't like it when I'm gone. James is coming along well, and he can handle most things on my behalf, but the clients expect to see me. Investors considering us expect to deal with me. And I need to look into some questionable transactions Ethan conducted while I was away. The stakes are high in this business, Elle. Success requires aggressive leadership."

I nodded. "James?"

"I'll introduce you. He's inside."

"I'd love to see your office sometime."

"I don't think the boss will mind." His smug wink made my heart flutter, as did his kiss when he slanted his mouth over mine, taking another. "I promise you this. I won't come back until we've spent a full day in bed." Then he flashed that marvelous grin.

Will held my hand tight as he led me inside where inquiring minds waited.

Thirteen

WILL AND I passed through the center of the room and headed straight for the bar, where he placed a glass of champagne in my hand without letting go of the other. I shifted my weight and squeezed his fingers to ground myself.

"Ease into it, Elle. They'll adore you."

"Why must they stare?" God, I was nervous.

"Who wouldn't? Christ. You're amazing."

"Will," I whined. I needed more than an expression of ego-driven pride.

"It's a rude society in comparison to your politically correct upbringing. You'll get used to it, baby." He took a drink of scotch. "They're curious. You've nothing to worry over." His gaze moved over my shoulder, and he nodded as he pulled me to his side.

James Jackson gestured for my hand with a teasing, knowing smile. "Ah, there she is. . . . The lovely lady I must thank for the job security. It's my honor to meet you. Welcome to England." He held my presented hand with affection.

"Thank you, James. It's so nice to meet you."

He was tall and elegant with light brown skin, warm brown eyes, and a showy grin. His head was bald and his facial hair groomed tight. His presence was similar to Will's—intelligence and authoritative charm whirled around him—though his immediate persona was warmer.

Will slapped him on the back and grinned. "She may as well sign your checks."

There was obvious trust and respect and even friendship between the two. James was a principal at the firm—Will's right arm. He directed the staff and operations under Will's areas of responsibility and researched ideas for investments and acquisitions. And then some.

Will called out to one of the clients. "David, come have a drink with us."

The two men shook hands in a manner that exceeded the boundaries of a cordial business greeting. Though their professional relationship was new, they had attended Oxford together. They had partied and chased women together, I'd bet.

"This is my wife, Caroline."

She extended her hand. "Quite pleased. David talks about you nonstop."

Will gave a slight bow and held her hand for a moment. "I'd like you to meet—"

She interrupted and turned to me. "Of course, the little gem you found abroad. You *are* lovely, darling. Shall we go have a chat while these men wade into their boring business conversations?"

Thanks to my implacable English gran, I could play the elite class social game as well as any Brit. I'd spent the afternoon preparing for forward behavior like Caroline's. After a quick check of my nerves, I reinforced my already-straight posture and set my glass on the bar, and in the same fashion she'd done to Will, offered my hand.

"Ellie James. Champagne?"

Stunned by my reciprocated presumptuousness, and then delighted, she grasped my fingers and grinned without uttering a word.

Will squeezed my other hand to express approval—and amusement—then kissed it before he allowed me to pull away.

I led Caroline arm in arm to one of the sofas. "Will, send some-one over, please." I threw the words over my shoulder at him with a playful smile.

He pulled his stare from my ass and winked, sending the bar-tender over with nothing more than a jerk of his chin.

Pretty, pretentious Caroline was a stay-at-home mom full of small talk about her girlfriends, great shoes—I gave her points for that—and her three young children. She pushed hard for a story about Will and me. My new friend admitted she'd seen the after-noon tabloids and knew who I was. Still, I offered nothing more than the old timeworn story of serendipity.

Those moments of shallow exchange reawakened my longing for Jess.

"Come on, darling. Give me something. Each of your families has rejected your God-given nobility. Others would kill for it. There must be more to the story." She had no idea how true her statement was.

Will carried on with an expanding group of men, leading a spir-ited conversation about a historic referendum the British would vote on in the coming year. "Aggressive policy development could fur-ther boost Britain's market—we'll possess one of the world's stron-gest economies by the end of next year anyway, despite claims of impending doom." A discussion about fast cars followed. I caught his hungered gaze as he spoke. He'd be insatiable, mind-blowing, later in bed.

Can't wait, I shot back at him with my eyes, biting my lip.

"Show me to the toilet, Ellie," Caroline said. She at once inter-rupted my silent conversation with Will and gave me an opportu-nity to gain a moment alone with him.

I sent Kirsty in my place and summoned Will with the curl of a finger. He quickly erased the distance between us and purred close to my ear as he tugged at his collar.

"*Elle.* I'm mad for you."

My hands glided up his arms. "If that's true, you should take me to bed." I removed the knot from his tie and slipped it from around his neck.

His throat rumbled as he forced back the idea.

"You're sweating. Take off your jacket." After he had, I unfastened the top buttons of his shirt while he worked his cufflinks. I held out my hand before he could put them into his pocket.

He raised a brow as he dropped the pavé-set black diamond cufflinks into my hand.

"I'll put them in your pocket myself." I smiled from beneath my lashes while stuffing my whole hand into the front of his trousers. He was already hard.

"You don't play fair, witch."

I shrugged and rolled up each of his sleeves into neat folds and then dragged my fingers along the inside of his forearms. "Better?"

"It's not enough."

"You know, when you come near me or even look my way, everyone watches."

He lowered his head and brushed his lips over mine. "And you know I don't care." I loved that about Will. It never mattered what others said or thought. He'd do what he wanted, take what he wanted, and that was that. "Give me ten minutes to get rid of the last few, and we'll get out of here."

Unwilling to sit through any more night-out-with-the-housewives recounting, I wandered into the fresh air near the open terrace by Thomas and the other familiar faces. He was going on about our run-in with paparazzi. I couldn't help but laugh at his embellished story, finally interjecting, "Thomas's version is far more entertaining. Most of that didn't happen. Not like that anyway."

Will appeared abruptly. "What the fuck is this?" His question was directed to Thomas, as was the newspaper he smacked against his brother's chest.

Ethan recognized Will's bloodthirsty tone and was between the two of them within seconds. He grabbed the newspaper and examined the front page while stiff-arming Thomas, pushing him out of Will's reach. "For fuck's sake. Where did this one come from? Christ." He arched up into Thomas's face and said something low.

Thomas raised both hands in surrender as he took several steps backward. He made his way across the room to Kirsty but kept one eye pinned on Will.

"Let me see." I pried the paper from Ethan's fingers.

I'd seen most of the tabloids earlier that day, but not this one. There was a photo on the front featuring Thomas and me. I knew the exact moment it had been snapped—after he'd pushed me into the alcove and shielded me from flying objects and fists with his own body. The deceiving headline about our alleged passionate embrace was ignorant at best.

Will snarled. "He knows better than to betray my trust."

I turned to him. His eyes revealed the same jealous rage he'd shown with Josh. His chest vibrated in warning beneath my palms.

"You know what happened, Will. You know it's another tabloid lie. It's nothing."

He removed my hands from his chest and held my wrists tight. "It's more than nothing—it's fucking inexcusable. Don't expect me to accept it for anything less. Go sit."

Ethan interrupted before I could respond. "Ellie, go on. Let me talk to him for a minute."

I pulled my wrists free and backed away from the monster Will was becoming and trusted Ethan to handle the situation. I watched Will follow Ethan to the bar as he glared over his shoulder at me and then across the room at Thomas. Ben joined them, and the two worked without success to calm Will.

I grabbed my sketchpad and doodled nonsense—anything to keep from looking his way.

Ethan startled me when he sat and offered a glass of champagne. "I need your help."

"How can I handle him if you can't?" I shook my head at the glass.

"You don't see it yet, but you own more influence than you understand. You must learn to tap into that gift when he gets out of hand. And don't test him again, not unless you're prepared to see him kill Thomas."

"Test him?"

Ethan's expression told me he understood the dubious nature of my tone.

My mouth did its thing and blurted a random thought before my brain could catch it. "Did you love her?" I yearned for another connection to my sister.

He paused with his whisky at his lips, frowned, and then threw back what was left in the glass. "We were different. You and Will can have what you both clearly desire. But it was more complicated for us."

I narrowed my eyes. "You didn't answer the question."

"Yes." He gave me the one word I needed to hear. "Goddamn it, don't cry. As much as I'd like to share your—our—grief, you know that's not possible." He waited until he saw my eyes. "I know you miss her. She loved you more than you know. Talked about you a lot." Ethan paused again. "I should have known, should have been there. It's on me—my fault, and I'm so sorry."

A single tear loosed itself.

"Stop it, Ellie. Save your tears for Will."

I wiped it away and swallowed the knot in my throat. He was right. Will had been gentle and comforting, caring for me with a profound tenderness while I worked through my grief and depression, and he still worked hard to protect me from the resulting anxiety. He was everything to me. It was Will's shoulder I wanted to cry on. Only his.

"We'll talk more about her soon. And Lissie. You have my word. You're family now, and anything I can do to ease your pain, I will. But right now, I need you to get over there and calm him. Go on," Ethan ordered. "I need both brothers alive tomorrow."

I pushed down the hem of my dress and headed for Will. He drained his glass and watched me approach. Jealousy and brutality dripped from him. Even so, I couldn't help but touch him—my hands went to his bared forearms, as they always seemed to do.

"What are you doing, Will?"

Hardened gunmetal eyes challenged mine.

I slipped my fingers higher beneath his folded sleeves and pushed harder for a response. "What are you doing to us?"

His eyes dropped to my hands, then fell to the floor. "Elle. Christ. If I hurt you—"

I snapped at him, interrupting. "You did. I'm not a dog. I do not *sit.*"

Will jerked his gaze back to mine. Tenderness and self-reproach mingled with the mess of anger and jealousy. "I'm sorry. Forgive me." He pushed a lock of hair away from my face. "I'll never speak to you that way again."

"No, you won't. Because if you do—" I abruptly halted, surprised by my own thoughts. I could imagine no scenario where an ultimatum turned out well. Will was the type of man who walked away without a second thought. His harsh words had stung, but it wasn't enough for me to push him away. It wasn't a deal breaker.

"It won't happen again, baby." He leaned in and pressed his lips to my temple, his words soft against my skin. "Come out into the corridor with me."

I stared at him as Ethan's words danced on my brain, realizing that while Will's emotions could become volatile, he would never walk away from me. His hand locked around mine, and we exited the lounge.

"Elle, I need you to understand something." His mood shifted, his expression growing dark again as he gripped my wrists and pulled me to his chest. "Look at me," he commanded. "Please."

I met his stare but with defiance.

"I can't live without you, and I *will* destroy any man who touches you or threatens to take you from me. You must never forget that. That's what I've become with you, and there's no way back from it."

It didn't matter if it were his enemy or his brother. Between the lines of his words was a warning for me as well. I needed to take care around other men, because even if my own behavior drove another to pursue me, his reaction would be the same. Someone would suffer, though it would never be me. It was a baser instinct I'd taken pleasure in drawing from his depths. I'd had no idea what it was at the time. An instinct—*a beast*—he could never again enslave. It was my beast, and only I could tame it. It would need to be reminded over and again that Will was my singular interest. And Will needed to know there was no longer a point of return for me either.

He reached for me with charged eyes. "Say something."

I don't know why, but I didn't. I couldn't stop myself from pushing him further.

Will dropped my wrists and pushed his fingers through his hair. He paced and cursed. When he found his resolve, he came back to me and curled a finger under my chin, luring my eyes to his. "Do I need to get down on my fucking knees and beg you to love me back? Is that it, Elle? Is that what you need from me? Tell me, and it's yours."

I gasped. Tears welled. My voice was no more than a broken whisper. "You did say it."

The muscles in his face relaxed, and his eyes softened. "I love you. I have from the moment you first looked up at me with those beautiful eyes."

I knew the moment he said the words they were the reason

I always pushed him. I needed him to love me. More than that, I needed him to love me to an absolute extreme. It was selfish.

The pooled tears rolled down my cheeks one at a time as though life were stuck in slow motion. I'd never exchanged a confession of love with another human being, and I didn't know how to push those words out for Will. I loved him wildly. Still, I was held captive by silence.

He jerked me from my feet. Our mouths collided.

I wound my arms tight around his neck as he held me against his hard body. I encouraged him with my own tongue to deepen our kiss, to leave me breathless.

In an instant, I was on my back on the floor, and he was on top of me.

"Don't move," he shouted into my ringing ears as he shielded my body with his.

An explosion had forced us from our feet.

Another volatile rumbling shockwave ripped through the fifth floor of the hotel, followed by the sounds of more splintering glass and wood. The lounge door blasted from its hinges and flew more than fifty feet beyond where we lay.

Will remained on top of me. "Don't move, baby," he repeated, though neither of us could hear much aside from the ringing aftermath of the explosions. He locked his gaze deep into mine and held it steady until he felt the grip of my fingers relax, releasing his flesh from my nails. "I've got you. Breathe out."

My lungs expelled a shuddering exhale. I was mindless, frozen.

"In. Out again," Will instructed.

Ethan, Thomas, and the others burst into the corridor. Some of them dripped with blood from lacerations caused by flying objects and glass. No one appeared to have life-threatening injuries.

Ethan's phone was pressed to his ear. He shouted information as he received it from the security command center. "Four is secure.

Hotel is locked down. Get her down to the room. No elevator—stairs only. Go!"

Will brought us to our feet, and we raced to the stairwell exit. Ben flew in front of us and kicked the steel door open, exiting first. The stairwell echoed with pounding feet as everyone else followed.

When we arrived at the entry to the fourth floor, Will shouted, "Wait! I won't take her in there without searching first, goddamn it."

"Thomas and I will do it. The rest of you stay here," Ethan ordered.

Ben followed Ethan and Thomas through the steel door anyway.

Blood dripped onto my arm. It wasn't mine.

"You're hurt. Let go, Will. Let me see!"

He released his tight grip but complained as I inspected his body. Blood trickled from the back of his neck. A piece of the door had hit him, but it was a superficial laceration. "Thank God," I breathed, wiping at the blood with the palm of my hand.

Thomas came back and held the door open. "All clear. Move it."

Everyone huddled in the center of the corridor on the fourth floor where there was no obvious impact or damage. Ethan was on his phone again but disconnected within seconds. "No one can get in or out of the hotel. All guests have been ordered to their rooms. I've delayed contacting police, but it won't be long before the neighboring establishments do. Two explosive devices were detonated on the roof, the second one made it to the terrace. There are no serious injuries within, and it will stay that way. We don't have much time to act independently."

Ethan shifted his eyes to Will, and the two shared a dark, knowing look. Ben and Thomas closed in at my sides when Ethan jerked his head at Will to pull him aside for a separate conversation. I heard only pieces of their exchange when their voices were raised.

"Fucking cowards, skulking around, terrorizing an innocent

woman because they're afraid of her DNA." Ethan palmed Will's shoulder. "Decide quickly, brother. We need to move now."

"I'll kill them all. You know me, Ethan. . . . I'll find a way. Motherfuckers are dead."

The reality of what happened—and what was to come—began to sink into my horrified, confused mind. I cried out for Will, and he immediately secured me in his arms.

"You can't fall apart on me, Elle. We'll handle this. I swear they'll not get to you. No one will take you from me." I felt it—that vibration deep within him. The calm before his storm.

I nodded to demonstrate my trust in him, my trust in the raging emotion that had become my lifeline, the side of my face rubbing against his chest. I was strong enough, I chanted in my head. We'd chosen this path together.

"How many?" he asked Ethan.

"Five that we know of. Our guy caught it on the cameras and locked down before they could get inside. Tossed four devices up. Only the two detonated. I need you, Will, you must trust Thomas or Ben to protect her. She'll be safe if you and I drive them away from here."

He'd stay if I pleaded. Will would choose me.

If our story were told by someone who never knew him well, it would be said that I ruined him. Because no matter the circumstances, he'd choose me. The truth is sometimes hard to see, but Will's truth was clear to me. Every piece of his life was an all-or-nothing decision he'd made. There was no gray, no space in between all or nothing, and his resolve never faltered. That's why I knew he'd choose me. That's how I knew he'd destroy the moon for me. I hadn't ruined him; I was one of his alls.

Will was the strongest fighter, and he needed to be in the fight if everyone were to survive. He could take down two men in the time it took the others to best one. Thomas was his close second. Ben was the sharpshooter, but his skills would be less useful on the busy streets of London.

I lifted my face from Will's chest and found his eyes. The incredible strength I discovered there powered my own. "Ben. I'll stay with Ben."

He inclined his head, and then the corner of his mouth twitched as he pushed that stubborn lock of hair behind my ear. He knew every thought I'd just had. "You must do exactly as he says. If you do that for me, then we'll all be safe. Promise me, baby."

"I promise."

Will went into our room and came out fast wearing jeans and a T-shirt. He held two leather holsters over his arm—one with his daggers and one with a gun.

I wondered how they would conceal their weapons and how the whole thing would play out with law enforcement. Were officers of Scotland Yard on the way? What would be written in tomorrow's newspapers? What would be reported on the broadcast news?

Will jolted me out of my head with a hard kiss. "Remember what I said. I meant it. . . . I love you."

I pulled his face into my hands. "Do whatever you must and come back to me, Will. Tell me then. Show me then."

His warm lips came to mine again, kissing me tenderly this time. He stepped aside, though he hesitated, ducking his head while gripping Ben's shoulder for a moment.

His best friend returned the gesture. "I won't let you down, my brother."

I steadied myself on Ben's arm. My trembling body fell into a cold sweat as I stared through a fog muddled with anxiety and horror. And awe. Three fierce, warrior-born brothers stood before me, shoulder to shoulder, primed for what their father had trained them to do—take the lives of others to save mine.

Will peered over his shoulder once more.

Although my heart beat too fast and vomit rose to the back of my throat, I lifted my shoulders and met his eyes with forced confidence.

"Let's go protect our girl, kill those terrorists," Ethan said.

And then the Hastings brothers, my shields, hit the streets of London.

Fourteen

THAT WAS THE night Will's world spun out of his control for the first time. The night he allowed rage to seep into his soul. The same night he set in motion the aggressive strategy he'd been pulling together since his first visit to Stonington ten years before.

A couple hours after Will left the hotel with his brothers, he'd instructed Ben to move me from London back to the estate in Hastings. We waited at Eastridge for word from London while journalists on television delivered breaking news of a small-scale domestic terrorist strike. The reports indicated the terror group remained unidentified and at large. Somehow my heart knew it would stay that way for the public—an unresolved act of violence. The truth hidden, another dark lie.

My phone and Ben's rang at the same time. His weary brown eyes met my nervous stare as he answered his and I answered mine. He mouthed Thomas's name.

"Elle." Will's voice was no more than a rasping whisper.

I breathed a sigh of relief. "Will."

"I lost him. Lost my brother. Ethan is gone. He's dead."

My relief became horror, and I choked on it as my legs gave way. John was at my side in a flash, winding both arms tight around me, supporting my weight. Mary's perceptive honey eyes targeted me, waiting to interpret the words I would deliver into the phone, but my breath refused to push anything out.

"Stay put. Wait for me there." The subjugated suffering in his voice dragged my mind from darkness back to him.

"Of course," I whispered. "I'm sorry, Will. . . . I'm so sorry."

"Talk to mother for me, baby. I can't do it."

"I'll take care of her," I breathed as I watched her watery eyes fill with pain.

I didn't know how to comfort Mary, and in fact, it was difficult to be near her. Guilt crept into my bones. It was my fault she'd lost her son—he lost his life protecting mine. She wept in a reserved manner as I held her, and then she pulled me with her to the bank of windows where gentle rain tapped a melancholy tune against the panes of glass.

"This is how it unravels, Ellie. Will's war." She was disconnecting from the world around us as she peered out into the dark landscape.

"Yes. This is . . . it . . . Will's. I'm . . . so sorry," I said, stumbling through the words.

John paced in silence about the drawing room and hall while he waited for Will and Thomas to return from London. Knowing the truth, I couldn't stomach anything more from the news and turned off the TV. I stopped John midstride and cradled that pained, youthful face in my palms. He looked so much like Will. "I'll be upstairs. If you need me for anything, come get me." He nodded, his teary eyes diving to the floor.

I passed time with the girls, hoping it would be a distraction from the anxiety that ripped through me in constant waves. Hoped Lissie's energetic spirit would strengthen me. I couldn't allow darkness to pull me back under. Will needed me strong while he grieved the loss of his brother, and nothing could keep me from being there for him. Just as he'd been there for me.

"He's back."

I leaped from the floor, stumbling over toys until Ben steadied me.

"How long has he been here? Are either of them hurt? How is he?"

Ben kissed the top of Chelsea's head and angled his own toward the open door. We stepped out of Lissie's room. "He's asking for you, but Ellie, he's not himself. They're not injured. Came in about an hour ago, and he hasn't stopped drinking since. Hasn't said a word other than to send for you. Thomas has gone to be with Mary in her room."

"Damn it, Ben. Why did you wait so long to get me?" I shouldn't have snapped at him. "Can you stay here until Sue comes back? Tell her we need her to stay through the night, and not a word to Lissie."

I didn't wait for his response. I sprinted along the corridor and raced down the stairs. Will was in the drawing room. He sat on the chesterfield and drank as he stared across the room with unfocused eyes. The whisky bottle on the table beside him was two-thirds empty.

I pried the glass from his hand and gave it to Mrs. Bates. "Take the rest of it out of here, please. Bring water and coffee. We'll need sandwiches or whatever your staff has available. He and Thomas haven't eaten anything since yesterday."

She dropped her somber eyes. Her lilting voice soothed. "Don't worry, dearest. I'll see to everything."

Will never spoke. When he finally looked up, grief-stricken eyes revealed the depth of his broken heart. My own heart splintered at the sight of his pain. I choked back a sob and bit down hard on the inside of my cheek, hard enough to draw blood. The metallic taste hit my tongue, causing me to swallow against the thickness in my throat and steel against the gag reflex.

He reached for my hand and pulled me into his lap, hugging my waist tight as he pressed his head to my chest. His face dropped deeper into the top of my breasts. Something unintelligible rumbled from his lips, and he squeezed me harder, turning his face just enough to breathe.

I wrapped him in my arms with courage and strength. My heart was strong enough to protect us both in that moment—the realization took me by surprise, though his vulnerable actions made me believe he'd expected it. It was a dreadful moment, and it was a wonderful moment—his heart was broken, and mine was full. Full because I knew I'd finally learned to love someone.

I held him that way while he swam through his sea of emotion and worked to beat it all back before anything breached the surface.

John, his nervousness finally submissive after the hours of pacing, came in and sat on the sofa with us. Heartbreak was evident in his eyes, too. And fear—he needed his brother. He was just a boy. A boy without a father. Will was the closest thing he'd had since Richard Hastings died nine years earlier.

Without thought, I reached out to John, offering my hand. He grabbed it and slid closer, and after meeting my eyes for reassurance, he rested his cheek on his brother's shoulder.

The acceleration of Will's breath against my skin was telling. He was affected by John's pain. He shifted, making me sink lower into his lap so we were face to face. "Elle, I—"

"Shhh . . . I know. We can talk later." I placed a tender kiss on his lips.

The muscles in his face and shoulders relaxed. He pressed his mouth against mine and brushed my cheek with the back of his fingers.

Mrs. Bates came back with a tray of sandwiches. She set up on the old mahogany serpentine sideboard and filled a plate with thick beef sandwiches for Will. Her large, warm hand touched my arm after she set the plate on the table beside us.

"Thank you, Mrs. Bates. Mary and Thomas have something upstairs?"

She nodded before bustling back to the kitchen.

Ben caught my silent plea for help with John and nodded. "Come mate, you'll have a sandwich with me."

John was beside himself and without guidance, so he did whatever he was told. The two of them ate in silence near one of the fireplaces while they waited for Will to come around. It was easy to see he was everything to them, just as he was to me.

"You must eat, too, Will," I said against his cheek after I kissed it. "You have nothing more than scotch in you."

He nodded and planted a lingering kiss on my neck.

I handed him the plate. "I'll just run upstairs quick and check on the girls."

"You will stay with me," he commanded sharply, setting his plate on the chesterfield and shifting so my bottom dropped into the small space between his and the sofa arm. He snaked an arm behind me and grabbed a sandwich in the other hand. I wasn't going anywhere.

Ben handed me a plate and a glass of water. "I talked to Nanny Sue. She'll stay with our girls indefinitely until dismissed."

I finished a sandwich while Will scarfed down four. Each time I looked at John, my heart sank deeper, if that was possible. He was attached to Will. He loved Ethan without question, but most of the pain he expressed seemed to be for Will. I wanted to reach out and hold him tight, but I couldn't. It wouldn't register with Will's possessive instinct that it was his young brother—it was another male, and it took nothing more than that to trigger his volatile behavior. His emotion simmered just beneath the surface. Anything could set him off.

The best way to help Will's brothers was for me to remain focused on combining my strength with his. I would give him whatever he needed, so he could find his way back to the family that needed him.

Will settled deeper into the leather cushions and pulled me in with him. Fatigue was obvious. He hadn't slept more than five or six hours over the past four nights.

"You should rest. Why don't we go upstairs?"

He threaded his fingers through my hair and pressed my face to his too-quiet chest. "Yeah. We'll go upstairs."

We checked on Lissie before stopping by my room so I could change and grab some things. When I stepped out from the closet, Will still leaned against the frame in the open doorway. I slipped my hand into his, and we headed down the corridor to his room.

Even though he was quiet, I sensed the storm that threatened to burst from his soul. "It's just us now. Say what you need to say. Do what you need to do."

"That's the thing, baby. I don't know what to say. Don't know what to do."

He wasn't ready to talk about Ethan or what happened out on those streets, and I wouldn't push. Maybe he'd never tell me how it went down, and if that's what he needed to get through his pain, I was all right with it.

"That's okay. Whatever it is you need, whatever you need to do, it'll come to you when you're ready." I wound my arms around his neck and lowered my head to the center of his chest. I tried to rein in a swell of emotion, but the effort failed me. I lifted wet eyes to his and pleaded. "For now, tell me you'll always come back. If anything were to happen to you—promise me. I love you, Will. Swear you'll always come back to me."

His beautiful blue eyes came alive, the dull haze clearing. "I swear it." Both hands knotted in my hair and applied pressure to the back of my head as he forced my mouth hard against his. I whimpered against his lips. He gentled but remained driven by strong emotion. "Christ, how I love you." He pushed the silk fabric from my shoulders and replaced it with his velvet kisses. "I swear to you, I'll come back. I'll never leave you."

That greedy mouth came back to mine, reasserting his claim. Everything he was, all that he had, went into making love to me. We went to the place where no one and nothing else existed. We burned everything—burned away his silent grief—and came out on the other side stronger as one whole.

Will roared through his climax and buried his face in my neck until his shuddering body calmed. He was still inside me when he lifted our bodies and sat back on his heels, unwilling to separate the physical intimacy from the emotional. His forehead rested against mine.

"I can't do this without you, baby."

My arms were locked around his neck and my legs around his hips. I pressed myself harder against his chest. "You don't have to, Will. I'm here."

He fell into a deep slumber and rested that way in the following hours—motionless, except for the slow, cadenced rise and fall of his chest.

Just as I began to drift, knuckles thwacked against the wooden door. "Let me in. Please." John's words were slurred. When I opened the door, he fell into my arms, whisky heavy on his breath. "Where's my brother?"

"Shhh . . . lower your voice. Don't wake him. Are you okay?"

His eyes widened, and then he covered his mouth and gagged.

"Here, lean on my shoulder."

I helped him stumble into the bathroom where he crouched in front of the toilet and vomited. I kneeled beside him, and he clung to my arm with the hand he didn't use to embrace the bowl. Each time he came up for air, I cleansed his face with a cool, wet cloth.

"S-sorry," he stuttered several times.

"Don't be, not to me. But you'll have to answer to your brother when he finds out."

Will appeared, looming above. I arched my neck back and examined his expression. No anger. Empathy.

"Go on, baby. You've done enough. I'll get him."

John clambered to the wall and thumped against it with wild, unfocused eyes. Within seconds, the drunken boy slid to the floor and passed out with a cheek pressed to the black-and-white marble tile.

Will carried him to the sofa and covered him with a quilt from the bed, tucking him in snug the way a father might swaddle a small child. But it was what he did next that etched another treasured mark into my heart. He placed a protective, loving kiss on his young brother's forehead. It was an unexpected, beautiful moment.

My eyes filled, and my throat tightened.

He turned and caught my watery smile, the back of his fingers caressing my cheek. Lost in reverence, I moved my hands up his arms and whispered his name. His lips parted as if he were going to say something, but instead, he lowered his head and drew my bottom lip between his with profound tenderness.

"Go see your mother and Thomas. They need you. I'll stay with John."

A weighted exhale crept from his lungs. He nodded. "I won't be long."

I never opened my eyes when he climbed back into bed sometime later. I snuggled into his side and lay my face on his chest. Our limbs instinctively tangled.

Sunlight and Will woke me. The sun warmed my skin, and he kissed it.

John groaned like a hungover sailor.

"Goddamn it," Will snapped.

"He doesn't know what to do with himself. Show him," I gently prodded as I traced Will's jawline with my fingertips and dragged my nails through the thick stubble.

"He's softer than we were at that age."

"Does it matter?"

"Yes, it matters. He's a Hastings."

"Do you plan to give him the same life you were given?"

The moment Ethan died, Will became the Hastings patriarch by default. Theirs was a venerable English family, anchored by aristocratic tradition. His decisions would determine how they lived and what each would become, and no one would oppose him.

He shut down inside his thoughts for a minute. "That's not what I want for him. He'll have more choices. He'll choose to wear the shield if that's what he wants. Either way, he must be a man of strength." A strand of hair fell onto my cheek, and he swept it away without hesitation. "See? Can't do it without you." His expression softened more. "Everything about you is so lovely. It forces me to find something better in myself."

"That's beautiful, Will."

"That's you, baby."

Losing him still weighed on my mind. Losing him would leave me with nothing. "Do you believe there's an afterlife—that our souls are eternal, that they go on, still knowing, still feeling? Do you think Ethan will find Isobel?"

"Hm."

"He loved her." We'd never know their story. Only that he loved her.

"I know. I'm sure that's why he never made other commitments."

"When we're gone, can we find each other? Is there more time?"

"I don't know, baby, but I don't subscribe to the belief of heaven and hell. Christ. If I believed that, I'd have yet another worry, because you and I certainly wouldn't go to the same place." He lifted my chin with his finger. "Neither of us is going anywhere. No one can take you from me, and I'll always come back to you. Rather than wading into philosophical reflection, I need you to trust that, trust me."

"I do trust you, Will." I had from the moment he lifted me from my hands and knees in that bloody foyer in Stonington. But it was hard not to worry, hard not to become insecure. He was forced to fight assassins of my personal death squad, forced to kill or be killed. And that wasn't your everyday run-of-the-mill relationship hurdle. We would never have those. It would never be that easy.

He crushed his mouth to mine. "Relationships scare you, and not just this kind—I can see that. In time, you'll trust what we have and feel safe with it." Then he threw his legs over the side of the bed and stared at his brother as he headed for the bathroom. His mood was shifting, his grief evolving. "John, get up. Hydrate and get to the gym."

And with that, John and I both understood he'd be punished for the whisky binge. I poured John a glass of water, and he pulled himself upright, grumbling and miserable.

"Will," Thomas called through the door.

"Come in," I called back.

Lissie slid down from his back and raced into the room in front of him, leaping onto the cushion between John and me before she hugged my neck.

"This one has been roaming about looking for you," Thomas said. He looked at his younger brother and shook his head. "Jesus. Did he order you to the gym?"

John bobbed his head with a scowl as he held out his water glass for a refill.

"How is Mary this morning?" I asked.

Steam and the woody scent of Tom Ford soap abruptly rushed from the bathroom as Will stepped out wearing nothing more than a towel around his hips.

"Are you fucking kidding me?"

"*Will.*" I covered Lissie's ears in case he complained more about the growing audience in his bedroom.

He rolled his eyes and went into the closet to dress. When he came out, he stood unmoving, staring at the four of us before dropping to the sofa and pulling me beneath his arm. Our eyes met, and his shoulders relaxed after a sigh broke free from his chest. I touched his cheek. We had just recognized our future.

"We need to tell her, Elle."

I'd hoped the next serious conversation with Lissie would be the one where she was introduced to her father. Instead, she would learn "Uncle Ethan" was gone. I couldn't imagine a better time than while she was enveloped in the strength of the three uncles she'd grown to love.

Lissie didn't take it well. She hid her tear-stricken face as she often did with bad news and refused to see the world. Death is hard enough for an adult to understand and accept. She was just seven, and she'd already lost more than her due. Ethan hadn't yet begun to spend time with her, but she still felt the loss and its harsh impact on her new family.

I held Lissie and stroked her messy, brown hair and waited for her to come back to us.

Will's eyes were filled with pain again, which caused my own to fill with tears. He kissed my temple and rubbed Lissie's back. She surprised us both when she reached for him. Will pulled her to his lap and placed a light kiss on top of her head after securing her in one big arm.

"Mother," Thomas said, rising.

I looked up and marveled at the strength I found in her eyes.

Mary Hastings stood in the doorway with both hands over her heart as she admired the tender, compassionate behavior of her three remaining sons. She gazed at me and smiled before grief reclaimed her and washed away the joy. "Come down soon, Ellie, and break your fast with Mrs. Bates and me in the drawing room." Then she turned and floated down the corridor, the flowing train of her black silk robe stretching behind her.

—

The men were still in the gym when I found them three hours later. Will was fighting both brothers at once. His strength was inconceivable. I'd never seen such power flow from one man.

"What's he doing?" I asked Ben.

"Teaching his brothers to respect him and follow his command."

"Ah. The new alpha. I know John's offense. What about Thomas's?"

"Maybe the photo, maybe something you and I will never know about. One thing I know for sure, Will doesn't do anything without purpose. And he's always been the alpha."

I jerked when Thomas suffered a heavy hit to his gut. As big and strong as he was, he still couldn't beat Will. It wasn't the fighting that shook me. It was how they fought each other with the same fierce determination as if the enemy were before them.

Ben noticed my reaction. "We're all subject to it when we mess up. It's his job now. You must learn to accept things for what they are without feeling guilt or anguish."

I let go of the breath I held. "I'm trying. I'll get there. So how is he this morning?"

"His entire life changed the minute Ethan died. He has a lot to come to terms with. He'll be the best leader and provider this family has ever had—once he fully accepts his role. And he will. Two years or even a year ago, I wouldn't have been so sure. But I warn you, Ellie, he'll be quite an arse for a bit. Don't let him get away with it. Be sure to go at him from a position of strength."

Ben knew Will better than most. They'd been together since they were boys, trained side by side from the age of twelve. Their fathers had worked together, and their mothers were close. The only time they'd spent apart was when Ben served in the Royal Air Force while Will studied at Oxford.

Will hit John hard, his body flying several feet before landing flat on his back. "Stay out of my whisky, boy. When you're man enough to handle it, you'll drink with me, not behind my fucking back."

I ran to John and kneeled on the mat beside him. He'd lost color in his face, and he wasn't breathing. The combination of Will's hard hit and his back slamming to the mat had thrust the air from his lungs.

John dug his heels in and launched himself backward while shaking his head. His thrashing to drive me away was confusing, but then I got it. I was making it worse for him. Will wouldn't tolerate one of his brothers accepting help, being soft. He'd hit him again harder, and John knew it.

Painful as it was to leave John alone fighting for his breath, I moved away.

"You will not coddle him," Will shouted, a menacing storm headed my way.

God, he was magnificent. And different—his sorrow had transformed to anger. I hooked my hands on my hips and narrowed my eyes as he advanced.

He left no space between us, though he kept his hands at his sides. "The only thing you'll find meddling down here, woman, is a smacked arse."

"Shall we step out and see?" I lifted onto tiptoes and pushed out my chin, moving my stare from his to the door and back.

His charged eyes followed mine, and he grew hard against my stomach. "Get out of my gym, witch. I have things to do."

His words often sounded crass to those unaccustomed to them. Witch wasn't to be compared to bitch. It wasn't the same thing to him. Not with me. *You own me. Everything I have, everything I am, it's all yours.* That's what it meant, and we both knew it.

I offered a compassionate smile. He didn't need another sparring partner, he needed someone to understand his pain. He needed time to work through losing Ethan. He hadn't taken my anger from me after my family was murdered, and I wouldn't take from him the anger he deserved after his loss.

His anger abated, and unmitigated pain filled his eyes. "I love you," he said against my lips after he bent to kiss them.

"I know. Me, too."

"Do you need me, baby?"

"Just checking in." I kissed his cheek. "Do whatever you must, but come back to me at the end of each day, Will."

His hands went to my hips, and he placed another warm kiss on my mouth. Just before he turned and strode away, the softness of his eyes receded and anger consumed them again.

My tongue traced my lips and tasted the salt he'd left behind as I crossed the length of the pale wooden floor. "Try not to hurt anyone else," I tossed over my shoulder.

I winced when I heard grunting and a heavy thud. Shouldn't have. Should have expected it. I counted to three and looked back without breaking my pace. Thomas was on his back next to his younger brother. Will was toweling sweat from his neck—his stare following the sway of my hips as he watched me leave the gym.

I swear his eyes were glowing.

From that moment, Will distanced himself from everyone, including me, spending his time either exhausting himself in the gym or on the phone with his lawyers. We didn't make love when he finally found his way to my bed that night, though he still locked me safe in his arms. He avoided my lips, kissing instead my forehead or temple.

No matter how hard I pushed, he didn't give in.

"Don't plead with me, Elle. As much as I want you, I can't right now."

It wasn't about me or us, I realized. He needed to manage the strength that surged through his body, and he couldn't do that until he found a way to purge the anger that burned him from the inside out. The denial was triggered by his protective instinct.

Rage continued to burrow deep into his soul.

Fifteen

WILL HAD BEEN quiet at the funeral. The words he spoke to guests after we returned to Eastridge for the luncheon were brief and cold. He didn't eat or sit. He chose to lurk in a dark corner, where he could keep an eye on me while working on a bottle of scotch.

When he'd had enough, he jerked his head toward the staircase and waited for me to walk in front of him, guiding me to my room with his hand at the small of my back. "Stay here until you're told the estate is clear." The kiss he placed on my mouth was distant and cold.

Before he managed to slip away, I grabbed his face and held it between my hands. Tears pushed hard, burning my eyes. His behavior had grown so dark it scared me. "Let me help you," I whispered.

He pulled away. "Go inside, Elle. Leave me alone."

I shook my head. "I won't." I couldn't. It was unbearable to see him suffer.

I followed him around the corner and through a door that led up another flight of stairs to the second story. There was a long corridor at the top of the narrow stairwell. It hadn't been renovated like the lower levels of the house. The oak floor planks were unfinished and worn and creaked beneath our weight. Uneven stone walls held dimly lit sconces. Old wood doors with small metal brackets that once held name cards lined up like soldiers at attention—servant quarters from a time long ago.

Will knew I was there but continued down the corridor without a word. We walked in silence until the first window appeared. Light rain drummed against it. Shadowy clouds circled the moon. He stopped walking, and I plowed into his back.

"*Elle*. It's not a good time for you to be near me." His voice was low and feral.

I didn't want to fight with him, but I was determined not to leave him alone in the state he was in. As I waited for his next move, I watched his broad shoulders move as breath pushed in and out of his body. We remained that way for several long moments—silent, and on edge.

He'd been there for me. He took care of me and carried my dark burden when I couldn't. There was no way I'd remain passive as he fell deeper into his own darkness, nor would I allow him to bear the grief alone any longer. I loved him. Madly. His pain was my pain.

I reached out and rested my fingertips on his back.

His breath stilled, and his back vibrated. When he finally turned to face me, warning was written in wild eyes. The beautiful blue had been eclipsed by black.

I'd never been intimidated by his incomparable size or aggressive behavior and could offer no explanation for it. I ignored the warning and straightened my back. Beast or not, I wasn't leaving him. "You need me."

He closed his eyes and nodded. The scent of burning sandalwood, his scent, filled the space around us. An eternity passed before he opened his eyes again, but when he did, he pushed them into mine and showed me everything. Pain. Guilt. Confusion. Fear. Anger. *Rage.*

I winced.

He stepped closer. Hunger joined the chaos in his gaze, and his hot breath touched my face as he spoke. "Good. You *should* be frightened."

"I'm not afraid of you, and you know that. I'm afraid you won't find your way back. I won't lose you, Will. I'll fight for you."

He erupted, the calm before his storm ending. He filled his hands with my hair and jerked my head back to cover my mouth with his. His tongue forced its way past my lips. His kiss was unyielding and savage.

I pressed against his hard body and fused myself to him. I wanted to ease his pain and chase away his anger. Wanted to give him whatever he needed. Nothing was too much. I'd give him everything.

The force of his kiss split my lip. He came down from the ruthless high when the metallic tang hit his tongue, but only for a moment to suck tenderly on my bleeding lower lip. "I'm sorry, baby." And then the storm returned. One hand moved from my hair down the front of my body and lingered on my thigh before he pushed under my skirt and into my panties.

I melted into his hand.

"I'll take you here if you don't walk away now," he snarled in my ear.

"I'm not leaving you."

"Then you'll scream for me, Elle. You will scream my fucking name." He pushed two fingers inside me, and with the third, he earned his name cried out loud.

Will's mastery of my body was irrefutable. I came fast after he moved those long fingers in and out while using his thumb to drive me over the edge. As I cried his name, he covered my mouth with his and thrust his tongue against mine, and when he was satisfied with the depth of our frenzied kiss, he found another fleeting moment of tenderness and placed a soft one on my swollen lips.

Without warning, he moved our bodies as if they were one, positioning us against the stone wall. He held me so tight nothing that wasn't us could survive in between.

The same wet fingers he'd had inside me went to his mouth, and then a growl ripped from his gut. It forced its way to the back of his throat where it waited impatiently. After tearing off my panties with a skilled yank, he lifted my skirt and pressed himself against me with even more force.

I tried to move him back so I could unbutton his shirt, but my strength was no match for his madness. I did the only thing I could to bare his chest—clawed at the buttons and ripped them from their tiny threads. He eased back just enough to give me access. His smooth, sculpted chest was my home, and he knew it.

My hands and mouth covered his skin. I pinched one of the cords in his neck. Hard. With my teeth. He grunted and grabbed fistfuls of my hair again, reclaiming my mouth with his. His erection strained and jerked between us.

I fumbled frantically with the fastenings of his trousers, and when he was free, I took his heavy erection into my hand and stroked. Another guttural sound escaped him when I squeezed, and it was clear then he was beyond any point of return—he would take what he wanted with abandon, and without regret.

Will snatched me from my feet and pushed my back against the wall. I wound myself around him, and when he shoved inside me with one severe thrust, I screamed his name again. He roared mine. Then he forced his vibrating body still and burrowed into my hair. I don't know how long we held each other that way, both panting and fevered, before he lifted his head and searched my eyes.

I pushed my fingers through his hair. "I love you, Will. Don't stop."

"Jesus, Elle." His voice was hoarse. He pushed against me harder to immobilize my rocking hips. "You know how mad it is, the way I love you, need you. You don't know what you're asking for. You can still go." He brushed my ear with his sweltering lips.

"I won't go."

The strength of his arms intensified as he began to move inside me. Then he threw that chaotic mix of his emotions into our fire and let it burn. The thrusting of his hips deepened beyond the force he'd ever allowed himself to use with me. He lost himself to rage. Rage was the one demon that grew when tossed into fire. The flames reached higher and higher as he thrust into me. It was as though fuel was poured on top of the mess that he was, engulfing him in a fiery, hell-like illusion.

Deeper. Harder. Faster. It was approaching too much. I raked my nails along his back and neck, drawing beads of blood, and screamed. The roar of his climax reverberated through the second story at the same time.

I collapsed onto his chest and shoulders, seared and drained, forcing him to support the weight of my limp body as we worked to catch our breath.

His arms, lungs, and voice trembled. "I'm so sorry. I've been too rough with you." He kissed my neck with remorseful tenderness.

"You were . . . lost."

Will steadied me on my feet but kept me tight in his arms. He dropped his head and pressed his face to my throat. "Forgive me. Say you'll forgive me. Please, baby. I'm so sorry." He dropped to his knees, burying his face in my stomach. "Baby, please."

His pleas shocked me as they slapped me across the face with his pain and exposed his one true vulnerability: hurting me. It was the one thing that could put him on his knees, and watching it play out horrified me.

He hadn't hurt me, but the intensity of his strength in those last moments was almost unbearable. Had he pushed me any harder, I would have stopped him. As far gone as he was, it may have taken a harsh blow to his face, but I had no doubt he would have stopped.

"Elle, I won't allow you to move away from me until you say something."

"Come back to me," I demanded.

He got back on his feet and lowered his still-pleading eyes to mine.

"You didn't hurt me, but you could have. You were close. Never lose yourself that way again. Not ever again, Will."

He shook his head. "Never. I swear. I'll never hurt you." He stepped back but maintained eye contact as he pulled down my skirt and fastened his trousers. His lips soothed mine with sweet kisses as he pulled me into a tender, protective embrace.

A sudden sting caused my back to arch in search of relief when he rested his hand there.

"What's wrong?"

I stalled. "It's been a long day. Neither of us has slept much. Come to bed with me."

"Tell me, goddamn it. Have I hurt you?"

"It's nothing. It's just—I think it's just from the wall."

Will spun me and lifted my blouse. "I did hurt you." The friction from the stone had torn the fabric and abraded my skin.

I tugged down my blouse and slipped into my heels. "I'm sure it's nothing." I looked around for my tattered panties. He'd stuck them in his pocket.

"Nothing?" He stared at me with wide eyes like I'd committed an egregious crime. "How can you say—don't dismiss what I've done to you."

"It's from the wall, not by your hand. Honestly, Will. You should see your own back."

My words made him angrier. "Not by my hand, but still my fault. I'm the last man who should ever leave a mark on you." He raked his hair and paced, cursing at himself and the God he wasn't convinced existed.

"Stop it, Will. Please. We have more important things to deal with."

His fury escalated. "*What?* There is *nothing* more important than you. I've been clear about that. Still, you test me."

I reached for him.

"You deserve so much better than this, than me." He backed away until he bumped into a door—he turned and punched it. The old wooden door flew off its hinges and crashed to the floor. He kicked it, sent it flying several feet beyond the doorway. Will charged into the room. He picked up the wrecked door, raised it above his head and threw it, smashing it against the wall. It splintered into countless, raining pieces.

I ran into the room and reached for him again, but he pulled away.

"Will, stop this. Please!"

He blew out slow, heavy breaths, though not from exertion. It was hard to tell if he was winding up further or working to calm himself.

"Ellie, step away from him," Thomas said behind me.

"This doesn't concern you. Get the fuck out of here," Will snapped. He stalked toward his brother.

"That's right. . . . Come at me, not her. What are you doing, brother?" Thomas snarled through his teeth, something I hadn't witnessed before. "You want to hurt her?"

Will stopped abruptly. He looked from Thomas to me, his eyes softening. "I love her. I'll never hurt her."

"You're losing it, and she's too fucking stubborn to leave you to it. She *will* get hurt."

Will stared at me for a moment before extending his hand. When I took it, he pulled me to his chest and held me tight against his heaving body. "Going to London for a while, Elle." He lifted my chin and found my eyes. "Stay with Thomas."

"No, I won't. You can't—"

"Please. I'm begging you, baby."

"How long?" Hot tears stung my cheeks.

He shook his head and then kissed my lips. "I'll come home as soon as I can."

I clutched his shirt with both hands and buried my face there. "No, you can't leave me. I won't let you." My breath stuttered as I sobbed the words. I choked when I heard them replay in my head— the same words I'd shouted at my dying sister.

"I'm not leaving you, baby. There's something I need to do—to fix this. I swear to you I'll make it right." Long fingers wiped at my cheeks, and warm lips kissed mine. We both tasted my tears. "Go on. My brother will keep you safe." He pried my clawing fingers from his shirt and eased me back into Thomas's hands. "Restrain her if you must, and keep the Six close at all times. She is their only purpose."

Thomas's capable hands gripped my arms from behind.

I twisted and pulled.

My heart refused to accept what Will had just said. It panicked and told my brain he was leaving me, just as everyone else in my life had.

I kicked and screamed.

I pushed Thomas until he had no choice but to secure his arms around me with force.

"Please don't leave me," I whispered.

Will picked up a document safe and walked away without looking back.

No one ever tells you love hurts. They tell you it heals your soul and gives you hope. You hear all the lovely stories, the fairy tales, the descriptions of euphoria, but the story about the pain goes untold.

Gran used to tell me love was equal parts risk and reward, but she never elaborated on either one. Of course she hadn't. She was old-school English, raised to be stone cold in the face of love.

Will loved me. He'd said the words several times since they first spilled from his lips in London. And he told Thomas. I saw it in his eyes when they burned into mine and felt it in his always-fevered skin when he touched me. He loved me beyond obsession—killed for me—and I believed him when he said he'd never stop.

Still, his leaving hurt.

He struggled with Ethan's death and the resulting responsibilities. When he said he'd make it right, he meant he'd make himself right. My heart fractured each time his words echoed inside my head. He was broken.

Even so, his leaving hurt.

Thomas and I were on the small, floral sofa in my room where he'd confined me. He sat on the edge and leaned forward, and I sat with my legs tucked beneath me and one side of my face pressed to the back. Two of the Six were armed and stood guard just outside the door while we waited for an all clear from Ben, indicating the estate was secure.

"He didn't leave you, Ellie."

"Stop saying that," I snapped.

"Then stop thinking it."

"I'm here, and he's gone. He wouldn't say why he was going or when he's coming back. So tell me, Thomas, what should I think?" I used the back of my hand to push at another tear muddied with mascara.

He reached for my hand and thumbed away the dark drop and then held it between both of his. "You're missing information that could help you better understand." He kept his eyes on the floor. "When our father was murdered, Ethan was there to immediately avenge his death. Will didn't have that. I know it sounds archaic to you, but it's what we know—what our father taught us."

"What are you saying?"

"The assassin who killed Ethan got away. Will won't have peace until he avenges our brother's death. He'll grow angrier as the guilt rides him harder. He knows the cost if he allows it to continue driving him. Everything. You."

"So he's gone to find the man who murdered Ethan. Why couldn't he tell me?"

I understood. I could relate to the desire for vengeance. It still burned within me, though I was forced to admit the magnitude of my enemy was beyond the scope of my ability, even if I learned to fight. The influence behind it was one of the world's most powerful. We worked hard to deny it—to accuse the queen would be high treason, punishable by life in prison, but my heart told me the Crown or someone very close was more than an innocent bystander.

"C'mon. You know he'll move mountains to spare you anything he can. Listen. You must understand we're at war here. It may not be a grand war of countrymen defending the kingdom, but it *is* war. Forget the romanticized stories found in history books. No matter the size of the war waged, it's never gallant, nor is it ever easy. And he worries about the nightmares. I hear it's quite awful."

I shrunk away from those eyes with which he watched me. They were too much like Will's. "Ethan told you?"

"Yeah. I can't stay in here with you, but if you choose to sleep downstairs in one of the open rooms, I can stay close."

The idea of anyone other than Will near me when I slept was uncomfortable. Thomas would always be my defender in Will's absence—the next Hastings in line who wore the inked shield on his shoulder. I had to get used to it. Will inherited more responsibility than most were challenged with over a lifetime, and I needed to be supportive, but my formidable desire to be with him would cause me to battle with myself over and again.

"I'll be fine up here, but thank you, Thomas."

He nodded. His half smile was hopeful, but his bouncing leg and wrinkled brow revealed something different. He knew I was lying.

—

"Have breakfast with me," Thomas said. "Coffee and two bites of toast in your room isn't enough. And yes, I asked Lily to show me."

I shrugged. "I'm not a breakfast person. And you know Mrs. Bates will take a switch to us both if she finds me in the kitchen with you men."

"Fuck that. Let's go." He pointed to the stairs.

I rolled my eyes and headed down to the kitchen.

John delivered a heated explanation to the table of men in their military-style training clothes. "I'm telling you, man, the Earls of Arundel and Sussex were one and the same. The names were inter-changeable for centuries."

"Kid's right," Thomas said. He handed me a plate and started to fill it.

"Stop. That's too much. Take the sausage away. I won't eat that."

He glared at me as he moved the sausage to his own plate.

"American women don't eat the way English women eat," John teased.

"She's not American, she's high-born English. The highest. Try to remember that, little brother, before Will beats your arse again."

Will hated it when others referred to me as American or *the* American. He pushed me to embrace my English heritage. "Your blood is the purest that exists," he often reminded me.

"She sounds like one."

"That'll change in time."

"I'm standing right here—knock it off, damn it. And by the way, many American women eat sausage. So what's this talk of earls?"

Thomas looked up from his plate-filling mission and stared at me. "You don't know?"

"Know what?"

"Christ. Maybe there's a reason he hasn't told you. Wait for Will to tell you."

"Or maybe it just hasn't come up yet with all that's happened. He swore no secrets. Spill it, Thomas. Now."

"Will is the Earl of Sussex. I mean he could be, if he chooses it. Our father disclaimed the title when our grandfather died, and as a matter of respect, Ethan honored that decision."

"What?" The bombshells never seemed to end.

The Hastings men descended not only from George Plantagenet, but also from an ancient line of fierce warriors, rewarded for their victories by kings and queens many times over. One of the countless spoils of war was a prominent position among the peerage—the Earldom of Sussex.

"He must see the queen's ministers and inform them of his intention. He's probably meeting with them this week."

"So he's back in London?"

"I didn't say that, Ellie."

"Maybe I should go to London. We'll see how he likes that."

"You're not going anywhere. Can't you just eat, and not give me shit all the time?"

"Go to hell, Thomas." I tossed my plate onto the table and stormed out of the kitchen.

I went to bed early that evening right after Lissie, and as I'd expected, tossed and turned for hours. When my phone rang at three in the morning, I was still awake. Stumbling through the darkness, I banged into the table with my hip and fumbled until finding the ring's source. I switched on the lamp and grabbed the phone but with caution—it had morphed into a ticking bomb. "That's your own heart drumming," I whispered as my legs weakened, lowering my bottom to the floor. I stared at his name without answering.

What if he wasn't coming back?

It rang a second time, revealing again his name and a photo of us on the beach. John had snapped it the day we all went to Old Town. The day Will supported me in his arms as I reached out to the sea, reclaiming myself. The day my head and heart finally connected as one, for England, for Will.

I swiped to take the call, but there was no air left in me to push out the sound of my voice when I mouthed his name.

"*Elle*," he breathed into the phone.

"Will."

"Forgive me. Please."

Tears welled, flooding my vision. The sob that clung to the back of my throat prevented words. Just one would release its hold and break me. I listened to him breathe instead.

"I'll be home today. Don't leave the house. Wait for me, baby."

Thomas had told him then, that I'd mouthed off about London. Anger burned away the pooled tears. I don't know why, but I couldn't resolve the unbidden pain his leaving caused.

"You heard. I threatened to leave, and now you're coming back to do your job."

"Jesus fucking Christ. That's not—" He released a heavy sigh and softened his words. "I'm coming home to you because I never left you. There were matters to be handled. None of which could challenge my desire for you. And I won't allow you to leave because I can't live without you. I know I hurt you . . . should have called. I'm sorry. I swear I'll make it up to you. I've proven I'll get on my knees for you, if that's what you need. Just say you'll forgive me. Please."

His pleading words dripped with sincerity and broke me. There was no holding back—I choked on the ambush of emotion.

"Goddamn it, Elle. Don't do that. Don't cry." He cleared his throat. "You'll wait for me. You will not leave the house without me." And then he hung up.

I blew my nose and dried my eyes, smiling as my heart recognized it had been *my* Will on the phone—the commanding, controlled warrior who refused to live without me.

He'd slain his demons.

The phone rang a third time.

"You're not a job. Never have been. I love you, baby."

"Tell me when you get home."

Sixteen

JOHN CORRECTED MY position before he demonstrated the proper technique for powering through with the left shoulder to throw a right cross. "Your reaction time has been great. Let's try it again. You duck, I throw this time. Let me know when you're ready."

"I've played a lot of tennis. That helps." I shifted into a defensive position. "I'm ready."

I'd started training on the mats with him the day after Will left. Will refused to teach me, insisting it was his job to fight, not mine. We'd argued for several days before I came up with another plan, and when he left, I was pissed off enough to implement it.

John could fight. Like his three brothers before him, John's training began when he was twelve, but unlike his brothers, he was easier to convince that I should know how to defend myself. I wasn't so naive to believe I'd manipulated a Hastings male into beating me with his fists. I knew he'd been given permission and unequivocal instructions, and only because he was much smaller than the others and had no real fighting experience outside the gym.

I'd approached Thomas first, but he'd given me a lecture similar to Will's. "There's a lot of pain that comes with hand-to-hand training. I won't allow you to suffer that way. You can't imagine the physical strength involved. When we fight, it takes over, and we become something . . . else. It has to be that way, or we die out there. Don't ask me again. I won't do it. Not ever."

But I could imagine. I'd seen it the day Will fought both brothers at once, and experienced it the night he took me hard against that stone wall. It was raw, animal-like strength, like nothing I'd ever witnessed.

"Forget about it, Ellie. Anything you've seen here in this house is nothing more than a scratch to the surface," Thomas had said after he'd read the thoughts written on my face.

"Get out of your head," John said, drawing my focus back to him. "Ready? Let's go."

Will appeared beyond his shoulder.

It was an immediate distraction, and I missed my cue to evade the hit, taking a blow to the face. The force of John's hit knocked me on my ass. I hadn't lost consciousness, although it took several seconds before I regained my vision, black slowly giving way to light.

The thump and Will's snarl registered in my ears before my rattled brain could grasp what was happening. He'd slammed John against the wall. "Take care not to hit her again if you want to live to see another fucking day."

John crouched forward after Will released him and placed his hands on his knees. He raised his head and stared at me as he worked to catch his breath.

"I'm fine. Sorry," I mouthed.

Will turned his charged eyes to mine and moved in. He pulled me to my feet and towered above, diving into my soul. "Are you hurt, baby?" His spiced heat saturated my senses.

I shook my head.

My heart banged around in my chest, wanting him with desperation, but hesitating. It hadn't yet found its resolve from the pain it was never entitled to in the first place. I had no right to be angry with him. Not only was he grieving and broken when he left, but he'd always been the broken one. It was through no fault of his own. His father and I—we broke him. Richard Hastings gave his son no choice, raising Will to fight, forcing him to take lives. To save mine.

Still, anger circumvented reason, and I hit him. Tears erupted as I pounded on his chest with both fists. I shouted at him, pounding, "Never do that to me again!"

He grabbed my wrists and pulled me tight against his chest, forcing me to reconnect with his eyes before he pushed his way into my mouth. His kiss was a tempest of emotion. Passionate and fierce, tender and apologetic. It was perfect.

I fought him anyway. I twisted and pulled back.

Those eyes burned into mine with determination while his fingers opened and released my wrists. "I'm sorry. Tell me what you want me to do. Tell me what you need." The gravel in his voice drove shivers along my spine.

I wanted him to kiss me again. I needed him to hold me. I slapped his face.

He accepted that harsh slap without a word, nodding to assure me he had. Then he took my wrists back and jerked me against his body again.

"Get the fuck out," Will said to our audience, his voice booming with authority, rumbling through the rafters. John and the other guys scurried into the locker room.

He slanted his mouth over mine and claimed it, allowing his emotions to drive him. There was no anger, no rage. Only love. Possessive, all-consuming love. Only one thing could have completed me more than that kiss—being tangled in bedsheets with him inside me.

"Forgive me." No longer a plea, it was a command. There would be no compromise. William Hastings, the conqueror, would get what he came for, even if he had to fight for it.

I was locked into his stare and wanted him with a madness that couldn't be explained. I wound my arms around his neck and breathed against his lips the one word he planned to take if it wasn't offered. "Forgiven."

He lifted me into his arms and held me with ease like a comfortable extension of his own body. I lost my breath when he took my mouth and slipped his tongue past my lips again. We kissed with unrestrained, fierce, breathless desire.

I once read you need only to breathe when you're not whole. I'd scoffed, called it rosy poetry. But the moment I forgave him—forgave myself—our combined strength became our breath, and I got it.

"You are everything. You're the purest part of me—the one piece that's good. The piece that holds the rest together. You are mine, and I'll never leave you, baby. Don't doubt me again."

I was high. Words escaped me.

"The world round us will change, Elle. But how I love you will not."

We pressed our mouths together again, and then I confessed: "I can't find myself when you're away."

"Look harder. You'll find us both. I promise." He kissed my forehead, temple, lips.

As individuals, we were broken and lost. But as a couple, we were whole. I cemented his pieces together, and he anchored me to the place where I belonged.

I smiled at the thought of how well we fit together. "Come shower with me."

Will's chest rumbled, and his warm mouth found my butterfly. "And then bed."

I wiggled my fingers through his shorter, spiky hair. I had loved his hair before, loved watching him rake it back when he was frustrated, but the textured, disheveled style he came back with was quite suitable to his handsome face.

John banged through the door. "Uncle Robert is here. . . . He insists on a family meeting."

"Goddamn it, John," Will said without moving his eyes from mine. He grinned. "Bunch of cockblockers round this house."

I laughed.

"I told him you are the only one who can call a family meeting, but he carried on until I couldn't stand it any longer. He's waiting with Mum at the table."

"Christ. All right. We'll be there soon. Go on—wait upstairs for me." He hesitated while his young brother left the gym. "First, there's something I want you to see, baby. If I don't get this off my arm, it'll drive me mad."

I hadn't noticed his left arm from elbow to wrist was wrapped with a thin layer of gauze. "You've been injured?" I slid down the front of his body.

One brow lifted and the corners of his mouth twitched as he unraveled the gauze.

I sucked in a sharp breath and gaped.

"It's not finished. When I called, when I heard you, I couldn't get out of that chair fast enough."

I swept my fingers over the inflamed skin. Couldn't pull my eyes away from the tattoo that swallowed the mass of his left inner forearm and snaked around it like a half sleeve.

It was a masterfully detailed dagger draped with an elegant, intricate vining rose. The artist used feminine details—butterflies and swirling patterns—to design the dagger's masculine hilt. Running along the length of the blade was my name, spelled the way he said it—Elle. The letters had been crafted so artfully they looked as if they were engraved into an actual blade. The overall detail was extraordinary in black and varying shades of gray. There were just two splashes of color. Deep crimson drops of blood clung to and dripped from the tip of the blade onto his wrist, and a brilliant green gem adorned the center of the hilt. If it wasn't finished, I couldn't imagine what he intended to add.

I pushed my eyes to his. "It's so beautiful, Will."

"You are more beautiful."

I couldn't stop touching it. My finger circled the gem. The color choice confused me, but after a few minutes it hit me. I recognized the icy shade of green, a variant of aquamarine. "Is that—"

"The color of your eyes."

My skin tingled. My breath caught. I shook my head. "I don't know what to say."

"Say you love me, Elle. There's nothing more I'll ever need."

I pushed my hands into the back pockets of his jeans and met his eyes from beneath my lashes, flashing the secret smile that belonged to him alone. "I love you, Will. I'll love you always."

A tiny flutter tickled the walls of my empty stomach when he smiled from his eyes for the first time since Ethan's death. He lowered his head and joined our lips, and then hand in hand, we walked out of the gym to slay together the next demon in our path.

Will stopped in front of a door obscured within a small alcove inside the billiard room. I had never noticed anyone using it before, and it hadn't been on any of Lissie's secret castle tours, so I had assumed it led to an unfinished room or storage.

"Ready?"

I nodded. "Whatever it is, I can handle it."

He winked and agreed. "You can. You'll learn things in this room you've not heard before, but it changes nothing. It doesn't make you less safe, baby." He pressed his mouth to my forehead and his palm to the electronic pad. The door slid open with a *whoosh* similar to that of the weapons room, revealing a high-tech conference room.

It was more like a situation room—*a war room.*

There were maps and photos pinned to the walls. Some old, some new. The security monitors I'd heard him reference consumed most of the space on the far wall. A carved wooden table and its twelve high-back executive leather chairs occupied the center. There were several keyboards around the table, and the low hum of a powerful CPU was present, though it wasn't visible.

Will placed his hand at the small of my back and guided me into his war room.

Robert Moore stood, cleared his throat, and rubbed his pointed, gray-stubbled chin as he stared at me. Warm, honey-brown eyes like his sister's twinkled beneath drooping lids. His wide mouth curved upward. Then he moved his gaze from me to Will. "Come, William. Take your place at the head of the table. Bring the little rose along to keep you in line."

Will ignored his uncle and pulled me with him to the other side of the room where his mother waited.

Mary hugged her son before positioning me in the chair to his left, instructing me with tact and discretion. She sat on my left and held my hand. Smiling eyes drifted to Will's tattooed arm and then lifted to meet mine. Her warm eyes crinkled more, though the slight upward curve of her lips remained subtle. She squeezed my hand in approval.

I returned the same and smiled to assure her Will's enthusiasm was reciprocated.

"Let's get on with it," Will said. "What news have you brought, Uncle Robert?"

"I found the leader inciting the Order. Jack Lewis is the name, and he seems to have aligned with someone within the community for information, but I've yet to hear any local names. Proceed with caution at tonight's dinner. Certainly that informant could be someone we've invited to Eastridge."

"Find him, Thomas." Will gripped his brother's shoulder. "Quickly." He turned his attention back to Robert. "Thank you. Your help is invaluable. Anything else?"

"Your mum and I have questions about your time away we'd like answered."

"I suppose you do, and I'll provide what's appropriate. But know you'll not press me the way you did my brother. You're a guest in my house, not its master."

Leader. Informants. Dinner. Anxiety knocked hard at my mind's door. I reminded myself not to open it. To defeat it, I needed to face it, but only through a locked window. I had what I needed to win, the one thing strong enough to keep me away from that door. Will's support. The bitter, metallic taste in my mouth dissolved, and my breathing slowed after I reached out to him, clutching his thigh beneath the table.

His hand found mine. He leaned in and spoke in a soothing tone. "You okay, baby?"

I pasted on a smile and inhaled the warmth of his breath. "Yes."

He raised his voice, anger and menace seeping into it. "The Order will soon learn with whom they're fucking. I'm neither my brother, nor my father. I'm the one without mercy. The one who planned for this day. I'll honor the pact, of course, but there's something more important that should be understood. Any man who threatens what is mine will die. And this—" he raised our entwined hands above the table, "is mine."

"I stand by your side, brother, always," Thomas said.

Ben raised his fist. "I stand with you as well, my brother."

"So do I," Joe Wright added.

After accepting the allegiances with a modest bow of his head, Will leaned forward and addressed Mary. "What questions do you have for me, Mother?"

She smiled, pride gleaming in her loving eyes. "Did you meet with the queen's ministers this week, dear?"

"Yes. The prince attended the meeting as well, though his only genuine interest was to discuss his investments. My terms were made clear. The Crown either eliminates the Order or uses its prerogative to allow me to do so without penalty or prosecution."

"But what leverage do you have to make a demand so great?" Robert asked.

"The queen and her son will aid me, or I'll break them financially. I can take the resulting hit—my wealth is greater. Ethan and I worked hard to pull their private assets into the firm and manipulate their investments, not because we needed their fortunes, but because I knew this day would come."

Thomas cleared his throat. "In what form do we come away from the attack and resulting deaths in London?"

"We're okay. The Crown exercised its influence with Scotland Yard and the NCA." Realizing I'd have no idea what the NCA was, he turned to me, and with a gentler voice said, "The National Crime Agency." Then he went on, addressing Thomas, "In order to preempt speculation and avoid additional public rumor—because the public now knows Ellie's home—the ministers pressured the director general to keep the case out of the hands of the National Counter Terrorism Security Office. It's been buried." He paused, looked at his mother, and softened his tone again. "What else, Mum?"

"They're all right with the fact she's here? Certainly they may never truly approve, but they're settled with it?" She placed her hand on my arm protectively.

Will nodded and exchanged an affectionate, perceptive smile with his mother. Their exchange, his hand holding mine and hers on my arm, caused my heart to flip.

Uncle Robert shifted restless legs. "What of her claim to the throne?"

"Ceded."

"Revocation clauses?"

"None."

"And the earldom?"

"I haven't yet decided."

My head was spinning. I couldn't have imagined the escalated depth of the situation. Will had anticipated it, and his knowledge and steadfast readiness was staggering.

Robert pushed his luck. "You're rather terse with your answers."

"I've shared what's appropriate. Anything else is our private business. And as for your disapproval—move past it. Elle and I decide what we want and how we'll live." Will looked at his watch as he stood and then offered me his hand. "Thomas, find me in two hours."

"Are the two of you joining us for lunch?" Mary asked as we attempted our getaway.

"No," we said at the same time.

"Have something sent up," Will added. He winked at his mother, and Mary Hastings, disarmed by her son's charisma, blushed. With that, I fell deeper in love with him.

We stopped near the bar in the billiard room where he discussed the Six's schedule and estate security with Ben, and I sorted through my thoughts, trying to wrap my mind around everything. He'd done as I had asked. Ceded my contentious claim to the throne. No matter what he chose to do with his own claim—ascend to his title or deny it—I would support him without question. I would follow Will anywhere. Give up everything to have him. Wasn't that what I'd already done?

"Elle?" Will said, drawing me out of my head.

"I'm sorry . . . what?"

"Come on, baby. I'm mad for you." He eased me against the bar and kissed my neck. "Go upstairs with me now, or I'll have you right here." His mouth roamed in a playful frenzy.

I shrieked, delighted with his relaxed behavior. "I'm getting into the shower first."

"You have ten minutes while I get my things from the car. Then you're mine, and I don't care where I find you—*mine*."

—

My room was filled with dozens of fragrant English roses. Again.

Lily followed me in with a tray of food. "Most people are afraid of him, but not me. I see how lovely he is with you. Oh, to be so lucky in love!" The housemaid was talkative and melodramatic when Mrs. Bates wasn't around. She made me smile.

"Would you mind taking that down to his room? He'll be coming up soon."

She left with the tray, and I raced into the bathroom. I showered and slipped into cropped jeans and a scarlet T-shirt, then plucked the pins from my upswept hair. Will's voice resounded out in the corridor. His presence was as immense and boundless as the estate. He was Eastridge, and it was him. Neither thrived without the other. I grinned and opened the door.

God, I'd missed him.

He'd been intercepted by the kids. Lissie clung piggyback-style to her superhero while John made a case for an afternoon of freedom at the beach with friends. I watched him interact like the father of two children who had lost theirs, and wanted him even more.

"Go on, John, but remember what I said about tonight." He swung Lissie around to his chest, kissed the top of her head, and nudged her in Nanny Sue's direction. Then, with scorching eyes and impatient hands, he pulled me into his embrace. "Already waited years for you, woman, and still you keep me waiting."

"You know what's said about those who wait . . . ? Now take me to bed, Will."

He swooped me into his arms with a grin and carried me to his room, locking the door behind us. The same heady fragrance from my room crashed into me. I stared at his bed. It was turned down and covered with a thick blanket of white rose petals.

"*Elle.*" He pulled the shirt over my head and unfastened my bra.

His tongue played with mine and then his kiss moved down to my breasts. "So beautiful," he said as he caressed them in his strong hands and lowered his head to take one and then the other into his mouth.

I moaned. My fingers twined through his hair.

He was fiercely gentle as he worked the button fly and pushed my jeans and panties to the floor in one swift move. "Turn. Let me see."

I stepped out of my jeans and heels, and turned around.

Will gathered my multicolored tresses and hooked them over one shoulder. He stared at my back before putting his hands on my hips and kissing the tender pink blemishes. "I'm so sorry, baby. It'll never happen again." He'd worked through his anger, but his heart still struggled with having been so lost that he'd allowed the stone to abrade my skin.

"I know."

More velvet kisses lined my spine.

I faced him and placed a kiss at the base of his throat, gripping the hem of his shirt. I pushed upward until he yanked it over his head and tossed it. My lips were magnets drawn to his steel chest. It was beautifully sculpted, broad and smooth, and bore two substantial scars. I kissed both and the shield inked on his shoulder.

His powerful arms with their fine, golden hair pulled me tight against his body, making me aware of the similar, sexy trail of hair that began at his navel and led into his jeans. I pulled back. He stared down at me, into me, from his towering height while my fingers worked his zipper. His fingers tangled in my hair and made sure my mouth couldn't escape his when he bent to kiss me. I slipped my hands beneath his waistband and shoved his jeans from his hips.

I dropped to my knees and kissed my way down that soft, golden path.

"Baby . . . don't do—"

He lost the words when I took him into my mouth. I'd never given oral to anyone other than Will—never had the desire before, but with him, it was something I couldn't imagine either of us doing without.

With a savage grunt, he worked to control himself, wrapping fistfuls of my hair around his hands as he fought the urge to thrust deep into my throat. His eyes glowed when I looked up to meet them. "Ah, God . . . *Christ* . . ." He jerked me to my feet and into his arms. He carried me to bed and fell on top of me, thrusting his tongue deep into my mouth. "Open," he commanded as he positioned my legs where he wanted them and pushed his fingers inside me.

I cried out. And even before I did, I knew he'd cover my mouth with his and swallow it. It wasn't meant to keep me quiet—not when we were in his room. He needed to control the sound so he could feel its vibration. When he saw or heard my reactions, it wasn't enough—he needed to feel it in his own soul. It was who he was. There was nothing violent or threatening about his desire for control in bed, so I gave it to him. There wasn't much I wouldn't give up for him. Still, I clawed at his shoulders, crazed for release.

A knowing smile claimed his face as he removed his fingers and gathered my wrists. "You've a long way to go, baby." He raised my hands above my head. "Hold on to the pillow. Do not release it. You'll want to. *Don't.*" I clung to the pillow, and he continued to wear that smirk while I pleaded with him.

"Will, please . . . I need . . ."

He shut me up with a fiery kiss. A kiss that wasn't destined to stay in one place. He used it to devour my body as he pushed it lower and harder. He buried his face between my thighs.

I screamed his name sooner than I wanted. He drove me so well, forcing me to shatter with such intensity that a billion stars danced throughout the galaxy in celebration.

Our eyes connected and a sense of urgency gripped him. He shot up and slammed into me with one fierce thrust, swallowing the sharp cry it tore from my lips. A growl vibrated upward from that arcane place and hitched in his throat, holding out for his climax.

He immediately restrained his shuddering body and pushed his stare into mine. "I can't live without you." It was an inhuman rumble. He kissed my lips and circled his hips before stilling himself again. Nothing less than full control would do. Even as his muscles strained, as his breath quickened and his eyes burned, he made deliberate, measured moves. He was proving to us both that he'd never again lose himself to rage or volatility when he made love to me.

I acknowledged his controlled behavior with a calculating smile. And then I pushed him to the one place he couldn't control. I demanded through our burning stare that he say more, do more, prove more.

He nodded, preparing to grant my silent request. Will never denied me when I demanded something of him. He understood my certifiable need to push him, just as I understood how reckless it was to push a man like him.

"I love you beyond words. Kill for you, without shame or regret. Never doubt me, Elle." He crushed his lips to mine with force and teased with his hips again. "You will marry me. Say it."

My soul fell deeper into his. "I will marry you," I said in a breathy whisper. My hands slipped down, driven by the intense emotion stirring in my chest. He captured them, pinning my arms to the bed, his fingers entwining with mine.

"Again." Another sharp command.

"I'll marry you, Will."

He bowed his head and locked in our commitment. Then, enraptured by my submission, he finally let go—my warrior loved me hard on a soft bed of roses.

—

"What would you have me do?" Will asked.

I traced the dagger's blade and watched goose bumps run up his arm. The details of his tattoo fascinated me. The ink slinger Will hired was more than that. He was a fellow artist.

"I won't tell you what to do, and you know that. Are you leaning in one direction?"

"If I accept reinstatement of the title, it would strengthen us."

"How? I mean, what does it really represent?"

"Well, in the present, titles are a mark of prestige and status, and a fascination by those without, not much more. The status doesn't hold the political or financial weight of times past. That makes no difference to me—I already have more financial influence than most, and care nothing for politics. I think the real benefit of accepting would be the draw of allies to us."

"How would it affect the Sussex counties?"

"It wouldn't. Some lands my father forfeited would come back with the title, but not a great deal. Lands generally aren't acquired that way anymore. The people using those properties transferred to me don't have to feel a thing."

I yawned. "Would you be willing to redirect the attached income back into the community? Provide support for a more sophisticated pier renovation, for instance."

"I'll deploy funding to whatever venture you desire." He yawned.

"That's crazy, Will. You know I don't have a lick of business sense." I rubbed my chin against the golden stubble on his jaw and kissed his neck.

He chuckled. "My lovely little artist—I wouldn't change a thing. Just paint me a picture, baby. I'll execute."

"You mean James Jackson will execute."

"James my arse." He tickled me, a good-humored reprimand for offending his ego, and I giggled like a little school girl.

"You're right, though. I need to do something."

"Work with me. Run one of my businesses, baby."

"We've established that's not my thing."

"I want you close to me."

We dropped it there and fell asleep in a tangled mess of sheets, arms, and legs. When I woke, it was to the restrained thunder of his voice as he spoke to Thomas. I lay there unmoving, feigning sleep while they had their meeting. It made no difference to me what their business was or what they said. I was unwilling to be roused physically or emotionally from my divine bliss.

"She'll rest as long as my voice is present, just keep it down. How was she?"

"Angry at first, then irritable. Couldn't get her to sleep downstairs where I could stay close. She wanted to do it her way, and I don't have to tell you what that's like. Had to tell her, man. She knows you hunted Ethan's murderer. There was nothing more I could do to hold her here without a fight. Then this rubbish with the hand-to-hand bouts. I don't want any part of it. She shouldn't be doing it."

"I know." Will sighed. "I don't like it either. If she continues, we'll need to ride John so he doesn't slip up and hit her again. I could see in her eyes how she'd suffered through those nights. That's on me, not you, brother. I appreciate how well you cared for her."

"You forget, brother. I wear the shield, same as you. I'll always protect her." Thomas hesitated, allowing his tone to relax. "I can tell you this—she's mad for you, and it has nothing to do with the situation. You're a lucky man."

"So lucky. Nothing is more important to me. Remember that."

"What's our next move?"

"Any leads on Jack Lewis?"

"Working on it. Need to get back to it. Do we need to deal with Immigration? I can put together a rootkit and access the system after a few test runs."

"Leave the Home Office alone. Her heritage is too strong for them to deny citizenship. I'm going to marry her, so it doesn't matter anyway."

"Not hard to figure out your plan after seeing that ink."

"It's not part of a plan," Will snapped. "Told you, I love her."

I smiled.

"Why do I feel like you've held something back?"

Will didn't respond, not audibly anyway.

"Ah, additional leverage. Why didn't they use MI5?"

"He was MI5. Drop it, Thomas."

"Concerns about dinner this evening?"

"Robert seems sure there's someone local providing intel. You need to be alert, circulate but stay close. Once the community leaders meet her, see how she's already thinking about what we can do for them, they'll be supportive."

"They better. We've put a lot in—money, protection. Christ, I just beat a man for Miller. Why should we give so much consideration? If they don't support her, we cut them off."

"If only it were that easy. After we shore up support here, we'll look to London for the same. You need to get on with joining the firm. Need you there. What's with Miller?"

"Scumbag from Westfield kept busting into his shop. Beat the arsehole bloody. He won't be back. I don't know how you're going to feel about this, but I didn't take Miller's offering."

"Good. No more pay for protection. And no more paid hits by this family—never again, not for anyone. I won't expose Elle to immorality beyond what's necessary to save her life. I won't have her living with a gang of nefarious mercenaries. Now that she and Lissie are with us, this family must move in a different direction. For mother's sake as well. Look into that flower shop Mum has her eye on. And get me Lewis."

After the door closed, Will returned to our nest of fragrant rose petals and pulled me to his chest. I drifted back into a sound, dreamless sleep.

Seventeen

JOHN WAITED OUTSIDE my bedroom door as I ran my cold hands along my hips once more and reassured myself the deep-blue dress I wore was appropriate.

I was careful to choose something that covered my back well enough to spare Will the discomfort of exposed, fading blemishes. It was a fitted, sleeveless gown with a conservatively draped V-neckline and ruched side seaming. The color reminded me of the moonlit sky over the Atlantic, while its shimmering metallic threads mimicked the twinkling of the stars. A fresh pedi and strappy Choos peeked from beneath the fluted, floor-length hem as I walked.

"Ellie, let's go. Will said you'd be ready."

Will was delayed by an extended call with an investor, so he sent John for me. It came as no surprise he chose his seventeen-year-old kid brother as his replacement. His ego wouldn't allow for me to make an entrance on the arm of another grown man.

I gave my formal but messy updo another once-over in the mirror, twisting a loose wisp around my finger to curl it, and then opened the door. "Okay, okay. Cut a girl some slack."

Dressed to kill in a tailored suit, John stood with perfect posture. He flashed a wide grin and winked, offering his arm. "I'll be your date until Will comes." When I failed to interlock our arms, he took my hand in his. He was becoming more and more like his bold brothers every day.

I pasted on a smile and pushed back at the rolling in my stomach.

When I stepped into the corridor, the savory aroma of roast beef hit me, and the air was already buzzing with conversations, clinking glasses, and the clanging of silverware on china. John ushered me down the staircase like the young aristocrat he was, hesitating at the bottom as he searched the three-story great hall for Thomas, just as he'd been instructed.

The hall was filled with long wooden tables covered in fine white linens. There were tall cocktail tables along two walls covered in the same fabric. The carpets had been removed, and the wood floor had been buffed to a shine. Lit candles flickered about while chandelier crystals sparkled and cast rainbows overhead. Harvest-colored floral arrangements accented with fragrant white roses adorned the entire ground floor. Buffet tables were filled with savory hors d'oeuvres and decadent desserts.

The billiard room was transformed to a full-service bar. I longed to slip in behind the bar to pour drinks and chat casually about nothing important. I missed Nick's. No, not Nick's—it was Jess and me together at Nick's that I missed. Images of her singing and the two of us bumping hips as we served up drinks during a full house on a Saturday evening filled my head. I needed to hear her voice. After Will finished his clean-up project in Stonington and my name was cleared, I'd be allowed to call her. Until then, I could only follow her tweets incognito.

"You look amazing. It'll drive him mad, you know." John's compliment—and affectionate insight—surprised me. It yanked me out of my head and back to Eastridge.

I squeezed his hand and smiled. "I'm lucky to be at your side right now, handsome."

Fifty or more people mingled, drinking, snacking, making small talk. Several more came through the foyer and brought a breath of fresh, cool night air with them.

Thomas stood near the center of the hall, and I decided shelter in his company was my best bet until Will turned up. I tugged on John's arm and headed for Thomas. He looked up from his conversation with a young couple and strode toward me, welcoming me with a warm smile.

Thomas possessed the same desirable traits as Will. He was fiercely protective, his charm was woven with arrogance, and he was generous and loyal, but somehow his presentation of those same qualities was different, lighter. Someday one lucky woman would win his heart, and he'd make her as happy as Will made me.

Thomas placed a thoughtful kiss on my hand and whisked me to the drawing room. "Don't want you in the hall until Will's here." Two of the Six followed and stood guard inside the door. The immense room was set up with a bar and reserved for family.

He asked the bartender for a double scotch and a glass of champagne and then changed his mind. "Just give me the glasses and a full bottle of each." He handed one bottle to John and guided me to the sofa by the nearest fireplace.

With each minute that passed in a house full of strangers and no sign of Will, I grew more anxious. I bit my lip. I fidgeted. I drank.

Thomas leaned against the mantle. "You're safe, Ellie. Security measures are in place." He opened his jacket to show me he was armed. "Slow down or you'll get pissed."

I gulped what was left in my glass and shrugged. I stood and extended my arm for a refill. "You're the guy pouring."

He lifted a brow and confiscated the glass. "You're too lovely for that."

Will's warm scent hit me. Then his strong hands gripped my waist. "*Elle.*" His breath washed over my neck, and his lips brushed my ear. "You're an exquisite little creature. *Mine.*"

Thomas and John headed for the hall. My guards moved to stand outside the door.

The tension in my body melted as I fell back against Will's. I dragged my fingertips along his tight beard, and smiled. "Finally."

He made no excuses, nor did he offer an explanation for being late. His lips brushed across my shoulder. I didn't know where he'd been or what he'd been doing, and I didn't care. He was there, pressing his arousal against my backside, and that was all that mattered.

"Your arse . . . looks so good in this gown."

"You . . . are a very naughty Englishman."

"And you quite like that, don't you, baby?" There was no mistaking the conceit and satisfaction—the sensuality—layered in Will's rasped words.

"Yes," I whispered.

He was the bad boy all the girls at college swooned over. The billionaire bad boy in the movies and romance novels women absorbed like it was their only source of oxygen. The badass man I never thought I'd want—until *he* rolled into town and pressed his lips to my hand.

"Turn. Let me see the rest of you."

When I faced him, he wore the sexy grin that would never be enough. His charged eyes lingered without care as they burned me from head to toe conducting their inspection.

My body screamed mindlessly for him. It begged me to spread my legs and demand he take me right there. I needed his touch like I needed air. I contracted my thigh muscles and reminded myself where we were. God, how insane—what was wrong with me?

His grin stretched wider.

"You've been up to something, Will."

"Still working on my return to your favor, yes?"

Since he was in a lighthearted mood, I decided to play along, smiling from under my lashes. "Maybe you should work a little harder."

"Let's see if this advances my position." He fished a bracelet from the inside breast pocket of his jacket and fastened it on my wrist before I realized what he was doing.

I stared at three sophisticated strands of perfectly aligned, alternating cushion-cut, marquise, and round brilliant diamonds and lost my breath for a moment. White light—similar to that in his eyes—reflected through the diamonds, making them twinkle with brilliance under the chandelier. There had to be thirty carats.

Then I stared at him. "What did you do?"

Someone out in the hall called his name.

"Will, why would you—"

"Because I wanted to. We've been through this." He moved his gaze to the doorway and snapped, "Just a fucking minute," then returned to our conversation. "Really, baby? We're going to do this?" He laid it out for me again. "I have a lot of money. I make a lot of money. It's only money, and I like to spend it. I'll buy you many things, and you will accept that. Shall we go upstairs and fight about it?"

It was a fight I wouldn't win. I narrowed my eyes anyway. "Well, could you at least give me the many things you insist on buying when we're alone so I can kiss you?"

He grabbed my waist and drew me in tight. "You can kiss me now."

"But—"

Will shut my mouth with his tongue. His amazing, wicked tongue. When he broke the kiss, he touched one of my blushing cheeks with the back of his fingers and smirked. "Let's get this done, Elle."

We entered the great hall holding hands.

Uncle Robert—who'd assumed the role of master of ceremonies—delivered the announcement that surprised me. "Ladies and gentlemen, the Eleventh Earl of Sussex and the Lady Eleanor of His Majesty King Edward the Fourth's House."

I squeezed Will's hand and gave him a dirty look.

"It wasn't me." He glared at Robert.

Panic stirred in my blood. "It will upset the queen."

"That's who you are, Elle. I'm surprised he didn't say her royal highness—*that* would upset the queen. Old supporters of the blood will never change. They'll talk about it until their deaths, and whisper the same from their graves. You'll always be the last white rose."

And there it was. The reality I needed to face in order to be free.

I thought of the herd of frolicking deer that continued to leap and play within view of my bedroom window. The little doe. How she taunted me with her freedom, showing me what could be mine. All I had to do was accept the truth. I'd done that to some degree, but I needed to be fully committed. No in-betweens, no gray. I was no longer the hidden girl across the sea, no longer living a lie.

Will kissed my hand.

My lips needed no instruction from my brain to smile in adoration at the one person who'd been honest with me. Will showed me who I was, revealed who I could be. I was madly in love with him. "You made your decision."

His mouth twitched with a controlled smile. "You asked me to fight for us. I chose to strengthen our position." Then he shook hands with the first guest in the queue that formed before us.

What the hell? Uncle Robert was at it again. He raised his glass and clanked it with silverware. "Friends, it's time for dinner. Please take your seats." He waived to Will and me. "They're quite wonderful. Lord Sussex is the youngest to ascend to the title in decades. He blessed England when he brought home her last daughter of the purest royal blood, certainly the loveliest ever to grace our presence. And—"

"Sit down, Robert," Will interrupted. His voice boomed through the hall as he stood. "Unlike my brother and our father, I've claimed my station as a peer of the realm." Grief washed over his face but vanished in an instant.

Champagne and whisky glasses clinked. Men and women shouted, "Hear, hear!"

"It would please me for all to refrain from addressing me as Earl or Lord Sussex."

He nodded at the waiting catering staff. Floorboards creaked and uniforms rustled as they dashed about delivering steaming dinner dishes to the tables.

"Anyone positioned on the properties returned to me in the Sussex counties will not be affected. You have my word. Business will continue as usual. Thomas and I will be available to you—anyone hurting needs only reach out to us. We're here to help. Spread the word."

Will extended his hand to me with a touch of dramatic flair.

My stomach rolled with nerves, but still, I needed to focus and stay out of his way, allowing him to work his plan. I found his eyes, slipped my hand into his, and stood at his side.

"It would please me most for you to welcome Ellie into your communities. As the incontestable heiress of the House of Plantagenet, the Crown offers to confer nationality by descent."

"But only if she gives up her rightful seat on the throne," someone shouted.

"True enough, my friend."

"Make her your countess," another called out.

He teased guests with one of his magnificent wide grins. "Do you think a woman of such grace would have me?"

There were hoots and howls of laughter.

"Long live the white rose," one table chanted.

"There have been attempts on her life and there will be more. Protect her." His last two words resonated above all sound.

Once more guests hailed, "Hear, hear!"

An adrenaline flush tingled through me. I was stunned. He commanded the room, captivating everyone in the hall with his unassailable charm. These people *wanted* him to stand among them as their earl. I'd heard stories about how the British still celebrated nobility, but never realized to what degree.

Will made a show of placing a protective kiss on my forehead and winked. "Let's sit and eat, baby."

Chairs scuffed wood, plates and silverware clanged, and the hall hummed with conversations again. Savory and sweet scents combined and created one delicious aroma. My empty stomach rumbled.

Someone called out Will's name.

"Go on," he said, searching the room for the caller as he stuffed another piece of roast beef into his mouth and chewed.

A white-haired, hunched man raised a shaky hand to identify himself. "My wife and I wish to thank you, sir. Your family saved mine. Our cash and stolen items were returned." It was Mr. Miller.

His son stood. "You have our support, sir."

"God save the white rose," the older Mr. Miller added.

Will graciously bowed his head at the two men.

I squeezed Will's thigh as I smiled at the Millers through the heat of another blush, receiving in return a devoted bend at the waist from each. Will captured my hand and raised it to his lips. The extravagant bracelet sparkled. As stunning as it was, it was no match for the scintillating light in his eyes at that moment.

"Now that's a fucking piece of jewelry," Thomas said. He flashed a complicit grin.

Mary Hastings narrowed her eyes and shook her head. "Must you boys always curse?" She patted my arm, and I caught the twinkle in her eye. "It's quite perfect, dear. My son has flawless taste."

All three of her sons leaned forward and eyed their mother as though she'd lost her mind. It was part of who they were, a mannerism imparted by their father. I rarely used the word, but it never offended me when it came from their mouths. She dismissed their incredulity with a delicate flick of her wrist.

Will stood and threw back his whisky in one swallow and pounded the glass on the table. "Something on your mind, Green?" His voice rumbled through the hall. He'd sussed out dissent among the ranks, though the rest of us had missed it.

My heart accelerated. Its hammering dropped into my stomach as it lurched in nervous rebellion, recognizing something dreadful was about to go down.

Thomas knew his brother well and understood the reason for his sudden outburst. He jumped to his feet and positioned himself behind me, receiving a curt nod of approval from Will.

"I won't ask again." Will removed his jacket and dropped his arms. His fists were balled. "Is there something on your fucking mind, Green?"

"Your reputation is indeed earned I see," Charles Green barked from a crowded table. "It's quite clear you're the seductive, barbarous hellion they say you are." He took a deep pull from his whisky glass, rising to his feet.

"Maybe. Yet here you stand in my house. You drink my scotch and seek whatever advantage you can gain. Go ahead—insult me. But know you straddle an important line of demarcation. Fall on the wrong side of that line by threatening what's mine, and you'll find out how barbarous this hellion can be."

Chairs screeched across wood planks as Green's three brothers got to their feet. The Six moved in and spread themselves around the perimeter of the hall. It grew quiet, and the air became still, laced with menace, contempt, and fear.

I held my breath, anxiety consuming me.

"Look at you. Uncompromising and sanctimonious. You will never maintain peace with the Crown. My family will no longer support your pact. One woman—" Charles Green pointed at me, slurring his words. "For the sake of many, let them have the last one. Give her up. Find another for your pleasure."

Will had the man's throat in his hands within seconds. "You're threatening her?" he asked in the collected manner I recognized as the unnatural calm before his control is lost. Green's face turned red as Will applied more pressure to his throat. "Since you're so familiar with my reputation, you must know I won't hesitate to retaliate when threatened." Will's nostrils flared, and the muscles in his face and jaw grew tighter.

"Fuck you, Hastings. You're not my lord. I doubt you can save her."

I stared at Will. Intense blue eyes were overcome with rage—the storm was about to hit. He lifted Green from the floor by the throat, and the breathless man's feet kicked at air. The sight, those flailing limbs, forced my brain from its lockdown, and I shouted at Thomas. "Do something. . . . Stop him!"

When Thomas and Ben sprang into action, crashing through tables and people to reach Will, so did Charles Green's three brothers.

Other men shouted, women screamed. People raced for the door.

I cried out for Will, but he couldn't hear me. Thomas and Ben struggled, unable to convince him to release the dangling man whose face was blue from lack of oxygen. Finally, Thomas wrapped his arms around Will's throat from behind and dragged him backwards.

My cries for Will only drew undesirable notice. Green's brothers crept through the chaos and surrounded me. The youngest held a long barrel revolver at his side. His words rattled close to my ear. "You can't be worth all this."

If he pointed that gun at me, if he touched me, he was a dead man. Fear climbed up the back of my throat. I swallowed it. No one would die if I could talk him down. "Walk away now. You know this won't end well for your family. Walk away while there's still time."

Another Green slithered closer, his stinking breath drifting into my face. "You're right, it won't. Not unless you make it so. Seems you have his number. He couldn't stop himself from falling all over you." His deep-set eyes moved up and down my body. "Can't say I blame him."

My gut lurched. I nearly gagged.

All three closed in tight.

"Please. Let me go to him before he looks your way. If he—"

My name blasted from Will's throat. It was too late. He was already moving across the hall, throwing tables out of his way. Plates and glasses shattered. Chairs sailed through the air. His eyes were locked on Seth Green, the man stupid enough to come near me with a gun.

I don't know why, but I stepped in front of Seth, shielding him for a moment from certain death. What I'd done was sense-less. He wrapped an arm around my waist and pressed the long barrel between my shoulder blades, and shouted, "Back off! I'll end this. . . . I'll kill her."

Time stopped, I think. I couldn't hear anything, not even my battering heartbeat.

As Will cleared the distance between us, I locked into his flaming eyes. I was immobilized but sickly comforted by the rage and violence burning there. That rage and violence represented my life, and as long as it burned in Will, I would live.

"Six," Thomas shouted.

"Come to me," Will shouted at the same time. His feet left the ground as he dove through the air toward me.

Ben was on his heels, making a dive of his own.

Will's heavy body took mine to the floor, though he'd twisted to keep from crushing me. Still, the air slammed violently from my lungs.

Ben's arms wrapped around Seth Green, his considerable weight taking them both down, causing the wood boards beneath us to kick back as they hit the floor next to Will and me. They wrestled for the gun.

When the gunshot blast exploded in my ears, my body jerked. The strength of Will's arms increased, enveloping me tighter, increasing the depth of the security he provided.

Crystals from a chandelier tinkled as they split into shards and rained down over us.

From beneath Will's arm, I saw Ben and Seth Green. Ben gripped the man's chin with one hand and the top of his head with the other. Seth was still thrashing, fumbling for the gun. Ben wrenched the man's head at an angle and snapped his neck, the sound of it horrifying, sickening.

The body convulsed. And then it stopped moving.

Panic-stricken and nauseated, I freaked out—I pushed my face deep into Will's neck, clutching frantically at his shirt and skin, and sobbed. I choked on the metallic taste filling my mouth.

"I've got you, Elle. I won't let go. Never let you go, baby," Will said, purring the words to soothe me. He maintained our position on the floor until Thomas and the Six surrounded us with weapons drawn. Then he held me tight in his arms as he brought us to our feet.

"Where is my mother?" Thomas shouted at someone.

"Robert," I said into Will's chest. He'd rushed Mary from the hall when hell broke loose.

As promised, Will didn't let go. He kept me tight against his body as he made decisions and directed his team. "John, upstairs. Pull mother and the girls into one room. Keep your weapon ready—stay put and protect them." He sent one of the Six with John.

I buried my face at the base of his throat and cried again.

He kissed the top of my head. "You're safe now. I promise."

"I can take her upstairs to your mum," someone—Uncle Robert, I think—offered.

One of the Six pushed him back. "Step away, sir." Once they were commanded to me, no one other than Will, Thomas, or John was permitted to touch me or come between their own bodies and mine.

"She stays with me," Will snapped, and then barked at someone else. "Get that fucking thing out of here. Outside. Police can pick it up later."

"That fucking thing" was the dead body of Seth Green, the man who'd held me at gunpoint. There was no way anyone would ever walk into Eastridge making threats—with or without a gun—and live to tell the story.

Will and I stood unmoving for several more minutes. I soaked his white shirt with my dirty tears and the blood from my broken lip, and he commanded his men as he protected me in his arms. "Get the rest of these people out of here. Secure all entrances and lock it down. Lock those three up, but don't touch them—not yet. Everyone to the war room afterward."

I had to get it together so I didn't impede Will's ability to do what he needed to do. This was what my life had become, and there was no alternative. I needed to toughen up and deal with it. "I'm sorry," I whispered, though I still clung to him with my wet face buried.

But I could do better than that, was stronger than that. I lifted my eyes to his.

He cradled my face in his steady hands. "Never apologize to me, Elle. You're not to blame. No one could be more innocent in this fucking mess than you. What happened here tonight is my fault. I did this. . . . I'm so sorry."

Will always blamed himself, although none of it was his fault. He never chose the life. His fate had been no different than mine, a predetermined circumstance into which we'd been born. Our ancestors bound us to the same legacy but bequeathed him the greater burden. I only had to live. He had to wage war to keep me alive. I thanked God every day for Will. I knew what would have become of us had we not fallen in love. Death would have claimed us, just as it claimed Isobel and Ethan.

"No. Never you, Will." I pressed my red-stained lips to his and pleaded. "Our families, their legacies are to blame. Tell me I'm right. Tell me you agree."

"Okay, baby. You're right." He said whatever I needed him to say. Then he secured a strong arm around my waist and led me to his war room.

It was on.

Eighteen

WILL SCRUTINIZED EVERY corner of the estate's security, eyeing each of the monitors on the wall while we waited for the others to complete their tasks and make their way to the war room. Strategic thoughts flashed in his eyes. His determination was a force unto itself.

That evening was the first time I saw the entire team assembled. Thomas and John would always be loyal. It was in their blood. The others were loyal of their own free will, and those are the faces I explored. I studied the hardened expressions of Ben Scott and Joe Wright. I examined the faces of Jonathan, Sam, Daniel, Peter, and Eric—indispensable members of the Six, their faces made hard by lines and creases that came from once carrying the weight of Britain's safety on their backs. I would pay more attention to these men in the future. They followed Will to protect me; they were dedicated to keeping me alive, and I owed them more respect than I'd given.

Uncle Robert had come in with the last man. "Can I be of some use?"

"Not here. Mother still grieves. Spend your time at Eastridge with her." Since there was an alleged local informant, Will wouldn't risk having anything he discussed with his men leaked into the community. I'd gathered from conversations with John that Robert and Richard Hastings had had a rocky relationship, which must have been the reason for Will's caution.

I wondered if I would be in his way. He worked hard to shield me from the details of the violence. Would my being in his war room hinder the conversations he needed to have? He needed to deal with the three remaining Green brothers and the police. He needed to strategize and plan the next moves against our enemy.

Truth be told, I never cared to be informed. I liked in equal measures knowing Will handled everything and not knowing how. Not knowing was one of the few things I could give him. God knows the scales of our relationship tipped significantly in his favor when it came to giving and sacrifice. He never asked for anything other than for me to say I loved him. So if staying out of his war-room business relieved him, then I'd provide that relief.

I folded back his sleeves. "Take me upstairs, Will. I want to see the girls and Mary. I'll wait for you in your room."

Satisfaction flickered in his eyes, and his shoulders relaxed. "Get started with a detailed rundown, cover every meter of this estate. Every corner must be secure. No mistakes. Put one of your drones in the air, Thomas. I'll be right back."

That strong, tattooed arm snaked around my waist again, and we headed upstairs.

"You've recovered remarkably tonight."

He was right. I'd fallen apart downstairs, but then pulled it together, realizing it was time to accept and overcome what I couldn't change. My connection to him revealed my strength—revealed me. I smiled and pulled his forehead to mine. "You deserve the credit for that. Go plan your war, Will."

Our lips connected for a lingering moment. The depth of his tenderness made me high.

Watching him go, I whispered, "William, my conqueror."

Will rubbed the back of his neck and cursed under his breath as he walked through the bedroom door. His voice was strained, and he was exhausted. "Didn't mean to wake you."

"You didn't. What is it?"

He sat on the edge of the bed and dropped his head. "This isn't going to be easy, baby—this life with me, the things I need to do."

I lifted onto my knees behind him and kneaded the muscles in his shoulders and neck. "I know. Our life together will never be easy. I've accepted that."

He reached up and found one of my hands and pulled it to his lips. "You deserve more than some fucking mercenary."

He didn't know I'd listened to his earlier conversation with Thomas. "You're no longer that. You make the rules now."

"If you want something else—"

"What?" He meant someone, not something else. We both knew the something could never be changed. "Don't. Don't do that to me."

"Just . . . goddamn it . . . take some time to think about what I am. What I've done. What I'm committed to doing again. You have the right to choose."

I climbed into his lap. "Yes, and I did choose. I know who you are. And I know every day since we met on that pier, and every day following this one, the lives you've taken or will take are those born from necessity—to save mine. You are my defender."

"Yes." He put his arms around me but still stared at the floor.

"More than that, you are my love."

Those blue eyes found mine.

"Don't destroy us. We're not Ethan and Isobel. We'll live, and we'll find our way through this mess. Take what you want—that's who you are. Take it, Will. Take my freedom from them, and give it back to me."

"Jesus, Elle," he whispered. His embrace strengthened as he pulled me snug against his body. He buried his face in my neck and inhaled. "There are no words. I can only hope you feel my need for you and know how I love you."

My heartbeat was steady and strong, and I wanted him to hear it before anxiety and fear robbed me of it once again. And they would. I wound my arms around his head and pulled his ear to my chest. "I do. I know."

We were face-to-face when I woke several hours later. Will's eyes were open, and he was staring at me. They were clear, beautiful. The dark circles beneath were almost gone, and the muscles in his face were relaxed.

"Why aren't you in the gym?"

He plucked several rose petals from my hair. "You slept so peacefully."

"You should wake me when you don't go downstairs."

"I'll never do that." He placed a hand on the back of my head and pulled me to his lips. "Promise me you'll have something more than coffee for breakfast."

"I promise. What will you do today?"

"Need to spend some time in the gym. The sun is shining, and it's warmer than usual. We'll go down to the beach and have dinner out."

A warm, ethereal feeling flowed through me. I smiled and reached for his face.

"I know you miss it, baby." His eyes charged. "I'll take what belongs to us. I swear." He kissed me hard and then climbed out of bed and stretched like the lion king he was. I watched as he strutted into the bathroom. He was without doubt aware of my contented stare at his tight, round ass.

Mrs. Bates's lilt drifted through the corridor and stopped outside the door. I rolled my eyes and sighed, then padded across the soft wool rug and slipped into my robe before she opened the door and called out for me.

Will and I were alone in his car at the front of our small army as it flooded convoy-style into Old Town. There were fifteen of us, and five more young men—friends of Thomas and John—joined us after we arrived. Girlfriends of the Six were invited, though there were just three. It was time we gave consideration to the personal lives of those who fought for us, the esteemed lives belonging to those faces I'd studied the night before. If we were going to step out of the shadows, we would eliminate as many restrictions as possible.

Will and Thomas were armed, and there was a weapons cache concealed in one of the vehicles—just in case.

After we'd filled the private car park behind Ethan's—Will's—pub, we walked down the busy cobbled streets to the beach and spent a quiet afternoon in the sunshine. The cool, salted breeze caressed our skin. The tide was high, the undercurrent strong, and the water cold, so we didn't swim, but it was still comforting to be there. Waves clapped like thunder and slapped the beach when they made it to shore.

I couldn't have been happier.

Will tossed me playfully onto the blanket and lowered himself on top after chasing me through the edge of the water. He hovered above my lips with his. "What do you hear?"

"Nothing. Only you." My whispering messenger went silent that day. I'd filled its place in my soul with something else. The sea had never been my home—it was the beacon tasked with getting me home.

"You're home, baby," he said as if he'd read my mind. Then he slanted his mouth over mine and claimed me with a relentless, devoted kiss.

"Let's go," Thomas shouted at the troops. He and Kirsty made their way east along the shoreline and approached Will and me in our favorite spot beneath Eastridge. "Christ. I'm starving. Let's go, brother."

Will pushed a soft kiss against my lips. "Why is it you all have such shitty timing?"

"It's not that. You can't keep your greedy fucking hands off her. Ever. Let's go. Information has been circulated."

The brick-paved street was filled with patrons dining and shopping and merchants selling their goods from the sidewalks. The energy of the community was intoxicating. Locals, government officials, business owners, and photographers flocked to the restaurant as we arrived. People behaved with respect and approached in a thoughtful manner, excited to see their new earl and curious about me. I recognized the mayor and a few city councillors from the night before at Eastridge, as well as several other faces—all were oddly blithe, as if they had erased the chaos of the night before from their minds.

Will bought every bottle of the local winery's VIP reserve from the restaurant. He shared it and the chef's best hors d'oeuvres with everyone who stopped at the front patio while we waited for our dinner table. The chef came out twice and offered a private dining room, but Will declined both invitations.

Will and Thomas flaunted our presence—they'd set it up—but remained cautious. The security detail was maintained around me at all times. A message had not only been sent, but hand delivered. Will wanted the town of Hastings, wanted it for the benefit of my freedom, and he was taking it. It was, after all, his namesake.

The food and drink demands of our party filled the charming seafood house with complete chaos. I'd never seen as much food on a restaurant table before.

"Ring Jess tomorrow."

"Really?"

Will winked. "Yeah."

"Everything is okay—in Stonington, I mean?"

"The cop got what he needed, and his captain was satisfied with the commissioner's interview. Closed the case."

I kissed his cheek. "Thank you, Will. The way you take care of everything, that I can talk to her again . . . you don't know how much it all means to me."

Satisfaction danced in his eyes. He did know.

The director of the art museum approached then and asked to speak with me. Will was unfriendly for the first time that day, grumbling with disapproval when I invited her to take John's seat next to me. He'd had enough for one day. Sharing was never easy for him.

"I'm sure her purpose is harmless," I whispered.

She was sincere, resting her hand on my arm as she spoke. Her kind smile reminded me of my beloved professor of nineteenth-century art history. She stayed only long enough to take a few sips of wine, closing with a predictable request for my support of the museum association.

Will threw his napkin onto the table and shot another whisky. He leaned back in his chair and pulled me into his side. "You look happy. You're so beautiful." He brushed his warm mouth against my shoulder. "Let's go home."

"It's been a lovely day. Thanks." I swept my fingers along his inked forearm and extorted a smile from him. "You don't plan to cover this when you're out?"

"Why would I do that?" He lifted my hand from his arm and kissed it. "Thomas, go settle this bill, and let's get out of here. Come sit here, John." He stood and waited for his youngest brother to take his chair and then headed for the restroom.

Three men appeared from a dark corner table and stepped into Will's path.

The Green brothers.

Ben flashed to his side in an instant. Wood scraped wood as the other guys in our party rose from their seats. Several headed that way until Will jerked his head and issued the single word command, sending the Six back to surround John and me in an impenetrable circle of guards. Thomas sprinted from the front, handed his pistol to John, and made his way to Will's side.

The thrashing of my heart dropped into my stomach and pitched up to my throat.

John held the Glock in his hand beneath the table. "Bet they're trying to wring more money from him. He's already paying for the funeral. Shouldn't even do that. Bastard came into our house with a gun and threatened you. He deserved death. Looks like the rest want it, too."

With one eye locked on his brothers, he went on to tell me the Greens agreed, after some harsh persuasion, to bury their dead brother quietly. Each claimed they didn't know their youngest brother had carried the gun to Eastridge and swore fealty after being reminded how Will killed the man who beat and raped their sister three years before.

Something about the faces and the body language of the Green brothers troubled me. Those men were not on board. Will's fisted hands, his clenched jaw and corded neck, and the way he moved with deliberate intent told me I was right.

The circle of men around John and me parted as Will came through the center. "Let's go, baby." He took my hand and led me out the door.

Later that night, Will and Thomas went back into town alone.

They hunted Greens.

It was almost noon, and Will still wasn't home. My mind was cluttered with angst, trepidation, and the persistence of those two head-wrecking words: *what if.* I called him again as I ran down the staircase, halting midstride when I heard his ringtone somewhere back on the first floor.

He was in the house somewhere, but he'd never bothered to let me know he was back. It made no sense—Will typically came to me first when he returned to Eastridge.

I darted back up the stairs.

Thomas and Ben stood in front of one of the guest bedroom doors, their expressions similar to deer caught in the headlights of a car. Thomas held Will's phone in his hand.

"Why aren't you with Will? And why do you have his phone?"

Thomas stared at me. His mouth opened but he said nothing. Something *had* happened.

My chest tightened. "Where is he, Thomas?" I whispered

"It's not a good time, Ellie."

"What? Where is he? What happened last night?"

"Listen—"

"What happened?" I cried. Images of Will lying lifeless somewhere cold and dark assaulted my mind, my heart, sending a shockwave of pain through my body. I hugged my abdomen as if it would hold me together.

"He's going to be fine, I promise." Thomas reached for me as he snapped at Ben, "Fuck this. He's too deep into his head—he doesn't realize what he's doing."

Ben tried to reason. "Ellie, he's just resting. Everything's all right. His shoulder will be fine."

"Was he shot?"

"Cut. It's not as bad as you think. He's had worse."

This wasn't about an injury—it was a glaring refusal to see me. Ben's words from one of our talks in the gym knocked around inside my head: *don't let him get away with it . . . position of strength.*

I dropped my arms and straightened my back. "Let me in, Thomas."

"Do you want me to go in with you?"

"No, we'll be okay."

Thomas nodded, gestured to the door, and headed for the staircase. Ben followed.

I stepped into the room and stared at Will. He lay propped against a stack of pillows, drinking from a lowball tumbler. One shoulder was bandaged, but otherwise, he was physically whole. He turned his face from me and searched outside the window for something to hold his eyes.

Tears welled, and a broken sob tried to rebuild in my throat, but I pushed back. Relief would have to wait. We had something to settle first. I drew a deep breath through my nose and pushed my shoulders back. Will had underestimated me. There was no way I would allow such behavior. Because like him, I would fight to protect what was mine.

I snatched the whisky from his hand. "I will not be replaced with this."

"You shouldn't be in here." He fought to keep his eyes trained outside the window.

"You don't belong in here either."

"Leave."

"You know I won't." I touched his bandaged shoulder. "Tell me what happened, Will."

"Leave, Elle. Just go."

Anger consumed my emotions. I wouldn't let him do that, wouldn't allow him to shut me out. I threw the glass at the fireplace, and it shattered against the stone surround. His eyes finally met mine when he grabbed me and pulled me down on top of him—he held my wrists so tightly it stung. The muscles in his shoulders and arms quivered.

I searched his eyes and found anger, roused by my own, but no rage lurked there. That anger was the beast that reared its head only when he believed something had hurt me. Knowing this, the reason behind his torment, I straddled his hips with confidence, determined not to back down.

When I turned my wrists to relieve the stinging sensation, he quickly opened his fingers and released me. "Baby, don't push me right now." He was wrecked. The situation with the Greens had dragged him somewhere deep and caused him to question himself, to retreat emotionally.

I took his face into my hands. "Why are you shutting me out? Taking a hit doesn't change anything between us. It's nothing. It changes nothing."

He pointed to his shoulder. "*This* is nothing." Then he pulled my hands from his face and locked onto my wrists again. "But what I've done, that's something. *That's* the fucking nightmare you should be concerned about."

"Now we're getting somewhere. Tell me, Will. What nightmare could be worse than those I already live with?" But he didn't need to say anything more. I could see what messed with his head. He blamed himself for the one-eighty by the Green brothers. Believed their rebellion was his creation. Worried others would follow.

"You are persuasive and successful in all you do—a powerful man. But the decision the Greens made to come after us? You don't get credit for that."

"I'll fix it," he snapped. His anger was still present but diminishing.

"Just remember. Whatever happens—whatever must be fixed—neither of us is whole without the other." I untied the string at the waist of his sweatpants. "Shall I remind you?"

He filled his hands with my hair and pulled me to his mouth. "I need you. Christ, how I need you." Will needed his pieces cemented back together—something I could fix. He pushed past my lips and kissed me hard. His strength was overwhelming.

I pressed on his injured shoulder. It was the only way I could best him. He jerked and lost his grip. I moved my mouth from his and kissed my way down his neck, his chest, dragged my mouth over his skin until reaching that golden trail of fine hair, and then I tugged like a savage at his sweatpants.

"Never shut me out again, Will."

"Never." The rhythm of his rising and falling chest amplified as his breath accelerated. "Never," he repeated, attempting to roll me onto my back.

I pushed on his shoulder again.

He fell flat on his back. "Goddamn it, Elle!" His voice crashed against the floral-papered walls of the small guest room we occupied. He stilled, and I stared at him. His handsome face. His sculpted body. His enormous erection.

"Fucking magnificent," I whispered.

His mood shifted fast, as it often did, and he smirked. "Did you just say fu—"

I locked my mouth around his wide crown.

He strangled the sound climbing up the back of his throat but loosed a primal grunt as his hips bucked. He threaded his fingers through my hair and tried not to pull, tried not to thrust. His wild eyes met mine with burning white fire.

The muscles in his chest rippled when he finally overthrew my rule and flung me onto my back across the width of the bed. "Be careful with that. You push me close to madness," he panted against my lips. He kissed my mouth and then dragged that kiss down my quivering body as he slid off my jeans. Smooth kisses teased as he trailed them over my thighs.

When he at last gave me what I wanted, I pulled his hair and arched my back, pressing hard against his mouth. A growl rumbled in his throat.

He had mastered the precise rhythm and intensity that would push me over the edge. He could send me over within seconds or draw it out as long as he desired. He'd also mastered determining the exact moment of my orgasms so he could do with them as he pleased. He was the master of my universe.

I shattered, screaming his name.

He shot up and drove himself inside me with a sharp thrust and swallowed the cry it tore from me, but then stopped moving to pull himself together. His breath was heavy as he apologized. "Only meant to spare you my dark mood. Should've known better. I'm sorry."

And with that, my anger resurfaced. I leveraged his injury once more—squeezed his shoulder so he'd roll onto his back again, and I could reclaim my position on top.

"Goddamn it, Elle. I said I'm sorry."

"Yes, and I've heard that one before." I dropped my head.

"Baby, don't be angry. Look at me."

My head whipped up, and I found his eyes. "Give me all of you—everything," I demanded, fighting against his hold on my hips.

A sudden wave of anxiety flowed through me, and I collapsed onto his chest.

He moved our bodies, reversing our positions until he hovered above me, and pressed his mouth to mine with tenderness. "I love you." Another of his gentle kisses caressed my lips. "I'll give you everything, my angel, always. But this . . . this we do my way when you're no longer angry with me . . . and willing to yield."

We stared into each other. Tears ran down the sides of my face, wetting my temples and sliding into my hair. He'd been stabbed. I could have lost him.

"You scared me."

"I'm an arsehole."

I nodded with enthusiasm. That was so much better than another "I'm sorry."

He grinned. "You're schooling me, baby. I used to be much worse."

"So I hear." My heart smiled first before it spread to my face.

The chuckles we shared against each other's mouths became a passionate kiss, and then he moved inside me, filling me over and over, loving me his way. Will was back and in control, just as he needed to be. Just as I needed him to be. Giving in—yielding to his dominance when he was inside me—eased my soul, took me home.

He controlled what went on in our bed and in our life together, but he gave me something in return that was more valuable. His key. It unlocked a power that was all mine. It was the power to push him until he was no longer the arrogant financier, nor the cold-blooded mercenary or the warrior born to protect me. I could turn that key until he was stripped down to the man behind it all. The man with a tender soul who loved me hard no matter the cost.

Nineteen

WILL HAULED HIS favorite worn leather sofa across the billiard room and placed it and his stack of newspapers close to the bank of windows where I'd begun to paint again. The room wasn't ideal with the bar and its traffic, and I disliked being exposed on the ground level, but it had the best north-facing windows in the house.

We were focused on the rehab of Will's shoulder and connecting the pieces of our life. We agreed it was one life and talked about how to move forward together. Will and I might never be free of the legacy of our ancestors, but we would change that for the following generations. We were committed to our fight to end an ancient war that somehow made its way to the twenty-first century. We would close the rabbit hole.

Apart from my distinct American accent, living in England felt like a natural fit. Eastridge was my home. Will was my home.

"Where's John with his education?" I had no clue how to approach the education system in England.

Will answered without looking up from *The Wall Street Journal.* "He's indulging in a gap year before university. Many kids here do that, take a gap year to travel or gain work experience. Not sure John should've been granted the luxury. I'm worried his enthusiasm will be lost. He doesn't show interest in anything other than football. Lissie needs to be enrolled in primary school. Mother can deal with that."

"Is he good?"

"He is."

Newspapers rustled as he continued to work through the stack. The smell of fresh ink mingled with the spike lavender I used with my oils. I imagined it was how our home would always smell. I loved that he preferred the paper medium to digital. Black and white, no shades of gray, no vibrant distractions.

"Maybe that's his way out. Isn't that what you want for him—a way out of the mess you and Thomas are bound to?"

"Yeah."

"Do you think the community—oh, damn it!"

"What's the matter, baby?"

"I'm trying to oil out *Neptune*, but she's not cooperating."

"The community will settle in."

"Your mother said you'll need to check your ego first." I peeked around the canvas.

He winked and took a sip from his coffee mug before he opened *The Times*. "*Neptune?*"

"The old fishing boat back in Stonington. You should remember her well."

"You've painted it from memory?" His newspaper dropped to the sofa, and he came around the canvas to watch me fine-tune my work. "Christ. It's perfect. Are you attached to it?"

"I'm almost done, which means I'll probably never look at it again."

"I'll have it framed, and we'll gift it to the seafood house where we had dinner. Don't sign it—that'll be done ceremonially once it hangs on their wall."

I looked away from *Neptune* and found another plan burning in Will's eyes. He would polish the best gems within the borders of his earldom, take them from our enemy and anyone else who challenged him, and give them to me. Those gems, places like that quaint seafood restaurant, would be the safe houses of my freedom.

He placed a sweet kiss on my mouth and left my heart racing before going back to the chesterfield to bury his nose in another daily.

"When will Thomas start at the firm?"

"Soon."

"I'll hunt you down, William Hastings. I won't be left alone day and night while you spend all your time in London."

"You would, baby, I know. We'll figure it out. I may have to do a lot of driving for a while—I'll do whatever it takes. You are my priority. Lissie, too."

We'd already decided to test Lissie's paternity using his DNA.

"What if she's not?"

"You have nothing to worry over." When he didn't get a response, he moved his eyes from the black-and-white print to my face. "Look at her. Watch how Mum looks at her."

"Your mother knows?"

"She suspects. It's rather hard to miss. How do you feel about adoption?"

"Adoption? You mean you would adopt her as your own?"

"We—ours. Mother can help raise her. And the nanny stays. Raising a child isn't something I want us to manage round the clock. I need you with me. You're mine." My possessive lover stared at me, waiting for an obedient response. "Don't fuck with me, Elle."

I was just as obsessed. I nodded and watched the tension drain from his handsome face. "I know you love her. And I know we need time. You come first, Will."

His broad shoulders relaxed as he exhaled.

"Lissie should have your name. She's your family. No one outside this house needs to know she's Isobel's daughter. I mean, I know she's safe. I know it ends with me—I'm all the Order wants now. Still, I can't help but worry for her."

Will was next to me in a flash, angered by my choice of words.

Words chosen subconsciously to test him. He pulled me to my feet. "Why are you talking this way? *You* are my family. *You* are safe. And it ends with *us*." He secured me in his arms and protected me with fierce affection. "Say the word, baby. . . . Us."

No matter how many steps forward we took, one of us always seemed to lose our footing, forcing the other to right us again. I pressed my ear to his chest. As a child, strange as it was, I was soothed by severe coastal thunderstorms in the night while tucked safe in my bed. That's what it was like to hear his heartbeat when he held me. "Us," I repeated.

"Lock down on it, baby. It's the only thing to keep us from stumbling." He pulled my chin up to kiss me. A soft kiss meant for reassurance bloomed with desire. He pushed his hardening length into my stomach and left me breathless. "I have something to show you." One corner of his mouth twitched before a striking grin consumed his face.

I pushed back against his arousal. "I've seen that before, you know."

His chest vibrated, and he owned my mouth again.

My body absorbed the feel of his touch. Absorbed his taste, his scent, even the sound of his voice, and infused my blood with it, producing the high I'd become so desperate for, day and night. I was a damned junkie.

Will led me through the hall and kissed me as we climbed the staircase. When we reached his room, he pulled me past the door. I tugged on his arm and whined. "Take me to bed, Will." I needed my fix.

He grinned and swept me into his arms. I tried to complain, but he shut my mouth with his—an effective tactic he used often. It became obvious he was on a mission. At the end of the corridor, he stopped in front of a set of double doors. His palm went to the electronic pad on the wall. A lock clicked, and the right side opened with a low hum.

He pushed the door open wide with his foot. "Welcome home, baby."

I squished my brows together. "What?"

"Our separate rooms are too small. And separate. We need more space." He stepped inside. "I won't have lath and plaster between us any longer."

"But—"

"*Elle.* You'll give me this," he commanded before setting me on my feet. He narrowed his eyes and stared—maybe reworking the lecture he'd given about the diamond bracelet.

The "but" wasn't about the load of cash he'd spent renovating the suite. I shook my head as if that would clear it and give me good sense. It was stupid to wonder why he hadn't asked me to move in with him. Stupid to fear living with him. We already lived together.

Living in Will's house wasn't my long-term plan when I agreed on England. I came because of my resolve to bide time and plot vengeance, and more importantly, it had been for Lissie's sake. That's what I'd told myself. Truth slapped me in the face as I stared up at him. I'd fallen in love with him before England. The proof was in how I thanked God it was Will who was thrown into my life before we ever flew across the Atlantic. As clichéd as it was—he had me at hello. That rumbling, accented hello on the pier unsettled the silence of my lost soul and changed me.

I gazed into his blue eyes. There was no fire, only love. And steely determination—that enormous, unbridled ego wasn't about to be denied. I swallowed hard, overwhelmed by a surge of emotion. I'd been over it in my head more than once—my love for him was insane. It was irrevocable. A smile stole across my lips at the thought, and I dragged my fingertips along his unshaven jawline. "Okay. You're right. It makes sense."

Will kissed my hand and then held it as he led me through our new suite.

Inside the entrance was a large living space that included a plush gray sectional and a beautiful wood dining table. The original fireplace was preserved, though converted to gas and surrounded with sleek built-in shelving. A generous wet bar was tucked into a corner. Its elegant carved cabinets with etched glass doors hung above white marble and were filled with shining cut-crystal barware. There was a stocked wine cooler on one side of the sink and a dishwasher on the other. Bottles of Will's favorite scotch and a multifunction espresso machine rested on the counter.

He led me through a door into an incredibly opulent bedroom. It had sweeping, deep-blue velvet draperies hanging from two ornate oriel windows that faced east and framed the English Channel. I wondered if I might see the lights of Boulogne-sur-Mer on a clear night. There was a masculine wooden desk on one side of the room where Will would work nights while he stayed close to me. The huge, four-poster bed had a grand headboard made of rich mahogany, and it was covered in layers of luxurious white and deep-blue linens. Blue-and-white silk Persian rugs covered much of the wood floor.

There were no words. I stared with a gaping mouth at the romantic boudoir.

Within the bedroom, there were three doors. The first led to the en suite—a master bathroom filled with white-and-gray marble. The second was his walk-in closet, already filled with clothing and weapons. One oversized rack displayed his many tailored Italian suits.

I lifted a brow. I hated the thought of him leaving me for London.

"Soon." He kissed my forehead. "We'll figure it out."

Beaming with satisfaction about what was soon to be revealed behind door number three, he opened it and nudged me inside. I stood in a posh, custom dressing room so large it would take decades to fill. It was an entire room itself, complete with its own fireplace, settee, white fur rugs, and crystal chandelier.

When he caught me eyeing the glass box that displayed Pearl, he put his arms around me. "It's a lovely family heirloom, baby, meant to be treasured, not fired." The old gun didn't mean much to me, but what he'd done with it meant everything. My eyes stung with unshed tears.

"Will, my God. It's . . . everything is . . . it's magical."

"You'll fill it in time." His face lit with pride.

"So that's the trick—build your woman an irresistible dressing room, and hold her captive by virtue of the temptation to fill it." I lifted onto tiptoes and nipped his earlobe.

He patted me on the ass. "Whatever it takes to tie you down. There's one more room." Holding both hands, he pulled me through the front living room to a set of French glass doors.

The space on the other side of those doors was flooded with natural light. The north wall was nothing more than a bank of windows. A stunning vintage easel and its blank canvas were strategically positioned, and a tall project table with built-in shelving was loaded with painting and sketching supplies.

Will stood pressed against my backside. His arms held me snug, and he rested his chin on top of my head. "What do you think? Is the light suitable?"

I stared without words once again, stunned by the wonderful little art studio he'd created with such obvious thought and care. The tears I swallowed burned my throat.

"We can change anything that doesn't suit you. A lot of traffic moves through this house. I need to know you're comfortable."

I whirled around to find his eyes. "Will," I squeaked. It took a moment for me to find my voice. "Everything is perfect. More than perfect. It's fabulous enough for the duke and his queen. Thank you. I would love to live here at Eastridge in this suite with you." I kissed him and hugged his neck tight.

"For an earl and his countess," he corrected with a whisper close to my ear.

I pulled back. "You were meant to protect me, *defensor mea,* not give me the world."

A warm smile played at his lips as he swept a flaxen strand of hair from my face. "I plan to do both." Smiling, indulgent lips touched my forehead. I shivered. He pushed deeper into his reserve of tenderness. The back of those long, talented fingers brushed my cheek. "You did say you'll marry me."

I'd meant it when I said the words, though I was unprepared for the conversation outside of bed. He hadn't mentioned it since, and it never occurred to me that he might want to get married so soon. I hit him with what had to have been a stupid expression. "It's too soon. Isn't this too fast?"

"No." His lips grazed mine.

"But—"

"I've loved you for a decade, Elle. You know that. I need this. Need you."

"You have me. I'm already yours."

"I need marriage vows. Need to know you're not going anywhere."

"Will, it's just that—" I couldn't breathe. Couldn't push out the words.

He wasn't interested in my opposition. Before I said another word, he gripped the back of my head and kissed me hard. "You and me . . . there's nothing else to it. My life, all that I have, it means nothing without you." He took my mouth again but with tenderness and devotion this time. His lips were intoxicating velvet, and when he kissed me that way, when he spoke in that soft tone, it was easy to forget my senses and forgive his offenses. I lost myself, moaning against his mouth as he growled into mine.

Then he pushed his hand into a pocket and pulled out the most beautiful ring I'd ever seen. He held it to his chest between us.

The ring was sophisticated, timeless. It had graduating pavé-set diamonds on the face and sides of a platinum band that led to a diamond halo of fourteen brilliant solitaires surrounding the center stone—a grand, fiery ruby. The ruby was a large cushion-cut gemstone, and the light that flashed from its crown reminded me of his passion when he made love to me.

William Hastings didn't get down on his knee or recite a practiced speech. Instead, he remained true to form—one of the many things I loved about him—and exhaled a sharp command. "Marry me."

My pulse raced. Fear driven by the unknown is the worst fear of all, and in my twenty-seven years, a marriage never existed in my home—it was my unknown. I opened and then closed my suddenly dry mouth.

For me, there had never been any husband-and-wife role models, no leading examples. I lost my parents when I was two, and my grandfather passed before that. Isobel's husband, David, left her after three short months. I'd held my pregnant, crying sister night after night when she could no longer bear the pain on her own. She cursed the institution and blamed it for his leaving. She and her long-time boyfriend married soon after they learned she was pregnant, but they never moved into the same home. The marriage was annulled.

He must have learned or suspected Lissie wasn't his child.

What if it changed us? What if it ruined what we had? I couldn't lose Will to a piece of paper. There was no way I could live without him.

I lowered my eyes.

From the moment we'd come together, Will had excelled at recognizing my internal battles. This time was no different, yet it was. It was the first time one of my emotional struggles hurt him. We both wiped at the tears streaking down my face.

I wanted to tell him I was scared. I wanted to tell him how I loved him, and how I couldn't live without him. That there would never be anyone for me but him. There was never anyone before him. But my head wouldn't allow me to say the words.

I should have looked at him, let him see into my soul, my heart, but something inside kept me from meeting his eyes, and I hurt him more.

"You'll wear this when you're ready, baby." He made sure I was watching as he placed it on the mantle. Then he headed for the gym without another word.

I leaned against the door and listened to his footsteps as they moved farther away. When I could no longer hear them, my gut wrenched and the emotion hurled itself from my soul. I fell to my knees and found myself recalling the pain I'd felt when I found Gran and Isobel lying on the floor in a pool of blood. This pain was different. It was worse.

According to my heart, hurting Will was a sin. It writhed in my chest and ripped itself to pieces to punish me. I wound my arms around myself in a foolish attempt to minimize the damage. I couldn't pull myself up from the floor, not even when Lissie's voice called out to me from the other side of the door.

"Aunt Ellie, you there? Thomas sent me. Can I come in?"

I couldn't let her in. I reasoned that since she now had the love and support of a strong family, it was okay if I pretended not to hear her. Thomas, John, or Mary would comfort her and keep her away from Will.

"Uncle Will looks really mad. Is he mad at you?"

Too late, damn it. When I opened the door, Lissie rushed in and hugged my waist.

"He's fine," I lied. "Everything is fine. You know how hard the men train. Will has a lot on his mind right now, that's all."

She regarded me with perceptive Hastings eyes. "Then why are you crying?"

Caught in my own web, I wiped my face on my sleeve and pulled her out the door. "Come on, girlie. Let's go find something to do in this castle of yours." We walked hand in hand down the corridor as one more ragged breath stung inside my chest. I released it. "Let's stop by the kitchen and ask Mrs. Bates if we can have pizza for dinner tonight."

"Yay!" she squealed, skipping along.

Mrs. Bates created a clever table in the dining room for the kids, crammed with handmade pizzas and iced wine chillers filled with bottles of different flavored sodas. Curled balloon strings dangled above our heads. Housekeeper or not, the overbearing Irish woman was part of the family, and she loved to make everyone happy.

Mary and I watched Lissie and John teach Chelsea how to eat pizza à la American. Their laughter floated through the air like a beautiful melody. It was impossible not to laugh with them.

Will was huddled in serious conversation with Thomas and Ben when I noticed him outside the dining room. It was obvious by the severe expressions on their faces they were headed for the war room.

Assassins were getting closer, coming for me—we were running out of time.

"Hold up a minute," Thomas said. He popped in and grabbed one of the pizzas still warming on the buffet, playfully reproaching his mother with a kiss on the cheek. "Where was all this when I was growing up, Mum?"

Her twinkling eyes gave her away. She was charmed by her son's attention. "Things have changed, yes, but I love you no less, Thomas."

Will's hot stare burned into me from the hall. I uncrossed one leg and crossed the other and then drew circles on my plate with a fork. I was afraid to look at him, afraid to see what I'd done.

Thomas sat down at the table across from me and made a low whistling sound to catch my attention. His mouth full of pizza, he encouraged me to go to Will with the tilt of his head. After he swallowed and smiled, I noticed the fresh bruise on his cheekbone.

I slid my chair from the table and went to Will.

Will stepped away from the dining room and offered his hand. The capacious tattoo lurched forward and caused my heart to twist and punish me again. Even after what I'd done, he was reaching out for me, still wanted me. The dagger bearing my name continued to call out until I placed my hand there and stepped into his space. My eyes remained on the floor. I felt like an ungrateful child who deserved a spanking.

Will lifted my chin and studied my eyes. "Christ. You've been crying."

I closed them. Couldn't bear the contact.

He pressed a gentle kiss to my forehead and then moved it to my lips. "Don't do that, baby. I can't take it when you cry."

I wanted more. More of him would make everything right again. I opened my eyes and met his stare, prepared to accept responsibility for what I'd done. I searched for his pain but couldn't find it. I searched for anger but didn't find that either. His eyes were flawless, invincible. My stomach rolled then—Thomas wore my punishment on his face.

"You should go in and enjoy your family," I whispered like a damned coward.

He shook his head, frowning as though I'd said something absurd. "I'll see you upstairs later. Carry only what you need for the night from your old room. I'll have the rest moved to our suite tomorrow." He let go of my chin and headed for his war room.

I twisted my hair into a messy bun and stepped into the shower after moving some of my things. The rich fragrance of the soap reminded me of the dozens of English roses Will had placed in our new bedroom.

Steaming water sluiced down my front when he slipped in behind me and pressed his hard body against mine. Breath rushed from my lungs, and my head dropped to his shoulder. We'd make love, and everything else would fade away.

My skin tingled in the wake of the delicate, stirring kisses he placed behind my ear, on my neck, and over my shoulder. His hands caressed every other part of me. My blood heated as he pressed his rigid length along my spine. "Need you," he breathed against the back of my neck before pulling my mouth around to his. Every touch, every kiss was deliberate and gentle.

I turned in his arms and met his eyes. As warm water rained over our bodies, a small voice whispered inside my head, encouraging me to give him what he needed. Marry him.

"Time is yours. I won't push. Whatever you want, Elle."

"What do you mean?"

"I told you—I'll deny you nothing." He paused for a moment, and his eyes dropped. "I'll wait as long as you need. Just tell me your hesitation isn't because you doubt me."

My heart punished me once more for the pain and confusion he was suffering. It thrashed inside my chest, forcing me to face the truth. It took a moment for me to push past the thickness of my throat. Then I pulled his eyes back to mine. "Will, I love you. There's no one I trust more. No one I believe in more. You're it for me. Always."

He stared deep into my eyes and explored my truth, and when he was satisfied, he leaned in and smiled against my lips. "I know you're scared. And I know you enjoy giving me shit, too. You drive me mad, woman." Smiling wide, he pounded off the water with the side of his fist.

I pulled the pins from my hair and released my long layers—something he always anticipated—then wound my arms around his neck. "You'd never be happy with a woman who didn't."

"You're it for me," Will tossed back, sweeping me into his arms. I kissed the bandage on his injured shoulder, and he carried me from the shower to our bed where our wet bodies fell into the sheets as one. His kiss was fierce but delicate, his passion bursting yet reserved.

When I reached between our bodies for him, he captured my wrists. "Don't push me tonight, witch." Then he buried his face in my neck and kissed my butterfly. "Not tonight." From that moment, his movements were slow and full of emotion. He spoke softer. His white-hot eyes were tempered by devotion as they lingered in mine and on my body. It seemed as if he were trying to capture and immortalize our time, like he was creating a photograph in his mind.

As he filled me, everything from that day burned to ashes, and we became whole once more. The love we shared was an obsession for each of us, it had no equal, and it was greater than my fear. I would wear his ring. And I would marry him. I would tell him before we left our bed.

My tender warrior wrapped me in his strength and made love to me again before we drifted to sleep. Our limbs were tangled, and my hair was fanned over his chest when we were dragged from a blissful slumber a few hours later.

Thomas beat at the door and shouted with urgency for his brother.

Twenty

"Will, goddamn it, get up now! Armed men are on property," Thomas shouted through the outer door of our suite as he pounded on it with his fists.

Before I could sort out in my sleepy brain what was happening, Will had already shoved into jeans and sprinted to meet Thomas at the door.

"How many?"

Thomas followed him into the closet. "At least eight, all armed. Sitting low at the north border. Don't know we've spotted them. Protocol's been implemented. Ben and the men who are here headed for the weapons room. The others will roll in within minutes. Hoping they won't be engaged as they come up the ridge—they're unarmed."

"*Fuck*. Prepare one of your drones so we can see from above. Send it up when we're ready to go out. Arm John and put him on the monitors with comms. Lock him in. Move it," Will commanded as he strapped a double chest holster across the width of his broad back and inserted two daggers. Before he turned to me, he fastened the holster strap across the butt of the Glock at his hip.

I stood behind him, trembling. I wore nothing more than the sheet from our bed.

"Elle, you must be quick. Get dressed and get your phone. I'll take you downstairs." He pocketed his own phone and grabbed another gun, tucking it into his waistband.

I wasn't moving, couldn't. . . . My body was cold with fear.

"You must move, Elle."

The time had arrived—our enemy had come. We were under siege. My mind was stuck, though my feet carried my frigid body to that posh dressing room, where I pulled on jeans and a bra. Will was there beside me within seconds.

"If the power is cut, a secured generator will support the important functions of the house. You will be safe." He pulled a sweater over my head and helped me slip into shoes.

There was no time for questions, no time to make sense of what was happening. I recognized the life-and-death urgency in his tone, and I knew it was assassins of the Order he was going out to fight. That had to be enough until he came back.

All that mattered was that he came back.

Will pulled me down the corridor and guided me to the basement training center. We entered the weapons room where the men were gathered, and then he pushed through a wall panel that led into an alcove housing a steel door. He pressed his palm to the electronic pad. A mechanical gear turned and clicked as though he'd unlocked a bank vault. The door hummed opened. One of his arms was locked around my waist, and the other held the door as he peered inside to take a head count.

Mrs. Bates held Chelsea. The little one slept soundly inside a bundle of blankets, wrapped in Mrs. Bates's strong arms. Mary sat engulfing a quiet but alert Lissie. She looked up from Lissie and pleaded with Will, using nothing more than her youngest son's name. Her eyes filled with tears.

"I need John's help with communications. He'll be in a secure room where no harm will come to him. I'll send him to you as soon as I can," Will told her before pulling the door shut. Then he pressed my back to the wall and kissed me.

Ben extended his arm into the alcove and handed Will my pistol.

"You won't need it, baby. Still, I won't leave you unarmed." He kept me pinned against the wall with his body as he ejected and inspected the magazine and reinserted it. "It's loaded—ten rounds—do you remember what I taught you? Do you remember how to chamber the first round by racking the slide? No chambering unless you feel threatened."

I nodded.

My heart thumped so hard I thought it might explode from my chest. Anxiety wrecked my stomach. Silent screams filled with terror banged around in my head.

"No one leaves this room. Allow no one other than a Hastings to enter. You'll see on the monitor next to the door who's on this side. If you can't see, do not open the door."

Outside the alcove, magazines clicked into place. Slides screeched over metal. Red laser beams bounced off walls. The voices of soldiers preparing for battle rumbled.

"Will?" I whispered.

"Do you understand what I've said?"

"Yes, but—"

He became an intense storm. "You must do exactly as I say, god-damn it!"

"Okay," I snapped.

"Nothing else matters right now, Elle." He placed the gun in my hand.

He was wrong. One thing mattered. And in that moment, to me, because he was heading out into what I could only imagine was like a war zone, it mattered more than anything. There was no way I'd allow him to fight before I could tell him what he needed to know—I wanted to marry him. I pulled the ruby ring from my pocket and placed it in the palm of his hand.

"Put it on my finger," I demanded.

"You're sure?" Hopeful eyes locked into mine, and everything else fell away.

"My answer is yes. I'll marry you. I want to wear your ring."

"When did you—"

"When you were inside me. I needed us to burn away my fear together, and we did."

Will shook his head and smiled. "Christ, you're a handful sometimes." Then he slipped the sparkling ruby onto my finger and kissed it. "I love you. No matter the circumstances, never forget that. You're the center of my world. You're everything," he breathed against my lips. He held his mouth there against mine as his hand moved to the electronic pad.

Before I could respond, tell him I loved him, he launched me into the safe room and pulled the door shut. I stumbled from the force and caught myself on a chair.

Lissie raced to me. She threw herself against my body with enough energy to knock me off balance again. We fell back against the door. I wrapped one arm around her and extended the other out to the side so Mary could take the gun from my hand.

Lissie was quiet until the moment she'd collided with me. While I held her, I wondered if she remembered her time in the secret room back in Stonington, when we lost Isobel and Gran. I wondered if she thought about our former life in Connecticut.

She'd fallen fast and hard for our new life and new family. She loved Will and his brothers, and they loved her. He was the closest thing to a father she'd ever had. Mary was already her grannie, and the connection they shared was remarkable. Though we had no legal proof she was Ethan's, it was hard to believe otherwise. Her turbulent Hastings eyes were undeniable, and she'd inherited not only his eyes, but also Ethan's warmth and sense of adventure. To have this family ripped away from her would devastate her still-healing soul.

I kissed the top of Lissie's head and held her tight while she hid her crying face in my sweater. "Your uncles will be back. I promise."

We finally moved from the door after she pulled my hands to her chest and found the ostentatious ring on my finger. She lifted her face and hit me with those eyes. "You're gonna get married . . . to Uncle Will?"

"Yes." I tucked a finger under her chin and caressed that tiny dimple beneath my thumb.

Her eyes sparkled.

"See? He must come back soon."

Anxiety won. Once Lissie settled on the sofa with Mary again, I locked myself in the bathroom and vomited. I went into that tiny bathroom and retched three different times.

We saw nothing. We heard nothing. We knew nothing until John came to the safe room more than two hours later. I ran to the door and crashed into him as he came through.

"It's okay—everyone is safe. The estate is secure." He held my arm even after he'd steadied me. He looked at Mary. "Thomas is inside, Mum, and he's fine. Everyone is fine."

"Where's Will?"

John gave his mother a slight nod and avoided my question.

"John?" I snapped.

"He's not hurt, Ellie. He was amazing—I could see him on camera. Thomas is right. Our brother is a beast. Thom is awesome, too. There were nine. Two got away."

I swallowed the acid that crept up my esophagus once more. My knees weakened so I clung harder to John's arm. Seven more dead—a fast-growing burden for Will to carry. But there was something else. "What are you not saying? Has he gone after them?"

John lowered his eyes and nodded.

I tore out of the room and darted up the stairs, taking two at a time until I reached ground level. I burst into the hall shouting for

Will. Eight men were there removing weapons from their bodies and toweling sweat and weather from their faces.

Will was not there.

I clutched the front of Thomas's rain- and blood-soaked shirt. "Thomas, go after him. Please!" I begged him, clawing at his chest.

Thomas handed his gun to Ben and pushed me back. "Someone give me a clean shirt." He was tugging the one he wore over his head while grappling with my mauling hands.

"Find him. . . . Go with him," I pleaded, my nails sinking into his bared flesh.

"Stop it, Ellie," he said low in my ear. Then Thomas wrapped his arms around me and hauled me into the war room, turning me loose once the door closed behind us. He pulled on a T-shirt that was too small for him, his massive size second only to Will's.

Anger leached into my veins, and I charged at him. "Where is he?" Thomas retreated, and I dogged him step for step around the conference table. "Tell me!"

Finally, he pushed his hands against my shoulders to keep me at arm's length, but that wasn't what stopped me. What caused me to stop dead in my tracks was how he stared at me with Will's eyes. John and Lissie had those eyes, too, as had Ethan. But there was something about Thomas that made his even more like Will's, and it frightened me on a level I didn't understand.

I crumbled onto the conference table and sobbed. He gave me a moment before gathering my boneless body from the tabletop and locking me in his arms.

"Is he hurt?"

"Jesus, you have a fucking temper."

"Thomas," I warned, my wet face buried in his shoulder.

"Not a scratch. He went after the two we lost. He'll track them and kill them, and he'll not come back until it's done. I need you to stop crying."

"Why is he alone?"

"He ordered everyone to stay with you."

It was my fault Will was out there alone. I broke again, clutching Thomas harder. Sobs overwhelmed me and caused my body and breath to shudder. Each skipped with unpredictability and without control over their respective natural rhythms. I was a mess.

Cursing beneath his breath, Thomas pressed me harder against his chest and waited for me to finish my ugly cry. He stroked my hair and pressed his cheek to my head.

"T-Thomas . . . go. . . . He's alone." I begged him to find his brother. *"Please."* There was no way to stop Will. The only thing I could do was get someone out there to fight with him.

"I can't leave you," he whispered. "If he's not here, I must be. You know that. You'll never be without one of us again. You'll never be alone again, Ellie."

I nodded against his chest, summoning strength, working to pull myself together. I lifted my head and allowed my hands to drop to his forearms. "Tell me what's going on. You must see how keeping things from me only makes the situation worse."

He jerked his arms away, and after pausing as if he needed to gather his thoughts, he handed me a towel. "He was already going. The Greens fell in with Jack Lewis. They were the informants Uncle Robert was tracking. We found only two of the three the night we went after them—Charles ran, leaving his brothers to die. Yesterday, we received intel indicating he and Lewis were working on a plan to draw you out. Will believes what he's doing is the best way to keep you safe."

I wiped my nose on the towel. "He planned to leave?"

"Yes. He's been torn up over this, Ellie. He allowed them into our home, gave them money."

Hot tears pooled in my eyes again.

"Stop it, we're not doing this again—he hasn't left you. He's on a mission, and you must think of it that way." Thomas grabbed my left hand and stared at the ring. The ruby and its diamonds twinkled beneath the florescent lighting. "You know who he is and what he must do."

I lowered my eyes to the ruby. Thomas was right. No one was stronger or more intelligent and determined than Will. "I'm sorry. I had no right to—"

"Don't apologize to me. Not ever. We take care of what's ours."

I sniffled and wiped at the last tears. "You sound like your brother."

He opened the door and waited for me to pass through, and as I did, he winked. "Yeah . . . but I'm better looking."

Will didn't answer his phone when I called again for the tenth time, and I didn't leave a message again. Voicemail messages were useless. Will never listened to them. I had gone up to rest, but without Will, not knowing where he was or when he was coming home, there was no way I could sleep. His scent still clung to the sheets, so I'd lie there if for no other reason.

I dropped my phone onto his pillow and stared at it, pushing the home button compulsively. The dazzling ruby and its bright halo caught my attention and sent me back to the moment I'd decided to wear the ring. I was cocooned in Will's arms, protected from the world by his power. He was moving inside me, filling me with his body while his possessive whispers filled my soul. "You're mine, my angel, and I'll love you until my last breath."

I flopped onto my back and held up my hand in a ray of golden sunlight, admiring my heavy engagement ring. It was more extravagant than the bracelet. I twisted the ring from side to side and watched the brilliant crown sparkle. The band was loose, so I slipped it from my finger and looked inside to see where the jeweler might cut for sizing.

I froze. There was an inscription.

Until my last breath. W

The script was elegant and poetic, flowing with grace, its romance transforming the W into butterfly wings. My fingers fell to my neck. I remembered what he'd said about my birthmark just before placing his first, sweet kiss on my lips, and realized his eyes had shown him a W, not a butterfly. I slipped the ring back on and covered my heart with both hands, locking the memory safe inside.

An aching lump continued to swell at the back of my throat.

Those four words were one more demonstration of his undeniable commitment. They showed me there was a decision to be made. Would I continue crying—God, I'd cried so much—or get out of bed and become the woman he deserved? I would never be his equal, but I could be his partner.

Will never left me. I'd abandoned him, left him alone in our fight. I could stay out of his war room if it eased his conscience, but could no longer add to his burden by remaining ignorant and passive. "Never again," I told the ruby. "I'll never do that to him again."

I swallowed the fat lump in my throat and got my ass out of bed.

On my way downstairs after a hot shower, I bumped into Mary in the corridor. She reached for my hand as we walked toward the staircase. "I spoke with Thomas."

I tried to think of something to derail the conversation but came up short.

"Who we are and where this life takes us, well, it never gets easier. There's nothing we can do to stop the madness when it finds us. But there are two things I know for certain, dear. William has the strongest mind and heart this family has seen in generations. And he will fight his way back to you. Nothing will stand in his way."

"He will. I believe that, too."

"Richard would have taken such delight in how you handle his son. You're very forgiving, Ellie. You soften him in all the right places." She pulled me to a stop, her honey eyes glistening. "Even as a boy, he'd make something worse before turning it into something better. It's the way of a lionhearted man. He'll endure more, but he'll accomplish a great deal more. His brother was the opposite. If something wasn't laid out perfectly before him, he'd give it up."

The way he'd given up Isobel.

"I miss Ethan terribly. Ah, but he and your sister left us something quite special."

"You know?"

"I do. Come with me."

We went to her room at the end of the south corridor wing where she removed a sealed envelope from a safe in the wall and handed it to me. "Open it, Ellie."

"Are you sure?"

"The solicitor wouldn't have given it to me if it were bad news. I imagine there's an unopened copy of the same lying around William's business office. Go on, open it."

I opened the envelope and found the results of Lissie's paternity. Ethan's signature appeared on the consent form—he'd initiated the test when we were in London. I skimmed through the pages explaining methodology and settled on the analysis conclusion. It was a bittersweet moment, a win and a loss at once.

Ethan died before knowing beyond any shadow of doubt that Lissie was his daughter.

Mary reached for my hand. "When shall we tell her?"

"Will should be here. I'd like him close when she learns the truth."

Lissie would need him. Will could give her the kind of strength and love she deserved. He would ease her broken heart with his tenderness and show her it could be mended again. Hers would have so many stitches before she turned eight years old.

"How long have the two of you known, dear?"

"We suspected. Will thought so from the moment he first saw her. Ethan agreed and planned to tell her. He wanted to be her father. She's never had that, and now . . ." I steeled myself against an intense wave of sorrow.

"I promise you he would have loved her well. And now . . . it's our job."

I nodded.

"Whatever you need, Ellie. Nothing would make me happier than to help raise my granddaughter. I can take on as much as you'll allow. We both know my son will remain possessive after the two of you marry. Speaking of the marriage . . ."

I squeezed my eyes shut tight and tried to block the crashing of my heartbeat inside my head. I could no longer hear the words of my soon-to-be mother-in-law—she'd freaked me out. The only person I'd ever had serious, life-changing conversations with was Will. I didn't know how to do it with anyone else.

She patted my arm and smiled. "Too much, too fast. It'll keep. But before we go down, there's one more thing." She pulled a wooden box from the safe. "This is an authentic piece from your line. Richard's mother came upon it somehow." Mary opened the box and displayed the treasure nestled in its blue velvet lining. It was a delicate tiara encrusted with shimmering diamonds and shining sapphires. It was enchanting. Seeing it, knowing it was something my ancestral grandmothers wore rendered me speechless.

"Most heirlooms were left behind for fear they might lead to your family's identity. When it's safe, we'll hunt down as many as we can. Wear this one when you become my daughter." She locked her kind eyes into mine, and as only a mother could do, she threw my words back at me. "See? He must come back soon."

Then she put her arm around my shoulders and steered me to the door, and just before she released me, she whispered in my ear, "It was I who sent him. I knew he loved you, and it was time for you to save him from what he was becoming."

Twenty-One

HE CAME AT me again, and I threw him to the floor. John and I had worked hard on different takedown techniques every day after Will left but without much luck. The seventh lesson and the turning technique did the trick. I finally got it.

That's what I did when Will left me—trained on the mats with John. I enjoyed the time we spent together, and the youngest Hastings was more than happy to demonstrate his "mad skills." Will couldn't stand to watch, so I never trained when he was home. Thomas also refused to watch. He'd left the gym when we came in. And since Will required either Thomas or Ben to supervise, Ben was stuck with the job.

John shot up from the mat. "Well done, Ellie. That's the one then. You're too delicate for the other takedowns."

I threw him down again. "Don't call me delicate, damn it."

"Well done, indeed." Ben pulled John to his feet and then gestured for me to submit my hands. He unraveled and started to rewrap. "These must remain snug if they're to prevent damage. And he's right—you are delicate. You're supposed to be. Shouldn't be fighting." It was as close as Ben came to affection. He never smiled at anyone other than Chelsea. I'd heard him laugh a time or two, but only after he and Will drank a lot.

"What if I'm attacked and no one is around?"

He rolled his eyes. "You'll never be without protection, and you know it. He's built an army round you."

It was my turn to roll my eyes. "Have either of you heard from him today?" I asked everyone, every day, several times a day. They hated it, but I didn't care—until I heard from Will, I would keep asking. Will instructed them to keep their mouths shut around me, and they never broke command, not even when my temper spiked.

"No," they said at the same time.

"Where is Thomas?" Thomas was most like Will and feared him the least—two reasons it was easier to manipulate him.

"Looking at the monitors," John said.

"Don't push him," Ben warned.

"I need to talk to Will. Why can't any of you get that? It's not like I can reach through the phone and drag him back by the ear."

"Can't you?"

I squared my shoulders. "You're right. I want him to come home."

"Exactly. He'll say no once, maybe twice. You'll plead with him, and he'll give you what you want, because no never means no when he says it to you. If he comes back before he finishes the job, you'll be at greater risk and he'll be distracted. One of you will die. So let him do what he needs to do for fuck's sake." He walked away, his gait smooth as a panther.

I'd just experienced Ben's shut-the-fuck-up kiss.

He was right. I needed to be an extension of Will's strength, not a distraction. Thomas would trust me to help if he knew that was what I wanted. I headed to the war room, stopping outside the door to pull my thoughts together. There had to be something I could do to help keep Will safe. Resolved, I pressed my palm to the pad and a slight gust hit my face as the door whooshed open.

Thomas's back was to the door as he stared at the monitors and spoke into his phone. "I'm quite serious. I can't take the fighting. I don't want her doing it on my watch." He paused, listening. "We're agreed then—it stops today?"

I covered my gaping mouth. It was Will. I ran at Thomas. "Give me the phone!" He leaped onto the table and continued listening into the phone. My legs weakened. I put a hand out, reaching for the wall.

Oh, God. What if he refused to talk to me?

Thomas shook his head. "Don't you do it. . . . Christ, Ellie. Yeah, she's about to—" Will's interjecting curses were loud enough for me to hear. Thomas jumped down and handed me the phone.

"Will. I miss you. Please say you're coming home now."

"*Elle.*" The sound of his voice crashed into me. I closed my eyes and clung to the way he said my name. "I'm not finished but soon, baby."

"If you can't come home yet, let me come to you."

"You will stay there."

"I can't bear another day."

"You can and you will."

I needed to get someone out there with him. "Send for Ben. Let him do this with you."

"I want him there to protect you."

"I have Thomas and the Six. I don't need them all."

"Baby, listen carefully—"

"Send for him, Will. I need to know you're not alone. I need this from you. You must give it to me. I'll accept nothing less."

He was quiet in thought for a moment. I could hear his breath and ached to feel it against my skin. I stifled a moan.

"I'll send for him. Promise me you'll settle down and wait for me to come home."

"Promise you'll come home."

"I swear."

"You must send for him without delay. And call me every night."

"You've become quite the negotiator, baby." There was a smile in his voice. "Thomas will give you another phone. When I can, I'll ring you on that one."

"I need you to get this done quickly—with Ben at your side—and come home to me."

"Yes. You'll stay put."

"Okay," I breathed into the phone. "Okay. How is your shoulder?"

"Shoulder's fine. Healed. Need to disconnect for now. I love you." He hung up.

I hugged the phone to my heart.

"All right?" Thomas asked softly.

"Fine. You heard?"

"I did." He smiled and held out his hand for the phone.

Will always kept his word. If he promised me something, he would make it happen. I wanted to be near Ben when he received Will's instructions, so I tugged on Thomas's arm and we headed back down to the training center. The men would be secretive about location and details, but I'd have the satisfaction of knowing Will was no longer fighting out there alone, wherever he was.

When we found Ben, he'd just ended the call. He unmasked a rare smile and bowed his head. "Well done, Ellie. Well done."

I leaped at him with a hug. "Bring him home to me safe and fast."

Ben and Thomas walked toward the weapons room with heads together and voices low, discussing the new plan. Thomas glanced back over his shoulder and smiled before the door slid shut behind them. He was as relieved as I was.

Ben left within the hour.

I fell asleep early that night staring at the burner phone Thomas had given me. I had only pleasant dreams, sleeping for five consecutive hours in our big bed, wrapped in sheets that still held Will's scent. I might have slept longer had I not received a frantic call from Jess at two-fifteen in the morning.

—

Jess shouted into the phone. "Ellie! Are you okay?" Panic and confusion were woven into her words. Loud music and mixed conversations boomed in the background. She was at Nick's.

"Jess, what's wrong?"

"Where are you? Wait, I'm going to step outside. Hold on—"

"What's going on? Talk to me."

"Are you okay? Are you still in England?"

"I'm at Eastridge, yes, and I'm fine. What's happened?"

"I don't know what's going on, but something's not right. I don't know how to explain it, but it just doesn't feel right. Tell me Will's there with you."

"I can't. He's not. Everything was okay when we last talked, but now you're scaring me. What is it—what's wrong?"

"Listen. Detective Parker is here. He never comes in. He showed me your picture and asked if I knew where to find you. He's definitely searching for you, but I think the case was closed, so it doesn't make sense for the police to be looking again. And I know Josh knows where you are."

"It makes absolutely no sense. Will spoke with Josh not long ago. I've been cleared."

"I went heavy on Parker's drinks, but he still wouldn't give up anything. Maybe they found something else, some new evidence." She hesitated and lowered her voice to a whisper. "And there's more."

"What is it?"

"Hold on a minute. Parker's leaving."

"Do not hang up, Jess."

"He's gone. So the guys from McFarland's year-round fishing crew were in earlier. That's what they do now when there's no work. Come here and drink all day. Anyway, they were talking about Will. I asked why, you know, since he's been gone for a while. Ellie, they told me he's here. Said they've seen him twice."

My breath hitched and every muscle in my body locked down.

"You okay?"

"I'm coming back, Jess. If Will's there . . . I'll get a flight and call you with the info as soon as I get to the airport. Don't say anything to anyone. Do not tell anyone you talked to me or that I'm on my way. Promise me."

"What's going on? Tell me!"

"I'm not sure. But promise me, Jess. I need your help. I'll explain when I call back."

"Okay. I'm here for you." Her voice broke. "I promise."

"Go straight home. Don't speak to anyone. I'll call you soon." I hung up before she could ask any more questions and leaped out of bed, running to my dressing room to throw some things into an overnight bag. I jerked a sweater from the shelf and jammed my bare feet into jeans.

Somehow going back to where it all began felt like a means to the end of a horrific nightmare—it was closure. And though I couldn't discern what or how, I sensed the coming retribution I had longed for. Will would understand. He'd be angry at first, but then he'd get it and forgive me. But it wasn't just about retribution and closure, and it would've been foolish to think so. I needed to see him, needed to feel him. I would do whatever it took to reach him.

My chest was tight and breathing difficult. Anxiety ripped through my blood and bones. Still, nothing could have stopped me. "Calm down. Focus." I paced our suite from room to room and hugged my clenching stomach. I had to get out of the house without being seen on the monitors. Thomas would never allow me to leave. He'd lock me up and call Will. I had to be on a plane to the United States before anyone realized I was no longer at Eastridge.

After digging through my Stella McCartney bag for an old credit card, I dialed the airline and reserved a seat to Hartford. If everything went well, I'd arrive in Stonington in thirteen or fourteen hours, which seemed like forever. Will's methods were so much more convenient.

There was one more thing I needed to do before leaving. Traitorous floorboards creaked as I crept through the corridor and slid a note under Thomas's bedroom door. The moment I spun on my toes, his sheets rustled. I froze. His feet hit the floor.

I closed my eyes, remained motionless. Could he hear the fierce hammering of my heart?

When his bathroom door banged into the wall, I ran down the corridor and stopped only when I reached the master suite. I waited. Listened. Prayed he hadn't yet stumbled upon the note.

Thomas never pursued me, so I grabbed my things and headed out. The taxi would arrive soon, and I had to make it to the road before anyone noticed. One of the Six was on guard near the front entrance. As soon as he turned his back, I slipped out of my shoes and stayed close to the wall as I crept through the darkness of the great hall to the kitchen.

I'd leave through the service entrance.

Damn it. Mrs. Bates was up. The back hem of her flowery house-coat disappeared into one of the pantries. Moments later, her slip-pered feet shuffled from the pantry to the rear staircase. I released my breath. She hadn't sensed my presence.

Once I'd made it outside, I avoided lit areas by ducking into the shadows and crawling behind trees and shrubs. A branch whipped against my thigh, slashing through my jeans and flesh. I covered my mouth and muffled a sharp cry.

When the lights of the house were no longer visible, I straight-ened and stumbled over the terrain. The scurrying of nocturnal creatures and rustling of tree leaves set my nerves on edge. Startled, I lost my footing and slid on the softness of the downward-sloping ridge several times.

Intense burning traveled from the fatigued muscles in my legs to my chest, where my heart alternated between hesitation and wild fluttering. Finally, the road appeared.

The driver was waiting as expected when I emerged from the dark landscape.

Incapacitating anxiety and the selfish, unrelenting ache in my soul for Will competed until I passed out from the meds and slept through the flight back to the States. His phantom scent, replaying the sound of his raspy voice in my head, and the image of me throwing myself into his arms were all that had kept me going.

The flight attendant's soft fingers gripped my arm. *"Mademoiselle, c'est l'heure. Les roues sont en baisse*—the wheels are down." She smiled with compassion and handed me a bottle of water.

"Merci."

When the captain announced our timely arrival into Hartford, I turned on my phone and jumped out of the seat. My head spun and knees buckled. I pushed a deep breath through my nose and gripped the seat in front of me. Another deep inhale, exhale. I was too close to Will to let go.

There were dozens of missed calls from Thomas and Jess, and missed calls from a blocked number, which must have been one of Will's burners. I tapped Jess's name first and prayed for her to answer right away.

"Ells, thank God. Where are you?"

"Just landed. Are you close?"

"Yes, I'm here. I'll meet you at the gate. But I'm warning you— there're a lot of people looking for you, including Will."

"You spoke to him?"

"No. I haven't taken any of their calls. But I was getting worried, and—"

"Jess, you know I'm fine. Don't take the calls. I need to think about how I'll handle this. Have you learned anything new?"

"Ben said in his message he's with Will, and if I see you, I should be sure to tell you so you didn't do anything else stupid. Detective Parker was at your house this morning."

"We're deplaning now. I'll see you at the gate."

I'd made a mess of things, and I wasn't sure what, if anything, could be done to clean it up. Everyone was angry with me, but at some point, they needed to realize I had no choice. I had to touch Will, had to feel him touching me to know I hadn't lost him. It was a desperate desire, and there was no rationalization.

I called Thomas next.

"Where the hell are you?" he shouted into the phone.

"Everything is fine. Calm down."

"No, nothing is fine, Ellie. Do you know what you've done? Not only have you put yourself in serious danger—running off without anyone to protect you, but you've also put me in a very bad place with my brother. He'll kill me for this, and he should. If anything happens to you—"

"I'm sorry. There's nothing I can say to make you understand. I'll handle Will."

"Where are you? Give me your location, and I'll come and get you. We can still fix this. Tell me where to find you. Please, Ellie."

"It's too late. I'll see him soon."

"Christ. You found him. Why didn't you just tell me?"

"You mean you didn't know?"

"No! He was sure you'd get it from me."

"Just landed in Connecticut. I'll call you again soon." I hung up.

Jess waited at the gate and caught me when I crumpled. She shouldered my weight as we made our way from the terminal to her car. "Come on, Ells. Let's get you out of here. I won't lecture you until you feel better." As she merged onto the southbound highway for Stonington, I dropped my face between my legs and retched with punishing force.

Jess patted me on the back. "We'll figure this out. We'll find him."

Forty minutes into the ride, I leaned back against the seat and took a sip of water. "Do you still have your guns—and access to your father's?"

Ben stood over the bed and watched me wipe the sleep from my eyes. Jess had called him while I slept. "Welcome back, sleeping beauty."

The sickness was finally subsiding. My body was slow to fire, but my brain was beginning to function as it should. "How long have I been out?"

"She said it's been eleven hours." He tapped out a message into his phone.

"Are you texting Will? Why isn't he here?"

"He wanted to know the moment you woke. Why do you think he's not here?"

"What is he doing?"

"What do you think he's doing?"

"Damn it, Ben. Stop answering my questions with questions."

"Just tell her what's going on. Do you know her at all? Look what she's done. Tell her or I will," Jess said.

Ben glared at me. "Jesus Christ, Ellie. You should be back in England. Do you know what you've done?"

I rubbed my temples. "Save the lecture. I've heard enough already. Where is Will and what's going on? You're supposed to be with him so he's not alone."

"That's fucking rich coming from you. You flew across the Atlantic alone."

"Yes, I screwed up. It's done, and I'm here. Let's move on."

"Jack Lewis and Charles Green are here. They're looking for ways to draw you out. Searching your personal belongings, public records, looking for connections to something or someone. They came over as a faction of eight to start. Will picked off several before I arrived. He's watching them now—waiting for the right opportunity to present itself."

"Go back to him, Ben. I don't want him fighting alone."

"He ordered me here."

"When will I see him?"

"Gee, he's a little busy right now. Hunting assassins and all, you know?" His shifting demeanor between anger and insolence was aggravating. And it was unlike him.

"You don't have to be unkind. I'm worried about him." Tears pushed at my lids, but I was stronger. "I love him—more than anything. Put yourself in my position for a minute."

He spent several moments examining the carpet before moving his eyes back to mine. "I'm sorry. You don't deserve that. This isn't your fault. I'm worried, too. He's certifiably mad when it comes to you. And that's not your fault either. He doesn't want to lead them to you, that's the only reason he's maintaining distance."

I accepted his apology with a nod. "Give me a few minutes, and I'll come downstairs."

Rounding the corner into the kitchen after throwing on dirty clothes and pulling my hair into a ponytail, I was determined to take charge. I made a beeline for Ben. "No one knows Will better or how to anticipate the movement of these assassins like you do. Go back to him. Jess will cover me."

Ben straightened his back and raised his brows, but neither of them said a word.

It was time I partnered with Will and took control when it was necessary. Being managed by him was one thing, but no longer would I allow his men to push me around. Not even Ben. So long as my directives were sound, the guys needed to respect my wishes. Will's safety was as important as mine. I would assert my position of strength.

"I'm going back up to shower. Jess, show him your collection. Convince him of your skill. Will needs him in the field." I grabbed a bottle of water and headed for the stairs. "Tell him I'm safe and that I love him. I won't take no for an answer, Ben. Go to him."

I didn't wait for their responses or look back, though a smile hit my lips when I heard their footsteps moving toward her father's hunting room. My best friend teased Will's best friend as she unlocked the door. "He may be an earl, but theoretically, she out-ranks him."

After a long, hot shower, I found Jess alone, still in the hunting room.

Jessica Miller knew how to handle a weapon. In order to gain her father's attention, she learned to share his enthusiasm for shooting and hunting. Two of the five pairs of mounted antlers on the wall belonged to her.

"Ben's gone?"

"Yeah. Let's see what happens. He was concerned Will would send him back." She continued to load a compact pistol and a revolver. "He was out of line. Glad you set him straight. Will might give you a hard time, but no one else should."

"Will doesn't speak to me that way. And if I ask for something, he gives it to me. Don't get me wrong. He's moody, and he can be a prick. But then he goes to the gym and works it out."

One of her robust laughs burst from her gut. "Are you saying the Hulk has been pussy-whipped?"

I laughed at her laugh. "It's not that. God, no woman likes *that*. It's more of a mutual thing. You'll just have to wait and see."

"So . . ." She cocked her head and lifted a brow. "He taught you to shoot?"

"Yes, he did. Don't be upset with me. I need to know how to use a gun now. Still learning. I didn't have the need when you tried. You know that."

"I get it. Everything has changed. Ben said you have a Glock 26, gen four."

"Yes."

"That's illegal over there."

"I know. I don't carry it. He keeps it under lock and key in the weapons room."

"I can't believe what I'm hearing, but I like it. Try my Ruger. See how it feels." She handed me her pistol. "It has a manual safety, not auto like yours."

It was about the same size as mine. I tested the sight. "How's the recoil?"

"Not bad, but more than your Baby Glock."

"Jess, listen. This is—" My hand went to my forehead after putting down the gun.

"Whatever it is, Ells, just say it."

"I need you to understand how dangerous these men are. They can't be offered the benefit of doubt. They will kill me without hesitation." I drew a stuttering breath.

"There's more. You know you can say anything to me. . . . I can handle it. We don't judge, we protect, remember?"

What would she think of Will? Would she see him differently—as a murderer? "All the men involved have killed others. All of them. . . . On both sides."

She nodded. "Some kill, some must kill. If the alternative is losing you, I'll do it myself."

Twenty-Two

I stared out the window into the darkness. "Damn you, Will." He was out there somewhere. I could feel him. He hadn't called or texted, nor had Ben. There'd been no relevant calls broadcast over the Stonington police scanner. Nothing in the newspaper or on television. We listened to the county's live emergency audio feed, but heard nothing of consequence reported there. Jess even called her supervisor at the hospital to see if anyone was brought in with knife or gunshot wounds. Nothing.

After more than forty-eight hours, I'd had enough. Jess holstered her revolver at her hip, and we headed out into the evening to find my missing warrior. We'd argued—and she'd won—about me carrying one of her guns without a license.

Stonington's ominous night with its waxing gibbous moon was eerie and quiet. It didn't feel like it used to—quaint, safe. Everything *had* changed. If war lurked, it wouldn't be hard to find. Jess drove past my abandoned house, but didn't stop. I would never step foot inside that house again. It wasn't about cowardice. It was about moving forward with a new life and leaving the pain of the past behind.

"Goodbye," I whispered as she hit the gas.

"You're sure?"

"Quite."

"You're beginning to sound like the English."

I smiled. The comment would have pleased Will. He encouraged me to grab my English heritage by the bollocks, as he'd say, and become it.

"That's a huge rock you're wearing. You're sure about that, too?"

"I've never been more certain about anything. He's everything, Jess. We're connected on a level I'm not sure others can see, and there are no words to describe it."

"It hasn't been long."

"I know. Time's become extraneous. It feels like we've already shared a lifetime."

"You've been through a lot together. And now you sound like an artist again."

"I'm painting again."

She nodded, but kept her eyes focused ahead on the street.

My heart twisted. I hated how she still waded in that stupid blue plastic swimming pool, hoping for that one connection to surface each time she stepped in. She deserved more. I wanted her to find what I'd found with Will—an explosion of bliss, obsessive, wonderful, and complete.

We drove back through town, circled to make one last pass down Water Street, and headed for the town dock.

"Lissie misses you. And your superhero movie and pizza binges."

"I miss her, too. Will I see her again?"

"Come back with me and you will. She loves England. She'll be grown—and English—before long. She's picking up the dialect and accent fast from her uncles."

"Uncles . . . so it's true. You've confirmed it?"

"It's true. I read the paternity results myself."

"Really sucks that he's gone. How nice it would've been for her to finally have a father."

"We haven't told her yet, that Ethan was her father. I'm so glad she loves Will. You should see how she adores him, loves them all. And they love her. It was the right call, Jess. She has so much more now than I could've given her on my own. She's safe, loved, and she'll never want for anything."

"What would Will say, if I came back with you?"

"He won't deny me my best friend."

Jess parked in the first lighted area. We stood in the middle of the empty visitors' lot, searching through the night for movement and sound. Much of Stonington's pier was built along a peninsula of land covered in asphalt, referred to as the town dock. There were boat and cold storage units and seafood processing warehouses— most were rusting metal buildings; a cultural center used for the arts, meetings, and celebrations; and a historical lighthouse, though not *the* historical lighthouse. That was located on the east side of the harbor.

"Let's go. There's light out there." I longed to walk that pier one more time.

"You're okay with the exposure?"

"You've got my back, and I've seen you shoot, so I'm good. If you're really worried, you should have let me carry your pistol."

Jess narrowed her blue eyes.

"You do remember what Will looks like?"

"He's a bit hard to forget. I won't shoot him. Or Ben. Anyone else might be shot first, questioned later. If they live."

"Now you sound like Will."

"This is serious shit, Ells. I won't risk someone taking you from me."

I righted after stumbling on a warped plank. "Now you *really* sound like him."

"Then I like him already," she teased.

We'd reached *Neptune*'s dock. I dragged my fingertips along the port side of her fading emerald-green hull. I'd missed the old girl. I don't know what it was about her. I cared nothing for the rest of the fleet.

"Shhh. Listen." Jess's flaming hair billowed behind her. "Did you hear that?" She wrapped both hands around the grip of her revolver and held it low, ready.

I listened but heard nothing. Then my body seized up as it released adrenaline into my bloodstream. And there it was. The subtle cadence of boots on asphalt. Someone was following us. There was a sudden grating screech. One of the rusty sliding doors on a metal warehouse had been opened. Light poured out, shadowing everything in its path.

I prompted myself to breathe in, breathe out.

"Keep your back against the boat," Jess said, her voice resolute. "Too late to turn back."

A creeping shadow crossed the small lot in front of the warehouse, and cold blood rushed through me, its frightened song humming in my ears.

"Freeze!" Jess aimed her gun at the shadow. "Hands over your head."

"I'm unarmed," the shadow called out, continuing in our direction.

"Liar. Stop walking and get on your knees. Do it!" She raised her gun higher, and the stout shadow fell to his knees, with his hands in the air above his head. "I'm going to approach. If you move a muscle, you're dead." Jess then lowered her voice. "Stay there with your back to that boat, Ells."

"I told you, I'm unarmed. I lost my piece back there." The silhouette of his head jerked toward the other warehouses. The voice was familiar, but I couldn't place it.

"What's your name, why are you out here, and who are you with? And oh, by the way, if you move, I'll blow your head off without your answers."

"There's some bad shit going on in this town. You should go home, red."

Jess moved closer to our shadowed detainee, one slow step at a time. She was too close—my God, she was getting too close.

"Son of a bitch . . . Parker! You're a cop for Christ's sake."

My heart crashed against my ribcage. My lungs quivered. Detective Parker and his murderous hunting knife had haunted my dreams for months. There were others, but it was his face I saw most often in those nightmares. Each time, he laughed and taunted, he touched me in ways too awful for words, and then he finally slit my throat. My feet moved without permission. I needed to see his face.

Parker grinned. "Ellie James." A depraved chuckle slid up his throat. "So you're back. My mates are going to love this. You should've stayed in hiding, dumb bitch." He spoke with the British accent he'd been effectively concealing.

The disguised pieces that drifted for months through my subconscious finally came together and made sense. How stupid it took so long—the facts had been there. Parker had been planted on the police force by the Order. He was the enemy.

Jess looked over her shoulder at me. "Get back against the boat, damn it, Ell—"

Parker was on his feet in a split second and nailed her in the face with his fist. Her gun flew from her hands and slid along the old wood planks of the pier as she landed on her back. He climbed on top of her and put a knife to her throat.

He was going to take her from me. I screamed her name.

Adrenaline rushed my body again, and something I'd never before experienced overwhelmed me. Fight conquered fear. It conquered the usual lockdown my brain bid. There was someone in my head, but it didn't sound like me. *Save her. Kill him.*

I picked up the gun and aimed at Parker. "You. Will. Not. Take. Her. From. Me."

He redirected his attention, his crude eyes meeting mine. "Oh, but I will. Just like I took your sister from you. That's right—I put that bullet through your sister's heart. Adopted sister, that is. She was meant to be a decoy, you know, and as it turns out, one more ineffective layer of protection. The gig worked until they tested her DNA some years back in London."

"What?" Words from the old tome bashed into the front of my skull: *unless his daughter acquires the throne as rightful queen.* Daughter. Singular. God, was it true? So many lies. Fury and hatred suddenly blasted through me, my blood boiling with it.

"But, of course, you didn't know. She was nothing more than unfortunate collateral damage. You're the one we want. *I* want. Joining forces with the Order was the only way I could get to you, to hurt him. What he and his brother did to my family was—"

As his shocking revelations hit me with the force of a hurricane, my mind screamed for vengeance. Screamed for the life of my best friend. Nothing else mattered. I closed the gap between Parker and me and pushed the gun into his temple. "Drop the knife," I snarled.

He let the knife fall from his hand. It clattered onto the pier. "If you make it out of this alive, ask him. Ask him what they did to my family. What *he* did to my sister."

"I won't ask. Now get off her—get on your knees."

Parker pushed back onto his knees, the revolver's short barrel still deep in his temple.

"Pick up the knife, Jess."

She steadied herself on her feet and retrieved the knife. "Step back, Ellie."

Another snarl—a vile sound I'd never before released tore itself from my throat, "He's mine."

"This isn't you. I won't let you do it. Step back, now."

"Don't worry yourself, red. She can't do it."

As I took two steps back, my mind—the voice—remained focused on Parker. I lowered the gun from his head and aimed for his chest. He'd wear a bullet in his own heart before the night ended.

"Two more, Ells. Please. Two more."

She was granted two more steps. Still, the thought that guided me and its desire to deliver Parker's punishment didn't waver. My fingers absorbed the comforting feel of the revolver's nylon grip. I smiled at the sensation. Evil climbed from my depths—Parker was a dead man.

And then Will stepped in front of me, stepped in front of my fucking gun.

He handed his to Jess and jerked his chin toward Parker. His eyes then burned into mine, unyielding blue challenging vengeful green. *"Elle."* I gasped at the way he said my name. "I'm here. You have a choice now. You can shoot him and become someone different . . . or choose my hand, baby." He cautiously reached for me.

I didn't move. Didn't reach for him. Didn't surrender my weapon. I stared into his eyes and measured his words. The stranger in my head pushed forward with her provocation.

Without breaking our connection, blue and green indivisible, Will stepped aside just enough to allow the sight of my gun to lock onto Parker's chest again. He knew better than anyone the battle raging inside my mind.

Boots pounded asphalt and halted somewhere near me. A magazine clicked into its well and the slide of a pistol scraped metal as a round was chambered. No threat. It was Ben.

Will's eyes pushed deeper into me. "I promise you justice. You must choose between that and vengeance. Either way, this man will never again see the light of day." His words were deliberate and powerful.

I blinked up at Will. I looked at Parker. The pig was sweating, and he stunk of fresh piss. His shifting eyes moved between Ben's gun and mine.

Ben's stinging voice as he said something sharp to Jess pulled my stare to his scarred face. He'd placed himself in front of her, shielding her, though his eyes and gun were fully trained on Parker.

The inexplicable energy that drew me to Will reached out and led my eyes back to his. I saw my future—our future, our life together in England—there in his eyes. Visions flooded my head. I saw him slip the ruby on my finger and kiss it as I married him in a gown of white lace. The white fire in his eyes as he made love to me. My lips, smiling down at him as he kneeled and kissed my pregnant stomach.

"I love you, Elle. Give me the gun," Will said, moving his hand closer.

My head cleared at the sound of his voice—the only voice that could command me—and I knew in that moment, if I made the wrong choice, it wouldn't be me who created those beautiful memories with him. It would be someone different. A hardened, fallen version of myself living my life, taking from me everything I wanted with Will. A sinful, murderous pretender taking from him the woman he wanted to love until his last breath. His angel.

I lowered the gun and put my hand in his. "You're here," I whispered.

Will shoved the revolver into his pocket and caught me as I collapsed into his arms. "I'll always be here for you," he said. His fingers weaved through my hair and pressed my ear to his thundering chest. "I'm here, baby. Right here."

Parker lashed out again. He was already a dead man with nothing more to lose. "Your reunion is touching. Enjoy the time you have. She won't last another six months."

A vicious snarl tore itself from the dark place where Will's beast dwelled, but before he could mete out punishment, vengeance reared her head one last time, and I beat him to it. Without thought, without granting my body permission, I pivoted into a swift sidekick and launched my heel into Parker's face. As bone crunched, blood flew from the bastard's nose and his back slammed to the asphalt a second later.

I panted, the sound of it hissing through my ears. I was insane and numb at once.

One corner of Will's mouth twitched, and then he anchored me tight in his strong arms, moving us close to *Neptune*. He crushed me against his body and slanted his mouth over mine, claiming me with his kiss. It was a spiraling, fiery kiss that revived my senses. I countered with the same fire, meeting his tongue with mine as I grasped his bearded face with both hands. His long fingers were threaded through the back of my hair, pressing me hard against his mouth. There were no separate breaths, no broken or lost pieces. Our souls reconnected, and there was only us, one whole again.

"God, how I love you," he breathed. He kissed me deeply again, murmuring against my lips, "I love you, Elle . . . love you beyond madness. . . ." And then he pulled back abruptly and cradled my face in his hands as he inspected me with wild, charged eyes. "Are you hurt?"

I lowered my eyes. "No, I'm not hurt. You must be so angry with me. I'm sorry, Will."

"No. Look at me, baby." When I did, he shook his head. "No, I'm not angry."

"I can't bear to be apart from you." My voice broke on the sob that tore from my chest.

"I know. I can't either. I'll never let it happen again." He wiped at the tears on my face with his thumbs. "I swear. I'll find another way. I will never separate us again." He pulled me to his chest—my home—where I soaked in the heat of his body and burrowed deeper into his warm leather jacket.

The sobbing caused my breath and words to stutter. "I l-love y-y-you."

"Stop crying, baby, please. It's tearing my heart out."

I moved my face up to the hollow at the base of his neck and strangled the tears.

Seconds later, a gunshot blast rang out as the world around me blurred. I found myself gasping for breath with my back flat against *Neptune*'s wooden deck, a thick, bruising chain digging into my spine. Jess sailed over the gunwale and landed on top of me.

Will had launched us over the side of the old fishing boat.

There was no time to think. No time to panic. Jess and I scurried on our hands and knees to the little cabin and shut ourselves in.

Another gunshot blasted and struck the boat's steel hull.

I heard a scream echo through my head and then realized it was my own. I screamed for Will, shoving at Jess as I clung to the cabin's rusted window frame. "Get off me! I have to see him!"

Jess gave up the fight to push me to the floor and pressed herself against my back. She wrapped her arms tight around my vibrating body as it imploded with fear.

"Oh, God, no . . . No!" I pounded on the glass with the sides of my fists. "Will! No!"

Will and Ben had their guns sighted on three assassins and Parker. The three assassins had their weapons sighted on Will and Ben. A red laser beam danced on Will's chest.

"He came," Jess whispered as Josh Mendes appeared behind the assassins and aimed his gun. The red glow disappeared from Will's chest as one assassin spun toward Josh and fired. He missed—and Josh put a bullet in his head.

Although my gut heaved from the sight, I couldn't look away. I couldn't turn from Will. I fumbled wildly with the latch on the window frame until the cloudy pane of glass slid open.

"Christ, it took you too fucking long to get here, cop."

"Stand down, Hastings," Josh ordered. He'd lunged and locked onto the remaining assassins, providing cover for Will and Ben. "Do your fucking job—go to her. I've witnessed no crime by your hand here today. Let's keep it that way."

"You'll give me that one," Will commanded. His menacing stare was locked on Parker. "I promised her justice."

Parker lurched forward, reaching for the weapon of the dead assassin.

Will and Josh reacted instinctively at once, but it was Josh's bullet that pierced Parker's chest. "Now get in the goddamned boat."

"You motherfucker," Will snarled.

The assassins took advantage of the pissing match and fired. A bullet grazed Josh's leg and another ricocheted off the boat's hull close to Will's head. Josh fired five rounds, taking out both hit men.

"Go! . . . Get her out of that boat and get out of here," Josh urged as he pulled his phone from his jacket and called the police department for assistance.

I exploded from the fly bridge and leaped into Will's arms after he boarded *Neptune*. He lifted me and held me against his warm body. Relief washed through my cold blood, cleansing it of vengeance, cleansing it of pain. It hit me as he strengthened his embrace. Will had needed that justice as much as I had. He hadn't made it to the house in time to save my family, so he blamed himself for their deaths.

On that fateful, haze-filled night, in the name of justice, Josh Mendes was our equalizer.

Will let me slide to my feet, but he didn't let go. I turned my head and watched Ben help Jess climb over the side of the fishing boat. "Come on, baby. We need to go before his backup arrives," he said close to my ear before he dragged his lips to mine and placed a soft kiss there.

Will vaulted over the side of the boat and held his arms out for me to fall into, and the moment my feet hit those familiar old planks, I knew I'd never again step foot on that pier.

Josh inclined his head when our eyes met but kept his distance. I'd hurt him. Still, he had risked his life to save mine. Somehow he'd

found a way to bury his pain and work with the arrogant English billionaire outlaw who took his girl. I didn't know when their relationship
began or even what it was. I knew only that Josh found Will in London,
and they'd worked together to clear my name and eradicate the assassins. Josh Mendes was a good man who tried hard to play by the rules,
and though he wasn't the man for me, I would never forget him.

As we passed by, the two of them clasped hands for a firm shake,
and each slapped the other's shoulder with respect. "Don't leave the
country yet, Hastings. I'll be in touch."

Will nodded.

We jogged hand-in-hand and met Ben and Jess at the car, the
four of us bone weary, ready to vanish quietly into the night. We
headed north out of Stonington.

"Pull over," Will said just minutes into the drive. There was a
desperate sense of urgency in his gravel tone. Before the car came
to a full stop, he pushed out the door, rolling off the seat to his feet.
Crouched low on the side of the highway, he vomited. Once he'd
finished, he stayed low with elbows resting on his thighs and wiped
his mouth on his sleeve.

I lifted his chin and stared into disoriented blue eyes. "You're
burning up. What's going on, Will?" Blood, violence, and murder
didn't typically affect him that way—they had become part of his
fabric. It was something else.

As he straightened to his full height, his breath accelerated and
sweat ran down his face. He shifted his weight several times. "I need
to sit, baby." The words were slurred.

I called out for Ben. There was no way I could keep him from
going down. "Something's wrong! He's going to—"

Ben was out of the car and supported Will's weight before I finished the sentence.

"Right side. Passed through," Will said. "Get me to a bed, my
brother."

"You've been shot—you knew?" I yanked at Will's shirt and found the entry wound under his arm. He'd taken the hit meant for me when he'd thrown me onto *Neptune's* deck. The bullet had torn through his muscled flesh near the top of his ribcage. Blood oozed down his side. I glanced at my own body where I'd been pressed against him. He'd bled on me though neither of us realized it at the time. I threw his jacket to the ground and lifted his shirt higher while Ben held him and raised his arm so I could pivot beneath to look for the exit wound. I shouted for Jess.

She leaned around my shoulders and inspected the wounds. "Clean pass through serratus anterior. Neither the lateral thoracic artery nor his lung took a direct hit since he kept going. Narrow. Twenty-two or maybe thirty-eight caliber. We need something clean to press to the wounds to stop the bleeding."

We had nothing. We were on a stretch of highway with nothing in sight. I tore off my jacket and jerked the long-sleeve cotton top I wore over my head, and pressed it strategically to both wounds. "Hold it there," I demanded of Jess. I grabbed my scarf from the ground and tied it around Will to hold the makeshift dressing in place.

Jess tugged on the scarf to make it tighter. "Good. Now keep pressure on both wounds. Push as hard as you can. We need to get medical help immediately."

Will grew weaker from the blood loss and could no longer stand on his own. "Cover her up," he ordered, directing his words to Ben after we had him in the back of the car. "Cottage."

Ben grabbed my jacket from the ground and held it for me with his head turned.

I slid my trembling arms into the leather sleeves and zipped to cover my bra. My body was freezing and in shock, but I wouldn't let it break me. I climbed into the back seat with Will and applied pressure to the wounds again. I was near fainting as I stared at his pale face. I closed my mouth and commanded breath in and out through my nose, forcing it to steady, knowing my erratic heart would follow.

"Hospital. He needs proper medical attention. We can't risk further blood loss and infection," Jess said. She looked from me to Ben, ignoring Will's "cottage" edict.

"You know how this works, Ben. I said go to the fucking cottage." His nostrils flared and his breathing accelerated again.

I kissed his cold lips. "Shhh . . . be calm. We'll go to the cottage, but you'll defer to me, and I'll do whatever it takes. Don't fight me. I won't lose you." I had a plan.

He nodded and closed his eyes.

We couldn't risk the involvement of law enforcement. The bullets Josh fired from his police-issued weapon were defensible, but we couldn't allow ourselves to be connected to the deaths that occurred prior to that. There was no way to know whether the jurisdiction of its citizenries assumed by British Parliament would prevail, and if it didn't, Will could go to prison in Connecticut, for life. The Crown would demand extradition and bring him home only to use the situation to gain the upper hand in our centuries-long silent war.

Ben pulled back onto the highway and headed for Lords Point.

"Jess, please. I can't lose him. Help me. I know you can do this—I know you can save his life." I was asking for more than I deserved, pulling her deeper into our world, where she would never live the same life she had. It was wrong, but I needed her. He was my everything—the one person I couldn't live without, and I'd do anything to save him. Anything. "I'm begging you. *Please.*"

She stared, measuring the commitment in my eyes. The entire side of her face was red and swelling fast. Tiny beads of blood dotted a small cut beneath her eye. Locked into my gaze, she said to Ben, "Hit the next exit and take a right. I know where to find the supplies we need."

Twenty-Three

Jᴇss ʙᴀʟᴀɴᴄᴇᴅ ᴏᴠᴇʀ the console between the two front seats and injected Will with penicillin and morphine. She yanked the scarf and shirt away from the wounds and poured a chemical hemostatic agent into each to aid the clotting process and then pressed sterile gauze against them. "Hold these and press hard. I'll start the drip. He's lost a lot of blood, and not only that, it'll combat the toxic effects of myoglobin from the muscle breakdown—I don't want to wait any longer."

I replaced her hands with mine. "Do it."

Jess had done everything she could for Will by the time we pulled up in front of the cottage. The rest was up to him.

We had dosed him with enough morphine to make him sleep so he couldn't fight us as we cared for him. When he realized what was going on, he made me promise I wouldn't allow anyone else to touch him, and Ben and Jess both pledged to stay armed while he was out. Just in case.

Jess walked me through proper cleaning and dressing of the wounds, and then I stripped him of his clothes, washed the blood and sweat from his body, and tucked him into bed.

His massive body burned through the morphine, and he drifted in and out of consciousness. He moved from the bed only when he needed to use the toilet, insisting he would do that on his own. Each time we dosed him with another round, he kissed my lips and mumbled how he loved me before drifting back into a deep sleep and sweating through it again.

I knew his body and mind were strong. He proved that as he pushed hard to come out on the other side. Still. Every second felt like a minute, and every minute felt like an hour. I wept when he was out, desperate for him to come back to me. I stayed in bed with him, leaving only when my bruised back ached from lack of movement. My bare body was something Will would fight for, so I curled into his and maintained contact with his fevered skin.

When I wasn't weeping or staring at him, I sketched. One image, in particular, continued to fix itself in my mind, demanding it be released onto paper. It was the wedding gown I'd seen in the vision back at the pier. It took almost no time to pencil its chic likeness.

"Here's one more," Jess said as she placed another box along the wall. She'd gone into town and stopped by my house to gather some things.

"You didn't have to do that."

"It's no big deal. I grabbed a few irreplaceable items. Birth certificates, photos, fabulous shoes. . . . You know, those sort of things. It's late. Get some sleep."

"That's more than a few. I'm so lucky to have you. Couldn't have done this without you. I love you, Jess."

She stopped and nailed me with her wide blue stare. "You've never said that before."

"Didn't know how."

She smiled and glanced at Will, her eyes growing watery. "Love you, too, Ells."

After Jess left the bedroom, I snuggled close to Will and tried to sleep but couldn't, so I dragged the box of photos close to the bed and started to trip down memory lane.

"Isobel . . . Oh, Isobel . . ." She'd hid her affair with Ethan well, though I finally stared at the truth—a photo of the two of them in a small album she'd never shared. Ethan had both arms around my sister, and they looked happy. They'd been in love. It was a beautiful photo; one I'd save for Lissie. My fingers traced the lines of her face. I couldn't recall Isobel ever looking as happy, not the way her eyes shined in that photo.

My heart knew in that moment what Parker had said was true, that she wasn't my sister, not by blood. I was furious with her for the lies, and I ached for her, missing everything about her. Though she hadn't shared my blood, she'd be my sister always.

I flipped the page and found another photo of Isobel and Ethan, but in this one, there was a third person. A man, his deceitful expression familiar, sickening. All three smiled and held drinks high as if celebrating something, and the hand of my sister's murderer rested warmly on Ethan's shoulder. I choked on my breath and slammed the album shut.

My mind spun with details that I'd never questioned but should have. I swallowed hard and forced myself to the truth. It had been staring me in the face for so long. Isobel's fascination with guns, knowing how to use them. Carrying one in her handbag. Meeting me at Nick's to walk me home every night. The paranoia and the overbearing, despotic behavior. She'd known the truth, and she had been protecting me.

And there was her secret involvement with Ethan. She'd fed information about me, about the security of our situation to the Hastings patriarch, to Ethan. How else could they have known if danger lurked on this side of the Atlantic? He hadn't found it necessary to keep tabs on her, to protect her the way Will protected me.

My God. Ethan had known all along.

They both knew she wasn't my biological sister. She'd been planted in my life—Isobel had been another defender of my blood.

Will stirred and grumbled something unintelligible. Did he know? He swore he had no secrets, that he'd never lie to me, and I believed him. No. Ethan had lied to him, too.

My eyes slammed shut, and I pushed my hand against my

forehead as if that would make it all disappear. I struggled to erase the unwanted image from my brain, that photo of Ethan and Isobel with Parker.

I reached out for Will, whispering hoarsely, "I'm here, my love. Right here."

I'd made the decision in that moment to keep the photo from Will until he made a full recovery. The meaning was unclear. Had my sister and Will's brother betrayed us? One thing was crystal clear. When the truth was revealed—whatever it might be—it would affect us both in a profound manner.

My mind spun further out of control.

What had Ethan and Will done to Parker's family, and what happened to his sister?

The abrupt ringing of my phone startled me. It was Thomas. Although he tried to disguise the distress in his voice, I picked up on his fear. Thomas adored his brother, and if anyone knew the hell he was going through, I did.

"He's getting everything he needs," I assured him. "Jess is well-trained."

"You sound shaken—what's happened? Are you all right?"

"It's nothing, Thomas. I'm fine. We'll be home in a few days. I promise."

"He hasn't called."

"He will. You know he's been sleeping. Give him another day."

Before hanging up, Thomas delivered my reprimand into the phone, "What you did—that fucked me up, Ellie. Never do that again."

It was sometime before sunrise on the third morning after Will had been shot, and I was stuck in the same loop, berating myself for selfish, reckless behavior.

Hindsight is a powerful and useless tool. I couldn't see it then, couldn't see past my determination to get to Will. I'd gambled with my life the day I left Eastridge—the life he worked so hard to protect. The fact that I'd made it through an international flight before falling ill, and worse, that I wasn't followed and murdered had been nothing more than luck itself. Worse still, my imprudence nearly cost us *his* life.

"I'm sorry. I'll never do it again," I whispered.

Will pulled my back tight against his chest and cupped my breasts. "It's all right, baby. No more apologies." Then his velvet lips brushed over my neck and shoulder, and his throbbing erection pushed into my back.

I turned in his arms and dragged my fingers along his jaw, smoothing an unruly beard. Even in the dark, it was evident the natural color of his face had returned and the fever had gone. "Oh, Will. You're back."

Determined to be finished with bedrest, he yanked the intravenous catheter from his arm. His strength surged, increasing with each breath. "Yeah. My woman needs me."

"I do. I've missed you so much."

He winced from the pain as he moved above me and claimed my mouth. As he balanced our weight, he held me tight and opened my legs wide with his knees. "I need you, too, Elle," he said near my ear before coming back to my lips and thrusting his tongue against mine again. His chest vibrated. "I need to be inside you. Been dreaming of it . . . dreamed it over and over."

His voice was nothing but gravel. Electrifying tingles raced along my spine and washed over my skin as my body anticipated the reconnection to his.

"I'm yours. All of me."

Will shoved into me with ravenous force and drew a sharp cry from my lips. Grasping for sanity and tenderness, he stilled his enormous body and buried his face in my hair. "I'm so sorry. I didn't mean to hurt you. Should have prepared you." His apology was about more than that harsh thrust. "I keep fucking up. Help me stop."

I stroked his cheek gently with my fingertips. "Everything's going to be okay. I love you, Will."

Despite his best effort and the tormenting pain of his gunshot wounds, he wasn't able to calm himself for long. We'd been separated too long. Too many emotions had been forced aside. He held me in trembling arms and drove hard.

I pushed against his chest with both hands and dug my nails into his flesh. His embrace relaxed some but remained too strong.

"You're crushing me. . . . Kiss me."

When he kissed me, the tension in his muscles eased, and he became my tender warrior again. "I love you, baby." Soothed by his bared soul, I lay my hands on the pillow above my head, and surrendered my soul. He settled into the position and rhythm that would shatter us both. His mouth covering mine, he swallowed his name when I cried it, and then lifted his head and roared mine through his own climax.

Once he'd caught his breath, Will lifted us and pushed back until we were sitting in our favorite ritualistic position. He was still inside me, and those strong arms held me tight through his refusal to separate our bodies. Our eyes locked and our breathing slowed. We were heart to heart and soul to soul, and I could feel the transcending depth of both. I ran my fingers through his hair and gently rocked my hips.

"Such grace. And beauty. I don't deserve you, Elle."

His reluctance to be with me in the beginning was never about what he believed I deserved. It went deeper than that. He'd judged himself unworthy of love. A self-inflicted punishment for his sins.

I took his face into my hands. "Being with someone isn't a matter of what's been earned, and love isn't meant to be denied as penance.

Being together is about how well we love, and no other man could love me as well as you do. I need you, Will. Only you."

He kissed me with warm, salty lips before resting his forehead against mine. "Christ, I love you. It just doesn't feel like enough to say words so common."

I held on to him—there was nothing else to be done. He was right. There were no words for our insane, obsessive love.

We eased back down to the mattress. He collapsed onto the pillows with a grimace and agonized groan. I snuggled into his body, and he anchored me to my home with his powerful arms. My head rested on his chest, and my ear found the heartbeat that was my lullaby.

We napped until the sun woke us. I rolled off Will's chest and stretched in a lazy manner, absorbing the sunshine that beamed across the bed. The sun worked hard at dazzling me with its warm, golden rays as they pierced the panes of glass. I'd missed it, but the brilliant East Coast sunrise over the Atlantic could no longer hold me as it once did.

"I want to go home, Will. Can you travel?"

"Yeah. You want to go tonight?" He lifted my hand and admired the ring he'd put on my finger a few weeks earlier. He turned it and watched the light shimmer across the lavish center stone.

I swear that ruby was carved from his heart. "I won't ever wear another ring." No other could bear as much love and sentiment as the one he was studying, inscribed with the words that meant more than the world to me.

He kissed the ruby with a smile on his lips. "Okay, baby."

I smiled, too, and scooted to the edge of the bed to snatch my phone from the table, handing it to him. "Thomas needs to hear your voice. Oh, wait. We need to talk about him first."

"What about him?" he snapped.

Guilt eclipsed my bliss. "Don't punish him, Will. Please. What I did—it's not his fault."

He was thoughtful before he responded, his silence wrecking my nerves. Finally, gentle resolve filled his eyes. "I don't blame my brother. And I don't blame you. What happened was my fault. Forgive me, Elle. I should have learned the first time."

"Don't do that. I won't let you do that. You can't accept responsibility for every foolish thing I do. I know I must learn to do as you say." Unshed tears blurred my vision.

"The day you stop challenging me, my rebellious little angel, I'll wonder if you've stopped loving me. I want you just as you are—defiance and all." Both corners of his mouth twitched, and his eyes flashed.

I sniffled and smiled. "We'll call this one a draw."

"There'll be many, I'm quite sure of it." With a full-on grin, he lifted the phone to his ear and waited for Thomas to answer.

My mind continued to drift while he and Thomas discussed arrangements for a plane to get us back to England, complete with an onboard medic this time. It was the first time anyone else had heard his voice since I'd tucked him into that bed. God, I had almost lost him.

"Tonight, goddamn it," Will said into the phone as I closed the bathroom door. When I came out, he was rummaging through his duffel bag. He complained and scratched at his bearded cheeks. "Jesus, I need a shower."

"Yep, you do." I snickered beneath my breath for a moment, then straightened my face. "But more importantly, you need to eat."

"Shower first," he grumbled on the way to the bathroom. He stole a kiss as he strutted past in all his naked glory.

—

Jess and Ben were making breakfast, and my stomach rumbled as the smell of bacon and coffee drifted beneath the bedroom door. I tied my robe and headed for the kitchen.

"Good morning," Jess exclaimed in a singsong.

They were sitting at the counter, side by side, each with a pistol stuffed into their waistband. She chewed on bacon and made some kind of list, while he read the newspaper and sipped from a mug of coffee. They looked like an old married couple but with guns.

"We heard the two of you," she said in her usual unabashed style. "Figured he should eat. Breakfast is still warm."

My emotions were too drained to manage a blush. I shrugged instead.

"We're to assume from the vigorous activity he's regained his strength?"

Ben's tight mouth curved in response to her question.

My gaping mouth wouldn't shut so I covered it with my hand. This time, my cheeks heated despite exhaustion.

Ben cleared his throat.

"He's growing stronger by the minute," I said. "Showering now. He and Thomas arranged our flight home. We're going tonight."

"Tonight? He's ready?"

"I think so. You should go talk to him. I'm sure the two of you have a lot to discuss. But wait, first—did either of you hear from Josh?"

"The cop was here twice. The case was reported as an unanticipated run-in with drug dealers. He said he'll call Will in a few days. We can leave."

"What? What do you mean drug dealers?"

As Ben hit the hallway to find Will, he said, "Don't dig, Ellie. Just let it go."

"Will did what he had to do, Ells. It was the only way to protect Josh. And it did take some heroin off the streets."

I shook my head in disbelief. What else didn't I know? I'd wondered if I would see Josh before we left, wondered if he was okay. Ben's words revealed that answer. Josh would continue to communicate with Will as needed, but I would never hear from him again. I chewed on a slice of bacon and let silence ride as I gathered my thoughts.

"You're leaving me again," my best friend blurted out.

"I can't stay here, Jess. You know that."

"But—"

"Come with me."

I'd turned her life upside down and was motivated by selfishness to shake it up even more. I wanted her with me. Needed her support. She was as much my sister as Isobel had been.

"Don't mess with me." She came around the counter and hovered three inches above me. "Are you serious?"

"Yes." I made a fist with my right hand and covered my heart, promising sincerity the way we had since ninth grade.

"Then I will come."

We squealed in concert and hugged it out, until Jess abruptly stiffened and moved to the side.

Will was watching. His hair was wet, and he wore nothing more than jeans and fresh bandages. He rubbed his clean-shaven jaw and pegged me with a grin. "It's settled then?" He winked as he made his way around the island to secure me in his arms. "*Elle*. I'm starving."

I stuffed a fat slice of bacon into his mouth. My fingers trailed along his silky jawline as he chewed and eventually landed on his arm. I traced the stunning tattoo bearing my name. He kissed my butterfly. We both purred.

Ben tugged Jess's arm. "We'll go wrap up in town."

"We leave for the airport at six," Will said.

Jess stared back at us, her eyes intense. "Do you want to go back to the house and get more of your things?"

I shook my head.

"She stays with me." Will's sharp words reminded me how insensitive he could be. For me, he pulled from his buried reserve of tenderness. Most people weren't as fortunate. He was known to be an abrasive prick for good reason. But it was who he'd been from the beginning, and asking him to change wasn't something I would ever do.

Jess was able to see beneath a person's surface when given a chance. She'd figure him out when she saw how devoted to me he was, how hard he worked to make me happy.

Will twirled me around and connected our bacon-flavored lips for a moment. "You never have to go back. Nothing in that house is worth revisiting a nightmare. We'll replace it. Buy anything you want."

He was right. Nothing left there held any real value, not to me. Memories—the good ones, those subtle but endearing moments with my grandmother and sister—were all I needed to take with me. I carried those deep inside, never to be lost.

"I want you to sell it."

"What about this one?"

"This place, too. Everything."

I would never delve back into the pain that forever damaged a large piece of my heart. There was no point. No reason to relive the horror when I had moved on months ago. Lissie and I would never stop grieving Isobel and Gran, would always carry those painful losses in our hearts, but we'd do so in our new home, surrounded by the love of our new family.

Will nodded. "Done." He understood, and he'd handle the business end of it. I'd never have to think about it again.

"What you did for Josh, to protect him from an internal investigation . . . that was lovely, Will. Thank you." I kissed his smooth cheek.

"It was a debt I needed to pay, baby."

"Sit and eat. You'll lose the strength you've regained. Then you can take me for a walk on the beach." He pulled up a stool and opened the newspaper, and I set a warm, brimming plate in front of him.

"I'll shower while you eat." My lips lingered longer than intended when I kissed his cheek again. It was the first time he'd shaved since we met. Will was the kind of man well-suited for facial hair, and I loved it on his handsome face, but the silkiness of his bare skin felt amazing to the lips. "I won't be long." I let down my hair and tossed him a smile as I sauntered across the kitchen floor.

Newspaper smacked granite and his fork hit the plate as he jumped up.

"Stay there—*eat*."

"Witch."

He sat and filled his mouth with another egg.

Twenty-Four

STROLLING ALONG THE shoreline at Lords Point where it all began for Will and me was like walking through an old dream. I was out of my mind for him from the moment he'd approached me on the pier. He was my world by the time we walked the beach together for the first time, but I never could have predicted how intense my feelings for him would become.

It was a gorgeous sunny day in October, and New England was bursting with its famed autumn colors. Cirrus clouds streaked across the horizon. The tide was low, and the Atlantic's surface was as smooth as polished glass. The nasal rasping call of a male snowy egret startled me. He'd wandered to the mainland from one of the marshy islands on his quest to find a suitable female to share his nest.

"Stick around, mate. It worked for me," Will said to the white heron as it waded fearlessly in shallow water just a few feet away. He squeezed my hand and grinned. "I found mine here."

I laughed from my gut, repaying the bird with a scare of his own. My heart cherished every rare moment when Will was able to let go of responsibility and war. I locked each one secure in my memory's safe like one would lock up gold and precious gems in an indestructible vault. "Don't take his advice . . . ," I told the bird, now preening his curvy plumes. "He stalked me for years before making a move."

Will winced as he lifted me and kissed my mouth. "I don't regret it, baby. I needed you strong. Look at you now—you're a beautiful force of will."

"The way you see me, the way you love me..." My whisper trailed off as I smashed my lips to his. He opened and led us into a deep kiss, and when we broke, breathless, I pushed my secret smile against his skin. "Put me down. If you open the wounds, we can't go home tonight."

We found a sunlit spot higher on the beach near some boulders. He sat in the sand and pulled me down on top facing him. I locked my legs around his lower back, rested my hands on his shoulders, and pressed my lips to his again. The fiery ruby on my finger connected with a ray of sun.

His energy commanded my gaze to his. Those blue eyes were charged, burning. "How long will you make me wait to marry you?"

I loved him insanely, and in truth, giving him the vows he desired wasn't a concession. There would never be anyone but him. There was no reason to torment him.

"I need time to find the gown."

"What?" A smile dangled from one corner of his open mouth.

"You heard me. The gown—that's your waiting period. Then I'll marry you."

His smile grew as he shook his head. "Fucking handful," he muttered. "What about all the other wedding things women do?"

"I don't care about any of that."

My mind functioned in an atypical, abstract manner. It wouldn't accept the intricate responsibilities of wedding planning. I wasn't opposed to weddings, nor did I dislike them. I just didn't want to plan one.

He delved into my eyes.

"I'm serious. The gown is all I need, though it won't be easy to find." Nothing other than the vision that played in my mind would do.

"You're an artist, baby. Draw what you want to wear. Choose a design house in London, and we'll have it handmade." He didn't know I'd already done that—put my vision on paper.

"You can't just force someone to make my wedding gown."

"I could, but I won't have to. Designers will fight for the opportunity. Think about it, Countess." He winked.

I narrowed my eyes. It would take time to get used to the English aristocracy and its never-ending love affair with titles. "You can't see it before the wedding. Not even the sketch."

"I won't peek. Mother will be more than happy to handle the rest. How big?"

"Whatever you want. *But . . .*"

His smile faded. "There's a *but*?"

"Yes. This is the second time you've left me. If you ever leave me again, for more than a few days to work in London, I will leave *you*. I swear, Will. You won't leave me a third time." He hadn't left me either time, and my heart knew that, but the reason for him going made no difference. I wouldn't be separated from him again, not unless we made the decision together.

He exhaled and shrugged. "Okay."

"Okay?" Just like that?

"Yes, I accept your condition. In fact, I made you that promise several days ago. I have a few conditions of my own—since we've gone there."

"Are you mocking me?"

"I'm quite serious."

He was worth billions. Some of his wealth was inherited, but he'd worked hard to earn most of it through his firm. Of course he'd protect his assets. "I'll sign it, Will."

"I'm not referring to a prenuptial agreement."

"Oh. Well, what are your conditions?"

"My time in London is necessary, so we'll get our own place there. When I need to work for extended periods, you'll go with me."

"Agreed." That wasn't a condition, it was fantastic. "What else?"

"Not so fast. Rules. You'll not be permitted to leave on your own for shopping or anything else. Not until I'm sure our enemy is completely eradicated. Probably not even then. You'll accept the protection of my men at all times when I'm not with you. And there will be domestic employees."

I expected the protection detail but rolled my eyes at the thought of another live-in housekeeper. "One qualification. In London—and at Eastridge—no housemaids in our bedroom in the morning and no more segregated breakfasts. I understand the value of tradition, but that one is too much."

"Agreed."

"What else?"

"The bishop of Chichester will marry us. I won't risk having the Crown or the government or even the Church disqualify our marriage the next time they're angry with me."

It was fitting since the bishop's diocese covered the same two counties as Will's earldom—East and West Sussex. I nodded. It made no difference to me who married us. "And?"

"You take my name. When we finish this conversation, you'll never again use James. And I name our children."

"What?" I chuckled.

"Traditional English names, baby. No made up names or twisted spelling deviations."

I swallowed another chuckle. "I accept your conditions. I have one more to add."

He narrowed his eyes.

"I get to be on top."

"Absolutely not."

"Once a month?"

"No."

"A few times a year?"

His forehead puckered with disapproval as he proffered his compromise. "Once a year—on your birthday."

Laughing hard, I rolled from his lap into the sand. "Okay, okay, condition withdrawn. We'll allow it to happen organically."

It wasn't something I needed, and he knew it. His desire for dominance in bed wasn't a problem for me. In fact, once I understood his need to possess me, it turned me on. I knew his heart, what drove him, and I loved him beyond sanity. There was no desire within me to change his bedding habits. It wasn't like he chained me and used whips and ball gags.

A spark of sunlight bounced around in his determined eyes as he claimed his position above me. "When you can overpower me, you can take the top." He demonstrated his power as he restrained my hands above my head and pushed his way into my mouth, taking all that was his with another of his smooth, passionate kisses.

"I have, and I will again."

"You cheated." He smirked. "How well did that work out for you, baby?"

We both smiled, remembering the time we spent in that little floral-papered guest room.

The muscles in his face tightened then, and his back stiffened. "The hell you live with is unbearable for me. I'll find a way—"

"Parker said you and Ethan hurt his family."

His mouth fell open and head jerked back. "What?"

I didn't say anything else. He needed a minute to grasp what he'd heard. He turned his face from mine and cursed.

"I didn't recognize him. Christ. Fuck."

I thought of the confession he'd made early on: his lucrative business deals often had consequences for others. Those deals sometimes ruined lives. It was something I'd told him I could live with, and I would.

"I'm sorry. So sorry, Elle. Christ, I've created more enemies, made it worse for you. The Greens, now this—yet another fuckup on my part. I swear it'll be the first thing I look into when we get back. I'll find a way to make it up to you."

"I know." There was nothing for him to make up to me, nothing to be fixed. But I knew Will, and in order for him to find peace, I had to allow him to believe otherwise.

I couldn't bring myself to ask about Parker's sister. I couldn't stomach the idea he might have had something serious with another woman. Stupid as it was, the damned jealousy, I would never ask that question.

"They knew Isobel was . . ." I gulped for air, the words stuck in my throat.

"Lewis confirmed it before he died. He and my brother both knew who she was. Ethan kept it from me. He lied to me." The pain in his eyes stung my heart, riled it.

"I'm sorry. I know how you loved him."

"It's a consequence of my loving you. I'll take it, all of it. This hurts you more, baby, I know. But remember, this lie, this betrayal or whatever the hell it is, it's also what keeps Lissie safe. She carries my blood, not yours, and mine alone poses no threat."

I pulled an image of Lissie's innocent face into my head. He was right. It hurt—another piece of my heart was wrecked—but this truth was a blessing for our little girl. She would never know the fear of being hunted.

Will maintained our intense connection. Through our eyes, he measured my suffering and drew it inward, attempting to shoulder my burden, just as he'd done in the darkest of my days when we first arrived in England.

But I wouldn't do that to him again. He was there, and I would live for him, not for the dead. I had learned to pull the pain forward, to feel it, so I could beat it.

I touched his silky cheek. "I'm okay. And you're wrong—it's

bearable. I've never been happier. And you did that, Will. The way you love me, the way I love you—that's what makes this hell tolerable for us."

He obscured his face in my neck and then nodded and kissed my butterfly. "You're amazing." His breath tickled my skin as he spoke. "We won't get a proper honeymoon, not right away, but when I'm certain it's safe, we'll go to Paris. Madrid. Berlin. Rome. Whatever you desire, it'll be yours. I swear I'll do whatever it takes to give you the life you deserve."

We hoped the death of the Order's leader, Jack Lewis, would preclude any remaining lone-wolf supporters from rising against us. Hoped another overlord wouldn't ascend and recruit. Will planned to make sure all relevant parties received a detailed recount of Lewis's demise. We would seek an understanding with the queen, forgiving the Crown and asking for the same favor in return.

"You know I'm not much good at travel anyway."

"I can get you to any of those European cities without leaving the ground, baby."

We laughed against each other's lips.

"Let's go inside. You should rest before we fly home."

"There's only one thing I need before we get on that plane." He rocked his hips and tried to hide the pained grimace by kissing me again.

I wedged my fingers between our lips. "You're the strongest man I know. Your strength is overwhelming, and it solidifies mine. It protects me in every way. But I want to be needed. Let me take care of you, just as you take care of me."

He kissed my fingers before moving them. "Don't you see? I draw that strength from you. My drive, determination, everything that's me . . . is you. You're everything that hurts, everything that gives me pleasure. My desperation for you is an addiction, it exceeds what words can express. I love you, Elle."

The way he loved me was inconceivable. Even more beyond reason was that I understood. Because I loved him the same. I had battled hard for him in the beginning, and he took lives for me in the end. Our bond was primal, beyond explanation. Neither of us would survive it.

"Until your last breath?"

He smiled from those gorgeous, steely eyes. "Yes, until my last breath." Then he pulled me to my feet and treated me to another of his cocky winks. "Come inside. I'll show you."

As we walked up the rocky hill path, high tide swept in and sent the heron squawking away from his hunt at the water's edge. A lavish breeze pushed at our backs and played in my hair. We didn't make it inside. Instead, we made love on the double-wide chaise lounge where he first pressed his lips to mine. Will pushed himself beyond the pain the gunshot wounds caused. There was no dominance, no submission. Every soft touch, every gentle thrust, every tender whisper avowing me his angel was deliberate and meaningful. It was an exquisite, soul-filling, unconditional love.

"We'll keep this place for now," he said as he drifted to sleep.

I stared at his handsome face as I had months before and listened to the thunder and crash of waves before they reached the shore and rolled back out with the current to rebuild. He was doing nothing more than breathing, though it seemed as if he were anchoring the earth to its place in the universe and me to mine on Earth. He was my place.

The sea became curt, its breeze flinging the blanket to expose my bare legs.

"Catch you on the other side—at home," I whispered.

Acknowledgments

I DREAMED OF DISTRAUGHT lovers, two silhouettes against a moonlit window in an otherwise dark place. The first passage I wrote for this novel was that dream, the emotional and sensual scene at the beginning of Chapter Fifteen. Discovering who these characters were before and after that encounter was a fantastic ride. Thank you, readers, for riding along with me.

Thank you to my editor, Elizabeth Kracht. You get what's inside my head. Because of that and your expertise in balancing patience and ass kickings, this novel exists as it is today.

I'm so grateful to the supportive members of my Women's Fiction Writers Association and Curtis Brown Creative writing tribes for the inspiring discussions and tough critiques.

Thank you, Kimberley Cameron, Bill Bernhardt, MM Finck, and Jennifer Longenberger for reading those ugly first drafts and reinforcing my confidence with your generous feedback.

To my incomparable publisher, Brooke Warner: you have my gratitude and admiration. You're a warrior every bit as fierce as Will. Lauren Wise, our editorial manager at SparkPress, deserves far more than this shout out for keeping us both on task with her exceptional oversight.

Thanks to Crystal Patriarche, my publicist, and her team of brilliant Sparks (like the fabulous Madison Rowbotham) for the fantastic presentation into the literary world. Your incredible vision and passion are unequaled.

For those brave souls who took a chance on this debut, you forever have my humble appreciation for your big-hearted endorsements.

Special thanks and much love to my parents and two children for their tolerance and encouragement. The four of you allow me to live inside my head and wait patiently while I travel between my two worlds.

About the Author

KELLI CLARE IS a former human resource executive and contributing writer for a *Forbes* and *TIME* recognized website for women. She has been a progressive voice for a global coalition of bloggers focused on issues involving women and girls, children, and world hunger. Clare lives in Northwest Ohio with her two children and sock-thieving spaniel. Connect with her at kelliclare.com or @kellideclare.

SELECTED TITLES FROM SPARKPRESS

SparkPress is an independent boutique publisher delivering high-quality, entertaining, and engaging content that enhances readers' lives, with a special focus on female-driven work.

Visit us at www.gosparkpress.com

Trouble the Water, Jackie Friedland,
$16.95, 978-1-943006-54-0.

When a young woman travels from a British factory town to South Carolina in the 1840s, she becomes involved with a vigilante abolitionist and the Underground Railroad while trying to navigate the complexities of Charleston high society and falling in love.

The Opposite of Never, Kathy Mehuron,
$16.95, 978-1-943006-50-2.

Devastated by the loss of their spouses, Georgia and Kenny think that the best times of their lives are long over until they find each other; meanwhile Kenny's teenage stepdaughter, Zelda, and Georgia's friend's son, Spencer, fall in love at first sight—only to fall prey to and suffer opiate addiction together.

Tracing the Bones, Elise A. Miller.
$17, 978-1-940716-48-0.

When forty-one-year-old Eve Myer—a woman trapped in an unhappy marriage and plagued by chronic back pain—begins healing sessions with her new neighbor Billy, she's increasingly drawn to him, despite the mysterious circumstances surrounding his wife and child's recent deaths.

The Absence of Evelyn, Jackie Townsend,
$16.95, 978-1-63152-244-4.

Nineteen-year-old Olivia's life takes a turn when she receives an overseas call from a man she doesn't know is her father; her mother Rhonda, meanwhile, haunted by her sister's ghost, must face long-buried truths. Four lives in all, spanning three continents, are now bound together and tell a powerful story about love in all its incarnations, filial and amorous, healing and destructive.

About SparkPress

SparkPress is an independent, hybrid imprint focused on merging the best of the traditional publishing model with new and innovative strategies. We deliver high-quality, entertaining, and engaging content that enhances readers' lives. We are proud to bring to market a list of *New York Times* best-selling, award-winning, and debut authors who represent a wide array of genres, as well as our established, industry-wide reputation for creative, results-driven success in working with authors. SparkPress, a BookSparks imprint, is a division of SparkPoint Studio LLC.

Learn more at GoSparkPress.com